R.A.

FORGOTTEN REALMS

SALVATORE

THE GHOST KING

III

TRANSITIONS

THE GHOST KING

TRANSITIONS

BOOK III

©2009 Wizards of the Coast LLC

Published by Wizards of the Coast LLC

FORGOTTEN REALMS, WIZARDS OF THE COAST, and their respective logos are trademarks of Wizards of the Coast LLC in the U.S.A. and other countries.

Printed in the U.S.A.

Cover art by Todd Lockwood

First Printing: October 2009

9 8 7 6 5 4 3 2 1

ISBN: 978-0-7869-5233-5
620-24195000-001-EN

Library of Congress Cataloging-in-Publication Data

Salvatore, R. A., 1959-
   The ghost king / R.A. Salvatore.
      p. cm. -- (Transitions ; bk. 3)
   ISBN 978-0-7869-5233-5
   1. Drizzt Do'Urden (Fictitious character)--Fiction. 2. Forgotten realms
(Imaginary place)--Fiction. I. Title.
   PS3569.A462345G47 2009
   813'.54--dc22
                              2009016151

U.S., CANADA,
ASIA, PACIFIC, & LATIN AMERICA
Wizards of the Coast LLC
P.O. Box 707
Renton, WA 98057-0707
+1-800-324-6496

EUROPEAN HEADQUARTERS
Hasbro UK Ltd
Caswell Way
Newport, Gwent NP9 0YH
GREAT BRITAIN
Save this address for your records.

Visit our web site at www.wizards.com

*To Diane, of course, the love of my life who has walked through
these years beside me and my dreams, and I beside her and hers.*

But there is someone else who gets a big thank you for this book—five
someones actually. This calling I have found, this purpose in my life, takes
me places. It is my duty to let it, to follow it. Sometimes those journeys are
not to places I want to go. Sometimes it hurts. When I finished *Mortalis,*
the fourth book of my DemonWars series, during a terrible time in my life,
I stated that I hoped I would never write a book like that again (though I
considered it the best piece I had ever written), that I would never again have
to go to that dark place.

When I started *The Ghost King,* I knew I had to go there, yet again. These
characters, these friends of twenty years, demanded no less of me. And so I
have spent the last months watching three videos, songs of my past from the
band and songstress that have walked beside me for most of my life.

Stevie Nicks once asked in a song, "Has anyone ever written anything for
you? And in your darkest hours, do you hear me sing?"

Ah, Ms. Nicks, you have been writing songs for me since my high school
years in the 1970s, though you don't know it. You were there with me during
those lonely and confusing days in high school, those awakening moments of
college. I watched the sun rise over Fitchburg State College, sitting in my car
and waiting for my class to begin, to the sounds of "The Chain." You were
there with me during that blizzard in 1978 when I found the works of Tolkien
and a whole new way of expressing myself suddenly came into view. You were
there with me when I met the woman who would be my wife, and on the
morning after our wedding, and at the births of our three children.

You went with us to hockey games and horse shows. To your concert at
Great Woods went my family, and my brother even as he neared the end of
his life.

And you were there with me as I wrote this book. "Sisters of the Moon,"
"Has Anyone Ever Written Anything for You?" and "Rhiannon," all three,
the songs that took me through my darkest hours and now let me go back to
that place, because my friends of two decades, the Companions of the Hall,
demanded no less of me.

So thank you, Stevie Nicks, and Fleetwood Mac, for writing the music
of my life.

—R. A. Salvatore

PRELUDE

The dragon issued a low growl and flexed his claws in close, curling himself into a defensive crouch. His eyes were gone, having been lost to the brilliant light bursting from a destroyed artifact, but his draconian senses more than compensated.

Someone was in his chamber—Hephaestus knew that beyond a doubt—but the beast could neither smell nor hear him.

"Well?" the dragon asked in his rumbling voice, barely a whisper for the beast, but it reverberated and echoed off the stone walls of the mountain cavern. "Have you come to face me or to hide from me?"

I am right here before you, dragon, came the reply—not audibly, but in the wyrm's mind.

Hephaestus tilted his great horned head at the telepathic intrusion and growled.

You do not remember me? You destroyed me, dragon, when you destroyed the Crystal Shard.

"Your cryptic games do not impress me, drow!"

Not drow.

That gave Hephaestus pause, and the sockets that once—not so long ago—housed his burned-out eyes widened.

"Illithid!" the dragon roared, and he breathed forth his murderous, fiery breath at the spot where he'd once destroyed the mind flayer and its drow companion, along with the Crystal Shard, all at once.

The fire blazed on and on, bubbling stone, heating the entire room. Many heartbeats later, fire still flowing, Hephaestus heard in his mind, *Thank you.*

Confusion stole the remaining breath from the dragon—confusion that lasted only an instant before a chill began to creep into the air around him, began to seep through his red scales. Hephaestus didn't like the cold. He was a creature of flame and heat and fiery anger, and the high frosts bit at his wings when he flew out of his mountain abode in the wintry months.

But this cold was worse, for it was beyond physical frost. It was the utter void of emptiness, the complete absence of the heat of life, the last vestiges of Crenshinibon spewing forth the necromantic power that had forged the mighty relic millennia before.

Icy fingers pried under the dragon's scales and permeated his flesh, leaching the life-force from the great beast.

Hephaestus tried to resist, growling and snarling, tightening sinewy muscles as if trying to repel the cold. A great inhale got the dragon's inner fires churning, not to breathe forth, but to fight cold with heat.

The crack of a single scale hitting the stone floor resounded in the dragon's ears. He swiveled his great head as if to view the calamity, though of course, he couldn't see.

But Hephaestus could feel . . . the rot.

Hephaestus could feel death reaching into him, reaching through him, grasping his heart and squeezing.

His inhale puffed out in a gout of cold flame. He tried to draw in again, but his lungs would not heed the call. The dragon started to swing his head forward, but his neck gave out halfway and the great horned head bounced down onto the floor.

Hephaestus had perceived only darkness around him since the first destruction of the Crystal Shard, and now he felt the same inside.

Darkness.

* * * * *

Two flames flickered to life, two eyes of fire, of pure energy, of pure hatred.

And that alone—sight!—confused the blind Hephaestus. He could see! But how?

The beast watched a blue light, a curtain of crawling lightning, crackle and sizzle its way across the slag floor. It had crossed the point of ultimate devastation, where the mighty artifact had long ago blasted loose its layers and layers of magic to blind Hephaestus, then again more recently, that very day, to emanate waves of murderous necromantic energy to assail the dragon and . . . ?

And do what? The dragon recalled the cold, the falling scales, the profound sensation of rot and death. Somehow he could see again, but at what cost?

Hephaestus drew a deep breath, or tried to, but only then did the dragon realize that he was not drawing breath at all.

Suddenly terrified, Hephaestus focused on the point of cataclysm, and as the strange curtain of blue magic thinned, the beast saw huddled forms, once contained within, dancing about the remnants of their artifact home. Stooped low, backs hunched, the apparitions—the seven liches who had created the mighty Crenshinibon—circled and chanted ancient words of power long lost to the realms of Faerûn. A closer look revealed the many different backgrounds of these men of ancient times, the varied cultures and features from all across the continent. But from afar, they appeared only as similar huddled gray creatures, ragged clothes dripping dullness as if a gray mist flowed from their every movement. Hephaestus recognized them for what they were: the life force of the sentient artifact.

But they had been destroyed in the first blast of the Crystal Shard!

The beast did not lift his great head high on his serpentine neck to breathe forth catastrophe on the undead. He watched, and he measured. He took note of their cadence and tone, and recognized their desperation. They wanted to get back into their home, back into Crenshinibon, the Crystal Shard.

The dragon, curious yet terrified, let his gaze focus on that empty vessel, on the once mighty artifact that he had inadvertently annihilated at the cost of his own eyes.

And he had destroyed it a second time, he realized. Unknown to him, there had remained residual power in the Crystal Shard, and when the tentacle-headed illithid had goaded him, he'd breathed forth fires that had again assaulted the Crystal Shard.

Hephaestus swiveled his head around. Rage engulfed the creature even more, a horror-filled revulsion that turned instantly from dismay to pure anger.

3

For his great and beautiful shining red scales were mostly gone, scattered about the floor. A few dotted the beast's mostly skeletal form here and there, pathetic remnants of the majesty and power he had once shown. He lifted a wing, a beautiful wing that had once allowed Hephaestus to sail effortlessly across the high winds curling up from the Snowflake Mountains to the northwest.

Bones, torn leathery tatters, and nothing more adorned that blasted appendage.

Once a beast of grandeur, majesty, and terrible beauty, reduced to a hideous mockery.

Once a dragon, earlier that very day a dragon, reduced to . . . what? Dead? Alive?

How?

Hephaestus looked at his other broken and skeletal wing to realize that the blue plane of strange magical power had crossed it. Looking more closely within that nearly opaque curtain, Hephaestus noted a second stream of crackling energy, a greenish dart within the blue field, backtracking and sparking inside the curtain. Low to the ground, that visible tether of energy connected the wing of the dragon to the artifact, joining Hephaestus to the Crystal Shard he thought he had long ago destroyed.

Awaken, great beast, said the voice in his head, the voice of the illithid, Yharaskrik.

"You did this!" Hephaestus roared. He started to growl, but was struck, suddenly and without warning, by a stream of psionic energy that left him babbling in confusion.

You are alive, the creature within that energy told him. *You have defeated death. You are greater than before, and I am with you to guide you, to teach you powers beyond anything you have ever imagined.*

With a burst of rage-inspired strength, the beast rose up on his legs, head high and swiveling to take in the cavern. Hephaestus dared not remove his wing from the magical curtain, fearing that he would again know nothingness. He scraped his way across the floor toward the dancing apparitions and the Crystal Shard.

The huddled and shadowy forms of the undead stopped their circling and turned as one to regard the dragon. They backed away—whether out of fear or reverence, Hephaestus could not determine. The beast approached the shard, and a clawed foreleg moved forward gingerly to touch the item.

As soon as his skeletal digits closed around it, a sudden compulsion, an overwhelming calling, compelled Hephaestus to swing his forelimb up, to smash the Crystal Shard into the center of his skull, right above his fiery eyes. Even as he performed that movement, Hephaestus realized that Yharaskrik's overwhelming willpower was compelling him so.

Before he could avenge that insult, however, Hephaestus's rage flew away. Ecstasy overwhelmed the dragon, a release of tremendous power and overwhelming joy, a wash of oneness and completeness.

The beast shuffled back. His wing left the curtain, but Hephaestus felt no horror at that realization, for his newfound sentience and awareness, and restored life energy, did not diminish.

No, not *life* energy, Hephaestus realized.

Quite the opposite . . . precisely the opposite.

You are the Ghost King, Yharaskrik told him. *Death does not rule you. You rule death.*

After a long while, Hephaestus settled back on his haunches, surveying the scene and trying to make sense of it all. The crawling lightning reached the cavern's far wall, the rock surface suddenly sparkling as if holding a thousand little stars. Through the curtain came the undead liches moving into a semi-circle before Hephaestus. They prayed in their ancient and long-forgotten languages and kept their horrid visages low, directed humbly at the floor.

He could command them, Hephaestus realized, but he chose to let them grovel and genuflect before him, for the beast was more concerned with the wall of blue energy dissecting his cavern.

What could it be?

"Mystra's Weave," the liches whispered, as if reading his every thought.

The Weave? Hephaestus thought.

"The Weave . . . collapsing," answered the chorus of liches. "Magic . . . wild."

Hephaestus considered the wretched creatures as he tried to piece together the possibilities. The apparitions of the Crystal Shard were the ancient wizards who had imbued the artifact with their own life-forces. At its essence, Crenshinibon radiated necromantic dweomers.

Hephaestus's gaze went back to the curtain, the strand of Mystra's Weave made visible, all but solid. He thought again of his last memories of sight, when he had brought forth his fiery breath over a drow and an illithid, and over the Crystal Shard. Dragonfire had detonated the mighty relic and had filled Hephaestus's eyes with brilliant, blinding light.

Then a cold wave of emptiness had slain him, had rotted the scales and the flesh from his bones. Had that spell . . . whatever it was . . . brought down a piece of Mystra's Weave?

"The strand was here before you breathed," the apparitions explained, reading his thoughts and dispelling that errant notion.

"Brought from the first fires that shattered the shard," Hephaestus said.

No, Yharaskrik said in the dragon's mind. *The strand released the necromancy of the ruined shard, giving me sentience once more and reviving the apparitions in their current state.*

And you invaded my sleep, Hephaestus accused.

I am so guilty, the illithid admitted. *As you destroyed me in that long-lost time, so I have returned to repay you.*

"I will destroy you again!" Hephaestus promised.

You cannot, for there is nothing to destroy. I am disembodied thought, sentience without substance. And I seek a home.

Before Hephaestus could even register that notion for what it was—a clear threat—another wave of psionic energy, much more insistent and overwhelming, filled his every synapse, his every thought, his every bit of reason with a buzzing and crackling distortion. He couldn't even think his name let alone respond to the intrusion as the powerful mind of the undead illithid worked its way into his subconscious, into every mental fiber that formulated the dragon's psyche.

Then, as if a great darkness were suddenly lifted, Hephaestus understood—everything.

What have you done? he telepathically asked the illithid. But the answer was there, waiting for him, in his own thoughts.

For Hephaestus needn't ask Yharaskrik anything ever again. Doing so would be no more than pondering the question himself.

Hephaestus was Yharaskrik and Yharaskrik was Hephaestus.

And both were Crenshinibon, the Ghost King.

Hephaestus's great intellect worked backward through the reality of his present state and the enthusiasm of the seven liches as his thoughts careened and at last convened, spurring him to certainty. The strand of blue fire, how ever it had come to be, had tied him to Crenshinibon and its lingering necromantic powers. Those powers were remnants but still mighty, he realized as

the Crystal Shard pulsed against his skull. It had fused there, and the necromantic energy had infused the remains of Hephaestus's physical coil.

Thus he had risen, not in resurrection, but in undeath.

The apparitions bowed to him, and he understood their thoughts and
intentions as clearly as they heard his own. Their sole purpose was to serve.

Hephaestus understood himself to be a sentient conduit between the
realms of the living and the dead.

The blue fire crawled out of the far wall and etched along the floor. It
crossed over where the Crystal Shard had lain, and over where Hephaestus's
wingtip had been. In the span of a few heartbeats, it exited the chamber
altogether, leaving the place dim, with only the dancing orange flames of the
liches' eyes, Hephaestus's eyes, and the soft green glow of Crenshinibon.

But the beast's power did not diminish with its passing, and the apparitions still bowed.

He was risen.

A dracolich.

PART
1

U N W E A V I N G

U N W E A V I N G

Where does reason end and magic begin? Where does reason end and faith begin? These are two of the central questions of sentience, so I have been told by a philosopher friend who has gone to the end of his days and back again. It is the ultimate musing, the ultimate search, the ultimate reality of who we are. To live is to die, and to know that you shall, and to wonder, always wonder.

This truth is the foundation of the Spirit Soaring, a cathedral, a library, a place of worship and reason, of debate and philosophy. Her stones were placed by faith and magic, her walls constructed of wonderment and hope, her ceiling held up by reason. There, Cadderly Bonaduce strides in profundity and demands of his many visitors, devout and scholarly, that they do not shy from the larger questions of existence, and do not shield themselves and buffet others with unreasoned dogma.

There is now raging in the wider world a fierce debate— just such a collision between reason and dogma. Are we no more than the whim of the gods or the result of harmonic process? Eternal or mortal, and if the former, then what is the relationship of that which is forever more, the soul, to that which we know will feed the worms? What is the next progression for consciousness and spirit, of self-awareness and—or—the loss of individuality in the state of oneness with all else? What is the relationship between the answerable and the unanswerable, and what does it bode if the former grows at the expense of the latter?

Of course, the act of simply asking these questions raises troubling possibilities for many people, acts of punishable heresy for others, and indeed even Cadderly once confided in me that life would be simpler if he could just accept what is, and exist in the present. The irony of his tale is not lost on me. One of the most prominent priests of Deneir, young Cadderly remained skeptical even of the existence of the god he served. Indeed he was an agnostic priest, but one mighty with powers divine. Had he worshipped any god other than Deneir, whose very tenets encourage inquisition, young Cadderly likely would never have found any of those powers, to heal or to invoke the wrath of his deity.

He is confident now in the evermore, and in the possibility of some Deneirrath heaven, but still he questions, still he seeks. At Spirit Soaring, many truths—laws of the wider world, even of the heavens above—are being unraveled and unrolled for study and inquisition. With humility and courage, the scholars who flock there illuminate details of the scheme of our reality, argue the patterns of the multiverse and the rules that guide it, indeed, realign our very understanding of Toril and its relationship to the moon and the stars above.

For some, that very act bespeaks heresy, a dangerous exploration into the realms of knowledge that should remain solely the domain of the gods, of beings higher than us. Worse, these frantic prophets of doom warn, such ponderings and impolitic explanations diminish the gods themselves and turn away from faith those who need to hear the word. To philosophers like Cadderly, however, the greater intricacy, the greater complexity of the multiverse only elevates his feelings for his god. The harmony of nature, he argues, and the beauty of universal law and process bespeak a brilliance and a notion of infinity beyond that realized in blindness or willful, fearful ignorance.

To Cadderly's inquisitive mind, the observed system supporting divine law far surpasses the superstitions of the Material Plane.

For many others, though, even some of those who agree with Cadderly's search, there is an undeniable level of discomfort.

I see the opposite in Catti-brie and her continued learning and understanding of magic. She takes comfort in magic, she has said, because it cannot be explained. Her strength in faith and spirituality climbs beside her magical prowess. To have before you that which simply is, without explanation, without fabrication and replication, is the essence of faith.

I do not know if Mielikki exists. I do not know if any of the gods are real, or if they are actual beings, whether or not they care about the day-to-day existence of one rogue dark elf. The precepts of Mielikki—the morality, the sense of community and service, and the appreciation for life—are real to me, are in my heart. They were there before I found Mielikki, a name to place upon them, and they would remain there even if indisputable proof were given to me that there was no actual being, no physical manifestation of those precepts.

Do we behave out of fear of punishment, or out of the demands of our heart? For me, it is the latter, as I would hope is true for all adults, though I know from bitter experience that such is not often the case. To act in a manner designed to catapult you into one heaven or another would seem transparent to a god, any god, for if one's heart is not in alignment with the creator of that heaven, then . . . what is the point?

And so I salute Cadderly and the seekers, who put aside the ethereal, the easy answers, and climb courageously toward the honesty and the beauty of a greater harmony.

As the many peoples of Faerûn scramble through their daily endeavors, march through to the ends of their respective lives, there will be much hesitance at the words that flow from Spirit Soaring, even resentment and attempts at sabotage. Cadderly's personal journey to explore the cosmos within the bounds of his own considerable intellect will no doubt foster fear, in particular of the most basic and terrifying concept of all, death.

From me, I show only support for my priestly friend. I remember my nights in Icewind Dale, tall upon Bruenor's Climb, more removed from the tundra below, it seemed, than from the stars above. Were my ponderings there any less heretical than the work of Spirit Soaring? And if the result for Cadderly and those others is anything akin to what I knew on that lonely mountaintop, then I recognize the strength of Cadderly's armor against the curses of the incurious and the cries of heresy from less enlightened and more dogmatic fools.

My journey to the stars, among the stars, at one with the stars, was a place of absolute contentment and unbridled joy, a moment of the most peaceful existence I have ever known.

And the most powerful, for in that state of oneness with the universe around me, I, Drizzt Do'Urden, stood as a god.

—Drizzt Do'Urden

CHAPTER

VISITING A DROW'S DREAMS

I will find you, drow.

The dark elf's eyes popped open wide, and he quickly attuned his keen senses to his physical surroundings. The voice remained clear in his mind, invading his moment of quiet Reverie.

He knew the voice, for with it came an image of catastrophe all too clear in his memories, from perhaps a decade and a half before.

He adjusted his eye patch and ran a hand over his bald head, trying to make sense of it. It couldn't be. The dragon had been destroyed, and nothing, not even a great red wyrm like Hephaestus, could have survived the intensity of the blast when Crenshinibon had released its power. Or even if the beast had somehow lived, why hadn't it arisen then and there, where its enemies would have been helpless before it?

No, Jarlaxle was certain that Hephaestus had been destroyed.

But he hadn't dreamed the intrusion into his Reverie. Of that, too, Jarlaxle was certain.

I will find you, drow.

It had been Hephaestus—the telepathic impartation into Jarlaxle's Reverie had brought the image of the great dragon to him clearly. He could not have mistaken the weight of that voice. It had startled him from his meditation, and he had instinctively retreated from it and forced himself back into the present, to his physical surroundings.

He regretted that almost immediately, and calmed long enough to hear the contented snoring of his dwarf companion, to ensure that all around him was secure, then he closed his eyes once more and turned his thoughts inward, to a place of meditation and solitude.

Except, he was not alone.

Hephaestus was there waiting for him. He envisioned the dragon's eyes, twin flickers of angry flame. He could feel the beast's rage, simmering and promising revenge. A contented growl rumbled through Jarlaxle's thoughts, the smirk of the predator when the prey was at hand. The dragon had found him telepathically, but did that mean it knew where he was physically?

A moment of panic swept through Jarlaxle, a moment of confusion. He reached up and touched his eye patch, wearing it that day over his left eye. Its magic should have stopped Hephaestus's intrusion, should have shielded Jarlaxle from all scrying or unwanted telepathic contact. But he was not imagining it. Hephaestus was with him.

I will find you, drow, the dragon assured him once more.

"Will" find him, so therefore had not yet found him . . .

Jarlaxle threw up his defenses, refusing to consider his current whereabouts in the recognition of why Hephaestus kept repeating his declaration. The dragon wanted him to consider his position so the beast could telepathically take the knowledge of his whereabouts from him.

He filled his thoughts with images of the city of Luskan, of Calimport, of the Underdark. Jarlaxle's principal lieutenant in his powerful mercenary band was an accomplished psionicist, and had taught Jarlaxle much in the ways of mental trickery and defense. Jarlaxle brought every bit of that knowledge to bear.

Hephaestus's psionically-imparted growl, turning from satisfaction to frustration, was met by Jarlaxle's chuckle.

You cannot elude me, the dragon insisted.

Aren't you dead?

I will find you, drow!

Then I will kill you again.

Jarlaxle's matter-of-fact, casual response elicited a great rage from the beast—as the drow had hoped—and with that emotion came a momentary loss of control by the dragon, which was all Jarlaxle needed.

He met that rage with a wall of denial, forcing Hephaestus from his thoughts. He shifted the eye patch to his right eye, his touch awakening the item, bringing forth its shielding power more acutely.

That was the way with many of his magical trinkets of late. Something was happening to the wider world, to Mystra's Weave. Kimmuriel had warned him to beware the use of magic, for reports of disastrous results from even simple castings had become all too commonplace.

The eye patch did its job, though, and combined with Jarlaxle's clever tricks and practiced defenses, Hephaestus was thrown far from the drow's subconscious.

Eyes open once more, Jarlaxle surveyed his small encampment. He and Athrogate were north of Mirabar. The sun had not yet appeared, but the eastern sky was beginning to leak its pre-dawn glow. The two of them were scheduled to meet, clandestinely, with Marchion Elastul of Mirabar that very morning, to complete a trading agreement between the self-serving ruler and the coastal city of Luskan. Or more specifically, between Elastul and Bregan D'aerthe, Jarlaxle's mercenary—and increasingly mercantile— band. Bregan D'aerthe used the city of Luskan as a conduit to the World Above, trading goods from the Underdark for artifacts from the surface realms, ferrying valuable and exotic baubles to and from the drow city-state of Menzoberranzan.

The drow scanned their camp, set in a small hollow amid a trio of large oaks. He could see the road, quiet and empty. From one of the trees a cicada crescendoed its whining song, and a bird cawed as if in answer. A rabbit darted through the small grassy lea on the downside of the camp, fleeing with sharp turns and great leaps as if terrified by the weight of Jarlaxle's gaze.

The drow slipped down from the low crook in the tree, rolling off the heavy limb that had served as his bed. He landed silently on magical boots and wove a careful path out of the copse to get a wider view of the area.

"And where're ye goin', I'm wantin' to be knowin'?" the dwarf called after him.

Jarlaxle turned on Athrogate, who still lay on his back, wrapped in a tangled bedroll. One half-opened eye looked back at him.

"I often ponder which is more annoying, dwarf, your snoring or your rhyming."

"Meself, too," said Athrogate. "But since I'm not much hearing me snoring, I'll be choosing the word-song."

Jarlaxle just shook his head and turned to walk away.

"I'm still asking, elf."

"I thought it wise to search the grounds before our esteemed visitor arrives," Jarlaxle replied.

"He'll be getting here with half the dwarfs o' Mirabar's Shield, not for doubting," said Athrogate.

True enough, Jarlaxle knew. He heard Athrogate shuffle out of his bedroll and scramble to his feet.

"Prudence, my friend," the drow said over his shoulder, and started away.

"Nah, it's more'n that," Athrogate declared.

Jarlaxle laughed helplessly. Few in the world knew him well enough to so easily read through his tactical deflections and assertions, but in the years Athrogate had been at his side, he had indeed let the dwarf get to know something of the true Jarlaxle Baenre. He turned and offered a grin to his dirty, bearded friend.

"Well?" Athrogate asked. "Yer words I'm taking, but what's got ye shaking?"

"Shaking?"

Athrogate shrugged. "It be what it be, and I see what it be."

"Enough," Jarlaxle bade him, holding his hands out in surrender.

"Ye tell me or I'll rhyme at ye again," the dwarf warned.

"Hit me with your mighty morningstars instead, I beg you."

Athrogate planted his hands on his hips and stared at the dark elf hard.

"I do not yet know," Jarlaxle admitted. "Something . . ." He reached around and retrieved his enormous, wide-brimmed hat, patted it into shape, and plopped it atop his head.

"Something?"

"Aye," said the drow. "A visitor, perhaps in my dreams, perhaps not."

"Tell me she's a redhead."

"Red scales, more likely."

Athrogate's face crinkled in disgust. "Ye need to dream better, elf."

"Indeed."

* * * * *

"My daughter fares well, I trust," Marchion Elastul remarked. He sat in a great, comfortable chair at the heavy, ornately decorated table his attendants had brought from his palace in Mirabar, surrounded by a dozen grim-faced dwarves of Mirabar's Shield. Across from him, in lesser thrones, sat Jarlaxle and Athrogate, who stuffed his face with bread, eggs, and all manner of delicacies. Even for a meeting in the wilderness, Elastul had demanded some manner of civilized discourse, which, to the dwarf's ultimate joy, had included a fine breakfast.

"Arabeth has adapted well to the changes in Luskan, yes," Jarlaxle answered. "She and Kensidan have grown closer, and her position within the city continues to expand in prominence and power."

"That miserable Crow," Elastul whispered with a sigh, referring to High Captain Kensidan, one of the four high captains who ruled the city. He knew well that Kensidan had become the dominant member of that elite group.

"Kensidan won," Jarlaxle reminded him. "He outwitted Arklem Greeth and the Arcane Brotherhood—no small feat!—and convinced the other high captains that his course was the best."

"I would have preferred Captain Deudermont."

Jarlaxle shrugged. "This way is more profitable for us all."

"To think that I'm sitting here dealing with a drow elf," Elastul lamented. "Half of my Shield dwarves would prefer that I kill you rather than negotiate with you."

"That would not be wise."

"Or profitable?"

"Nor healthy."

Elastul snorted, but his daughter Arabeth had told him enough about the creature Jarlaxle for him to know that the drow's quip was only half a joke, and half a deadly serious threat.

"If Kensidan the Crow and the other three high captains learn of our little arrangement here, they will not be pleased," Elastul said.

"Bregan D'aerthe does not answer to Kensidan and the others."

"But you do have an arrangement with them to trade your goods through their markets alone."

"Their wealth grows considerably because of the quiet trade with Menzoberranzan," Jarlaxle replied. "If I decide it convenient to do some dealing outside the parameters of that arrangement, then . . . I am a merchant, after all."

"A dead one, should Kensidan learn of this."

Jarlaxle laughed at the assertion. "A weary one, more likely, for what shall I do with a surface city to rule?"

It took a moment for the implications of that boast to sink in to Elastul, and the possibility brought him little amusement, for it served as a reminder and a warning that he dealt with dark elves.

Very dangerous dark elves.

"We have a deal, then?" Jarlaxle asked.

"I will open the tunnel to Barkskin's storehouse," Elastul replied, referring to a secret marketplace in the Undercity of Mirabar, the dwarf section. "Kimmuriel's wagons can move in through there alone, and none shall be allowed beyond the entry hall. And I expect the pricing exactly as we discussed, since the cost to me in merely keeping the appropriate guards alert for drow presence will be no small matter."

" 'Drow presence?' Surely you do not expect that we will deign to move further into your city, good marchion. We are quite content with the arrangement we have now, I assure you."

"You are a drow, Jarlaxle. You are never 'quite content.' "

Jarlaxle simply laughed, unwilling and unable to dispute that point. He had agreed to personally broker the deal for Kimmuriel, who would oversee the set-up of the operation, since Jarlaxle's wanderlust had returned and he wanted some time away from Luskan. In truth, Jarlaxle had to admit to himself that he wouldn't really be surprised at all to return to the North after a few months on the road and find Kimmuriel making great inroads in the city of Mirabar, perhaps even becoming the true power in the city, using Elastul or whatever other fool he might prop up to give him cover.

Jarlaxle tipped his great hat, then, and rose to leave, signaling Athrogate to follow. Snorting like a pig on a truffle, the dwarf kept stuffing his mouth, egg yolk and jam splattering his great black beard, a braided and dung-tipped mane.

"It has been a long and hungry road," Jarlaxle commented to Elastul.

The marchion shook his head in disgust. The dwarves of Mirabar's Shield, however, looked on with pure jealousy.

* * * * *

Jarlaxle and Athrogate had marched more than a mile before the dwarf stopped belching long enough to ask, "So, we're back for Luskan?"

"No," Jarlaxle replied. "Kimmuriel will see to the more mundane details now that I have completed the deal."

"Long way to ride for a short talk and a shorter meal."

"You ate through half the morning."

Athrogate rubbed his considerable belly and issued a belch that scared a flock of birds from a nearby tree, and Jarlaxle gave a helpless shake of his head.

"My tummy hurts," the dwarf explained. He rubbed his belly and burped again, several times in rapid succession. "So we're not back to Luskan. Where, then?"

That question gave Jarlaxle pause. "I am not sure," he said honestly.

"I won't be missing the place," said Athrogate. He reached over his shoulder and patted the grip of one of his mighty glassteel morningstars, which he kept strapped diagonally on his back, handles up high, their spiked ball heads bouncing behind his shoulders as he bobbed along the trail. "Ain't used these in months."

Jarlaxle, staring absently into the distance, simply nodded.

"Well, wherever we're to go, if even ye're to know, I'm thinkin' and talkin', it's better ridin' than walkin'. Bwahaha!" He reached into a belt pouch where he kept a black figurine of a war boar that could summon a magical mount to his side. He started to take it out, but Jarlaxle put a hand over his and stopped him.

"Not today," the drow explained. "Today, we meander."

"Bah, but I'm wantin' a bumpy road to shake a few belches free, ye damned elf."

"Today we walk," Jarlaxle said with finality.

Athrogate looked at him with suspicion. "So ye're not for knowin' where we're to be goin'."

The drow looked around at the rough terrain and rubbed his slender chin. "Soon," he promised.

"Bah! We could've gone back into Mirabar for more food!" Athrogate blanched as he finished, though, a rare expression indeed for the tough dwarf, for Jarlaxle fixed him with a serious and withering glare, one that reminded him in no uncertain terms who was the leader and who the sidekick.

"Good day for a walk!" Athrogate exclaimed, and finished with a great belch.

They set their camp only a few miles northeast of the field where they had met with Marchion Elastul, on a small ridge among a line of scraggly, short trees, many dead, others nearly leafless. Below them to the west loomed the remains of an old farm, or perhaps a small village, beyond a short rocky field splashed with flat, cut stones, most lying but some standing on end, leading Athrogate to mutter that it was probably an old graveyard.

"That or a pavilion," Jarlaxle replied, hardly caring.

Selûne was up, dancing in and out of the many small clouds that rushed overhead. Under her pale glow, Athrogate was soon snoring contentedly, but for Jarlaxle, the thought of Reverie was not welcomed.

He watched as the shadows under the moon's pale glow began to shrink, disappear, then stretch toward the east as the moon passed overhead and started its western descent. Weariness crept in upon him, and he resisted it for a long while.

The drow silently berated himself for his foolishness. He couldn't stay present and alert forever.

He leaned against a dead tree, a twisted silhouette whose shadow looked like the skeleton of a man who reached, pleading, to the gods. Jarlaxle didn't climb it—the old tree likely wouldn't have held his weight—but instead remained standing, leaning against the rough trunk.

He let his mind fall away from his surroundings, let it fall inward. Memories blended with sensations in the gentle swirl of Reverie. He felt his own heartbeat, the blood rushing through his veins. He felt the rhythms of the world, like a gentle breathing beneath his feet, and he embraced the sensation of a connection to the earth, as if he had grown roots into the deep rock. At the same time, he experienced a sensation of weightlessness, as if he were floating, as the wonderful relaxation of Reverie swept through his mind and body.

Only there was Jarlaxle free. Reverie was his refuge.

I will find you, drow.

Hephaestus was there with him, waiting for him. In his mind, Jarlaxle saw again the fiery eyes of the beast, felt the hot breath and the hotter hatred.

Be gone. You have no quarrel with me, the dark elf silently replied.

I have not forgotten!

'Twas your own breath that broke the shard, Jarlaxle reminded the creature.

Through your trickery, clever drow. I have not forgotten. You blinded me, you weakened me, you destroyed me!

That last clause struck Jarlaxle as odd, not just because the dragon obviously wasn't destroyed, but because he still had the distinct feeling that it wasn't Hephaestus he was communicating with—but it was Hephaestus!

Another image came into Jarlaxle's thoughts, that of a bulbous-headed creature with tentacles waving menacingly from its face.

I know you. I will find you, the dragon went on. *You who stole from me the pleasures of life and the flesh. You who stole from me the sweet taste of food and the pleasure of touch.*

So the dragon is dead, Jarlaxle thought.

Not I! Him! the voice that resonated like Hephaestus roared in his mind. *I was blind, and slept in darkness! Too intelligent for death! Consider the enemies you have made, drow! Consider that a king will find you—has found you!*

That last thought came through with such ferocity and such terrible implications that it startled Jarlaxle from his Reverie. He glanced around frantic, as if expecting a dragon to swoop down upon him and melt his camp into the dirt with an explosion of fiery breath, or an illithid to materialize and blast him with psionic energy that would scramble his mind forever.

But the night was quiet under the moon's pale glow.

Too quiet, Jarlaxle believed, like the hush of a predator. Where were the frogs, the night birds, the beetles?

Something shifted down to the west, catching Jarlaxle's attention. He scanned the field, seeking the source—a rodent of some sort, likely.

But he saw nothing, just the uneven grasses dancing in the moonlight on the gentle night breeze.

Something moved again, and Jarlaxle swept his gaze across the abandoned stones littering the field, reached up and lifted his eye patch so he could more distinctly focus. Across the field stood a shadowy, huddled figure, bowing and waving its arms. It occurred to the drow that it was not a living man, but a wraith or a specter or a lich.

In the open ground between them, a flat stone shifted. Another, standing upright, tilted to a greater angle.

Jarlaxle took a step toward the ancient markers.

The moon disappeared behind a dark cloud and the darkness deepened. But Jarlaxle was a creature of the Underdark, blessed with eyes that could see in the most meager light. In the nearly lightless caverns far below the stone, a patch of luminous lichen would glow to his eyes like a high-burning torch. Even in those moments when the moon hid, he saw that standing stone shift again, ever so slightly, as if something scrabbled at its base below the ground.

"A graveyard . . ." he whispered, finally recognizing the flat stones as markers and understanding Athrogate's earlier assessment. As he spoke, the moon came clear, brightening the field. Something churned in the dirt beside the shifting stone.

A hand—a skeletal hand.

A greenish blue crackle of strange ground lightning blasted tracers across the field. In that light, Jarlaxle saw many more stones shifting, the ground churning.

I have found you, drow! the beast whispered in Jarlaxle's thoughts.

"Athrogate," Jarlaxle called softly. "Awaken, good dwarf."

The dwarf snored, coughed, belched, and rolled to his side, his back to the drow.

Jarlaxle slipped a hand crossbow from the holster on his belt, expertly drawing back the string with his thumb as he moved. He focused on a particular type of bolt, blunted and heavy, and the magical pouch beside the holster dispensed it into his hand as he reached for it.

"Awaken, good dwarf," the drow said again, never taking his gaze from the field. A skeletal arm grasped at the empty air near the low-leaning headstone.

When Athrogate did not reply, Jarlaxle leveled the hand crossbow and pulled the trigger.

"Hey, now, what's the price o' bacon!" the dwarf yelped as the bolt thumped him in the arse. He rolled over and scrambled like a tipped crab, but jumped to his feet. He began circling back and forth with short hops on bent legs, rubbing his wounded bum all the while.

"What do ye know, elf?" he asked at length.

"That you are indeed loud enough to wake the dead," Jarlaxle replied, motioning over Athrogate's shoulder toward the stone-strewn field.

Athrogate leaped around.

"I see . . . dark," he said. As he finished, not only did the moon break free of the clouds, but another strange lightning bolt arced over the field like a net of energy had been cast over it. In the flash, whole skeletons showed themselves, standing free of their graves and shambling toward the tree-lined ridge.

"Coming for us, I'm thinking!" Athrogate bellowed. "And they look a bit hungry. More than a bit! Bwahaha! Starved, I'd wager!"

"Let us be gone from this place, and quickly," said Jarlaxle. He reached into his belt pouch and produced an obsidian statue of a gaunt horse with twists like fire around its hooves.

Athrogate nodded and did likewise, producing his boar figurine.

They both dropped their items and called forth their steeds together, an equine nightmare for Jarlaxle, snorting smoke and running on hooves of flame, and a demonic boar for Athrogate that radiated heat and belched the fire of the lower planes. Jarlaxle was first up in his seat, turning his mount to charge away, but he looked over his shoulder to see Athrogate take up his twin morningstars, leap upon the boar, and kick it into a squealing charge straight down at the graveyard.

"This way's faster!" the dwarf howled, and he set the heavy balls of his weapons spinning at the ends of their chains on either side. "Bwahaha!"

"Oh, Lady Lolth," Jarlaxle groaned. "If you sent this one to torment me, then know that I surrender, and just take him back."

Athrogate charged straight down onto the field, the boar kicking and bucking. Another green flash lit up the stony meadow before him, showing dozens of walking dead climbing from the torn earth, lifting skeletal hands at the approaching dwarf.

Athrogate bellowed all the louder and clamped his powerful legs tightly on the demon-boar. Seeming no less crazy than its bearded rider, the boar charged straight at the walking horde, and the dwarf sent his morningstars spinning. All around him they worked, heavy glassteel balls smashing against bone, breaking off reaching fingers and arms, shattering ribs with powerful swipes.

The boar beneath him gored, kicked, and plowed through the mindless undead that closed in hungrily. Athrogate drove his heels in hard against the boar's flanks and it leaped straight up and brought forth the fires of the lower planes, a burst of orange flame blasting out beneath its hooves as it landed, boiling into a radius half again wider than the dwarf was tall and curling up in an eruption of flame. The grass all around Athrogate smoked, licks of flame springing to life on the taller clumps.

While the flames bit at the nearest skeletons, they proved little deterrence to those coming from behind. The creatures closed, showing not the slightest sign of fear.

An overhead swing from Athrogate brought a morningstar down atop a skull, exploding it in a puff of white powder. He swung his other morningstar in a wide sweep, back to front, clipping three separate reaching skeletal arms and taking them off cleanly.

The skeletons seemed not to notice or care, and kept coming. Closing, always closing.

Athrogate roared all the louder against the press, and increased the fury of his swings. He didn't need to aim. The dwarf couldn't have missed smashing bones if he tried. Clawing fingers reached out at him, grinning skulls snapped their jaws.

Then the boar shrieked in pain. It hopped and sent out another circle of flames, but the unthinking skeletons seemed not to notice as their legs blackened. Clawing fingers raked the boar, sending it into a bucking frenzy, and Athrogate was thrown wide, clearing the front row of skeletons, but many more rushed at him as he fell.

* * * * *

Jarlaxle hated this kind of fight. Most of his battle repertoire, both magical and physical, was designed to misdirect, to confuse, and to keep his opponent off-balance.

You couldn't confuse a brainless skeleton or zombie.

With a great sigh, Jarlaxle plucked the huge feather from his hat and threw it to the ground, issuing commands to the magical item in an arcane language. Almost immediately, with a great puff of smoke, the feather became a gigantic flightless bird, a diatryma, ten feet tall and with a neck as thick as a strong man's chest.

Responding to Jarlaxle's telepathic commands, the monstrous bird charged onto the field and buffeted the undead with its short wings, pecking them to pieces with its powerful beak. The bird pushed through the throng of undead, kicking and buffeting and pecking with abandon. Every attack rattled a skeleton to pieces or smashed a skull to powder.

But more rose from the torn soil, and they closed and clawed.

On the side of the ridge, Jarlaxle casually slipped a ring onto his finger and drew a thin wand from his pack.

He punched out with the ring and its magic extended and amplified his strike many times over, blowing a path of force through the nearest ranks of skeletons, sending bones flying every which way. A second punch shattered three others as they tried to close from his left flank.

His immediate position secured, the drow lifted the wand, calling upon its powers to bring forth a burst of brilliantly shining light, warm and magical and ultimately devastating to the undead creatures.

Unlike the flames of the magical boar, the wand's light could not be ignored by the skeletons. Where fire could but blacken their bones, perhaps wound them slightly, the magical light struck at the core of the very magic that gave them animation, countering the negative energy that had lifted them from the grave.

Jarlaxle centered the burst in the area where Athrogate had fallen, and the dwarf's expected yelp of surprise and pain—pain from stinging eyes—sounded sweet to the drow.

He couldn't help but laugh when the dwarf finally emerged from the rattle of collapsing skeletons.

The fight, however, remained far from won. More and more skeletons continued to rise and advance.

Athrogate's boar was gone, slain by the horde. The magic of the figurine could not produce another creature for several hours. Jarlaxle's bird, too, had fallen victim to slashing digits and was being torn asunder. The drow lifted his fingers to the band on his hat, where the nub of a new feather was beginning to sprout. But several days would pass before another diatryma could be summoned.

Athrogate turned as if he meant to charge into another knot of skeletons, and Jarlaxle yelled, "Get back here!"

Still rubbing his stinging eyes, the dwarf replied, "There be more to hit, elf!"

"I will leave you, then, and they will tear you apart."

"Ye're askin' me to run from a fight!" Athrogate yelled as his morning-stars pulverized another skeleton that reached for him with clawing hands.

"Perhaps the magic that raised these creatures will lift you up as a zombie," Jarlaxle said as he turned his nightmare around, facing up the ridge. Within a few heartbeats, he heard mumbling behind him as Athrogate approached. The dwarf huffed and puffed beside him, holding the onyx boar figurine and muttering.

"You cannot call another one now," Jarlaxle reminded him, extending a hand that Athrogate grasped.

The dwarf settled behind the drow on the nightmare's back and Jarlaxle

27

kicked the steed away, leaving the skeletons far, far behind. They rode hard, then more easily, and the dwarf began to giggle.

"What do you know?" the drow asked, but Athrogate only bellowed with wild laughter.

"What?" Jarlaxle demanded, but he couldn't spare the time to properly look back, and Athrogate sounded too amused to properly answer.

When they finally reached a place where they could safely stop, Jarlaxle pulled up abruptly and turned around.

There sat Athrogate, red-faced with laughter as he held a skeletal hand and forearm, the fingers still clawing in the air before him. Jarlaxle leaped from the nightmare, and when the dwarf didn't immediately follow, the drow dismissed the steed, sending Athrogate falling to the ground through an insubstantial swirl of black smoke.

But Athrogate still laughed as he thumped to the ground, thoroughly amused by the animated skeletal arm.

"Be rid of that wretched thing!" Jarlaxle said.

Athrogate looked at him incredulously. "Thought ye had more imagination, elf," he said. He hopped up and unstrapped his heavy breastplate. As soon as it fell aside, the dwarf reached over his shoulder with the still-clawing hand and gave a great sigh of pleasure as the fingers scratched his back. "How long do ye think it'll live?"

"Longer than you, I hope," the drow replied, closing his eyes and shaking his head helplessly. "Not very long, I imagine."

"Bwahaha!" Athrogate bellowed, then, "Aaaaaaaah."

* * * * *

"The next time we face such creatures, I expect you to follow my lead," Jarlaxle said to Athrogate the next morning as the dwarf fiddled once more with his skeletal toy.

"Next time? What do ye know, elf?"

"It was not a random event," the drow admitted. "I have been visited, twice now, in my Reverie by a beast I had thought destroyed, but one that has somehow transcended death."

"A beast that brought up them skeletons?"

"A great dragon," Jarlaxle explained, "to the south of here and . . ." Jarlaxle paused, not really certain where Hephaestus's lair was. He had gone there, but magically with a teleportation spell. He knew the general features of that distant region, but not the specifics of the lair, though he thought of someone who would surely know the place. "Near to the Snowflake Mountains," he finished. "A great dragon whose thoughts can reach across hundreds of miles, it seems."

"Ye thinking we need to run farther?"

Jarlaxle shook his head. "There are great powers I can enlist in defeating this creature."

"Hmm," said the dwarf.

"I just have to convince them not to kill us first."

"Hmm."

"Indeed," said the drow. "A mighty priest named Cadderly, a Chosen of his god, who promised me death should I ever return."

"Hmm."

"But I will find a way."

"So ye're sayin', and so ye're prayin', but I'm hoping I'm not the one what'll be payin'."

Jarlaxle glared at the dwarf.

"Well, then ye can't be going back where ye're wanting—though I canno' be thinking why ye're wanting what ye're wantin'! To go to a place where the dragons are hauntin'!"

The glare melted into a groan.

"I know, I know," said Athrogate. "No more word-songin'. But that was a good one, what?"

"Needs work," said the drow. "Though considerably less so than your usual efforts."

"Hmm," said the dwarf, beaming with pride.

CHAPTER

THE BROKEN CONTINUUM

Drizzt Do'Urden slipped out of his bedroll and reached his bare arms up high, fingers wide, stretching to the morning sky. It was good to be on the road, out of Mithral Hall after the dark winter. It was invigorating to smell the fresh, crisp air, absent the smoke of the forges, and to feel the wind across his shoulders and through his long, thick white hair.

It was good to be alone with his wife.

The dark elf rolled his head in wide circles, stretching his neck. He reached up high again, kneeling on his blankets. The breeze was chill across his naked form, but he didn't mind. The cool wind invigorated him and made him feel alive with sensation.

He slowly moved to stand, exaggerating every movement to flex away the kinks from the hard ground that had served as his mattress, then paced away from the small encampment and outside the ring of boulders to catch a view of Catti-brie.

Dressed only in her colorful magical blouse, which had once been the enchanted robe of a gnome wizard, she stood on a hillside not far away, her palms together in front of her in a pose of deep concentration. Drizzt marveled at her simple charm. The colorful shift reached only to mid-thigh, and Catti-brie's natural beauty was neither diminished nor outshone by the finely crafted garment.

They were on the road back to Mithral Hall from the city of Silverymoon, where Catti-brie's wizard mentor, the great Lady Alustriel, ruled. It had not been a good visit. Something was in the air, something dangerous and frightening, some feeling among the wizards that all was not well with the Weave of magic. Reports and whispers from all over Faerûn spoke of spells gone horribly awry, of magic misfiring or not firing at all, of brilliant spellcasters falling to apparent insanity.

Alustriel had admitted that she feared for the integrity of Mystra's Weave itself, the very source of arcane energy, and the look on her face, ashen, was something Drizzt had never before witnessed from her, not even when the drow had gone to Mithral Hall those many years ago, not even when King Obould and his great horde had crawled from their mountain holes in murderous frenzy. It was indeed a crestfallen and fearful look that Drizzt would never have thought possible on the face of that renowned champion, one of the Seven Sisters, Chosen of Mystra, beloved ruler of mighty Silverymoon.

Vigilance, observation, and meditation were Alustriel's orders of the day, as she and all others scrambled to try to discern what in the Nine Hells might be happening, and Catti-brie, less than a decade a wizard but showing great promise, had taken those orders to heart.

That's why she had risen so early, Drizzt knew, and had moved away from the distractions of the encampment and his presence, to be alone with her meditation.

He smiled as he watched her, her auburn hair still rich in color and thick to her shoulders, blowing in the breeze, her form, a bit thicker with age, perhaps, but still so beautiful and inviting to him, swaying gently with her thoughts.

She slowly spread her hands out wide as if in invitation to magic, the sleeves of her blouse reaching only to her elbows. Drizzt smiled as she rose from the ground, floating upward a few feet in easy levitation. Purple flames of faerie fire flickered to life across her body, appearing as extensions of the violet fabric of the blouse, as if its magic joined with her in a symbiotic completion. A magical gust of wind buffeted her, blowing her auburn mane out wide behind her.

Drizzt could see that she was immersing herself in simple spells, in safe magic, trying to create more intimacy with the Weave as she contemplated the fears Alustriel had relayed.

A flash of lightning in the distance startled Drizzt and he jerked his head toward it as a rumble of thunder followed.

He crinkled his brow in confusion. The dawn was cloudless, but lightning it had been, reaching from high in the sky to the ground, for he saw the crackling blue bolt lingering along the distant terrain.

Drizzt had been on the surface for forty-five years, but he had never seen any natural phenomenon quite like that. He had witnessed terrific storms from the deck of Captain Deudermont's *Sea Sprite*, had watched a dust storm engulf the Calim Desert, had seen a squall pile snow knee-deep on the ground in an hour's time. He had even seen the rare event known as ball lightning once, in Icewind Dale, and he figured the sight before him to be some variant of that peculiar energy.

But this lightning traveled in a straight line, and trailed behind it a curtain of blue-white, shimmering energy. He couldn't gauge its speed, other than to note that the curtain of blue fire expanded behind it.

It appeared to be crossing the countryside to the north of his position. He glanced up at Catti-brie, floating and glowing on the hilltop to the east, and he wondered whether he should disturb her meditation to point out the phenomenon. He glanced at the line of lightning and his lavender eyes widened in shock. It had accelerated suddenly and had changed course, angling in his direction.

He turned from the lightning to Catti-brie, to realize that it was running straight at her!

"Cat!" Drizzt yelled, and started running.

She seemed not to hear.

Magical anklets sped Drizzt on his way, his legs moving in a blur. But the lightning was faster, and he could only cry out again and again as it sizzled past him. He could feel its teeming energy. His hair rose up wildly from the proximity of the powerful charge, white strands floating on all sides.

"Cat!" he yelled to the hovering, glowing woman. "Catti-brie! Run!"

She was deep in her meditation, though she did seem to react, just a bit, turning her head to glance at Drizzt.

But too late. Her eyes widened just as the speeding ground lightning engulfed her. Blue sparks flew from her outstretched arms, her fingers jerking spasmodically, her form jolting with powerful discharges.

The edge of the strange lightning remained for a few heartbeats, then continued onward, leaving the still-floating woman in the shimmering blue curtain of its wake.

"Cat," Drizzt gasped, scrambling desperately across the stones. By the time he got there, the curtain was moving along, leaving a scarred line crackling with power on the ground.

Catti-brie still floated above it, still trembled and jerked. Drizzt held his breath as he neared her, to see that her eyes had rolled up into her head, showing only white.

He grabbed her hand and felt the sting of electrical discharge. But he didn't let go and he stubbornly pulled her aside of the scarred line. He hugged her close and tried unsuccessfully to pull her down to the ground.

"Catti-brie," Drizzt begged. "Don't you leave me!"

A thousand heartbeats or more passed as Drizzt held her, then the woman finally relaxed and gently sank from her levitation. Drizzt leaned her back to see her face, his heart skipping beats until he saw that he was staring into her beautiful blue eyes once more.

"By the gods, I thought you lost to me," he said with a great sigh of relief, one that he bit short as he noted that Catti-brie wasn't blinking. She wasn't really looking at him at all, but rather looking past him. He glanced over his shoulder to see what might be holding her interest so intently, but there was nothing.

"Cat?" he whispered, staring into her large eyes—eyes that did not gaze back at him nor past him, but into nothingness, he realized.

He gave her a shake. She mumbled something he could not decipher. Drizzt leaned closer.

"What?" he asked, and shook her again.

She lifted off the ground several inches, her arms reaching out wide, her eyes rolling back into her head. The purple flames began anew, as did the crackling energy.

Drizzt moved to hug her and pull her down again, but he fell back in surprise as her entire form shimmered as if emanating waves of energy. Helplessly the drow watched, mesmerized and horrified.

"Catti-brie?" he asked, and as he looked into her white eyes, he realized that something was different, very different! The lines on her face softened and disappeared. Her hair seemed longer and thicker—even her part changed to a style Catti-brie had not worn for years! And she seemed a bit leaner, her skin a bit tighter.

Younger.

" 'Twas a bow that found meself in the halls of a dwarven king," she said, or something like that—Drizzt could not be certain—and in a distinctly

34

Dwarvish accent, like she'd once had when her time had been spent almost exclusively with Bruenor's clan in the shadows of Kelvin's Cairn in faraway Icewind Dale. She still floated off the ground, but the faerie fire and the crackling energy dissipated. Her eyes focused and returned to normal, those rich, deep blue orbs that had so stolen Drizzt's heart.

"Heartseeker, yes," Drizzt said. He stepped back and pulled the mighty bow from his shoulder, presenting it to her.

"Can't be fishing Maer Dualdon with a bow, though, and so it's Rumble-belly's line I'm favorin'," she said, still looking into the distance and not at Drizzt.

Drizzt crinkled his face in confusion.

The woman sighed deeply. Her eyes rolled back into her head, showing only white to Drizzt. The flames and energy reappeared and a gust of wind came up from nowhere, striking only Catti-brie, as if those waves of energy that had come forth from her were returning to her being. Her hair, her skin, her age—all returned, and her colorful garment stopped blowing in the unfelt wind.

The moment passed and she settled to the ground, unconscious once more.

Drizzt shook her again, called to her many times, but she seemed not to notice. He snapped his fingers in front of her eyes, but she didn't even blink. He started to lift her, to carry her toward the camp so they could hurry on their way to Mithral Hall, but as he extended her arm, he saw a tear in her magical blouse just behind the shoulder. Then he froze as he noticed bruises under the fabric. With a shiver of panic, Drizzt gently slid the ripped section aside.

He sucked in his breath in fear and confusion. He had seen Catti-brie's bare back a thousand times, had marveled at her unblemished, smooth skin. But it was marked, scarred even, in the distinctive shape of an hourglass as large as Drizzt's fist. The lower half was almost fully discolored, the top showing only a small sliver of bruising, as if almost all of the counting sand had drained.

With trembling fingers, Drizzt touched it. Catti-brie did not react.

"What?" he whispered helplessly.

He carried Catti-brie along briskly, her head lolling as if she were half-asleep.

CHAPTER

It was a place of soaring towers and sweeping stairways, of flying buttresses and giant, decorated windows, of light and enlightenment, of magic and reason, of faith and science. It was Spirit Soaring, the work of Cadderly Bonaduce, Chosen of Deneir. Cadderly the Questioner, he had been labeled by his brothers of Deneir, the god who demanded such inquiry and continual reason from his devoted.

Cadderly had raised the grand structure from the ruins of the Edificant Library, considered by many to be the most magnificent library in all of Faerûn. Indeed, architects from lands as far and varied as Silverymoon and Calimport had come to the Snowflake Mountains to glimpse this creation, to marvel in the flying buttresses—a recent innovation in the lands of Faerûn, and never before on so grand a scale. The work of magic, of divine inspiration, had formed the stained glass windows, and also rendered the great murals of scholars at work in their endless pursuit of reason.

Spirit Soaring had been raised as a library and a cathedral, a common ground where scholars, mages, sages, and priests might gather to question superstition, to embrace reason. No place on the continent so represented the wondrous joining of faith and science, where one need not fear that logic, observation, and experimentation might take a learner away from edicts of the divine. Spirit Soaring was a place where truth was considered divine, and not the other way around.

Scholars did not fear to pursue their theories there. Philosophers did not fear to question the common understanding of the pantheon and the world. Priests of any and all gods did not fear persecution there, unless the very concept of rational debate represented persecution to a closed and small mind.

Spirit Soaring was a place to explore, to question, to learn—about everything. There, discussions of the various gods of the world of Toril always bordered on heresy. There, the nature of magic was examined, and so there, at a time of fear and uncertainty, at the time of the failing Weave, rushed scholars from far and wide.

And Cadderly greeted them, every one, with open arms and shared concern. He looked like a very young man, much younger than his forty-four years. His gray eyes sparkled with youthful luster and his mop of curly brown hair bounced along his shoulders. He moved like a much younger man, loose and agile, a distinctive spring in his step. He wore a typical Deneirrath outfit, tan-white tunic and trousers, and added his own flair with a light blue cape and a wide-brimmed hat, blue to match the cape, with a red band, plumed on the right side.

The time was unsettling, the magic of the world possibly unraveling, yet Cadderly Bonaduce's eyes reflected excitement more than dread. Cadderly was forever a student, his mind always inquisitive, and he did not fear what was simply not yet explained.

He just wanted to understand it.

"Welcome, welcome!" He greeted a trio of visitors one bright morning, who were dressed in the green robes of druids.

"Young Bonaduce, I presume," said one, an old graybeard.

"Not so young," Cadderly admitted.

"I knew your father many years ago," the druid replied. "Am I right in assuming that we will be welcomed here in this time of confusion?"

Cadderly looked at the man curiously.

"Cadderly still lives, correct?"

"Well, yes," Cadderly answered, then grinned and asked, "Cleo?"

"Ah, your father has told you of . . . me . . ." the druid answered, but he ended with wide eyes, stuttering, "C-Cadderly? Is that you?"

"I had thought you lost in the advent of the chaos curse, old friend!" Cadderly said.

"How can you be . . . ?" Cleo started to ask, in utter confusion.

"Were you not destroyed?" the youthful-seeming priest asked. "Of course you weren't—you stand here before me!"

"I wandered in the form of a turtle, for years," Cleo explained. "Trapped by insanity within the animal coil I most favored. But how can you be Cadderly? I had heard of Cadderly's children, who should be as old . . ."

As he spoke, a young man walked up to the priest. He looked very much like Cadderly, but with exotic, almond-shaped eyes.

"And here is one," Cadderly explained, sweeping his son to him with an outstretched arm. "My oldest son, Temberle."

"Who looks older than you," Cleo remarked dryly.

"A long and complicated story," said the priest. "Connected to this place, Spirit Soaring."

"You are wanted in the observatory, Father," Temberle said with a polite salute to the new visitors. "The Gondsmen are declaring supremacy again, as gadget overcomes magic."

"No doubt, both factions think I side with their cause."

Temberle shrugged and Cadderly breathed a great sigh.

"My old friend," Cadderly said to Cleo, "I should like some time with you, to catch up."

"I can tell you of life as a turtle," Cleo deadpanned, drawing a smile from Cadderly.

"We have many points of view in Spirit Soaring at the time, and little agreement," Cadderly explained. "They're all nervous, of course."

"With reason," said another of the druids.

"And reason is our only way through this," said Cadderly. "So welcome, friends, and enter. We have food aplenty, and discussion aplenty more. Add your voices without reserve."

The three druids looked to each other, the other two nodding approvingly to Cleo. "As I told you it would be," Cleo said. "Reasonable priests, these Deneirrath." He turned to Cadderly, who bowed, smiled widely, and took his leave.

"You see?" Cadderly said to Temberle as the druids walked past into Spirit Soaring. "I have told you many times that I am reasonable." He patted his son on the shoulder and followed after the druids.

"And every time you do, Mother whispers in my ear that your reasonableness is based entirely on what suits your current desires," Temberle said after him.

Cadderly skipped a step and seemed almost to trip. He didn't look back, but laughed and continued on his way.

* * * * *

Temberle left the building and walked to the southern wall, to the great garden, where he was to meet with his twin sister, Hanaleisa. The two had planned a trip that morning to Carradoon, the small town on the banks of Impresk Lake, a day's march from Spirit Soaring. Temberle's grin widened as he approached the large, fenced garden, catching sight of his sister with his favorite uncle.

The green-bearded dwarf hopped about over a row of newly-planted seeds, whispering words of encouragement and waving his arms—one severed at his elbow—like a bird trying to gain altitude in a gale. This dwarf, Pikel Bouldershoulder, was most unusual for his kind for having embraced the ways of the druids—and for many other reasons, most of which made him Temberle's favorite uncle.

Hanaleisa Maupoissant Bonaduce, looking so much like a younger version of their mother, Danica, with her strawberry blond hair and rich brown eyes, almond-shaped like Temberle's own, looked up from the row of new plantings and grinned at her brother, as clearly amused by Pikel's gyrations as was Temberle.

"Uncle Pikel says he'll make them grow bigger than ever," Hanaleisa remarked as Temberle came through the gate.

"Evah!" Pikel roared, and Temberle was impressed that he had apparently learned a new word.

"But I thought that the gods weren't listening," Temberle dared say, drawing an "Ooooh" of consternation and a lot of finger-wagging from Pikel.

"Faith, brother," said Hanaleisa. "Uncle Pikel knows the dirt."

"Hee hee hee," said the dwarf.

"Carradoon awaits," said Temberle.

"Where is Rorey?" Hanaleisa asked, referring to their brother Rorick, at seventeen, five years their junior.

"With a gaggle of mages, arguing the integrity of the magical strands that empower the world. I expect that when this strangeness is ended, Rorey will have a dozen powerful wizards vying to serve as his mentor."

Hanaleisa nodded at that, for she, like Temberle, knew well their younger brother's propensity and talent at interjecting himself into any debate. The young woman brushed the dirt from her knees and slapped her hands together to clean them.

"Lead on," she bade her brother. "Uncle Pikel won't let my garden die, will you?"

"Doo-dad!" Pikel triumphantly proclaimed and launched into his rain dance . . . or fertility dance . . . or dance of the sunshine . . . or whatever it was that he danced about. As always, the Bonaduce twins left their Uncle Pikel with wide, sincere smiles splayed on their young faces, as it had been since their toddler days.

* * * * *

Her forearms and forehead planted firmly on the rug, the woman eased her feet from the floor, drawing her legs perpendicular to her torso. With great grace, she let her legs swing wide to their respective sides, then pulled them together as she straightened in an easy and secure headstand.

Breathing softly, in perfect balance and harmony, Danica turned her hands flat and pressed up, rising into a complete handstand. She posed as if underwater, or as if gravity itself could not touch her in her deep meditative state. She moved even beyond that grace, seeming as if some wire or force pulled her upward as she rose up from palms to fingers.

She stood inverted, perfectly still and perfectly straight, immune to the passage of time, unstrained. Her muscles did not struggle for balance, but firmly held her in position so her weight pressed down uniformly onto her strong hands. She kept her eyes closed, and her hair, showing gray amidst the strawberry hues, hung to the floor.

She was deep in the moment, deep within herself. Yet she sensed an approach, a movement by the door, and she opened her eyes just as Ivan Bouldershoulder, yellow-bearded brother of Pikel, poked his hairy head through.

Danica opened her eyes to regard the dwarf.

"When all their magic's gone, yerself and meself'll take over the world, girl," he said with an exaggerated wink.

Danica rolled down to her toes and gracefully stood upright, turning as she went so that she still faced the dwarf.

"What do you know, Ivan?" she asked.

"More'n I should and not enough to be sure," he replied. "Yer older brats went down to Carradoon, me brother's telling me."

"Temberle enjoys the availability of some young ladies there, or so I've heard."

"Ah," the dwarf mused, and a very serious look came over him. "And what o' Hana?"

Danica laughed at him. "What of her?"

"She got some boy sniffin' around?"

"She's twenty-two years old, Ivan. That would be her business."

"Bah! Not until her Uncle Ivan gets to talk to the fool, it won't!"

"She can handle herself. She's trained in the ways of—"

"No, she can'no'!"

"You don't show the same concern for Temberle, I see."

"Bah. Boys'll do what boys're supposed to be doin', but they best not be doin' it to me girl, Hana!"

Danica put a hand up over her mouth in a futile attempt to mask her laughter.

"Bah!" Ivan said, waving his hand at her. "I'm takin' that girl to Bruenor's halls, I am!"

"I don't think she'd agree to that."

"Who's askin'? Yer young ones be runnin' wild, they be!"

He continued to grumble, until the laughing Danica finally managed to catch her breath long enough to inquire, "Was there something you wished to ask me?"

Ivan stared at her blankly for a moment, confused and flustered. "Yeah," he said, though he seemed uncertain. After another moment of reflection, he added, "Where's the little one? Me brother was thinkin' o' jogging down to Carradoon, and he missed them older brats when they left."

"I haven't seen Rorick all day."

"Well, he didn't go with Temberle and Hana. Is it good by yerself that he goes with his uncle?"

"I cannot think of a safer place for any of my children to be, good Ivan."

"Aye, and that's what's what," the dwarf agreed, hooking his thumbs under the suspenders of his breeches.

"I fear that I cannot say the same for my future children-in-law, however. . . ."

"Just the son-in-law," Ivan corrected with a wink.

"Don't break anything," Danica begged. "And don't leave any marks."

Ivan nodded, then brought his hands together and cracked his knuckles loudly. With a bow, he took his leave.

Danica knew Ivan was harmless, at least as far as suitors to her daughter were concerned. It occurred to her just then that Hanaleisa would have a hard time indeed maintaining any relationships with Ivan and Pikel hovering over her.

Or maybe, those two would serve as a good test of a young man's intentions. His heart would surely have to be full for him to stick around once the dwarves started in on him.

Danica giggled and sighed contentedly, reminding herself that, other than the few years they had been away serving King Bruenor in Mithral Hall, Ivan and Pikel Bouldershoulder had been the best guardians any child could ever know.

* * * * *

The shadowy being, once Fetchigrol the archmage of a great and lost civilization, didn't even recognize himself by that name, having long ago abandoned his identity in the communal joining ritual that had forged the Crystal Shard. He had known life; had known undeath as a lich; had known a state of pure energy as part of the Crystal Shard; had known nothingness, obliteration.

And even from that last state, the creature that was once Fetchigrol had returned, touched by the Weave itself. No more was he a free-willed spirit, but merely an extension, an angry outreach of that curious triumvirate of power that had melded into a singular malevolent force in a fire-blasted cavern many miles to the southeast.

Fetchigrol served the anger of Crenshinibon-Hephaestus-Yharaskrik, of the being they had become, the Ghost King.

And like all seven of the shadowy specters, Fetchigrol searched the night, seeking those who had wronged his masters. In the lower reaches of the Snowflake Mountains, overlooking a large lake shining under the moonlight to the west, and on a trail leading deeper into the mountains and to a great library, he sensed that he was close.

When he heard the voices, a thrill coursed Fetchigrol's shadowy substance, for above all, the undead specter sought an outlet for his malevolence,

43

a victim of his hatred. He drifted to the deeper shadows behind a tree overlooking the path as a pair of young humans came into view, walking tentatively in the dim light among the roots that crisscrossed the trail.

They passed right before him, not noticing at all—though the young woman did cock her head curiously and shiver.

How the undead creature wanted to leap out and devour them! But Fetchigrol was too far removed from their world, was too much within the Shadowfell, the intruding realm of shadow and darkness that had come to Faerûn. Like his six brothers, he had not the substance to affect material creatures.

Only spirits. Only the diminishing life energies of the dead.

He followed the pair down the mountain until they at last found a place they deemed suitable for an encampment. Confident that they would stay there at least until pre-dawn, the malevolent spirit rushed into the wilds, seeking a vessel.

He found it only a couple of miles from the young humans' camp, in the form of a dead bear, its half-rotted carcass teeming with maggots and flies.

Fetchigrol bowed before the beast and began to chant, to channel the power of the Ghost King, to call to the spirit of the bear.

The corpse stirred.

* * * * *

His steps slow, his heart heavier than his weary limbs, Drizzt Do'Urden crossed the Surbrin River Bridge. The eastern door of Mithral Hall was in sight, as were members of Clan Battlehammer, scurrying to join him as he bore his burden.

Catti-brie lay listless in his arms, her head lolling with every step, her eyes open but seeing nothing.

And Drizzt's expression, so full of fear and sadness, only added to that horrifying image.

Calls to "Get Bruenor!" and "Open the doors and clear the road!" led Drizzt through that back door, and before he had gone ten strides into Mithral Hall, a wagon bounced up beside him and a group of dwarves helped get him and the listless Catti-brie into the back.

Only then did Drizzt realize how exhausted he was. He had walked for miles with Catti-brie in his arms, not daring to stop, for she needed help he could not provide. Bruenor's priests would know what to do, he'd prayed, and so the dwarves who gathered around repeatedly assured him.

The driver pushed the team hard across Garumn's Gorge and down the long and winding tunnels toward Bruenor's chambers.

Word had passed ahead, and Bruenor was in the hall waiting for them. Regis and many others stood beside him as he paced anxiously, wringing his strong hands or pulling at his great beard, softened to orange by the gray that dulled its once-fiery red.

"Elf?" Bruenor called. "What d'ye know?"

Drizzt nearly crumbled under the desperate tone in his dear friend's voice, for he couldn't offer much in the way of explanation or hope. He summoned as much energy as he could and flipped his legs over the side rail of the wagon, dropping lightly to the floor. He met Bruenor's gaze and managed a slight and hopeful nod. He struggled to keep up that optimism as he moved around the wagon and dropped the gate, then gathered his beloved Catti-brie in his arms.

Bruenor was at his side as Drizzt hoisted her. The dwarf's eyes widened and his hands trembled as he tried to reach up and touch his dear daughter.

"Elf?" he asked, his voice barely a whisper, and so shaky that the short word seemed multisyllabic.

Drizzt looked at him, and there he froze, unable to shake his head or offer a smile of hope.

Drizzt had no answers.

Catti-brie had somehow been touched by wild magic, and as far as he could tell, she was lost to them, was lost to the reality around her.

"Elf?" Bruenor asked again, and he managed to run his fingers across his daughter's soft face.

* * * * *

She stood perfectly still, staring at the jutting limb of the dead tree, her hands up before her, locked in striking form. Hanaleisa, so much her mother's daughter, found her center of peace and strength.

She could have reached up and grasped the end of the branch, then used her weight and leverage to break it free. But what would have been the fun in that?

45

So instead, the tree became her opponent, her enemy, her challenge.

"Hurry up, the night grows cold!" Temberle called from their camp near the trail.

Hanaleisa allowed no smile to crease her serious visage, and blocked out her brother's call. Her concentration complete, she struck with suddenness and with sheer power, striking the branch near the trunk with a left jab then a right cross, once, twice, then again with a snapping left before falling back into a defensive lean, lifting her leg for a jolting kick.

She rose up in a spinning leap and snapped out a strike that severed the end of the branch much farther out from the trunk, then again to splinter the limb in the middle. She finished with another leaping spin, bringing her leg up high and wide then dropping it down hard on the place she had already weakened with her jabs.

The limb broke away cleanly, falling to the ground in three neat pieces.

Hanaleisa landed, completely balanced, and brought her hands in close, fingers touching. She bowed to the tree, her defeated opponent, then scooped the broken firewood and started for the camp as her brother called out once more.

She had gone only a few steps before she heard a shuffling in the forest, not far away. The young woman froze in place, making not a sound, her eyes scouring the patches of moonlight in the darkness, seeking movement.

Something ambled through the brush, something heavy, not twenty strides away, and heading, she realized, straight for their camp.

Hanaleisa slowly bent her knees, lowering herself to the ground, where she gently and silently placed the firewood, except for one thick piece. She stood and remained very still for a moment, seeking the sound again to get her bearings. With great agility she brought her feet up one at a time and removed her boots, then padded off, walking lightly on the balls of her bare feet.

She soon saw the light of the fire Temberle had managed to get going, then noted the form moving cumbersomely before her, crossing between her and that firelight, showing itself to be a large creature indeed.

Hanaleisa held her breath, trying to choose her next move, and quickly, for the creature was closing on her brother. She had been trained by her parents to fight and fight well, but never before had she found herself with lethal danger so close at hand.

The sound of her brother's voice, calling her name, "Hana?" jarred her from her contemplation. Temberle had heard the beast, and indeed, the beast was very close to him, and moving with great speed.

Hanaleisa sprinted ahead and shouted out to catch the creature's attention, fearing that she had hesitated too long. "Your sword!" she cried to her brother.

Hanaleisa leaped up as she neared the beast—a bear, she realized—and caught a branch overhead, then swung out and let go, soaring high and far, clearing the animal. Only then did Hanaleisa understand the true nature of the monster, that it was not just a bear that might be frightened away. She saw that half of its face had rotted away, the white bone of its skull shining in the moonlight.

She struck down as she passed over it, her open palm smacking hard against the snout as the creature looked up to react. The solid blow jolted the monster, but did not stop its swipe, which clipped Hanaleisa as she flew past, sending her into a spin.

She landed lightly but off balance and stumbled aside, and just in time as Temberle raced past her, greatsword in hand. He charged straight in with a mighty thrust and the sword plunged through the loose skin on the undead creature's back and cracked off bone.

But the bear kept coming, seeming unbothered by the wound, and walked itself right up the blade to Temberle, its terrible claws out wide, its toothy maw opened in a roar.

Hanaleisa leaped past Temberle, laying flat out in mid-air and double-kicking the beast about the shoulders and chest. Had it been a living bear, several hundred pounds of muscle and tough hide and thick bone, she wouldn't have moved it much, of course, but its undead condition worked in her favor, for much of the creature's mass had rotted away or been carried off by scavengers.

The beast stumbled back, sliding down the greatsword's blade enough for Temberle to yank it free.

"Slash, don't stab!" Hanaleisa reminded him as she landed on her feet and waded in, laying forth a barrage of kicks and punches. She batted aside a swatting paw and got behind the swipe of deadly claws, then rattled off a series of heavy punches into the beast's shoulders.

She felt the bone crunching under the weight of those blows, but again, the beast seemed unbothered and launched a backhand that forced the young woman to retreat.

47

The bear went on the offensive, and it attacked with ferocity, moving to tackle the woman. Hanaleisa scrambled back, nearly tripping over an exposed root, then getting caught against a birch stand.

She cried out in fear as the beast fell over her, or started to, until a mighty sword flashed in the moonlight above and behind it, coming down powerfully across the bear's right shoulder and driving through.

The undead beast howled and pursued the dodging Hanaleisa, crashing into the birch stand and taking the whole of it down beneath its bulky, tumbling form. It bit and slashed as if it had its enemy secured, but Hanaleisa was gone, out the side, rolling away.

The bear tried to follow, but Temberle moved fast behind it, relentlessly smashing at it with his heavy greatsword. He chopped away chunks of flesh, sending maggots flying and smashing bones to powder.

Still the beast came on, on all fours and down low, closing on Hanaleisa.

She fought away her revulsion and panic. She placed her back against a solid tree and curled her legs, and as the beast neared, jaws open to bite at her, she kicked out repeatedly, her heel smashing the snout again and again.

Still the beast drove in, and still Temberle smashed at it, and Hanaleisa kept on kicking. The top jaw and snout broke away, hanging to the side, but still the animated corpse bore down!

At the last moment, Hanaleisa threw herself to the side and backward into a roll. She came around to her feet, every instinct telling her to run away.

She denied her fear.

The bear turned on Temberle ferociously. His sword crashed down across its collarbone, but the monster swatted it with such strength that it tore the sword from Temberle's hand and sent it flying away.

Up rose the monster to its full height, its arms raised to the sky, ready to drop down upon the unarmed warrior.

Hanaleisa leaped upon its back and with the momentum of her charge, with every bit of focus and concentration, with all the strength of her years of training as a monk behind her strike, drove her hand—index and middle fingers extended like a blade—at the back of the beast's head.

She felt her fingers break through the skull. She retracted and punched again and again, pulverizing the bone, driving her fingers into the beast's brain and tearing pieces out.

The bear swung around and Hanaleisa went flying into the trees, crashing hard through a close pair of young elms, bouncing from one to the other, her momentum pushing her so she fell to the ground right behind them.

But as she slid down the narrowing gap, her ankle caught. Desperate, she looked at the approaching monster.

She saw the sword descend behind it, atop its skull, splitting the head in half and driving down the creature's neck.

And still it kept coming! Hanaleisa's eyes widened with horror. She couldn't free her foot!

But it was only the undead beast's momentum that propelled it forward, and it crashed into the elms and fell to the side.

Hanaleisa breathed easier. Temberle rushed up and helped her free her foot, then helped her stand. She was sore in a dozen places—her shoulder was surely bruised.

But the beast was dead—again.

"What evil has come to these woods?" the young woman asked.

"I don't . . ." Temberle started to answer, but he stopped. Both he and his sister shivered, their eyes going wide in surprise. A sudden coldness filled the air around them.

They heard a hissing sound, perhaps laughter, and jumped back to back into a defensive posture, as they had been trained.

The chill passed, and the laughter receded.

In the firelight of their nearby camp, they saw a shadowy figure drift away.

"What was that?" Temberle asked.

"We should go back," Hanaleisa breathlessly replied.

"We're much closer to Carradoon than Spirit Soaring."

"Then go!" Hanaleisa said, and the pair rushed to the camp and scooped up their gear.

Each took a burning branch to use as a torch, then started along the trail. Cold pockets of air found them repeatedly as they ran, with hissing laughter and patches of shadow darker than the darkest night shifting around them. They heard animals screech in fear and birds flutter from branches.

"Press on," each urged the other repeatedly, and they whispered more insistently when at last their torches burned away and the darkness closed in tightly.

They didn't stop running until they reached the outskirts of the town of Carradoon, dark and asleep on the shores of Impresk Lake, still hours before the dawn. They knew the proprietor at Cedar Shakes, a fine inn nearby, and went right to the door, rapping hard and insistently.

"Here, now! What's the racket at this witching hour?" came a sharp response from a window above. "What and wait, ho! Is that Danica's kids?"

"Let us in, good Bester Bilge," Temberle called up. "Please, just let us in."

They relaxed when the door swung open. Cheery old Bester Bilge pulled them inside, telling Temberle to throw a few logs on the low-burning hearth and promising a strong drink and some warm soup in short order.

Temberle and Hanaleisa looked to each other with great relief, hoping they had left the cold and dark outside.

They couldn't know that Fetchigrol had followed them to Carradoon and was even then at the old graveyard outside the town walls, planning the carnage to come with the next sunset.

CHAPTER

A throgate held the skeletal arm aloft. He grumbled at its inactivity, and gave it a little shake. The fingers began to claw once more and the dwarf grinned and reached the bony arm over his shoulder, sighing contentedly as the scraping digits worked at a hard-to-reach spot in the middle of his itchy back.

"How long ye think it'll last, elf?" he asked.

Jarlaxle, too concerned to even acknowledge the dwarf's antics, just shrugged and continued on his meandering way. The drow wasn't sure where he was going. Any who knew Jarlaxle would have read the gravity of the situation clearly in his uncertain expression, for rarely, if ever, had anyone ever witnessed Jarlaxle Baenre perplexed.

The drow realized that he couldn't wait for Hephaestus to come to him. He didn't want to encounter such a foe on his own, or with only Athrogate at his side. He considered returning to Luskan—Kimmuriel and Bregan D'aerthe could certainly help—but his instincts argued against that. Once again, he would be allowing Hephaestus the offensive, and would be pitted against a foe that could apparently raise undead minions to his command with ease.

Above all else, Jarlaxle wanted to take the fight to the dragon, and he believed that Cadderly might well prove the solution to his troubles. But how could he enlist the priest, who was surely no willing ally of the dark elves? Except one particular dark elf.

And wouldn't it be grand to have Drizzt Do'Urden and some of his mighty friends along for the hunt?

But how?

So at Jarlaxle's direction, the pair traveled eastward, meandering across the Silver Marches toward Mithral Hall. It would take them easily a tenday, and Jarlaxle wasn't sure he had that kind of time to spare. He resisted Reverie that first day, and when night came, he meditated lightly, standing on a precarious perch.

A cold breeze found him, and as he shifted to curl against it, he slipped from the narrow log upon which he stood and the resulting stumble startled him. His hand already in his pocket, Jarlaxle pulled forth a fistful of ceramic pebbles. He spun a quick circle, spreading them around, and as each hit the ground, it broke open and the enchantment within, dweomers of bright light, spewed forth.

"What the—?" Athrogate cried, startled from his sleep by the sudden brightness.

Jarlaxle paid him no heed. He moved fast after a shadowy figure racing away from the magical light, a painful thing to undead creatures. He threw another light bomb ahead of the fleeing, huddled form, then another as it veered toward a shadowy patch.

"Hurry, dwarf!" the drow called, and he soon heard Athrogate huffing and puffing in pursuit. As soon as Athrogate passed him, Jarlaxle drew out a wand and brought forth a burst of brighter and more powerful light, landing it near the shadowy form. The creature shrieked, an awful, preternatural keening that sent a shiver coursing down Jarlaxle's spine.

That howl didn't slow Athrogate in the least, and the brave dwarf charged in with abandon, his morningstars spinning in both hands, arms outstretched. Athrogate called upon the enchantment of the morningstar in his right hand and explosive oil oozed over its metallic head. The dwarf leaped at the cowering creature and swung with all his might, thinking to end the fight with a single, explosive smite.

The morningstar hit nothing substantial, just hummed through the empty night.

Then Athrogate yelped in pain as a sharp touch hit his shoulder, a point of sudden and burning agony. He fell back, swinging with abandon, his morningstars crisscrossing, again hitting nothing.

The dwarf saw the specter's dark, cold hands reaching toward him, so he tried a different tactic. He swung his morningstars in from opposite sides, aiming the heads to collide directly in the center of the shadowy darkness.

Jarlaxle watched the battle with a curious eye, trying to gauge this foe. The specter was a minion of Hephaestus, obviously, and he knew well the usual qualities of incorporeal undead denizens.

Athrogate's weapon should have harmed it, at least some—the dwarf's morningstars were heavily enchanted. Even the most powerful undead creatures, the ones that existed on both the Prime Material Plane and a darker place of negative energy, should not have such complete immunity to his assault.

Jarlaxle winced and looked away when Athrogate's morningstar heads clanged together, the volatile oil exploding in a blinding flash, a concussive burst that forced the dwarf to stumble backward.

When the drow looked again, the specter seemed wholly unbothered by the burst. Jarlaxle took note of something unusual. Precisely as the morningstar heads collided, the specter seemed to diminish. In the moment of explosion, the creature appeared to vanish or shrink.

As the undead creature approached the dwarf, it grew substantial again, those dark hands reaching forth to inflict more cold agony.

"Elf! I can't be hitting the damned thing!" The dwarf howled in pain and staggered back.

"More oil!" Jarlaxle yelled, a sudden idea coming to him. "Smash them together again."

"That hurt, elf! Me arms're numb!"

"Do it!" Jarlaxle commanded.

He fired off his wand again, and the burst of light caused the specter to recoil, buying Athrogate a few heartbeats. Jarlaxle pulled off his hat and reached inside, and as Athrogate swung mightily with his opposing morningstars, the drow pulled forth a flat circle of cloth, like the black lining of his hat. He threw it out and it spun, elongating as it sailed past the dwarf.

The morningstars collided in another explosion, throwing Athrogate backward again. The specter, as Jarlaxle expected, faded, began to diminish to nothingness—no, not to nothingness, but to some other plane or dimension.

And the fabric circle, the magical extra-dimensional pocket created by the power of Jarlaxle's enchanted hat, fell over the spot.

The sudden glare caused by waves of energy—purple, blue, and green—rolled forth from the spot, pounding out a hum of sheer power.

The fabric of the world tore open.

Jarlaxle and Athrogate floated, weightless, staring at a spot that was once a clearing in the trees but seemed to have been replaced with . . . starscape.

"What'd'ye do, elf!" the dwarf cried, his voice modulating in volume as if carried on gigantic intermittent winds.

"Stay away from it!" Jarlaxle warned, and he felt a slight push at his back, compelling him toward the starry spot, the rift, he knew, to the Astral Plane.

Athrogate began to flail wildly, suddenly afraid, for he was not far from that dangerous place. He began to spin head over heels and all around, but the gyrations proved irrelevant to his inexorable drift toward the stars.

"Not like that!" Jarlaxle called.

"How, ye stupid elf?"

For Jarlaxle, the solution was easy. His drift carried him beside a tree, still rooted solidly in the firmament. He grabbed on with one hand and held himself easily in place, and knew that an easy push would propel him away from the rift. That was exactly what it was, Jarlaxle knew, a tear in the fabric of the Prime Material Plane, the result of mixing the energies of two extra-dimensional spaces. For Jarlaxle, who carried items of holding that created extra-dimensional pockets larger than their apparent capacity, a pair of belt pouches that did the same, and several other trinkets that could facilitate similar dweomers, the consequences of mingling them was not unknown or unexpected.

What surprised him, though, was that his extra-dimensional hole had reacted in such a way with that shadowy being. All he'd hoped to do was trap the thing within the magical hole when it tried to flow back into the plane of the living.

"Throw something at it!" Jarlaxle cried, and as Athrogate lifted his arm as if to launch one of his morningstars, the drow added, "Something you never need to retrieve!"

Athrogate held his throw at the last moment then pulled his heavy pack off his back. He waited until he spun around, then heaved it at the rift. The opposite reaction sent the dwarf floating backward, away from the tear—far enough for Jarlaxle to take a chance with a rope. He threw an end out toward Athrogate, close enough for the dwarf to grasp, and as soon as Athrogate held on, the drow tugged hard and brought the dwarf sailing toward him, then right past.

Jarlaxle took note that Athrogate drifted only a few feet before exiting the area of weightlessness and falling hard to his rump. His eyes never leaving the curious starscape that loomed barely ten strides away, Jarlaxle pushed himself back and dropped to stand beside Athrogate as the dwarf pulled himself to his feet.

"What'd'ye do?" the dwarf asked in all seriousness.

"I have no idea," Jarlaxle replied.

"Worked, though," Athrogate offered.

Jarlaxle, not so certain of that, merely smirked.

They kept watch over the rift for a short while, and gradually the phenomenon dissipated, the wilderness returning to its previous firmament with no discernable damage. All was as it had been, except that the specter was gone.

* * * * *

"Still going east?" Athrogate asked as he and Jarlaxle started out the next day.

"That was the plan."

"The plan to win."

"Yes."

"I'm thinkin' we won last night," the dwarf said.

"We defeated a minion," Jarlaxle explained. "It has always been my experience that defeating a minion of a powerful foe only makes that foe angrier."

"So we should've let the shadow thing win?"

Jarlaxle's sigh elicited a loud laugh from Athrogate.

On they went through the day, and at camp that night, Jarlaxle dared to allow himself some time in Reverie.

And there, in his own subconscious, Hephaestus found him again.

Clever drow, the dracolich said in his mind. *Did you truly believe you could so easily escape me?*

Jarlaxle threw up his defenses in the form of images of Menzoberranzan, the great Underdark city. He concentrated on a distinct memory, of a battle his mercenary band had waged on behalf of Matron Mother Baenre. In that fight, a much younger Jarlaxle had engaged two separate weapons masters right in front of the doors of Melee-Magthere, the drow school of martial training. It was perhaps the most desperate struggle Jarlaxle had ever known, and one he would not have survived were it not for the intervention of a third weapons master, one of a lower-ranked House—House Do'Urden, actually, though that battle had been fought many decades before Drizzt drew his first breath.

That memory had long been crystallized in the mind of Jarlaxle Baenre, with images distinct and clear, and a level of tumult enough to keep his thoughts occupied. And with such emotional mental churning, the drow hoped he wouldn't surrender his current position to the intrusive Hephaestus.

Well done, drow! Hephaestus congratulated him. *But it will not matter in the end. Do you truly believe you can so easily hide from me? Do you truly believe your simple, but undeniably clever trick, would destroy one of the Seven?*

One of *what* 'Seven'? Jarlaxle asked himself.

He put the question to the back of his mind quickly and resumed his mental defense. He understood that his bold stand did little or nothing to shake the confidence of Hephaestus, but he remained certain that the hunting dragon wasn't making much headway. Then a notion occurred to him and he was jolted from his confrontation with the dragon, and from his Reverie entirely. He stumbled away from the tree upon which he was leaning.

"The Seven," he said, and swallowed hard, trying to recall all that he had learned about the origins of the Crystal Shard—

—and the seven liches who had created it.

"The Seven . . ." Jarlaxle whispered again, and a shiver ran up his spine.

* * * * *

Jarlaxle set the pace even swifter the next day, nightmare and hell boar running hard along the road. When they saw the smoke of an encampment not far ahead, Jarlaxle pulled to a halt.

"Orcs, likely," he explained to the dwarf. "We are near the border of King Obould's domain."

"Let's kill 'em, then."

Jarlaxle shook his head. "You must learn to exploit your enemies, my hairy little friend," he explained. "If these are Obould's orcs, they are not enemies of Mithral Hall."

"Bah!" Athrogate said, and spat on the ground.

"We go to them not as enemies, but as fellow travelers," Jarlaxle ordered. "Let us see what we might learn." Noting the disappointment on Athrogate's face, he added, "But do keep your morningstars near at hand."

It was indeed a camp of Many Arrow orcs, who served Obould, and though they sprang to readiness, brandishing weapons, at the casual approach of the curious pair—dwarf and drow—they held their arrows.

"We are travelers from Luskan," Jarlaxle greeted them in perfect command of Orcish, *"trade emissaries to King Obould and King Bruenor."* Out of the corner of his mouth, he bade Athrogate to remain calm and to keep his mount's pace steady and slow. *"We have good food to share,"* Jarlaxle added. *"And better grog."*

"What'd'ye tell 'em?" Athrogate asked, seeing the porcine soldiers brighten and nod at one another.

"That we're all going to get drunk together," Jarlaxle whispered back.

"In a pig's fat rump!" the dwarf protested.

"Wherever you please," the drow replied. He slid down from his saddle and dismissed his hell-spawned steed. "Come, let us learn what we may."

It all started rather tentatively, with Jarlaxle producing both food and "grog" aplenty. The drink went over well with the orcs, even more so when the dwarf spat out his first taste of it with disgust. He looked to Jarlaxle as if dumbstruck, as if he never could have imagined anything potent tasting so wretched. Jarlaxle responded with a wink and held out his flask to replenish Athrogate's mug, but with a different mixture, the dwarf noted.

Gutbuster.

Not another word of complaint came from Athrogate.

"You friends with Drizzt Do'Urden?" one of the orcs asked Jarlaxle, the creature's tongue loosened by the drink.

"You know of him?" the drow replied, and several of the orcs nodded. *"As do I! I have met him many times, and fought beside him on occasion—and woe to those who stand before his scimitars!"*

That last bit didn't go over well with the orcs, and one of them growled threateningly.

"Drizzt is wounded in his heart," said the orc, and the creature grinned as if that fact pleased him immensely.

Jarlaxle stared hard and tried to decipher that notion. "Catti-brie?"

"A fool now," the orc explained. *"Touched by magic. Daft by magic."*

A couple of the others chuckled.

The Weave, Jarlaxle realized, for he was not ignorant of the traumatic events unfolding around him. Luskan, too, a city that once housed the Hosttower of the Arcane and still named many of the wizards of that place as citizens—and allies of Bregan D'aerthe—had certainly been touched by the unraveling Weave.

"Where is she?" Jarlaxle asked, and the orc shrugged as if it hardly cared.

But Jarlaxle surely did, for a plan was already formulating. To defeat Hephaestus, he needed Cadderly. To enlist Cadderly, he needed Drizzt. Could it be that Catti-brie, and so Drizzt, needed Cadderly as well?

* * * * *

"Guenhwyvar," the young girl called. Her eyes leveled in their sockets, showing their rich blue hue.

Drizzt and Bruenor stood dumbfounded in the small chamber, staring at Catti-brie, whose demeanor had suddenly changed to that of her pre-teen self. She had floated off the bed again, rising as her eyes rolled to white, purple flames and crackling energy dancing all around her, her thick hair flowing in a wind neither Drizzt nor Bruenor could feel.

Drizzt had seen this strange event before, and had warned Bruenor, but when his daughter's posture and demeanor, everything about the way she held herself, had changed so subtly, yet dramatically, Bruenor nearly fell over with weakness. Truly she seemed a different person at that moment, a younger Catti-brie.

Bruenor called to her, his voice thick with desperation and remorse, but she seemed not to notice.

"Guenhwyvar?" she called again.

She seemed to be walking then, slowly and deliberately, though she didn't actually move. She held out one hand as if toward the cat—the cat who wasn't there.

Her voice was gentle and quiet when she asked, "Where's the dark elf, Guenhwyvar? Can ye take me to him?"

"By the gods," Drizzt muttered.

"What is it, elf?" Bruenor demanded.

The young girl straightened, then slowly turned away from the pair. "Be ye a drow?" she asked. Then she paused, as though she heard a response. "I've heard that drow be evil, but ye don't seem so to me."

"Elf?" Bruenor begged.

"Her first words to me," Drizzt whispered.

"Me name's Catti-brie," she said, still talking to the wall away from the pair. "Me dad is Bruenor, King o' Clan Battlehammer."

"She's on Kelvin's Cairn," said Bruenor.

"The dwarves," Catti-brie said. "He's not me real dad. Bruenor took me in when I was just a babe, when me real parents were . . ." She paused and swallowed hard.

"The first time we met, on Kelvin's Cairn," Drizzt breathlessly explained, and indeed he was hearing the woman, then just a girl, exactly as he had that unseasonably warm winter's day on the side of a faraway mountain.

Catti-brie looked over her shoulder at them—no, not at them, but above them. "She's a beautiful ca—" she started to say, but she sucked in her breath suddenly and her eyes rolled up into her head and her arms went out to her sides. The unseen magical energy rushed back into her once more, shaking her with its intensity.

And before their astonished eyes, Catti-brie aged once again.

By the time she floated down to the floor, both Drizzt and Bruenor were hugging her, and they gently moved her to her bed and laid her down.

"Elf?" Bruenor asked, his voice thick with desperation.

"I don't know," replied the trembling Drizzt. He tried to fight back the tears. The moment Catti-brie had recaptured was so precious to him, so burned into his heart and soul. . . .

They sat beside the woman's bed for a long while, even after Regis came in to remind Bruenor that he was due in his audience chamber. Emissaries had arrived from Silverymoon and Nesmé, from Obould and from the wider world. It was time for Bruenor Battlehammer to be king of Mithral Hall again.

But leaving his daughter there on her bed was one of the toughest things Bruenor Battlehammer had ever done. To the dwarf's great relief, after ensuring that the woman was sleeping soundly, Drizzt went out with him, leaving the reliable Regis to watch over her.

* * * * *

The black-bearded dwarf stood in line, third from the front, trying to remember his lines. He was an emissary, a formal representative to a king's court. It was not a new situation to Athrogate, for he had once lived a life that included daily audiences with regional leaders.

Once, long ago.

"Don't rhyme," he warned himself quietly, for as Jarlaxle had pointed out, any of his silly word games would likely tip off Drizzt Do'Urden to the truth about the disguised dwarf. He cleared his throat loudly, wishing he had his morningstars with him, or some other weapon that might get him out of there if his true identity were discovered.

The first representative had his audience with the dwarf king and moved out of the way.

Athrogate rehearsed his lines again, telling himself that it was really simple, assuring himself that Jarlaxle had prepared him well. He went through the routine over and over.

"Come forward, then, fellow dwarf," King Bruenor said, startling Athrogate. "I've too much to do to be sittin' here waitin'!"

Athrogate looked at the seated Bruenor, then at Drizzt Do'Urden, who stood behind the throne. As he locked gazes with Drizzt, he saw a hint of recognition, for they had matched weapons eight years before, during the fall of Deudermont's Luskan.

If Drizzt saw through his disguise, the drow hid it well.

"Well met, King Bruenor, for all the tales I heared of ye," Athrogate greeted enthusiastically, coming forward to stand before the throne. "I'm hopin' that ye're not put out by me coming to see yerself directly, but if I'm returning to me kinfolk without having had me say to yerself, then suren they'd be chasing me out!"

"And where might home be, good . . . ?"

"Stuttgard," Athrogate replied. "Stuttgard o' the Stone Hills Stuttgard Clan."

Bruenor looked at him curiously and shook his head.

"South o' the Snowflakes, long south o' here," the dwarf bluffed.

"I am afraid that I know not of yer clan, or yer Stone Hills," said Bruenor. He glanced at Drizzt, who shrugged and shook his head.

"Well, we heared o' yerself," Athrogate replied. "Many're the songs o' Mithral Hall sung in the Stone Hills!"

"Good to know," Bruenor replied, then he prompted the emissary with a rolling motion of his hand, obviously in a rush to be done with the formalities. "And ye're here to offer trade, perhaps? Or to set the grounds for an alliance?"

"Nah," said Athrogate. "Just a dwarf walkin' the world and wantin' to meet King Bruenor Battlehammer."

The dwarf king nodded. "Very well. And ye're wishing to remain with us in Mithral Hall for some time?"

Athrogate shrugged. "Was heading east, to Adbar," he said. "Got some family there. I was hopin' to come to Mithral Hall on me return back to the west, and not plannin' to stop through now. But on the road, I heared whispers about yer girl."

That perked Bruenor up, and the drow behind him as well.

"What of me girl?" Bruenor asked, suspicion thick in his voice.

"Heared on the road that she got touched by the falling Weave o' magic."

"Ye heared that, did ye?"

"Aye, King Bruenor, so I thought I should come through as fast as me short legs'd be taking me."

"Ye're a priest, then?"

"Nah, just a scrapper."

"Then why? What? Have ye anything to offer me, Stuttgard o' the Stone Hills?" Bruenor said, clearly agitated.

"A name, and one I think ye're knowin'," said Athrogate. "Human name o' Cadderly."

Bruenor and Drizzt exchanged glances, then both stared hard at the visitor.

"His place's not too far from me home," Athrogate explained. "I went right through it on me way here, o' course. Oh, but he's got a hunnerd wizards and priests in there now, all trying to get what's what, if ye get me meaning."

"What about him?" Bruenor asked, obviously trying to remain calm but unable to keep the urgency out of his tone—or out of his posture, as he leaned forward in his throne.

"He and his been workin' on the problems," Athrogate explained. "I thought ye should know that more'n a few that been brain-touched by the Weave've gone in there, and most've come out whole."

Bruenor leaped up from his seat. "Cadderly is curing those rendered foolish by the troubles?"

Athrogate shrugged. "I thinked ye'd want to be knowin'."

Bruenor turned fast to Drizzt.

"A month and more of hard travel," the drow warned.

"Magical items're working," Bruenor replied. "We got the wagon me boys're building for Silverymoon journeys. We got the zephyr shoes . . ."

Drizzt's eyes lit up at the reference, for indeed the dwarves of Clan Battlehammer had been working on a solution to their isolation, even before the onset of magical afflictions. Without the magical teleportation of their neighboring cities, or creations of magic like Lady Alustriel's flying chariots of fire, the dwarves had taken to a more mundane solution, constructing a wagon strong enough to handle the bumps and stones of treacherous terrain. They had sought out magical assistance for teams that might be pulling the vehicle.

The drow was already starting off the dais before Bruenor could finish his sentence. "On my way," Drizzt said.

"Can I wish ye all me best, King Bruenor?" Athrogate asked.

"Stuttgard o' the Stone Hills," Bruenor repeated, and he turned to the court scribe. "Write it down!"

"Aye, me king!"

"And know that if me girl finds peace in Spirit Soaring, that I'll be visiting yer clan, good friend," Bruenor said, looking back to Athrogate. "And know that ye're fore'er a friend o' Mithral Hall. Ye stay as long as ye're wantin', and all costs fall to meself! But beggin' yer pardon, the time's for me to be goin'."

He bowed fast and was running out of the room before Athrogate could even offer his thanks in reply.

* * * * *

Full of energy and enthusiasm for the first time in a few long days, the hope-filled Drizzt and Bruenor charged down the hall toward Catti-brie's door. They slowed abruptly as they neared, seeing the sizzling purple and blue streaks of energy slipping through the cracks in the door.

"Bah, not again!" Bruenor groaned. He beat Drizzt to the door and shoved it open.

There was Catti-brie, standing in mid air above the bed, her arms out to her sides, her eyes rolled to white, trembling, trembling. . . .

"Me girl . . ." Bruenor started to say, but he bit back the words when he noted Regis against the far wall, curled up on the floor, his arms over his head.

"Elf!" Bruenor cried, but Drizzt was already running to Catti-brie, grabbing her and pulling her down to the bed. Bruenor grumbled and cursed and rushed over to Regis.

Catti-brie's stiffness melted as the fit ended, and she fell limp into Drizzt's arms. He eased her down to a sitting position and hugged her close, and only then did he notice the desperate Regis.

The halfling flailed wildly at Bruenor, slapping the dwarf repeatedly and squirming away from Bruenor's reaching hands. Clearly terrified, he seemed to be looking not at the dwarf, but at some great monster.

"Rumblebelly, what're ye about?" Bruenor asked.

Regis screamed into the dwarf's face in response, a primal explosion of sheer terror. As Bruenor fell back, the halfling scrambled away, rising up to his knees, then to his feet. He ran headlong, face-first, into the opposite wall. He bounced back and fell with a groan.

"Oh, by the gods," said Bruenor, and he reached down and scooped something up from the floor. He turned to Drizzt and presented the item for the drow to see.

It was the halfling's ruby pendant, the enchanted gemstone that allowed Regis to cast charms upon unwitting victims.

Regis recovered from his self-inflicted wallop and leaped to his feet. He screamed again and ran past Bruenor, flailing his arms insanely. When Bruenor tried to intercept him, the halfling slapped him and punched him, pinched him and even bit him, and all the while Bruenor called to him, but Regis seemed not to hear a word. The dwarf might as well have been a demon or devil come to eat the little one for dinner.

"Elf!" Bruenor called. Then he yelped and fell back, clutching his bleeding hand.

Regis sprinted for the door. Drizzt beat him there, hitting him with a flying tackle that sent them both into a roll into the hall. In that somersault, Drizzt deftly worked his hands so that when they settled, he was behind Regis, his legs clamped around the halfling's waist, his arms knifed under Regis's, turning and twisting expertly to tie the little one in knots.

There was no way for Regis to break out, to hit Drizzt, or to squirm away from him. But that hardly slowed his frantic gyrations, and didn't stop him from screaming insanely.

The hallway began to fill with curious dwarves.

"Ye got a pin stuck in the little one's arse, elf?" one asked.

"Help me with him!" Drizzt implored.

The dwarf came over and reached for Regis, then quickly retracted his hand when the halfling tried to bite it.

"What in the Nine Hells?"

"Just ye take him!" Bruenor yelled from inside the room. "Ye take him and tie him down—and don't ye be hurting him!"

"Yes, me king!"

It took a long time, but finally the dwarves dragged the thrashing Regis away from Drizzt.

"I could slug him and put him down quiet," one offered, but Drizzt's scowl denied that course of action.

"Take him to his chamber and keep him safe," the drow said. He went back into the room, closing the door behind him.

"She didn't even notice," Bruenor explained as Drizzt sat on the bed beside Catti-brie. "She's not knowing the world around her."

"We knew that," Drizzt reminded.

"Not even a bit! Nor's the little one now."

Drizzt shrugged. "Cadderly," he reminded the dwarf king.

"For both o' them," said the dwarf, and he looked at the door. "Rumble-belly used the ruby on her."

"To try to reach her," Drizzt agreed.

"But she reached him instead," the dwarf said.

CHAPTER

ANGRY DEAD

"I t will be at Spirit Soaring," the Ghost King proclaimed.

The specter chasing Jarlaxle had worked out the drow's intentions even before the clever dark elf's dastardly trick had sent the creature on its extraplanar journey. And anything the specters knew, so knew the dracolich.

The enemies of Hephaestus, Yharaskrik, and mostly of Crenshinibon would congregate there, in the Snowflake Mountains, where a pair of the Ghost King's specters were already causing mischief.

Then there would be only one more, the human southerner. The Crystal Shard knew he could be found, though not as easily as Jarlaxle. After all, Crenshinibon had shared an intimate bond with the dark elf for many tendays. With Yharaskrik's psychic powers added to the shard's, locating the familiar drow had proven as simple as it was necessary. Jarlaxle had become the focus of anger that served to bring the trio of mighty beings together, united in common cause. The human, however tangential, would be revealed soon enough.

Besides, to at least one of the three vengeful entities— the dragon—the coming catastrophe would be enjoyable.

To Yharaskrik, the destruction of its enemies would be practical and informative, a worthy test for the uncomfortable but likely profitable unification.

And Crenshinibon, which served as conduit between the wildly passionate dragon and the ultimately practical mind flayer, would share in all the sensations the destruction of Jarlaxle and the others would bring to both of them.

* * * * *

"Uncle Pikel!" Hanaleisa called when she saw the green-bearded dwarf on a street in Carradoon late the next morning. He was dressed in his traveling gear, which meant that he carried a stick and had a cooking pot strapped on his head as a helmet.

Pikel flashed her a big smile and called into the shop behind him. As the dwarf advanced to give Hanaleisa a great hug, Hanaleisa's younger brother Rorick exited the shop.

"What are you doing here?" she called over Pikel's shoulder as her grinning sibling approached.

"I told you I wanted to come along."

"Then spent the rest of the morning arguing with wizards about the nature of the cosmos," Hanaleisa replied.

"Doo-dad!" Pikel yelled, pulling back from the young woman, and when both she and Rorick looked at him curiously, he just added, "Hee hee hee."

"He has it all figured out," Rorick explained, and Hanaleisa nodded.

"And do the wizards and priests have it all figured out as well?" Hanaleisa asked. "Because of your insights, I mean?"

Rorick looked down.

"They kicked you out," Hanaleisa reasoned.

"Because they couldn't stand to be upstaged by our little brother, no doubt!" greeted Temberle, rounding the corner from the blacksmith he'd just visited. His greatsword had taken a nasty nick the previous night when bouncing off the collarbone of the undead bear.

Rorick brightened a bit at that, but when he looked up at his brother and sister, an expression of confusion came over him. "What happened?" he asked, noting that Temberle had his greatsword in hand and was examining the blade.

"You left Spirit Soaring late yesterday?" Temberle asked.

"Midday, yes," Rorick answered. "Uncle Pikel wanted to use the tree roots to move us down from the mountains, but father overruled that, fearing the unpredictability and instability of magic, even druidic."

"Doo-dad," Pikel said with a giggle.

"I wouldn't be traveling magically either," said Hanaleisa. "Not now."

Pikel folded his arm and stump over his chest and glared at her.

"So you camped in the forest last night?" Temberle went on.

Rorick answered with a nod, not really understanding where his brother might be going, but Pikel apparently caught on a bit, and the dwarf issued an "Ooooh."

"There's something wrong in those woods," said Temberle.

"Yup, yup," Pikel agreed.

"What are you talking about?" Rorick asked, looking from one to the other.

"Brr," Pikel said, and hugged himself tightly.

"I slept right through the night," said Rorick. "But it wasn't that cold."

"We fought a zombie," Hanaleisa explained. "A zombie bear. And there was something else out there, haunting the forest."

"Yup, yup," Pikel agreed.

Rorick looked at the dwarf, curious. "You didn't say anything was amiss."

Pikel shrugged.

"But you felt it?" Temberle asked.

The dwarf gave another, "Yup, yup."

"So you did battle—*real* battle?" Rorick asked his siblings, his intrigue obvious. The three had grown up in the shadow of a great library, surrounded by mighty priests and veteran wizards. They had heard stories of great battles, most notably the fight their parents had waged against the dreaded chaos curse and against their own grandfather, but other than the few times when their parents had been called away for battle, or their dwarf uncles had gone to serve King Bruenor of Mithral Hall, the lives of the Bonaduce children had been soft and peaceful. They had trained vigorously in martial arts—hand-fighting and sword-fighting—and in the ways of the priest, the wizard, and the monk. With Cadderly and Danica as their parents, the three had been blessed with as comprehensive and exhaustive an education as any in Faerûn could ever hope for, but in practical applications of their lessons, particularly fighting, the three were neophytes indeed, completely untested until the previous night.

Hanaleisa and Temberle exchanged concerned looks.

"Tell me!" Rorick pressed.

"It was terrifying," his sister admitted. "I've never been so scared in my entire life."

"But it was exciting," Temberle added. "And as soon as the fight began, you couldn't think about being afraid."

"You couldn't think about anything," said Hanaleisa.

"Hee hee hee," Pikel agreed with a nod.

"Our training," said Rorick.

"We are fortunate that our parents, and our uncles," said Hanaleisa, looking at the beaming Pikel, "didn't take the peace we've known for granted, and taught us—"

"To fight," Temberle interrupted.

"And to react," said Hanaleisa, who was always a bit more philosophical about battle and the role that martial training played in a wider world view. She was much more akin to her mother in that matter, and that was why she had foregone extensive training with the sword or the mace in favor of the more disciplined and intimate open-hand techniques employed by Danica's order. "Even one who knew how to use a sword well would have been killed in the forest last night if his mind didn't know how to tuck away his fears."

"So you felt the presence in the forest, too," Temberle said to Pikel.

"Yup."

"It's still there."

"Yup."

"We have to warn the townsfolk, and get word to Spirit Soaring," Hanaleisa added.

"Yup, yup." Pikel lifted his good arm before him and straightened his fingers, pointing forward. He began swaying that hand back and forth, as if gliding like a fish under the waters of Impresk Lake. The others understood that the dwarf was talking about his plant-walking, even before he added with a grin, "Doo-dad."

"You cannot do that," Hanaleisa said, and Temberle, too, shook his head.

"We can go out tomorrow, at the break of dawn," he said. "Whatever it is out there, it's closer to Carradoon than to Spirit Soaring. We can get horses to take us the first part of the way—I'm certain the stable masters will accompany us along the lower trails."

"Moving fast, we can arrive before sunset," Hanaleisa agreed.

"But right now, we've got to get the town prepared for whatever might come," said Temberle. He looked at Hanaleisa and shrugged. "Though we don't really know what is out there, or even if it's still there. Maybe it was just that one bear we killed, a wayward malevolent spirit, and now it's gone."

"Maybe it wasn't," said Rorick, and his tone made it clear that he hoped he was right. In his youthful enthusiasm, he was more than a little jealous of his siblings at that moment—a misplaced desire that would soon enough be corrected.

* * * * *

"Probably wandering around for a hundred years," muttered one old water-dog—a Carradoon term for the many wrinkled fishermen who lived in town. The man waved his hand as if the story was nothing to fret about.

"Eh, but the world's gone softer," another in the tavern lamented.

"Nay, not the world," yet another explained. "Just our part of it, living in the shadow of them three's parents. We've been civilized, I'm thinking!"

That brought a cheer, half mocking, half in good will, from the many gathered patrons.

"The rest of the world's grown tougher," the man continued. "It'll get to us, and don't you doubt it."

"And us older folk remember the fights well," said the first old water-dog. "But I'm wondering if the younger ones, grown up under the time of Cadderly, will be ready for any fights that might come."

"His kids did well, eh?" came the reply, and all in the tavern cheered and lifted tankards in honor of the twins, who stood at the bar.

"We survived," Hanaleisa said loudly, drawing the attention of all. "But likely, some sort of evil is still out there."

That didn't foster the feeling of dread the young woman had hoped for, but elicited a rather mixed reaction of clanking mugs and even laughter. Hanaleisa looked at Temberle, and they both glanced back when Pikel bemoaned the lack of seriousness in the crowd with a profound, "Ooooh."

"Carradoon should post sentries at every gate, and along the walls," Temberle shouted. "Start patrols through the streets, armed and with torches. Light up the town, I beg you!"

Though his outburst attracted some attention, all eyes turned to the tavern door as it banged open. A man stumbled in, crying out, "Attack!

Attack!" More than his shouts jarred them all, though, for filtering in behind the stranger came cries and screams, terrified and agonized.

Tables upended as the water-dogs leaped to their feet.

"Uh-oh," said Pikel, and he grabbed Temberle's arm with his hand and tapped Hanaleisa with his stump before they could intervene. They had come to the tavern to warn people and to organize them, but Pikel was astute enough to realize the folly of the latter intention.

Temberle tried to speak anyway, but already the various crews of the many Carradden fishing boats were organizing, calling for groups to go to the docks to retrieve weapons, putting together gangs to head into the streets.

"But, people . . ." Temberle tried to protest. Pikel tugged at him insistently.

"Shhh!" the dwarf cautioned.

"The four of us, then," Hanaleisa agreed. "Let's see where we can be of help."

They exited alongside a score of patrons, though a few remained behind—fishing boat captains, mostly—to try to formulate some sort of strategy. With a few quick words, Pikel tucked his black oaken cudgel—his magical shillelagh—under his half-arm and waggled his fingers over one end, conjuring a bright light that transformed the weapon into a magical, fire-less torch.

Less than two blocks from the tavern door, back toward the gateway through which they had entered Carradoon, the four learned what all the tumult was about. Rotting corpses and skeletons swarmed the streets. Human and elf, dwarf and halfling, and many animal corpses roamed freely. The dead walked—and attacked.

Spotting a family trying to escape along the side of the wide road, the group veered that way, but Rorick stopped short and cried out, then stumbled and pulled up his pant leg. As Pikel moved his light near, trickles of blood showed clearly, along with something small and thrashing. Rorick kicked out and the attacking creature flew to the side of the road.

It flopped weirdly back at him, a mess of bones, skin, and feathers.

"A bird," Hanaleisa gasped.

Pikel ran over and swung the bright end of his cudgel down hard, splattering the creature onto the cobblestones. The light proved equally damaging to the undead thing, searing it and leaving it smoldering.

"Sha-la-la!" Pikel proudly proclaimed, lifting his club high. He turned fast, adjusting his cooking pot helmet as he did so, and launched himself into the nearest alleyway. As soon as the light of the cudgel crossed the alley's threshold, it revealed a host of skeletons swarming at the dwarf.

Temberle threw his arm around his brother's back and propped him up, hustling him back the way they had come, calling for the fleeing Carradden family to catch up.

"Uncle Pikel!" Hanaleisa cried, running to support him.

She pulled up short as she neared the alleyway, assaulted by the sound of crunching bones and by bits of rib and skull flying by. Pikel's light danced wildly, as if a flame in a gale, for the doo-dad dwarf danced wildly, too. It was as ferocious a display as Hanaleisa had ever seen, and one she had never imagined possible from her gentle gardener uncle.

She refocused her attention back down the street, to the retreating family, a couple and their trio of young children. Trusting in Pikel to battle the creatures in the alley, though he was outnumbered many times over, the woman sprinted away, crossing close behind the family. Hanaleisa threw herself at two skeletons moving in close pursuit. She hit them hard with a flat-out body block, knocking them back several steps, and she tucked and turned as she fell to land easily on her feet.

Hanaleisa went up on the ball of one foot and launched into a spinning kick that drove her other foot through the ribcage of an attacker. With a spray of bone chips, she tugged her foot out, then, without bringing it down and holding perfect balance, she leaned back to re-angle her kick, and cracked the skeleton in its bony face.

Still balanced on one foot, Hanaleisa expertly turned and kicked again, once, twice, a third time, into the chest of the second skeleton.

She sprang up and sent her back foot into a high circle kick before the skeleton's face, not to hit it, but as a distraction, for when she landed firmly on both feet, she did so leaning forward, in perfect position to launch a series of devastating punches at her foe.

With both skeletons quickly dispatched, Hanaleisa backed away, pursuing the family. To her relief, Pikel joined her as she passed the alleyway. Side by side, the two grinned, pivoted back, and charged into the pursuing throng of undead, feet, fists, and sha-la-la pounding.

More citizens joined them in short order, as did Temberle, his greatsword shearing down skeletons and zombies with abandon.

But there were so many!

The dead had risen from a cemetery that had been the final resting place for many generations of Carradden. They rose from a thick forest, too, where the cycle of life worked relentlessly to feed the hunger of such a powerful and malignant spell. Even near the shores of Impresk Lake, under the dark waters, skeletons of fish—thousands of them thrown back to the waters after being cleaned on the decks of fishing boats—sprang to unlife and knifed up hard against the undersides of dark hulls, or swam past the boats and flung themselves out of the water and onto the shore and docks, thrashing in desperation to destroy something, anything, alive.

And standing atop the dark waters, Fetchigrol watched. His dead eyes flared to life in reflected orange as a fire grew and consumed several houses. Those eyes flickered with inner satisfaction whenever a cry of horror rang out across the dark, besieged city.

He sensed a shipwreck not far away, many shipwrecks, many long-dead sailors.

* * * * *

"I'm all right!" Rorick insisted, trying to pull his leg away from his fretting Uncle Pikel.

But the dwarf grabbed him hard with one hand, a grip that could hold back a lunging horse, and waggled his stumpy arm at the obstinate youngster.

They were back in the tavern, but nothing outside had calmed. Quite the opposite, it seemed.

Pikel bit down on a piece of cloth and tore off a strip. He dipped it into his upturned cookpot-helmet, into which he'd poured a bit of potent liquor mixed with some herbs he always kept handy.

"We can't stay here," Temberle called, coming in the door. "They approach."

Pikel worked fast, slapping the bandage against Rorick's bloody shin, pinning one end with his half-arm and expertly working the other until he had it knotted. Then he tightened it down with his teeth on one end, his hand on the other.

"Too tight," Rorick complained.

"Shh!" scolded the dwarf.

72

Pikel grabbed his helmet and dropped it on his head, either forgetting or ignoring the contents, which splashed down over his green hair and beard. If that bothered the dwarf, he didn't show it, though he did lick at the little rivulets streaming down near his mouth. He hopped up, shillelagh tucked securely under his stump, and pulled Rorick up before him.

The young man tried to start away fast, but he nearly fell over with the first step on his torn leg. The wound was deeper than Rorick apparently believed.

Pikel was there to support him, though, and they rushed out behind Temberle. Hanaleisa was outside waiting, shaking her head.

"Too many," she explained grimly. "There's no winning ground, just retreat."

"To the docks?" Temberle asked, looking at the flow of townsfolk in that direction and seeming none too pleased by that prospect. "We're to put our backs to the water?"

Hanaleisa's expression showed that she didn't like that idea any more than he, but they had no choice. They joined the fleeing townsfolk and ran on.

They found some organized defense forming halfway to the docks and eagerly found positions among the ranks. Pikel offered an approving nod as he continued past with Rorick, toward a cluster of large buildings overlooking the boardwalk and wharves. Built on an old fort, it was where the ship captains had decided to make their stand.

"Fight well for mother and father," Hanaleisa said to Temberle. "We will not dishonor their names."

Temberle smiled back at her, feeling like a veteran already.

They got their chance soon enough, their line rushing up the street to support the last groups of townsfolk trying hard to get ahead of the monstrous pursuit. Fearlessly, Hanaleisa and Temberle charged among the undead, smashing and slashing with abandon.

Their efforts became all the more devastating when Uncle Pikel joined them, his bright cudgel destroying every monster that ventured near.

Despite their combined power, the trio and the rest of the squad fighting beside them were pushed back, moving inexorably in retreat. For every zombie or skeleton they destroyed, it seemed there were three more to take its place. Their own line thinned whenever a man or woman was pulled down under the raking and biting throng.

And those unfortunate victims soon enough stood up, fighting for the other side.

Horrified and weak with revulsion, their morale shattered as friends and family rose up in undeath to turn against them, the townsfolk gave ground.

They found support at the cluster of buildings, where they had no choice but to stand and fight. Eventually, even that defense began to crumble.

Hanaleisa looked to her brother, desperation and sadness in her rich brown eyes. They couldn't retreat into the water, and the walls of the buildings wouldn't hold back the horde for long. She was scared, and so was he.

"We have to find Rorick," Temberle said to his dwarf uncle.

"Eh?" Pikel replied.

He didn't understand that the twins only wanted to make sure that the three siblings were together when they died.

CHAPTER

THE POLITICS OF ENGAGEMENT

6

It was the last thing Bruenor Battlehammer wanted to hear just then.

"Obould's angry," Nanfoodle the gnome explained. "He thinks we're to blame for the strange madness of magic, and the silence of his god."

"Yeah, we're always to blame in that one's rock-head," Bruenor grumbled back. He looked at the door leading to the corridor to Garumn's Gorge and the Hall's eastern exit, hoping to see Drizzt. Morning had done nothing to help Catti-brie or Regis. The halfling had thrashed himself to utter exhaustion and since languished in restless misery.

"Obould's emissary—" Nanfoodle started to say.

"I got no time for him!" Bruenor shouted.

Across the way, several dwarves observed the uncharacteristic outburst. Among them was General Banak Brawnanvil, who watched from his chair. He'd lost the use of his lower body in the long-ago first battle with Obould's emerging hordes.

"I got no time!" Bruenor yelled again, though somewhat apologetically. "Me girl's got to go! And Rumblebelly, too!"

"I will accompany Drizzt," Nanfoodle offered.

"The Nine Hells and a tenth for luck ye will!" Bruenor roared at him. "I ain't for leaving me girl!"

"But ye're the king," one of the dwarves cried.

"And the whole world is going mad," Nanfoodle answered.

75

Bruenor simmered, on the edge of an explosion. "No," he said finally, and with a nod to the gnome, who had become one of his most trusted and reliable advisors, he walked across the room to stand before Banak.

"No," Bruenor said again. "I ain't the king. Not now."

A couple of dwarves gasped, but Banak Brawnanvil nodded solemnly, accepting the responsibility he knew to be coming.

"Ye've ruled the place before," said Bruenor. "And I'm knowin' ye can do it again. Been too long since I seen the road."

"Ye save yer girl," the old general replied.

"Can't give ye Rumblebelly to help ye this time," Bruenor went on, "but the gnome here's clever enough." He looked back at Nanfoodle, who couldn't help but smile at the unexpected compliment and the trust Bruenor showed in him.

"We've many good hands," Banak agreed.

"Now don't ye be startin' another war with Obould," Bruenor instructed. "Not without me here to swat a few o' his dogs."

"Never."

Bruenor clapped his friend on the shoulder, turned, and started to walk away. A large part of him knew that his responsibilities lay there, where Clan Battlehammer looked to him to lead, particularly in that suddenly troubling time. But a larger part of him denied that. He was the king of Mithral Hall, indeed, but he was the father of Catti-brie and the friend of Regis, as well.

And little else seemed to matter at that dark moment.

He found Drizzt at Garumn's Gorge, along with as smelly and dirty a dwarf as had ever been known.

"Ready to go, me king!" Thibbledorf Pwent greeted him with enthusiasm. The grisly dwarf hopped to attention, his creased battle armor, all sharpened plates and jagged spikes, creaking and squealing with the sudden motion.

Bruenor looked at the drow, who just closed his eyes, long ago having quit arguing with the likes of the battlerager.

"Ready to go?" Bruenor asked. "With war brewing here?"

Pwent's eyes flared a bit at that hopeful possibility, but he resolutely shook his head. "Me place is with me king!"

"Brawnanvil's the Steward o' Mithral Hall while I'm gone."

A flash of confusion in the dwarf's eyes couldn't take hold. "With me King Bruenor!" Pwent argued. "If ye're for the road, Pwent and his boys're for the road!"

At that proclamation, a great cheer came up and several nearby doors banged open. The famed Gutbuster Brigade poured into the wide corridor.

"Oh no, no," Bruenor scolded. "No, ye ain't!"

"But me king!" twenty Gutbusters cried in unison.

"I ain't taking the best brigade Faerûn's e'er known away from Steward Brawnanvil in this troubled time," said Bruenor. "No, but I can't." He looked Pwent straight in the eye. "None o' ye. Ain't got room in the wagon, neither."

"Bah! We'll run with ye!" Pwent insisted.

"We're goin' on magical shoes and we ain't got no magical boots for the lot of ye to keep up," Bruenor explained. "I ain't doubtin' that ye'd all run till ye drop dead, but that'd be the end of it. No, me friend, yer place is here, in case that Obould thinks it's time again for war." He gave a great sigh and looked to Drizzt for support, muttering, "Me own place is here."

"And you'll be back here swiftly," the drow promised. "Your place now is on the road with me, with Catti-brie and Regis. We've no time for foolishness, I warn. Our wagon is waiting."

"Me king!" Pwent cried. He waved his brigade away, but hustled after Drizzt and Bruenor as they quickly moved to the tunnels that would take them to their troubled friends.

In the end, only four of them left Mithral Hall in the wagon pulled by a team of the best mules that could be found. It wasn't Pwent who stayed behind, but Regis.

The poor halfling wouldn't stop thrashing, fending off monsters that none of them could see, and with all the fury and desperation of a halfling standing on the edge of the pit of the Abyss itself. He couldn't eat. He couldn't drink. He wouldn't stop swinging and kicking and biting for a moment, and no words reached his ears to any effect. Only through the efforts of a number of attendants were the dwarves able to get any nourishment into him at all, something that could never have been done on a bouncing wagon moving through the wilds.

Bruenor argued taking him anyway, to the point of hoarseness, but in the end, it was Drizzt who said, "Enough!" and led the frustrated Bruenor away.

"Even if the magic holds, even if the wagon survives," Drizzt said, "it will be a tenday and more to Spirit Soaring and an equal time back. He'll not survive."

They left Regis in a stupor of exhaustion, a broken thing.

"He may recover with the passage of time," Drizzt explained as they hustled along the tunnels and across the great gorge. "He was not touched directly by the magic, as was Catti-brie."

"He's daft, elf!"

"And as I said, it may not hold. Your priests will reach him—" Drizzt paused and skidded to a stop "—or I will."

"What do ye know, elf?" Bruenor demanded.

"Go and ready the wagon," Drizzt instructed, "but wait for me."

He turned and sprinted back the way they'd come, all the way to Regis's room, where he burst in and dashed to the small coffer atop the dresser. With trembling hands, Drizzt pulled forth the ruby pendant.

"What're ye about?" asked Cordio Muffinhead, a priest of high repute, who stood beside the halfling.

Drizzt held up the pendant, the enchanting ruby spinning enticingly in the torchlight. "I have an idea. Pray, wake the little one, but hold him steady, all of you."

They looked at the drow curiously, but so many years together had taught them to trust Drizzt Do'Urden, and they did as he bade them.

Regis came awake thrashing, his legs moving as if he were trying to run away from some unseen monster.

Drizzt moved his face very close to the halfling, calling to him, but Regis gave no sign of hearing his old friend.

The drow brought forth the ruby pendant and set it spinning right before Regis's eyes. The sparkles drew Drizzt inside, so alluring and calming, and a short while later, within the depths of the ruby, he found Regis.

"Drizzt," the halfling said aloud, and also in Drizzt's mind. *"Help me."*

Drizzt got only the slightest glimpse of the visions tormenting Regis. He found himself in a land of shadow—the very Plane of Shadow, perhaps, or some other lower plane—with dark and ominous creatures coming at him from every side, clawing at him, open maws full of sharpened teeth biting at his face. Clawed hands slashed at him along the periphery of his vision, always just a moment ahead of him. Instinctively, Drizzt's free hand went to a scimitar belted at his hip and he cried out and began to draw it forth.

Something hit him hard, throwing him aside, right over the bed he couldn't see. It sent him tumbling to a floor he couldn't see.

In the distance, Drizzt heard the clatter of something bouncing across the stone floor and knew it to be the ruby pendant. He felt a burning sensation in his forearm and closed his eyes tightly to grimace away the pain. When he opened his eyes again, he was back in the room, Cordio standing over him. He looked at his arm to see a trickle of blood where it had caught against his half-drawn scimitar as he tumbled.

"What—?" he started to ask the dwarf.

"Apologies, elf," said Cordio, "but I had to ram ye. Ye was seein' monsters like the little one there, and drawing yer blade . . ."

"Say no more, good dwarf," Drizzt replied, pulling himself up to a sitting position and bringing his injured arm in front of him, pressing hard to try to stem the flow of blood.

"Get me a bandage!" Cordio yelled to the others, who were hard at work holding down the thrashing Regis.

"He's in there," Drizzt explained as Cordio wrapped his arm. "I found him. He called out for help."

"Yeah, that we heared."

"He's seeing monsters—shadowy things—in a horrible place."

Another dwarf came over and handed the ruby pendant to Cordio, who presented it to Drizzt, but the drow held up his hand.

"Keep it," Drizzt explained. "You might find a way to use it to reach him, but do take care."

"Oh, I'll be having a team o' Gutbusters ready to knock me down in that case," Cordio assured him.

"More than that," said Drizzt. "Take care that you can escape the place where Regis now resides." He looked with great sympathy at his poor halfling friend, for the first time truly appreciating the horror Regis felt with every waking moment.

Drizzt caught up to Bruenor in the eastern halls. The king sat on the bench of a fabulous wagon of burnished wood and solid wheels, with a sub-carriage that featured several strong springs of an alloy Nanfoodle had concocted, almost as strong as iron, but not nearly as brittle. The wagon showed true craftsmanship and pride, a fitting representation of the art and skill of Mithral Hall.

The vehicle wasn't yet finished, though, for the dwarves had planned an enclosed bed and perhaps an extension bed for cargo behind, with a greater harness that would allow a team of six or eight. But upon Bruenor's call for urgency, they had cut the work short and fitted low wooden walls and a tailgate quickly. They had brought out their finest team of mules, young and strong, fitting them with magical horseshoes that would allow them to move at a swift pace throughout the entirety of a day.

"I found Regis in his nightmares," Drizzt explained, climbing up beside his friend. "I used the ruby on him, as he did with Catti-brie."

"Ye durned fool!"

Drizzt shook his head. "With all caution," he assured his companion.

"I'm seein' that," Bruenor said dryly, staring at the drow's bandaged arm.

"I found him and he saw me, but only briefly. He is living in the realm of nightmares, Bruenor, and though I tried to pull him back with me, I could not begin to gain ground. Instead, he pulled me in with him, a place that would overwhelm me as it has him. But there is hope, I believe." He sighed and mouthed the name they had attached to that hope, "Cadderly." That notion made Bruenor drive the team on with more urgency as they rolled out of Mithral Hall's eastern gate, turning fast for the southwest.

Pwent moved up to ride on the seat with Bruenor. Drizzt ran scout along their flanks, though he often had to climb aboard the wagon and catch his breath, for it rolled along without the need to rest the mules. Through it all, Catti-brie sat quietly in the back, seeing nothing that they could see, hearing nothing that they could hear, lost and alone.

* * * * *

"Ye're knowin' them well," Athrogate congratulated Jarlaxle later that day when the pair, lying on top of a grassy knoll, spied the wagon rambling down the road from the northeast.

Jarlaxle's expression showed no such confidence, for he had been caught completely by surprise at the quick progress the wagon had already made; he hadn't expected to see Bruenor's party until the next morning.

"They'll drive the mules to exhaustion in a day," he mumbled, shaking his head.

Off in the distance, a dark figure moved among the shadows, and Jarlaxle knew it to be Drizzt.

"Running hard for their hurt friend," Athrogate remarked.

"There is no power greater than the bonds they share, my friend," said the drow. He finished with a cough to clear his throat, and to banish the wistfulness from his tone. But not quickly enough, he realized when he glanced at Athrogate, to keep the dwarf from staring at him incredulously.

"Their sentiments are their weakness," Jarlaxle said, trying to be convincing. "And I know how to exploit that weakness."

"Uh-huh," said Athrogate, then he gave a great "Bwahaha!"

Jarlaxle could only smile.

"We goin' down there, or we just following?"

Jarlaxle thought about it for a moment, then surprised himself and the dwarf by hopping up from the grass and brushing himself off.

* * * * *

"Stuttgard o' the Stone Hills?" Bruenor asked when the wagon rolled around a bend in the road to reveal the dwarf standing in their way. "I thought ye was stayin' in Mithral . . ." he called as he eased the wagon to a stop before the dwarf. His voice trailed off as he noted the dwarf's impressive weapons, a pair of glassteel morningstars bobbing behind his sturdy shoulders. Suspicion filled Bruenor's expression, for Stuttgard had shown no such armament in Mithral Hall. His suspicion only grew as he considered how far along the road he was already—for Stuttgard to have arrived meant that the dwarf must have departed Mithral Hall immediately after meeting with Bruenor.

"Nah, but well met again, King Bruenor," Athrogate replied.

"What're ye about, dwarf?" Bruenor asked. Beside Bruenor, Pwent stood flexing his knees, ready to fight.

A growl from the side turned them all to look that way, and up on a branch in the lone tree overlooking the road perched Guenhwyvar, tamping her paws as if she meant to spring down upon the dwarf.

"Peace, good king," Athrogate said, patting his hands calmly in the air before him. "I ain't no enemy."

"Nor are you Stuttgard of the Stone Hills," came a call from farther along the road, behind Athrogate and ahead of the wagon.

Bruenor and Pwent looked past Stuttgard and nodded, though they couldn't see their drow companion. Stuttgard glanced over his shoulder, knowing it to be Drizzt, though the drow was too concealed in the brush to be seen.

"I should have recognized you at Bruenor's court," Drizzt called.

"It's me morningstars," Stuttgard explained. "I'm lookin' bigger with them, so I'm told. Bwahaha! Been a lot o' years since we crossed weapons, eh Drizzt Do'Urden?"

"Who is he?" Bruenor called to Drizzt, then he looked straight at the dwarf in the road and said, "Who are ye?"

"Where is he?" Drizzt called out in answer, drawing looks of surprise from both Bruenor and Pwent.

"He's right in front o' us, ye blind elf!" Pwent called out.

"Not him," Drizzt replied. "Not . . . Stuttgard."

"Ah, but suren me heart's to fall, for me worthy drow me name can't recall," said the dwarf in the road.

"Where is who?" Bruenor demanded of Drizzt, anger and impatience mounting

"He means me," another voice answered. On the side of the road opposite Guenhwyvar stood Jarlaxle.

"Oh, by Moradin's itchy arse," grumbled Bruenor. "Scratched it, he did, and this one fell out."

"A pleasure to see you again as well, King Bruenor," Jarlaxle said with a bow.

Drizzt came out of the brush then, moving toward the group. The drow had no weapons drawn—indeed, he leaned his bow over his shoulder as he went.

"What is it, me king?" Pwent asked, glancing nervously from the dwarf to Jarlaxle. "What?"

"Not a fight," Bruenor assured him and disappointed him at the same time. "Not *yet* a fight."

"Never that," Jarlaxle added as he moved beside his companion.

"Bah!" Pwent snorted.

"What's this about?" Bruenor demanded.

Athrogate grumbled as Drizzt walked by, and gave a lamenting shake of his head, his braided beard rattling as its small beads bounced.

"Athrogate," Drizzt whispered as he passed, and the dwarf howled in laughter.

"Ye're knowin' him?" asked Bruenor.

"I told you about him. From Luskan." He looked at Jarlaxle. "Eight years ago."

The drow mercenary bowed. "A sad day for many."

"But not for you and yours."

"I told you then and I tell you now, Drizzt Do'Urden. The fall of Luskan, and of Captain Deudermont, was not the doing of Bregan D'aerthe. I would have been as happy dealing with him—"

"He never would have dealt with the likes of you and your mercenaries," Drizzt interrupted.

Jarlaxle didn't finish his thought, just held his hands out wide, conceding the point.

"And what's this about?" Bruenor demanded again.

"We heard of your plight—of Catti-brie's," Jarlaxle explained. "The right road is to Cadderly, so I had my friend here go in—"

"And lie to us," said Drizzt.

"It seemed prudent in the moment," Jarlaxle admitted. "But the right road *is* to Cadderly. You know that."

"I don't know anything where Jarlaxle is concerned," Drizzt shot back, even as Bruenor nodded. "If this is all you claim, then why would you meet us out here on the road?"

"Needin' a ride, not to doubt," Pwent said, and his bracers screeched as they slid together when he crossed his burly arms over his chest.

"Hardly that," the drow replied, "though I would welcome the company." He paused and looked at the mules then, obviously surprised at how fresh they appeared, given that they had already traveled farther than most teams would go in two days.

"Magical hooves," Drizzt remarked. "They can cover six days in one."

Jarlaxle nodded.

"Now he's wanting a ride," Pwent remarked, and Jarlaxle did laugh at that, but shook his head.

"Nay, good dwarf, not a ride," the drow explained. "But there is something I would ask of you."

"Surprising," Drizzt said dryly.

"I am in need of Cadderly, too, for an entirely different reason," Jarlaxle explained. "And he will be in need of me, or will be glad that I am there, when he learns of it. Unfortunately, my last visit with the mighty priest did not fare so well, and he requested that I not return."

"And ye're thinking that he'll let ye in if ye're with us," Bruenor reasoned, and Jarlaxle bowed.

"Bah!" snorted the dwarf king. "Ye better have more to say than that."

"Much more," Jarlaxle replied, looking more at Drizzt than Bruenor. "And I will tell you all of it. But it is a long tale, and we should not tarry, for the sake of your wife."

"Don't ye be pretendin' that ye care about me girl!" Bruenor shouted, and Jarlaxle retreated a step.

Drizzt saw something then, though Bruenor was too upset to catch it. True pain flashed in Jarlaxle's dark eyes; he did care. Drizzt thought back to the time Jarlaxle had allowed him, with Catti-brie and Artemis Entreri, to escape from Menzoberranzan, one of the many times Jarlaxle had let him walk away. Drizzt tried to put it all in the context of the current situation, to reveal the possible motives behind Jarlaxle's actions. Was he lying, or was he speaking the truth?

Drizzt felt it the latter, and that realization surprised him.

"What're ye thinking, elf?" Bruenor asked him.

"I would like to hear the story," Drizzt replied, his gaze never leaving Jarlaxle. "But hear it as we travel along the road."

Jarlaxle nudged Athrogate, and the dwarf produced his boar figurine at the same time that Jarlaxle reached into his pouch for the obsidian nightmare. A moment later, their mounts materialized and Bruenor's mules flattened their ears and backed nervously away.

"What in the Nine Hells?" Bruenor muttered, working hard to control the team.

On a signal from Jarlaxle, Athrogate guided his boar to the side of the wagon, to take up a position in the rear.

"I want one o' them!" Thibbledorf Pwent said, his eyes wide with adoration as the fiery demon boar trotted past. "Oh, me king!"

Jarlaxle reined his nightmare aside and moved it to walk beside the wagon. Drizzt scrambled over that side to sit on the rail nearest him. Then he called to Guenhwyvar.

The panther knew her place. She leaped down from the tree, took a few running strides past Athrogate, and leaped into the wagon bed, curling up defensively around the seated Catti-brie.

"It is a long road," Drizzt remarked.

"It is a long tale," Jarlaxle replied.

"Tell it slowly then, and fully."

The wagon wasn't moving, and both Drizzt and Jarlaxle looked at Bruenor, the dwarf staring back at them with dark eyes full of doubt.

"Ye sure about this, elf?" he asked Drizzt.

"No," Drizzt answered, but then he looked at Jarlaxle, shook his head, and changed his mind. "To Spirit Soaring," he said.

"With hope," Jarlaxle added.

Drizzt turned his gaze to Catti-brie, who sat calmly, fully withdrawn from the world around her.

CHAPTER

NUMBERING THE STRANDS

This is futile!" cried Wanabrick Prestocovin, a spirited young wizard from Baldur's Gate. He shoved his palms forward on the table before him, ruffling a pile of parchment.

"Easy, friend," said Dalebrentia Promise, a fellow traveler from the port city. Older and with a large gray beard that seemed to dwarf his skinny frame, Dalebrentia looked the part of the mage, and even wore stereotypical garb: a blue conical hat and a dark blue robe adorned with golden stars. "We are asked to respect the scrolls and books of Spirit Soaring."

A few months earlier, Wanabrick's explosion of frustration would have been met by a sea of contempt in the study of the great library, where indeed, the massive collections of varied knowledge from all across Faerûn, pulled together by Cadderly and his fellows, were revered and treasured. Tellingly, though, as many wizards, sages, and priests in the large study nodded their agreement with Wanabrick as revealed their scorn at his outburst.

That fact was not lost on Cadderly as he sat across the room amidst his own piles of parchment, including one on which he was working mathematical equations to try to inject predictability and an overriding logic into the seeming randomness of the mysterious events.

His own frustrations were mounting, though Cadderly did well to hide them, for that apparent randomness seemed less and less like a veil to be unwound and more and more like an actual collapse of the logic that held

Mystra's Weave aloft. The gods were not all dark, had not all gone silent, unlike the terrible Time of Troubles, but there was a palpable distance involved in any divine communion, and an utter unpredictability to spell-casting, divine or wizardly.

Cadderly rose and started toward the table where the trio of Baldur's Gate visitors studied, but he purposely put a disarming smile on his face, and walked with calm and measured steps.

"Your pardon, good Brother Bonaduce," Dalebrentia said as he neared. "My friend is young, and truly worried."

Wanabrick turned a wary eye at Cadderly. His face remained tense despite Cadderly's calm nod.

"I don't blame you, or Spirit Soaring," Wanabrick said. "My anger, it seems, is as unfocused as my magic."

"We're all frustrated and weary," Cadderly said.

"We left three of our guild in varying states of insanity," Dalebrentia explained. "And a fourth, a friend of Wanabrick's, was consumed in his own fireball while trying to help a farmer clear some land. He cast it long—I am certain of it—but it blew up before it ever left his hand."

"The Weave is eternal," Wanabrick fumed. "It must be . . . stable and eternal, else all my life's work is naught but a cruel joke!"

"The priests do not disagree," said a gnome, a disciple of Gond.

His support was telling. The Gondsmen, who loved logic and gears, smokepowder and contraptions built with cunning more than magic, had been the least affected by the sudden troubles.

"He is young," Dalebrentia said to Cadderly. "He doesn't remember the Time of Troubles."

"I am not so young," Cadderly replied.

"In mind!" Dalebrentia cried, and laughed to break the tension. The other two Baldurian wizards, one middle-aged like Cadderly and the other even older than Dalebrentia, laughed as well. "But so many of us who feel the creak of knees on a rainy morning do not much sympathize, good reju-venated Brother Bonaduce!"

Even Cadderly smiled at that, for his journey through age had been a strange one indeed. He had begun construction of Spirit Soaring after the terrible chaos curse had wrought the destruction of its predecessor, the Edificant Library. Using magic given him by the god Deneir—nay, not given him, but chan-neled through him—Cadderly had aged greatly, to the point of believing that the construction would culminate with his death as an old, old man. He and Danica had accepted that fate for the sake of Spirit Soaring, the magnificent tribute to reason and enlightenment.

But the cost had proven a temporary thing, perhaps a trial of Deneir to test Cadderly's loyalty to the cause he professed, the cause of Deneir. After the completion of Spirit Soaring, the man had begun to grow younger physically—much younger, even younger than his actual age. He was forty-four, but appeared as a man in his young twenties, younger even than his twin children. That strange journey to physical youth, too, had subsequently stabilized, Cadderly believed, and he appeared to be aging more normally with the passage of the past several months.

"I have traveled the strangest of journeys," Cadderly said, putting a comforting hand on Wanabrick's shoulder. "Change is the only constant, I fear."

"But surely not like this!" Wanabrick replied.

"So we hope," said Cadderly.

"Have you found any answers, good priest?" Dalebrentia asked.

"Only that Deneir works as I work, writing his logic, seeking reason in the chaos, applying rules to that which seems unruly."

"And without success," Wanabrick said, somewhat dismissively.

"Patience," said Cadderly. "There are answers to be found, and rules that will apply. As we discern them, so too will we understand the extent of their implications, and so too will we adjust our thinking, and our spellcasting."

The gnome at a nearby table began to clap his hands at that, and the applause spread throughout the great study, dozens of mages and priests joining in, most soon standing. They were not cheering for him, Cadderly knew, but for hope itself in the face of their most frightening trial.

"Thank you," Dalebrentia quietly said to Cadderly. "We needed to hear that."

Cadderly looked at Wanabrick, who stood with his arms crossed over his chest, his face tight with anxiety and anger. The wizard did manage a nod to Cadderly, however.

Cadderly patted him on the shoulder again and started away, nodding and smiling to all who silently greeted him as he passed.

Outside the hall, the priest gave a sigh full of deep concern. He hadn't lied when he'd told Dalebrentia that Deneir was hard at work trying to unravel the unraveling, but he hadn't relayed the whole truth, either.

Deneir, a god of knowledge and history and reason, had answered Cadderly's prayers of communion with little more than a sensation of grave trepidation.

* * * * *

"Keep faith, friend," Cadderly said to Wanabrick later that same night, when the Baldurian contingent departed Spirit Soaring. "It's a temporary turbulence, I'm sure."

Wanabrick didn't agree, but he nodded anyway and headed out the door.

"Let us hope," Dalebrentia said to Cadderly, approaching him and offering his hand in gratitude.

"Will you not stay the night at least, and leave when the sun is bright?"

"Nay, good brother, we have been away too long as it is," Dalebrentia replied. "Several of our guild have been touched by the madness of the pure Weave. We must go to them and see if anything we have learned here might be of some assistance. Again, we thank you for the use of your library."

"It's not my library, good Dalebrentia. It's the world's library. I am merely the steward of the knowledge contained herein, and humbled by the responsibilities the great sages put upon me."

"A steward, and an author of more than a few of the tomes, I note," Dalebrentia said. "And truly we are all better off for your stewardship, Brother Bonaduce. In these troubled times, to find a place where great minds might congregate is comforting, even if not overly productive on this particular occasion. But we are dealing with unknowns here, and I am confident that as the unraveling of the Weave, if that is what it is, is understood, you will have many more important works to add to your collection."

"Any that you and your peers pen would be welcome," Cadderly assured him.

Dalebrentia nodded. "Our scribes will replicate every word spoken here today for Spirit Soaring, that in times to come when such a trouble as this visits Faerûn again, Tymora forefend, our wisdom will help the worried wizards and priests of the future."

They held their handshake throughout the conversation, each feeding off the strength of the other, for both Cadderly—so wise, the Chosen of Deneir—and Dalebrentia—an established mage even back in the Time of Troubles some two decades before—suspected that what they'd all experienced of late was no temporary thing, that it might lead to the end of Toril as they knew it, to turmoil beyond anything they could imagine.

"I will read the words of Dalebrentia with great interest," Cadderly assured the man as they finally broke off their handshake, and Dalebrentia moved out into the night to join his three companions.

They were a somber group as their wagon rolled slowly down Spirit Soaring's long cobblestone entry road, but not nearly as much so as when they had first arrived. Though they had found nothing solid to help them solve the troubling puzzle that lay before them, it was hard to leave Spirit Soaring without some measure of hope. Truly the library had become as magnificent in content as it was in construction, with thousands of parchments and tomes donated from cities as far away as Waterdeep and Luskan, Silverymoon, and even from great Calimport, far to the south. The place carried an aura of lightness and hope, a measure of greatness and promise, as surely as any other structure in all the lands.

Dalebrentia had climbed into the wagon beside old Resmilitu, while Wanabrick rode the jockey box with Pearson Bluth, who drove the two ponies.

"We will find our answers," Dalebrentia said, mostly to the fuming Wanabrick, but for the sake of all three.

Hooves clacking and wheels bouncing across the cobblestones were the only sounds that accompanied them down the lane. They reached the packed dirt of the long road that would lead them out of the Snowflakes to Carradoon.

The night grew darker as they moved under the thick canopy of overhanging tree limbs. The woods around them remained nearly silent—strangely so, they would have thought, had they bothered to notice—save for the occasional rustle of the wind through the leaves.

The lights of Spirit Soaring receded behind them, soon lost to the darkness.

"Bring up a flame," Resmilitu bade the others.

"A light will train enemies upon us," Wanabrick replied.

"We are four mighty wizards, young one. What enemies shall we fear this dark and chilly night?"

"Not so chilly, eh?" Pearson Bluth said, and glanced over his shoulder.

Though the driver's statement was accurate, he and the other two noted with surprise that Resmilitu hugged his arms around his chest and shivered mightily.

"Pop a light, then," Dalebrentia bade Wanabrick.

The younger wizard closed his eyes and waggled his fingers through a quick cantrip, conjuring a magical light atop his oaken staff. It flared to life, and Resmilitu nodded, though it shed no heat.

Dalebrentia moved to collect a blanket from the bags in the wagon bed. Then it was dark again.

"Ah, Mystra, you tease," said Pearson Bluth, as Wanabrick offered stronger curses to the failure.

A moment later, Pearson's good nature turned to alarm. The darkness grew more intense than the night around them, as if Wanabrick's dweomer had not only failed, but had transformed somehow into an opposing spell of darkness. The man pulled the team to a stop. He couldn't see the ponies, and couldn't even see Wanabrick sitting beside him. He had no way of knowing if they, too, were engulfed in the pitch blackness.

"Damn this madness!" Wanabrick cried.

"Oh, but you've erased the stars themselves," said Dalebrentia in as light-hearted a tone as he could manage, confirming that the back of the wagon, too, had fallen victim to the apparent reversal of the dweomer.

Resmilitu cried out then through chattering teeth, "So chill!" and before the others could react to his call, they felt it too, a sudden, unnatural coldness, profound and to the bone.

"What?" Pearson Bluth blurted, for he knew as the others knew that the chill was no natural phenomenon, and he felt as the others felt a malevolence in that coldness, a sense of death itself.

Resmilitu was the first to scream out in pain as some unseen creature came over the side of the wagon, its raking hands clawing at the old mage.

"Light! Light!" cried Dalebrentia.

Pearson Bluth moved to heed that call, but the ponies began to buck and kick and whinny terribly. The poor driver couldn't hold the frantic animals in check. Beside him, Wanabrick waved his arms, daring to dive into the suddenly unpredictable realm of magic for an even greater enchantment. He brought forth a bright light, but it lasted only a heartbeat—enough to reveal the hunched and shadowy form assailing Resmilitu.

The thing was short and squat, a misshapen torso of black flesh and wide shoulders, with a head that looked more like a lump without a neck. Its legs were no more than flaps of skin tucked under it, but its arms were long and sinewy, with long-fingered, clawing hands. As Resmilitu rolled away, the creature followed by propelling itself with those front limbs, like a legless man dragging himself.

"Be gone!" cried Dalebrentia, brandishing a thin wand of burnished wood tipped in metal. He sent forth its sparkling bolts of pure energy just as Wanabrick's magical light winked out.

The creature wailed in pain, but so too did poor Resmilitu, and the others heard the tearing of the old wizard's robes.

"Be gone!" Dalebrentia cried again—the trigger phrase for his wand—and they heard the release of the missiles even though they couldn't see any flash in the magical darkness.

"More light!" Dalebrentia cried.

Resmilitu cried out again, and so did the creature, though it sounded more like a shriek of murderous pleasure than of pain.

Wanabrick threw himself over the seat atop the fleshy beast and began thrashing and pounding away with his staff to try to dislodge it from poor Resmilitu.

The monster was not so strong, and the wizard managed to pry one arm free, but then Pearson Bluth screamed out from in front, and the wagon lurched to the side. It rolled out of the magical darkness at that moment, and the light atop Wanabrick's oaken staff brightened the air around them. But the wizards took little solace in that, for the terrified team dragged the wagon right off the road, to go bouncing down a steep embankment. They all tried to hold on, but the front wheels turned sharply and dug into a rut, lifting the wagon end over end.

Wood splintered and the mages screamed. Loudest of all came the shriek of a mule as its legs shattered in the roll.

Dalebrentia landed hard in some moss at the base of a tree, and he was certain he'd broken his arm. He fought through the pain, however, forcing himself to his knees. He glanced around quickly for his lost wand but found instead poor Resmilitu, the fleshy beast still atop him, tearing at his broken frame in a frenzy.

Dalebrentia started for him, but fell back as a blast of lightning blazed from the other side, lifting the shadowy beast right off his old friend and throwing it far into the night. Dalebrentia looked to Wanabrick to nod his approval.

But he never managed that nod. Looking at the man, the magically-lit staff lying near him, Dalebrentia saw the shadowy beasts crawling in behind the younger mage, huddled, fleshy beasts coming on ravenously.

To the side, Pearson Bluth stumbled into view, a beast upon his back, one of its arms wrapped around his neck, its other hand clawing at his face.

Dalebrentia fell into his spellcasting and brought forth a fiery pea, thinking to hurl it past Wanabrick, far enough so its explosion would catch the approaching horde but not engulf his friend.

But the collapsing Weave deceived the old mage. The pea had barely left his hand when it exploded. Waves of intense heat assailed Dalebrentia and he fell back, clutching at his seared eyes. He rolled around wildly on the ground, trying to extinguish the flames, too far lost to agony to even hear the cries of his friends, and those of the fleshy beasts, likewise shrieking in burning pain.

Somewhere in the back of his mind, old Dalebrentia could only hope that his fireball had eliminated the monsters and had not killed his companions.

His hopes for the former were dashed a heartbeat later when a clawed hand came down hard against the side of his neck, the force of the blow driving a dirty talon through his skin. Hooked like a fish, blinded and burned by his own fire and battered from the fall, Dalebrentia could do little to resist as the shadowy beast tugged at him.

* * * * *

Had he remained at the door where he'd sent the wizards off more than an hour before, Cadderly might have seen the sudden burst of fire far down the mountain trail, with one tall pine going up in flames like the fireworks the priest had often used to entertain his children in their younger days. But Cadderly had gone back inside as soon as the four from Baldur's Gate had departed.

Their inability to discover anything pertinent had spurred the priest to his meditation, to try again to commune with Deneir, the god who might, above all others in the pantheon, offer some clues to the source of the unpredictable and troubling events.

He sat in a small room lit only by a pair of tall candles, one to either side of the blanket he had spread on the floor. He sat cross-legged on that blanket, hands on his knees, palms facing up. For a long while, he focused only on his breathing, making his inhalations and exhalations the same length, using the count to clear his mind of all worry and trials. He was alone in his cadence, moving away from the Prime Material Plane and into the realm of pure thought, the realm of Deneir.

He'd done the same many times since the advent of the troubles, but never to great effect. Once or twice, he thought he had reached Deneir, but the god had flitted out of his thoughts before any clear pictures might emerge.

This time, though, Cadderly felt Deneir's presence keenly. He pressed on, letting himself fall far from consciousness. He saw the starscape all around him, as if he floated among the heavens, and he saw the image of Deneir, the old scribe, sitting in the night sky, long scroll spread before him, chanting, though Cadderly could not at first make out the words.

The priest willed himself toward his god, knowing that good fortune was on his side, that he had entered that particular region of concentration and reason in conjunction with the Lord of All Glyphs and Images.

He heard the chant.

Numbers. Deneir was working the *Metatext,* the binding logic of the multiverse.

Gradually, Cadderly began to discern the slightly-glowing strands forming a net in the sky above him and Deneir, the blanket of magic that gave enchantment to Toril. The Weave. Cadderly paused and considered the implications. Was it possible that the *Metatext* and the Weave were connected in ways more than philosophical? And if that were true, since the Weave was obviously flawed and failing, could not the *Metatext* also be flawed? No, that could not be, he told himself, and he moved his focus back to Deneir.

Deneir was numbering the strands, Cadderly realized, was giving them order and recording the patterns on his scroll. Was he somehow trying to infuse the failing Weave with the perfect logic and consistency of the *Metatext?* The thought thrilled the priest. Would his god, above all others, be the one to repair the rents in the fabric of magic?

He wanted to implore his god, to garner some divine inspiration and instruction, but Cadderly realized, to his surprise, that Deneir was not there to answer his call to commune, that Deneir had not brought him to that place. No, he had arrived at that place and time as Deneir had, by coincidence, not design.

He drifted closer—close enough to look over Deneir's shoulder as the god sat there, suspended in emptiness, recording his observations.

The parchment held patterns of numbers, Cadderly noted, like a great puzzle. Deneir was trying to decode the Weave itself, each strand by type and form. Was it possible that the Weave, like a spider's web, was comprised of various parts that sustained it? Was it possible that the unraveling, if that's what the time of turbulence truly was, resulted from a missing supporting strand?

Or a flaw in the design? Surely not that!

Cadderly continued to silently watch over Deneir's shoulder. He committed to memory a few sequences of the numbers, so he could record them later when he was back in his study. Though certainly no god, Cadderly still hoped he might discern something in those sequences that he could then communicate back to Deneir, to aid the Scribe of Oghma in his contemplations.

When at last Cadderly opened his physical eyes again, he found the candles still burning beside him. Looking at them, he deduced that he had been journeying the realm of concentration for perhaps two hours. He rose and moved to his desk, to transcribe the numbers he had seen, the representation of the Weave.

The collapsing Weave.

Where were the missing or errant strands? he wondered.

* * * * *

Cadderly hadn't seen the firelight down the mountain trail, but Ivan Bouldershoulder, out collecting wood for his forge, surely had.

"Well, what mischief's about?" the dwarf asked. He thought of his brother, then, and realized that Pikel would be angry indeed to see so majestic a pine go up in a pillar of flame.

Ivan moved to a rocky outcropping to gain a better vantage. He still couldn't make out much down the dark trails, but his new position put the wind in his face, and that breeze carried with it screams.

The dwarf dropped his pack beside the hand-sled on which rested the firewood, adjusted his helmet, which was adorned with great deer antlers, and hoisted Splitter, his double-bladed battle-axe, so named—by Ivan, after Cadderly had enchanted it with a powerfully keen edge—for its work on logs and goblin skulls alike. Without so much as a glance back at Spirit Soaring, the yellow-bearded dwarf ran down the dark trails, his short legs propelling him at a tremendous pace.

Fleshy beasts of shadow were feeding on the bodies of the Baldurian wizards by the time he arrived.

Ivan skidded to an abrupt halt, and the nearest creatures noticed him and came on, dragging themselves with their long forelimbs.

Ivan thought to retreat, but only until he heard a groan from one of the wizards.

"Well, all righty then!" the dwarf decided, and he charged at the beasts, Splitter humming as he slashed it back and forth with seeming abandon. The keen axe sheared through black skin with ease, spilling goo from the shrieking crawlers. They were too slow to get ahead of those powerful swipes, and too stupid to resist their insatiable hunger and simply flee.

One after another fell to Ivan, splattering with sickly sounds as Splitter eviscerated them. The dwarf's arms did not tire and his swings did not slow, though the beasts did not stop coming for a long, long while.

When finally there seemed nothing left to hit, Ivan rushed to the nearest mage, the oldest of the group.

"No helpin' that one," he muttered when he rolled Resmilitu over to find his neck torn out.

Only one of them wasn't quite dead. Poor Dalebrentia lay shivering, his skin all blistered, his eyes tightly closed.

"I got ye," Ivan whispered to him. "Ye hold that bit o' life and I'll get ye back to Cadderly."

With that and a quick glance around, the dwarf set Splitter in place across his back and bent low to slide one hand under Dalebrentia's knees, the other under his upper back. Before he lifted the man, though, Ivan felt such a sensation of coldness—not the cold of winter, but something more profound, as if death itself stood behind him.

He turned, slowly at first, as he reached around to grasp his weapon.

A shadowy form stood nearby, staring at him. Unlike the fleshy beasts that lay dead all around him—indeed, the four mages had also killed quite a few—it appeared more like a man, old and hunched over.

Such a cold chill went through Ivan then that his teeth began to chatter. He wanted to call out to the man, or shadow, or specter, or whatever it was, but found that he could not.

And found that he didn't have to.

Images of a long-ago time swirled in Ivan's mind, of dancing with his six mighty friends around an artifact of great power.

Images of a red dragon came clear to him, so clear that he began to duck as if the beast circled right above his head.

An image of another creature erased the others, an octopus-headed monstrosity with tentacles waggling under its chin like the braided strands of an old dwarf's beard.

A name was whispered into his ear, carried on unseen breezes. "Yharaskrik."

Ivan stood up straight, lifting Dalebrentia in his arms.

Then he dropped the man to the ground before him, lifted his heavy boot, and pressed it down on Dalebrentia's throat until the wheezing and the squirming stopped.

With a satisfied grin, Ivan, who was not Ivan, looked all around. He held out his hand toward each of the Baldurian wizards in turn, and each rose up to his call.

Throats torn, arms half-eaten, great holes in their bellies, it did not matter. For Ivan's call was the echo of the Ghost King, and the Ghost King's call beckoned souls from the land of the dead with ease.

His four gruesome bodyguards behind him, Ivan Bouldershoulder started off along the trails, moving farther away from Spirit Soaring.

He didn't reach his intended location that night. Instead, he found a cave nearby where he and his bodyguards could spend the daylight hours.

There would be plenty of time to kill when the darkness fell once more.

CHAPTER

BATTLE OF THE BLADE AND OF THE MIND

Hanaleisa snap-kicked to the side, breaking the tibia of a skeleton that had gotten inside the reach of Temberle's greatsword. The young woman leaned low to her left, raising her right leg higher, and kicked again, knocking the skull off the animated skeleton as it turned toward her.

At the same time, she punched out straight at a second target, her flying fist making a grotesque splattering sound as it smashed through the rotting chest of a zombie.

The blow would have knocked the breath from any man, but zombies have no need for breath. The creature continued its lumbering swing, its heavy arm slamming against Hanaleisa's blocking left arm and shoulder, driving her a step to her right, closer to her brother.

Exhausted after a long night of fighting, Hanaleisa found a burst of energy yet again, stepping forward and rocking the zombie with a barrage of punches, kicks, and driving knees. She ignored the gory results of every blow, almost all of them punching through rotting skin and breaking brittle bones, leaving holes through which fell rotted organs and clusters of maggots. Again and again the woman pounded the zombie until at last it fell away.

Another lumbered up—an inexhaustible line of enemies, it seemed.

Temberle's greatsword cut across in front of Hanaleisa just before she advanced to meet the newest foe. Temberle hit the creature just below the shoulder, taking its arm, and the sword plowed through ribs with ease, throwing the zombie aside.

"You looked like you needed to catch your breath," Hanaleisa's brother explained. Then he yelped, his move to defend Hanaleisa costing him a parry against the next beast closing with him. His right arm bloody from a long, deep wound, he stepped back fast and punched out with the pommel of his sword, slamming and jolting the skeleton.

Then Hanaleisa was there. She leaped up and ahead, rising between the skeleton closing on her and the one battling Temberle. Hanaleisa kicked out to the sides, both feet flying wide. With a jolting rattle of bones, the two skeletons flew apart.

Hanaleisa landed lightly, rising up on the ball of her left foot and spinning a powerful circle-kick into the gut of the next approaching zombie.

Her foot went right through it, and when she tried to retract, she discovered herself hooked on the monster's spine. She pulled back again, having little choice, and found herself even more entangled as the zombie, not quite destroyed by the mighty blow, reached and clawed at her.

Temberle's sword stabbed in hard from the side, taking the monster in the face and skewering it.

Hanaleisa stumbled back, still locked with the corpse. "Protect me!" she yelled to her brother, but she bit the words back sharply as she noted Temberle's arm covered in blood, and with more streaming from the wound. As he clenched his sword to swing again, his forearm muscles tightening, blood sprayed into the air.

Hanaleisa knew he couldn't go on for long. None of them could. Exhausted and horrified, and with their backs almost against the wall of the wharf's storehouse, they needed a break from the relentless assault, needed something to give them time to regroup and bandage themselves—or Temberle would surely bleed to death.

Finally pulling free and leaping to both feet, Hanaleisa glanced around for Pikel, or for an escape route, or for anything that might give her hope. All she saw was yet another defender being pulled down by the undead horde, and a sea of monsters all around them.

In the distance, just a few blocks away, more fires leaped to angry life as Carradoon burned.

With a sigh of regret, a grunt of determination, and a sniffle to hold back her tears, the young woman went back into the fray ferociously, pounding the monster nearest her and the one battling Temberle with blow after blow. She leaped and spun, kicked and punched, and her brother tried to match her.

But his swings were slowing as his blood continued to drain.

The end was coming fast.

* * * * *

"They're too heavy!" a young girl complained, straining to lift a keg with little success. Suddenly, though, it grew lighter and rose up through the trapdoor as easily as if it were empty. Indeed, when she saw that no one was pushing from below, the girl did glance underneath at the bottom of the keg, thinking its whiskey must have all drained out.

On the roof nearby, Rorick kept his focus, commanding an invisible servant to hold fast to the keg and help the little one. It wasn't much of a spell, but Rorick wasn't yet much of a wizard, and in times of unpredictable and often backfiring magic, he dared not attempt more difficult tricks.

He found satisfaction in his efforts, though, reminding himself that leaders needed to be clever and thoughtful, not just strong of arm or Art. His father had never been the greatest of fighters, and it wasn't until near the end of the troubles that had come to Edificant Library that Cadderly had truly come into his own Deneir-granted power. Still, Rorick wished he'd trained more the way his sister and brother had. Leaning heavily on a walking stick, his ankle swollen and pus oozing from the dirty wound, he was reminded with every pained step that he really wasn't much of a warrior.

I'm not much of a wizard, either, he thought, and he winced as his unseen servant dissipated. The girl, overbalanced with the keg, tumbled down. The side of the container broke open and whiskey spilled over the corner of the storehouse roof.

"What now, then?" a sailor asked, and it took Rorick a moment to realize that the man, far older and more seasoned than he, was speaking to him, was looking to him for direction.

"Be a leader," Rorick mumbled under his breath, and he pointed toward the front of the storehouse, to the edge of the low roof, where below the battle was on in full.

* * * * *

"Doo-dad!" came a familiar cry from far to Hanaleisa's right, much beyond Temberle. She started to glance that way, but saw movement up above and fell back, startled.

Out over the heads of the defenders came the whiskey kegs—by the dozen! They sailed out and crashed down, some atop zombies and other wretched creatures, others smashing hard on the cobblestones.

"What in the—?" more than one surprised defender cried out, Temberle included.

"Doo-dad!" came the emphatic answer.

All the defenders looked that way to see Pikel charging at them. His right arm was stretched out to the side, shillelagh pointed at the horde. The club threw sparks, and at first the bright light alone kept the undead back from Pikel, clearing the way as he continued his run. But more importantly, those sparks sizzled out to the spilled alcohol, and nothing burned brighter than Carradden whiskey.

The dwarf ran on, the enchanted cudgel spitting its flares, and flames roared up in response.

Despite her pain, despite her fear for her brothers, Hanaleisa couldn't help but giggle as the dwarf passed, his stumpy arm flapping like the wing of a wounded duck. He was not running, Hanaleisa saw—he was skipping.

An image of a five-year-old Rorick skipping around her mother's garden outside Spirit Soaring, sparkler in hand, flashed in Hanaleisa's mind, and a sudden contentment washed over her, as if she was certain that Uncle Pikel would make everything all right.

She shook the notion away quickly, though, and finished off a nearby monster that was caught on their side of the fire wall. Then she ran to Temberle, who was already calling out to organize the retreat. Hanaleisa reached into her pouch and pulled forth some clean cloth, quickly tying off Temberle's torn arm.

And not a moment too soon. Her brother nodded appreciatively, then swooned. Hanaleisa caught him and called for help, directing a woman to retrieve Temberle's greatsword, for she knew—they all knew—he would surely need it again, and very soon.

Into the storehouse they went, a line of weary and battered defenders—battered emotionally as much as physically, perhaps even more so, for they knew to a man and woman that their beloved Carradoon was unlikely to survive the surprise onslaught.

* * * * *

"You saved us all," Hanaleisa said to Rorick a short while later, when they were all together once more.

"Uncle Pikel did the dangerous work," Rorick said, nodding his chin toward the dwarf.

"Doo-dad, hee hee hee," said the dwarf. He presented his shillelagh and added, "Boom!" with a shake of his hairy head.

"We're not saved yet," Temberle said from a small window overlooking the carnage on the street. Conscious again, but still weakened, the young man's voice sounded grim indeed. "Those fires won't last for long."

It was true, but the whiskey-fueled conflagration had turned the battle and saved their cause. The stupid undead knew no fear and had kept coming on, their rotting clothes and skin adding fuel to the flames as they crumpled and burned atop their fellows.

But a few stragglers were getting through, scratching at the storehouse walls, battering the planks, and the fires outside were burning low.

One zombie walked right through the fires and came out ablaze. Still it advanced, right to the storehouse door, and managed to pound its fists a few times before succumbing to the flames. And as bad luck would have it, those flames licked at the wood. They wouldn't have been of consequence, except from the roof above, one of the kegs had overturned, spilling its volatile contents across the roof and down the side.

Several people screamed as the corner of the storehouse flared up. Some went to try to battle the flames, but to no avail. Worse, the keg throwers hadn't emptied about a third of the whiskey stocks from the storehouse. Whiskey was one of Carradoon's largest exports—boats sailed out with kegs of the stuff almost every tenday.

More than a hundred people were in that storehouse, and panic spread quickly as the flames licked up over their heads to the roof, fanning across the ceiling.

"We've got to get out!" one man called.

"To the docks!" others yelled in agreement, and the stampede for the back door began in full.

"Uh oh," said Pikel.

Temberle hooked Rorick's arm over his shoulder and the brothers leaned heavily on each other for support as they moved toward the exit, both calling for Hanaleisa and Pikel to follow.

Pikel started to move, but Hanaleisa grabbed him by the arm and held him back.

"Eh?"

Hanaleisa pointed to a nearby keg and rushed for it. She popped the top and hoisted it, then ran to the front door, where skeletons and zombies pounded furiously. With a look back at Pikel, Hanaleisa began splashing the keg's contents all along the wall.

"Hee hee hee," Pikel agreed, coming up beside her with a keg of his own. First he lifted it to his lips for a good long swallow, but then he ran along the wall, splashing whiskey all over the floor and the base of the planks.

Hanaleisa looked across the storehouse. The brave townsfolk had regained a measure of calm and were moving swiftly and orderly out onto the docks.

The heat grew quickly. A beam fell from the roof, dropping a line of fire across the floor.

"Hana!" Rorick cried from the back of the storehouse.

"Get out!" she screamed at him. "Uncle Pikel, come along!"

The dwarf charged toward her and hopped the fallen beam alongside her, both heading fast for the door.

More fiery debris tumbled from the ceiling, and the whiskey-soaked side wall began to burn furiously. The flames spread up the walls behind them.

But the undead hadn't broken through, Hanaleisa realized when she reached the exit. "Go!" she ordered Pikel, and pushed him through the door. To the dwarf's horror, to the horror of her brothers, and to the horror of everyone watching, Hanaleisa turned and sprinted back into the burning building.

Smoke filled her nostrils and stung her eyes. She could barely see, but she knew her way. She leaped the beam burning in the middle of the floor, then ducked and rolled under another that tumbled down from above.

She neared the front door, and just as she leaped for it, a nearby keg burst in a ball of fire, causing another to explode beside it. Hanaleisa kicked out at the heavy bar sealing the door, all her focus and strength behind the blow. She heard the wood crack beneath her foot, and a good thing that was, for she had no time to follow the move. At that moment, the fires reached the whiskey she and Pikel had poured out, and Hanaleisa had to sprint away to avoid immolation.

But the door was open, and the undead streamed in hungrily, stupidly.

More kegs exploded and half the roof caved in beside her, but Hanaleisa maintained her focus and kept her legs moving. She could hardly see in the heavy smoke, and tripped over a burning beam, painfully smashing her toes in the process.

She scrambled along, quickly regaining her footing.

More kegs exploded, and fiery debris flew all around her. The smoke grew so thick that she couldn't get her bearings. She couldn't see the doorway. Hanaleisa skidded to a halt, but she couldn't afford to stop. She sprinted ahead once more, crashing into some piled crates and overturning them.

She couldn't see, she couldn't breathe, she had no idea which way was out, and she knew that any other direction led to certain death.

She spun left and right, started one way, then fell back in dismay. She called out, but her voice was lost in the roar of the flames.

In that moment, horror turned to resignation. She knew she was doomed, that her daring stunt had succeeded at the cost of her life.

So be it.

The young woman dropped down onto all fours and thought of her brothers. She hoped she had bought them the time they needed to escape. Uncle Pikel would lead them to safety, she told herself, and she nodded her acceptance.

* * * * *

To his credit, Bruenor didn't say anything. But it was hard for Thibbledorf Pwent and Drizzt not to notice his continual and obviously uncomfortable glances to either side, where Jarlaxle and Athrogate weaved in and out of the trees on their magical mounts.

"He's the makings of a Gutbuster," remarked Pwent, who sat beside Bruenor on the wagon's jockey box, while Drizzt walked along beside them. The Gutbuster nodded his hairy chin toward Athrogate. "Bit too clean, me's thinkin', but I'm likin' that pig o' his. And them morningstars!"

"Gutbusters play with drow, do they?" Bruenor replied, but before the sting of that remark could sink in to Pwent, Drizzt beat him to the reply with, "Sometimes."

"Bah, elf, ye ain't no drow, and ain't been one, ever," Bruenor protested. "Ye know what I'm meaning."

"I do," Drizzt admitted. "No offense intended, so no offense taken. But neither do I believe that Jarlaxle is what you've come to expect from my people."

"Bah, but he ain't no Drizzt."

"Nor was Zaknafein, in the manner you imply," Drizzt responded. "But King Bruenor would have welcomed my father into Mithral Hall. Of that, I'm sure."

"And this strange one's akin to yer father, is he?"

Drizzt looked through the trees to see Jarlaxle guiding his hellish steed along, and he shrugged, honestly at a loss. "They were friends, I've been told."

Bruenor paused for a bit and similarly considered the strange creature that was Jarlaxle, with his outrageously plumed hat. Everything about Jarlaxle seemed unfamiliar to the parochial Bruenor, everything spoke of the proverbial "other" to the dwarf.

"I just ain't sure o' that one," the dwarf king muttered. "Me girl's in trouble here, and ye're asking me to trust the likes o' Jarlaxle and his pet dwarf."

"True enough," Drizzt admitted. "And I don't deny that I have concerns of my own." Drizzt hopped up and grabbed the rail behind the seat so he could ride along for a bit. He looked directly at Bruenor, demanding the dwarf's complete attention. "But I also know that if Jarlaxle had wanted us dead, we would likely already be walking the Fugue Plain. Regis and I would not have gotten out of Luskan without his help. Catti-brie and I would not have been able to escape his many warriors outside of Menzoberranzan those years ago, had he not allowed it. I have no doubt that there's more to his offer to help us than his concern for us, or for Catti-brie."

"He's got some trouble o' his own," said Bruenor, "or I'm a bearded gnome! And bigger trouble than that tale he told about needing to make sure the Crystal Shard was gone."

Drizzt nodded. "That may well be. But even if that is true, I like our chances better with Jarlaxle beside us. We wouldn't even have turned toward Spirit Soaring and Cadderly, had not Jarlaxle sent his dwarf companion to Mithral Hall to suggest it."

"To lure us out!" Bruenor snapped back, rather loudly.

Drizzt patted one hand in the air to calm the dwarf. "Again, my friend, if that was only to make us vulnerable, Jarlaxle would have ambushed us on the road right outside your door, and there we would remain, pecked by the crows."

"Unless he's looking for something from ye," Bruenor argued. "Might still be a pretty ransom on Drizzt Do'Urden's head, thanks to the matron mothers of Menzoberranzan."

That was possible, Drizzt had to admit to himself, and he glanced over his shoulder at Jarlaxle once more, but eventually shook his head. If Jarlaxle had wanted anything like that, he would have hit the wagon with overwhelming force outside of Mithral Hall, and easily enough captured all four, or whichever of them might have proven valuable to his nefarious schemes. Even beyond that simple logic, however, there was within Drizzt something else: an understanding of Jarlaxle and his motives that surprised Drizzt every time he paused to consider it.

"I do not believe that," Drizzt replied to Bruenor. "Not any of it."

"Bah!" Bruenor snorted, hardly seeming convinced, and he snapped the reins to coax the team along more swiftly, though they had already put more than fifty miles behind them that day, with half-a-day's riding yet before them. The wagon bounced along comfortably, the dwarven craftsmanship more than equal to the task of the long rides. "So ye're thinking he's just wanting us for a proper introduction to Cadderly? Ye're buying his tale, are ye? Bah!"

It was hard to find a proper response to one of Bruenor's "bahs," let alone two. But before Drizzt could even try, a scream from the back of the wagon ended the discussion.

The three turned to see Catti-brie floating in the air, her eyes rolled back to show only white. She hadn't risen high enough to escape the tailgate of the wagon, and was being towed along in her weightless state. One of her arms rose to the side, floating in the air as if in water, as they had seen before during her fits, but her other arm was forward, her hand turned and grasping as if she were presenting a sword before her.

Bruenor pulled hard on the reins and flipped them to Pwent, heading over the back of the seat before the Gutbuster even caught them. Drizzt beat the dwarf to the wagon bed, the agile drow leaping over the side in a rush to grab Catti-brie's left arm before she slipped over the back of the rail. The drow raised his other hand toward Bruenor to stop him, and stared intently at Catti-brie as she played out what she saw in her mind's eye.

Her eyes rolled back to show their deep blue once more.

Her right arm twitched, and she winced. Her focus seemed to be straight ahead, though given her distant stare, it was hard to be certain. Her extended hand slowly turned, as if her imaginary sword was being forced into a downward angle. Then it popped back up a bit, as if someone or something had slid off the end of the blade. Catti-brie's breath came in short gasps. A single tear rolled down one cheek, and she quietly mouthed, "I killed her."

"What's she about, then?" Bruenor asked.

Drizzt held his hand up to silence the dwarf, letting it play out. Catti-brie's chin tipped down, as if she were looking at the ground, then lifted again as she raised her imaginary sword.

"Suren she's looking at the blood," Bruenor whispered. He heard Jarlaxle's mount galloping to the side, and Athrogate's as well, but he didn't take his eyes off his beloved daughter.

Catti-brie sniffled hard and tried to catch her breath as more tears streamed down her face.

"Is she looking into the future, or the past?" Jarlaxle asked.

Drizzt shook his head, uncertain, but in truth, he was pretty sure he recognized the scene playing out before him.

"But she's floated up and almost o'er the aft. I ain't for sayin', but that one's daft," said Athrogate.

Bruenor did turn to the side then, throwing a hateful look at the dwarf.

"Beggin' yer pardon, good King Bruenor," Athrogate apologized. "But that's what I'm thinking."

Catti-brie began to sob and shake violently. Drizzt had seen enough. He pulled the woman close, hugging her and whispering into her ear.

And the world darkened for the drow. For just an instant, he saw Catti-brie's victim, a woman wearing the robes of the Hosttower of the Arcane, a mage named Sydney, he knew, and he knew then without doubt the incident his beloved had just replayed.

Before he could fully understand that he saw the body of the first real kill Catti-brie had ever known, the first time she had felt her victim's blood splash on her own skin, the image faded from his mind and he moved deeper, as if through the realm of death and into . . .

Drizzt did not know. He glanced around in alarm, looking not at the wagon and Bruenor, but at a strange plain of dim light and dark shadows, and dark gray—almost black— fog wafting on unfelt breezes.

They came at him there, in that other place, dark, fleshy beasts like legless, misshapen trolls, pulling themselves along with gangly, sinewy arms, snarling through long, pointed teeth.

Drizzt turned fast to put his back to Catti-brie and went for his scimitars as the first of the beasts reached out to claw at him. Even the glow of Twinkle seemed dark to his eyes as he brought the blade slashing down. But it did its work, taking the thing's arm at the elbow. Drizzt slipped forward behind the cut, driving Icingdeath into the torso of the wretched creature.

He came back fast the other way and spun around. To his horror, Catti-brie was not there. He sprinted out, bumping hard into someone, then tripped and went rolling forward. Or he tried to roll, but discovered that the ground was several feet lower than he'd anticipated, and he landed hard on his lower back and rump, rattling his teeth.

Drizzt stabbed and slashed furiously as the dark beasts swarmed over him. He managed to get his feet under him and came up with a high leap, simply trying to avoid the many slashing clawed hands.

He landed in a flurry and a fury, blades rolling over each other with powerful and devastating strokes and stabs, and wild slashes that sent the beasts falling away with terrible shrieks and screeches, three at a time.

"Catti-brie!" he cried, for he could not see her, and he knew that they had taken her!

He tried to go forward, but heard a call from his right, and just as he spun, something hit him hard, as if one of the beasts had leaped up and slammed him with incredible force.

He lost a scimitar as he flew backward a dozen feet and more, and came down hard against some solid object, a tree perhaps, where he found himself stuck fast—completely stuck, as if the fleshy beast or whatever it was that had hit him had just turned to goo as it had engulfed him. He could move only one hand and couldn't see, could hardly breathe.

Drizzt tried to struggle free, thinking of Catti-brie, and he knew the fleshy black beasts were closing in on him.

CHAPTER

A T I M E F O R H E R O E S

A light appeared, a bright beacon cutting through the smoke, beckoning her. Hanaleisa felt its inviting warmth, so different from the bite of the fire's heat. It called to her, almost as if it were enchanted. When she at last burst out the door, past the thick smoke, rolling out onto the wharves, Hanaleisa was not surprised to see a grinning Uncle Pikel standing there, holding aloft his brilliantly glowing shillelagh. She tried to thank him, but coughed and gagged on the smoke. Nearly overcome, she managed to reach Pikel and wrap him in a great hug, her brothers coming in to flank her, patting her back to help her dislodge the persistent smoke.

After a long while, Hanaleisa finally managed to stop coughing and stand straight. Pikel quickly ushered them all away from the storehouse, as more explosions wracked it, kegs of Carradden whiskey still left to explode.

"Why did you go in there?" Rorick scolded her once the immediate danger was past. "That was foolish!"

"Tut tut," Pikel said to him, waggling a finger in the air to silence him.

A portion of the roof caved in with a great roar, taking down part of the wall with it. Through the hole, the four saw the continuing onslaught of the undead, the unthinking monsters willingly walking in the door after Hanaleisa had opened it. They were fast falling, consumed by the flames.

"She invited them in," Temberle said to his little brother. "Hana bought us the time we'll need."

"What are they doing?" Hanaleisa asked, looking past her brothers toward the wharves, her question punctuated by coughs. The question was more of surprise than to elicit a response, for the answer was obvious. People swarmed aboard the two small fishing vessels docked nearby.

"They mean to ferry us across the lake to the north, to Byernadine," Temberle explained, referring to the lakeside hamlet nearest to Carradoon.

"We haven't the time," Hanaleisa replied.

"We haven't a choice," Temberle said. "They have good crews here. They'll get more boats in fast."

Shouting erupted on the docks. It escalated into pushing and fighting as desperate townsfolk scrambled to get aboard the first two boats.

"Sailors only!" a man shouted above the rest, for the plan had been to fill those two boats with experienced fishermen, who could then retrieve the rest of the fleet.

But the operation wasn't going as planned.

"Cast her off!" many people aboard one of the boats shouted, while others still tried to jump on board.

"Too many," Hanaleisa whispered to her companions, for indeed the small fishing vessel, barely twenty feet long, had not near the capacity to carry the throng that had packed aboard her. Still, they threw out the lines and pushed her away from the wharf. Several people went into the water as she drifted off, swimming hard to catch her and clinging desperately to her rail, which was barely above the cold waters of Impresk Lake.

The second boat went out as well, not quite as laden, and the square sails soon opened as they drifted out from shore. So packed was the first boat that the crewmen aboard couldn't even reach the rigging, let alone raise sail. Listing badly, weaving erratically, her movements made all on shore gasp and whisper nervously, while the shouting and arguing on the boat only increased in desperation.

Already, many were shaking their heads in dismay and expecting catastrophe when the situation fast deteriorated. The people in the water suddenly began to scream and thrash about. Skeletal fish knifed up to stab hard into them like thrown knives.

The fishing boat rocked as the many hangers-on let go, and people shrieked as the waters churned and turned red with blood.

Then came the undead sailors, rising up to some unseen command. Bony hands gripped the rails of both low-riding ships, and people aboard and on shore cried out in horror as the skeletons of long-dead fishermen began to pull themselves up from the dark waters.

The panic on the first boat sent several people splashing overboard. The boat rocked and veered with the shifting weight, turning uncontrollably—and disastrously. Similarly panicked, the sailors on the second boat couldn't react quickly enough as the first boat turned toward her. They crashed together with the crackle of splintering wood and the screams of scores of townsfolk realizing their doom. Many went into the water, and as the skeletons scrambled aboard, many others had no choice but to leap into Impresk Lake and try to swim to shore.

Long had men plied the waters of Impresk Lake. Its depths had known a thousand thousand turns of the circle of life. Her deep bed churned with the rising dead, and her waters roiled as more skeletal fish swarmed the splashing Carradden.

And those on the wharves, Hanaleisa, her bothers, and Uncle Pikel as well, could only watch in horror, for not one of the eighty-some people who had boarded those two boats made it back to shore alive.

"Now what?" Rorick cried, his face streaked with tears, his words escaping through such profound gasps that he could hardly get them out.

Indeed, everyone on the wharves shared that horrible question. Then the storehouse collapsed with a great fiery roar. Many of the undead horde were destroyed in that conflagration, thanks to the daring of Hanaleisa, but many, many more remained. And the townsfolk were trapped with their backs to the water, a lake they dared not enter.

Rag-tag groups ran to the north and south as all semblance of order broke down. A few boat crews managed to band together along the shore, and many townsfolk followed in their protective wake.

Many more looked to the children of Cadderly and Danica, those two so long the heroes of the barony. In turn, the three siblings looked to the only hope they could find: Uncle Pikel.

Pikel Bouldershoulder accepted the responsibility with typical gusto, punching his stump into the air. He tucked his cudgel under that short-ened arm and began to hop around, tapping his lips with one finger and mumbling, "umm" over and over again.

"Well, what then?" a fishing boat captain cried. Many people closed in on the foursome, looking for answers.

"We find a spot to defend, and we order our line," Temberle said after looking to Pikel for answers that did not seem to be forthcoming. "Find a narrow alleyway. We cannot remain down here."

"Uh-uh," Pikel disagreed, even as the group began to organize its retreat.

"We can't stay here, Uncle Pikel!" Rorick said to the dwarf, but the indomitable Pikel just smiled back at him.

Then the green-bearded dwarf closed his eyes and tapped his shillelagh against the boardwalk, as if calling to the ground beneath. He turned left, to the north, then hesitated and turned back before spinning to the north again and dashing off at a swift pace.

"What's he doing?" the captain and several others asked.

"I don't know," Temberle answered, but he and Rorick hooked arms again and started after.

"We ain't following the fool dwarf blindly!" the captain protested.

"Then you're sure to die," Hanaleisa answered without hesitation.

Her words had an effect, for all of them swarmed together in Pikel's wake. He led them off the docks and onto the north beach, moving fast toward the dark rocks that sheltered Carradoon's harbor from the northern winds.

"We can't get over those cliffs!" one man complained.

"We're too near the water!" another woman cried, and indeed, a trio of undead sailors came splashing at them, forcing Temberle and Hanaleisa and other warriors to protect their right flank all the way.

All the way to an apparent dead end, where the rocky path rose up a long slope, then ended at a drop to the stone-filled lake.

"Brilliant," the captain complained, moving near Pikel. "Ye've killed us all, ye fool dwarf!"

It surely seemed as if he spoke the truth, for the undead were in pursuit and the group had nowhere left to run.

But Pikel was unbothered. He stood on the edge of the drop, beside a swaying pine, and closed his eyes, chanting his druidic magic. The tree responded by lowering a branch down before him.

"Hee hee hee," said Pikel, opening his eyes and handing the branch to Rorick, who stood beside him.

"What?" the young man asked.

Pikel nodded to the drop, and directed Rorick's gaze to a cave at the back of the inlet.

"You want me to jump down there?" Rorick asked, incredulous. "You want me to *swing* down?"

Pikel nodded, and pushed him off the ledge.

The screaming Rorick, guided by the obedient tree, was set down—as gently as a mother lays her infant in its crib—on a narrow strip of stone beside the watery inlet. He waited there for the captain and two others, who came down on the next swing, before heading toward the cave.

Pikel was the last one off the ledge, with a host of zombies and skeletons closing in as he leaped. Several of the monsters jumped after him, only to fall and shatter on the stones below.

His cudgel glowing brightly, Pikel moved past the huddled group and led the way into the cave, which at first glance seemed a wide, high, and shallow chamber, ankle deep with water. But Pikel's instincts and his magical call to the earth had guided him well. On the back wall of that shallow cave was a sidelong corridor leading deeper into the cliffs, and deeper still into the Snowflake Mountains.

Into that darkness went two score of Carradoon's survivors, half of them capable fighters, the other half frightened citizens, some elderly, some too young to wield a weapon. Just a short while into the retreat, they came to a defensible spot where the corridor ended at a narrow chimney, and through that chimney was another chamber.

There they decided to make their first camp, a circle of guards standing at the cave entrance, which they covered with a heavy stone, and more guarding the two corridors that led out of the chamber, deeper into the mountains.

No more complaints were shouted Uncle Pikel's way.

* * * * *

Jarlaxle slid his wand away, shouting to Athrogate, "Just his face!"

The drow leaped from his mount to the back of the wagon, charging right past Bruenor, who was down on one knee, his right hand grasping his left shoulder in an attempt to stem the flow of spraying blood.

Twinkle had cut right through the dwarf's fine armor and dug deeply into the flesh beneath.

Jarlaxle seized Catti-brie just as she floated over the back of the wagon, having been jostled hard by the thrashing and running Drizzt. Jarlaxle pulled her in and hugged her closely, as Drizzt had done, and started that same journey to insanity.

Jarlaxle knew the distortions for what they were, the magic of his eye patch fighting back the deception. So he held Catti-brie and whispered softly to her as she sobbed. Gradually, he was able to ease her down to the floorboards of the wagon, moving her to a sitting position against the side wall.

He turned away, shaking his head, to find Thibbledorf Pwent hard at work tearing off Bruenor's blood-soaked sleeve.

"Ah, me king," the battlerager lamented.

"He's breathing," Athrogate called from the side of the trail, where Drizzt remained stuck fast by the viscous glob Jarlaxle's wand had launched at him. "And seethin', thrashing and slashin', not moving at all but wantin' to be bashin'!"

"Don't ask," Jarlaxle said as both Bruenor and Pwent looked Athrogate's way, then questioningly back at Jarlaxle.

"What just happened?" Bruenor demanded.

"To your daughter, I do not know," Jarlaxle admitted. "But when I went to her, I was drawn through her into a dark place." He glanced furtively at Drizzt. "A place where our friend remains, I fear."

"Regis," Bruenor muttered. He looked at Jarlaxle, but the drow was staring into the distance, lost in thought. "What d'ya know?" Bruenor demanded, but Jarlaxle just shook his head.

The drow mercenary looked at Catti-brie again and thought of the sudden journey he had taken when he'd touched her. It was more than an illusion, he believed. It was almost as if his mind had walked into another plane of existence. The Plane of Shadow, perhaps, or some other dark region he hoped never to visit again.

But even on that short journey, Jarlaxle hadn't really gone away, as if that plane and the Prime Material Plane had overlapped, joined in some sort of curious and dangerous rift.

He thought about the specter he'd encountered when Hephaestus had come looking for him, of the dimensional hole he had thrown over the creature, and of the rift to the Astral Plane that he'd inadvertently created.

Had that specter, that huddled creature, been physically passing back and forth from Toril to that shadowy dimension?

"It's real," he said quietly.

"What?" Bruenor and Pwent demanded together.

Jarlaxle looked at them and shook his head, not sure how he could explain what he feared had come to pass.

* * * * *

"He's calming down," Athrogate called from the tree. "Asking for the girl, and talking to me."

With Pwent's help, Bruenor pulled himself to his feet and went with the drow and the dwarf to Drizzt's side.

"What're ye about, elf?" Bruenor asked when he got to Drizzt, who was perfectly helpless, stuck fast against the tree.

"What happened?" the drow ranger replied, his gaze fixed on Bruenor's arm.

"Just a scratch," Bruenor assured him.

"Bah, but two fingers higher and ye'd have taken his head!" Athrogate cut in, and both Bruenor and Jarlaxle glared at the brash dwarf.

"I did—?" Drizzt started to ask, but he stopped and scowled with a perplexed look.

"Just like back at Mithral Hall," muttered Bruenor.

"I know where Regis is," Drizzt said, looking up with alarm. He was sure the others could tell that he was even more afraid for his little friend at that dark moment. And his face twisted with more fear and pain when he glanced over at Catti-brie. If Regis's mind had inadvertently entered and been trapped in that dark place, then Catti-brie was surely caught between the two worlds.

"Yerself came back, elf, and so'll the little one," Bruenor assured him.

Drizzt wasn't so confident of that. He had barely set his toes in that umbral dimension, but with the ruby, Regis had entered the very depths of Catti-brie's mind.

Jarlaxle flicked his wrist, and a dagger appeared in his hand. He motioned for Athrogate to move aside, and stepped forward, bending low, carefully cutting Drizzt free.

"If you mean to go mad again, do warn me," Jarlaxle said to Drizzt with a wink.

Drizzt neither replied nor smiled. His expression became darker still when Athrogate walked over, holding the drow's lost scimitar, red with the blood of his dearest friend.

PART
2

PRYING THE RIFT

PRYING THE RIFT

I know she is in constant torment, and I cannot go to her. I have seen into the darkness in which she resides, a place of shadows more profound and more grim than the lower planes. She took me there, inadvertently, when I tried to offer some comfort, and there, in so short a time, I nearly broke.

She took Regis there, inadvertently, when he tried to reach her with the ruby, and there he broke fully. He threw the drowning Catti-brie a rope and she pulled him from the shore of sanity.

She is lost to me. Forever, I fear. Lost in an oblivious state, a complete emptiness, a listless and lifeless existence. And those rare occasions when she is active are perhaps the most painful of all to me, for the depth of her delusions shines all too clearly. It's as if she's reliving her life, piecemeal, seeing again those pivotal moments that shaped this beautiful woman, this woman I love with all my heart. She stood again on the side of Kelvin's Cairn back in Icewind Dale, living again the moment when first we met, and while that to me is among my most precious of memories, that fact made seeing it play out again through the distant eyes of my love even more painful.

How lost must my beloved Catti-brie be to have so broken with the world around her?

And Regis, poor Regis. I cannot know how deeply into that darkness Catti-brie now resides, but it's obvious to me that Regis went fully into that place of shadows. I can attest to the convincing nature of his delusions, as can Bruenor, whose shoulder now carries the scar of my blade as I fought off imaginary monsters. Or were they imaginary? I cannot begin to know. But that is a moot point to Regis, for to him they are surely real, and they're all around him, ever clawing at him, wounding him and terrifying him relentlessly.

We four—Bruenor, Catti-brie, Regis, and I—are representative of the world around us, I fear. The fall of Luskan, Captain Deudermont's folly, the advent of Obould—all of it were but the precursors. For now we have the collapse of that which we once believed eternal, the unraveling of Mystra's Weave. The enormity of that catastrophe is easy to see on the face of the always calm Lady Alustriel. The potential results of it are reflected in the insanity of Regis, the emptiness of Catti-brie, the near-loss of my own sanity, and the scar carried by King Bruenor.

More than the wizards of Faerûn will feel the weight of this dramatic change. How will diseases be quelled if the gods do not hear the desperate pleas of their priests? How will the kings of the world fare when any contact to potential rivals and allies, instead of commonplace through divination and teleportation, becomes an arduous and lengthy process? How weakened will be the armies, the caravans, the small towns, without the potent power of magic-users among their ranks? And what gains will the more base races, like goblins and orcs, make in the face of such sudden magical weakness? What druids will tend the fields? What magic will bolster and secure the exotic structures of the world? Or will they fall catastrophically as did the Hosttower of the Arcane, or long-dead Netheril?

Not so long ago, I had a conversation with Nanfoodle the gnome in Mithral Hall. We discussed his cleverness in funneling explosive gasses under the mountain ridge where Obould's giant allies had set up devastating artillery. Quite an engineering feat by the gnome and his crew of dwarves, and one that blew the mountain ridge apart more fully than even a fireball from Elminster could have done. Nanfoodle is much more a follower of Gond, the god of inventions, than he is a practitioner of the Art. I asked him about that, inquiring as to why he tinkered so when so much of what he might do could be accomplished more quickly by simply touching the Weave.

I never got an answer, of course, as that is not Nanfoodle's wont. Instead, he launched into a philosophical discussion of the false comfort we take in our dependence on, and expectation of, "that which is."

Never has his point been more clear to me than it is now, as I see "that which is" collapsing around us all.

Do the farmers around the larger cities of Faerûn, around Waterdeep and Silverymoon, know how to manage their produce without the magical aid of the druids? Without such magical help, will they be able to meet the demands of the large populations in those cities? And that is only the top level of the problems that will arise should magic fail! Even the sewers of Waterdeep are complicated affairs, built over many generations, and aided at certain critical points, since the city has so expanded, by the power of wizards, summoning elementals to help usher away the waste. Without them—what?

And what of Calimport? Regis has told me often that there are far too many people there, beyond any sensible number for which the ocean and desert could possibly provide. But the fabulously rich Pashas have supplemented their natural resources by employing mighty clerics to summon food and drink for the markets, and mighty wizards to teleport in fresh sustenance from faraway lands.

Without that aid, what chaos might ensue?

And, of course, in my own homeland of Menzoberranzan, it is magic that keeps the kobolds enslaved, magic that protects the greater Houses from their envious rivals, and magic that holds together the threads of the entire society. Lady Lolth loves chaos, they say, and so she may see it in the extreme if that magic fades!

The societies of the world have grown over the centuries. The systems we have in place have evolved through the many generations, and in that evolution, I fear, we have long forgotten the basic foundations of society's structures. Worse, perhaps, even re-learning those lost arts and crafts will not likely suffice to meet the needs of lands grown fatter and more populous because of the magical supplements to the old ways. Calimport could never have supported her enormous population centuries ago.

Nor could the world, a much wider place by far, have attained such a level of singularity, of oneness, of community, as it has now. For people travel and communicate to and with distant lands much more now than in times long past. Many of the powerful merchants in Baldur's Gate are often seen in Waterdeep, and vice versa. Their networks extend over the leagues because their wizards can maintain them. And those networks are vital in ensuring that there will be no war between such mighty rival cities. If the people of Baldur's Gate are dependent upon the craftsmen and farmers of Waterdeep, then they will want no war with that city!

But what happens if it all collapses? What happens if "that which is" suddenly is not? How will we cope when the food runs out, and the diseases cannot be defeated through godly intervention?

Will the people of the world band together to create new realities and structures to fulfill the needs of the masses?

Or will all the world know calamity, on a scale never before seen?

The latter, I fear. The removal of "that which is" will bring war and distance and a world of pockets of civilization huddled defensively in corners against the intrusion of murderous insanity.

I look helplessly at Catti-brie's lifelessness, at Regis's terror, and at Bruenor's torn shoulder and I fear that I am seeing the future.

—Drizzt Do'Urden

CHAPTER

B E A R D E D P R O X Y

Y ou garner too much enjoyment from so simple a trick," Hephaestus said
to his companion in a cave south of Spirit Soaring.

"It is a matter of simple efficiency and expedience, dragon, from which
I take no measure of enjoyment," Yharaskrik answered in the voice of Ivan
Bouldershoulder, whose body the illithid had come to reside in—partially,
at least.

Any who knew Ivan would have scratched their heads in surprise at the
strange accent in the dwarf's gravelly voice. A closer inspection would only
have added to the onlooker's sense of strangeness, for Ivan stood too calmly.
He refrained from tugging at the hairs of his great yellow beard, shifting
from one foot to the other, or thumping his hands against his hips or chest,
as was typical.

"I am still within you," Yharaskrik added. "Hephaestus, Crenshinibon,
and Yharaskrik as one. Holding this dwarf under my control allows me
to give external voice to our conversations, though that is rarely a good
thing."

"While you are reading my every thought," the dragon replied, no small
amount of sarcasm in his tone, "you have externalized a portion of your
consciousness to shield your own thoughts from me."

The dwarf bowed.

"You do not deny it?" Hephaestus asked.

"I am in your consciousness, dragon. You know what I know. Any question you ask of me is rendered rhetorical."

"But we are no longer fully joined," Hephaestus protested, and the dwarf chuckled. The dragon's confusion was apparent. "Are you not wise enough to segment your thoughts into small compartments, some within and some, in the guise of that ugly little dwarf, without?"

The Yharaskrik in Ivan's body bowed again. "You flatter me, great Hephaestus. Trust that we are inexorably joined. I could no more hurt you than harm myself, for to do to one is truly to do to the other. You know this is true."

"Then why did you reach out to the dwarf, this proxy host?"

"Because for you, particularly, who have never known such mental intimacy," the illithid answered, "it can become confusing as to where one voice stops and the other begins. We might find ourselves battling for control of the body we both inhabit, working each other to exhaustion over the simplest of movements. It is better this way."

"So you say."

"Look within yourself, Hephaestus."

The dracolich did exactly that and for a long while did not reply. Finally, he looked the dwarf straight in the eye and said, "It is a good thing."

Yharaskrik bowed again. He glanced to the side of the chamber, past the four animated corpses of the Baldurian wizards, to the pair of huddled creatures in the deeper shadows.

"As Crenshinibon has externalized parts of itself," the illithid said in the dwarf's voice.

Fetchigrol stepped forward before Hephaestus could respond. "We are Crenshinibon," the specter said. "Now we are apart in body, sundered by the magic of the falling Weave, but we are one in thought."

Hephaestus nodded his gigantic head, but Yharaskrik, who had felt a strange evolution over the last few days, disagreed. "You are not," the illithid argued. "You are tentacles of the squid, but there is independence in your movements."

"We do as we are commanded," Fetchigrol protested, but it rang hollow to the Ghost King. The illithid was correct in his assessment. The seven apparitions were gaining a small measure of independent thought once more, though neither feared that the Ghost King could be threatened by such an occurrence.

"You are fine soldiers for the cause of Crenshinibon," said Yharaskrik. "Yet within the philosophy that guides you there is independence, as you have shown here in these mountains."

The specter let out a low groan.

"We exist in two worlds," Yharaskrik explained. "And a third, because of Crenshinibon, because of the sacrifice of Fetchigrol and his six brethren. How easy it was for you, how easy it is for us all, to reach into the realm of death and bring forth mindless minions, and so Fetchigrol did."

"Carradoon is in chaos," the specter's voice said, though the dark humanoid's face gave no indication that it spoke. "As the fleeing humans are killed, they join our ranks."

Yharaskrik waved his hand to the side, to the four undead wizards he had lifted from their death, one even before the flames of a fireball had stopped crinkling its blackened skin. "And how easy it is!" the illithid said, the even cadence of its voice thrown aside for the first time in the conversation. "With this power alone, we are mighty."

"But we have more than this singular power," Hephaestus said.

Fetchigrol's spectral companion floated forward, willed by the Ghost King.

"The fodder of Shadowfell are ours for the calling," Solmé said. "The gate is not thick. The door is not locked. The crawlers hunger for the flesh of Toril."

"And as they kill, our ranks grow," Fetchigrol said.

Yharaskrik nodded and closed his dwarf eyes, pondering the possibilities. This curious twist of circumstance, this fortuitous blending of magic, intellect, and brute power, of Crenshinibon, Yharaskrik, and Hephaestus, had created seemingly unlimited possibilities.

But had it also created a common purpose?

To conquer, or to destroy? To meditate, to contemplate, to explore? What fruit had the tree of fate served? To what end?

Hephaestus's growl brought Yharaskrik from his contemplation, to see the dragon staring at him with suspicion.

"Where we eventually wander is not the immediate concern," the dragon warned, his voice thick with pent up rage. "I will have my revenge."

Yharaskrik heard the dragon's internal dialogue quite clearly, flashing with images of Spirit Soaring, the home of the priest who had aided in the demise of all three of the joined spirits. On that place, the dragon focused its hatred and wrath. They had flown over the building the night before, and even then, Yharaskrik and Crenshinibon had to overrule the reflexive anger of Hephaestus. Had it not been for those two mediating internal voices, the dragon would have swooped down upon the place in an explosive fit of sheer malevolence.

Yharaskrik did not openly disagree, and didn't even allow its mind to show any signal of contrary thought.

"Straightaway!" Hephaestus roared.

"No," the illithid then dared argue. "Magic is unwinding, arcane at least, and in some cases divine, but it has not fully unwound. It is not lost to the world, but merely undependable. This place, Spirit Soaring, is filled with mighty priests and wizards. To underestimate the assemblage of power there is fraught with peril. In the time of our choosing, it will fall, and they will fall. But no sooner."

Hephaestus growled again, long and low, but Yharaskrik feared no outburst from the beast, for he knew that Crenshinibon continually reinforced its reasoning within Hephaestus. The dragon wanted action, devastating and catastrophic, wanted to rain death upon all of those who had helped facilitate his downfall. Impulsive and explosive was Hephaestus's nature, was the way of dragonkind.

But the way of the illithid required patience and careful consideration, and no sentient creature in the world was more patient than Crenshinibon, who had seen the span of millennia.

They overruled Hephaestus and calmed the beast. Their promises of a smoldering ruin where Spirit Soaring stood were not without merit, intent, and honest expectation, and of course, Hephaestus knew that as surely as if the thought was his own.

The dracolich curled up with those fantasies. He, too, could be a creature of patience.

To a point.

* * * * *

"Hold that flank!" Rorick yelled to the men on the left-hand wall of the cave, scattered amidst a tumble of rocks. They stood in ankle-deep water and battled hard against a throng of skeletons and zombies. The center of the defensive line, bolstered by the three Bonaduce children and Pikel, held strong against the attacking undead. The water was nearly knee-deep there, its drag affecting the advancing monsters more than the defenders.

To the right, the contours and bends of the tunnel also favored the defenders. Before them, where the tunnel opened even wider, lay a deep pool. Skeletons and zombies alike that ventured there went completely underwater, and those that managed to claw back up were rained on by heavy clubs. That pool was the primary reason the defenders had chosen to make their stand there when at last the hordes had found them. Initially, it had seemed a prudent choice, but the relentlessness of their enemies was starting to make many, including Temberle and Hanaleisa, think that maybe they should have chosen a more narrow choke point than a thirty-foot expanse.

"They won't hold," Rorick said to his siblings even as Hanaleisa kicked the head off a skeleton and sent it flying far down the tunnel.

Hanaleisa didn't need clarification to know what he meant. Her gaze went immediately to the left, to the many rocks along that broken section of tunnel. They had believed those rocks to be an advantage, forcing the undead press of monsters to carve up their advancing line to get past the many obstacles. But since the monsters had engaged, those many scattered boulders were working against the defenders, who too often found themselves cut off from their allies.

Hanaleisa slapped Temberle on the shoulder and splashed away to the side. She had barely gone two steps, though, before Rorick cried out in pain. She spun back as Rorick fell, lifting his already injured leg, blood streaming anew. Temberle reached for him, but a splash sent Temberle tumbling. A skeletal fish broke the water and smacked him hard in the face.

All across the middle of the line, defenders began shifting and groaning as undead fish knifed through the water and found targets.

"Retreat!" one man cried. "Run away!"

"Nowhere to run!" shouted another.

"Back down the tunnel!" the first screamed back, and began splashing his way deeper into the cave with several others in his wake. The integrity of their center collapsed behind them.

Rorick and Temberle regained their footing at the same time. Rorick waved his brother away. Temberle, blood running freely from his broken nose, turned back fast and hoisted his heavy greatsword.

Hanaleisa glanced to the left flank just in time to see a man pulled down under a dozen rotting hands. Out of options, all of it crumbling before her eyes, she could only cry out, "Uncle Pikel!" as she had done so many times in her life, whenever confronted by a childhood crisis.

If Pikel was listening, it didn't show, for the green-bearded dwarf stood away from the front line, his eyes closed. He held his hand out before him, gripping his magical cudgel, and he waved his stump in slow circles. Hanaleisa started to call out to him again, but saw that he was already chanting.

The young monk glanced toward the left wall and back to the center. Realizing she had to trust her uncle, she bolted for the rocks, toward the group of skeletons pummeling and tearing the fallen defender. She leaped into their midst, fists and feet flailing with power and precision. She kicked one skeleton aside and crushed the chest of a zombie. She immediately went up on the ball of her foot, the other leg extended and pumping furiously as she turned a fast circle.

"Come to me!" she called to the fallen man's companions, many of whom seemed to be turning to flee, as had several of those from the center of the line.

Hanaleisa winced then as a skeletal hand clamped upon her shoulder, bony fingers digging a deep gash. She threw back an elbow that shattered the creature's face and sent it falling away.

Then she redoubled her kicking and punching, determined to fight to the bitter end.

The men and women deeper in the cave abandoned all thoughts of retreat and came on furiously. Hanaleisa had inspired them. Hanaleisa had shamed them.

The warrior monk took some satisfaction in that as the horde was beaten back and the fallen man was pulled from the undead grasp. She doubted it would matter in the end, but still, for some reason, it mattered to her. They would die with honor and courage, and that had to count for something.

She glanced at her brothers just as Pikel, on his fourth try, finally completed his spell. A shining white orb as big as Hanaleisa's fist popped from the dwarf's shillelagh and sailed over the heads of the lead defenders. The orb hit a skeleton and bounced off. Hanaleisa's mouth dropped open in surprise as the skeleton that had been hit locked up and iced over.

"What—?" she managed to say as the small orb splashed into the water. Then she and everyone else gasped in shock as the radius of the pond around the orb froze solid.

The fighters in front yelled out in surprise and pain as the icy grasp spread to them and knocked them backward or grabbed them and froze them in place. An unintended consequence, no doubt, but no matter, for the monstrous advance, including the insidious undead fish, was immediately halted.

Frigid trails spread from the center of the ice, moving to the sides and away from the defenders, following Pikel's will.

"Now!" Hanaleisa called to her fellows at the left wall, and they moved furiously to turn back the undead tide.

Those not caught in the ice chopped vigorously to free their companions. They moved with desperation when they saw newly arrived undead from behind the frozen area coming on undeterred, climbing up on the ice and using their stuck companions as handholds to help them navigate across the slippery surface.

But Pikel had bought the defenders enough time, and the battered and bruised group retreated down the tunnel, deeper under the mountains, until they crossed through a narrow corridor, a single-file passageway that finally opened—mercifully—into a wider chamber some hundred strides along. At the exit to that tunnel, they made their stand. Two warriors met the undead as they tried to come through.

And when those two grew weary or suffered injuries, two others took their place.

Meanwhile, behind them, Rorick organized a line of defenders who had found large rocks, and when he was certain he had enough, he called out for the defenders to stand aside. One by one, his line advanced and hurled rocks into the tunnel, driving back skeletons and zombies. As soon as each had let fly, they ran off to find another rock.

This went on for some time, until the rocks hit only other rocks, until the monsters were driven back and blocked behind a growing wall of stone. When it ended, the stubborn monsters still clawing on the back side of the barricade, Pikel stepped forward and began to gently rub the stone and dirt of the tunnel walls. He called to the plants, bidding them to come forth, and so they sent their vines and their roots, intertwining behind and among the stones, locking them ever so securely.

For the moment, at least, it seemed that the threat had ended. It had come with many cuts and bruises and even more serious wounds, and the man who had been pulled down amid the undead wouldn't be fighting any time soon, if he managed to survive his injuries. And the defenders were deep into the tunnels, in a place of darkness they did not know. How many other tunnels might they find under the foothills of the Snowflakes, and how many monsters might find those as well, and come against them yet again?

"So what are we to do?" a man asked as the enormity of their situation settled upon them.

"We hide, and we fight," said a determined Temberle, sniffling through his shattered nose.

"And we die," said another, an old, surly, gray-bearded fishing boat captain.

"Aye, then we get back up and fight for th'other side," another added.

Temberle, Hanaleisa, and Rorick all looked to each other, but had no rebuttal.

"Ooooh," said Pikel.

CHAPTER

LIVING NIGHTMARE

I need to get you new mounts," Jarlaxle said with an exaggerated sigh.

"We done a thousand miles and more from Mithral Hall," Bruenor reminded. "And pushed them hard all the way. Even with the shoes. . . ." He shook his head. Indeed, the fine mules had reached their limit, for the time being at least, but had performed brilliantly. From dawn to dusk, they had pulled the wagon, every day. Aided by the magical shoes and the fine design and construction of their load, they had covered more ground each and every day than an average team might cross in a tenday.

"True enough," the drow admitted. "But they are weary indeed."

Drizzt and Bruenor looked at each other curiously as Pwent shouted, "I want one o' them!" and pointed at Athrogate's fire-spitting boar.

"Bwahaha!" Athrogate yelled back. "Be sure that I'm feeling big, ridin' into battle on me fiery pig! And when them orcs figure out me game, I squeeze him on the flanks and fart them into flame! Bwahaha!"

"Bwahaha!" Thibbledorf Pwent echoed.

"Can we just harness them two up to pull the damned wagon?" Bruenor asked, waving a hand at the other two dwarves. "I'll nail the magical shoes on their feet."

"You understand the pain I've known for the last decade," Jarlaxle said.

"Yet you keep him around," Drizzt pointed out.

"Because he is strong against my enemies and can hold back their charge," said Jarlaxle. "And I can outrun him should we need to retreat."

Jarlaxle handed the mule off to Drizzt, who slowly walked the weary beast around to the back of the wagon, where he had just tethered its partner. Their days of pulling the wagon were over, for a while at least.

The hells-born nightmare resisted Jarlaxle's tug as he tried to put it in the harness.

"He's not liking that," said Bruenor.

"He has no choice in the matter," Jarlaxle replied, and he managed at last to harness the beast. He clapped the dirt off his hands and moved to climb up beside Pwent and Bruenor on the jockey box. "Keep the pace strong and steady, good dwarf. You will find the demon horse more than up to the . . ." He paused, and in pulling himself up, encountered the skeptical expressions of both dwarves. "I give you my mount, and you would have me walk?" Jarlaxle asked as if wounded.

Pwent looked to Bruenor.

"Let him up," Bruenor decided.

"I'll protect ye, me king!" Pwent declared as Jarlaxle took his seat next to the battlerager, with Pwent between the mercenary and Bruenor.

"He'd kill you before you ever knew the fight had started," Drizzt remarked as he walked past.

Pwent's eyes went wide with alarm.

"Oh, it is true," Jarlaxle assured him.

Pwent started to stutter and stammer, but Bruenor nudged him hard.

"What, me king?" the battlerager asked.

"Just shut up," said Bruenor, and Jarlaxle laughed.

The dwarf king snapped the reins, but instead of moving ahead, the nightmare snorted fire and turned its head around in protest.

"Please, allow me," Jarlaxle said with obvious alarm as he grabbed at the reins, which Bruenor relinquished.

With no movement of the reins at all, Jarlaxle willed the nightmare forward. The demonic creature had no trouble pulling the wagon. The only thing that slowed the pace was the drow's deference to the two mules tied to the back, both exhausted from the long road.

And indeed it had been long, for they had covered most of the leagues by morning, and the Snowflake Mountains were in sight, though fully a day's travel away.

Jarlaxle assured them that his magical beast could continue after the sun had set, that it could even see in the dark, but out of continued deference to the mules, who had given the journey their all, Bruenor called for a halt that mid afternoon. They went about setting their camp in the foothills.

Jarlaxle dismissed his nightmare back to its home on a lower plane, and Athrogate did likewise with his demonic boar. Then Athrogate and Pwent went out to find logs and boulders to fashion some defenses for their camp. They had barely started moving, though, and Jarlaxle and Bruenor had just untied the mules when the beasts began shifting nervously and snorting in protest.

"What's that about?" Bruenor asked.

Jarlaxle tugged the reins of his mule straight down, hard, but the creature snorted in protest and pulled back.

"Wait," Drizzt said to them. He was in the wagon, standing beside the seated Catti-brie, and when the others looked to him for clarification, they went silent, seeing the ranger on his guard, his eyes locked on the trees across the road.

"What're ye seeing, elf?" Bruenor whispered, but Drizzt just shook his hand, which was outstretched toward the dwarf, bidding him to silence.

Jarlaxle quietly retied the mules to the wagon, his gaze darting between Drizzt and the trees.

Drizzt slid Taulmaril off his shoulder and strung it.

"Elf?" Bruenor whispered.

"What in the Nine Hells?" Thibbledorf Pwent howled then, from behind the trio.

Bruenor and Jarlaxle both looked back at him to see a long-armed, short-legged creature with bloated gray and black skin dragging itself over the boulders toward Pwent and Athrogate. Drizzt never turned his gaze from the trees, and soon enough saw another of the same monster crash out of the underbrush.

The drow froze—he knew those strange creatures all too well, those clawing, huddled, shadowy things. He had gone to their umbral home.

Catti-brie was there.

And Regis.

Had he gone there again? He lifted his bow and leveled it for a shot, but took a deep breath, thinking that he might again be in that state of mental confusion. Would he let fly only to put an arrow through Bruenor's heart?

"*Shoot it, Drizzt,*" he heard Jarlaxle say in Deep Drow—a language Drizzt hadn't heard spoken in a long time. It was as if Jarlaxle had read his thoughts perfectly. *"You are not imagining this!"*

Drizzt pulled back and let fly, and the magical bow launched a searing line of energy, like lightning, at the fleshy beast, splattering its chest and throwing it back into the brush.

But where there was one, there were many, and a shout behind from the two dwarves clued Drizzt in to that fact even as more of them crashed out onto the road before him.

The ranger pumped his arms furiously, reaching into his magical quiver to draw forth arrow after arrow, nock it, and let it fly, tearing the darkness with sizzling lines of bright lightning. So thick were the beasts that almost every arrow hit a fleshy mass, some burning through to strike a second monster behind the first. The stench of burning flesh fouled the air, and a sickly bubbling and popping sound filled the dead calm between the thunderous blasts of Taulmaril.

Despite the devastation he rained on the crawlers, they came on. Many crossed the road and neared the wagon. Drizzt let fly another shot, then had to drop Taulmaril and draw out his blades to meet the onslaught.

Beside him, Bruenor leaped down from the wagon, banging his old, trusted shield, emblazoned with the foaming mug of Clan Battlehammer. He gripped his many-notched axe, a weapon he had carried for decades upon decades. As the dwarf leaped down, Jarlaxle sprang up onto the seat and drew out a pair of thin wands, including the one he had used earlier to restrain Drizzt.

"Fireball," he explained to Bruenor, who looked at him, about to ask why he wasn't on the ground with a weapon in his hand.

"Then light 'em up!"

But Jarlaxle considered for a moment, and shook his head, unsure of the casting. If his other wand malfunctioned, he might glue himself to the wagon, but if this one backfired, he'd light himself up, and Bruenor and Catti-brie, too.

To the dwarf's surprise, Jarlaxle shifted both wands to his left hand, then snapped his right wrist, bringing forth a blade from his magical bracer. A second snap of his wrist elongated that blade to a short sword. A third and final thrust made it a long sword.

Jarlaxle moved to put the fireball wand away, but changed his mind and slid the other one into his belt. If the situation deteriorated to where he needed to use a device, he decided, he'd have to take the chance.

* * * * *

Athrogate worked his morningstars magnificently, the heavy spiked balls humming at the ends of their chains, weaving out before him, to this side and that, and over his head.

"Get out yer weapon!" he yelled at Thibbledorf Pwent.

"I *am* me weapon, ye dolt!" the battlerager yelled back, and as the fleshy creature crawled nearer, just before Athrogate stepped forward to launch a barrage of flying morningstars, Pwent charged and dived upon the enemy, fists pumping, knees thumping. Locked in place with his fist spikes, the trapped creature flailing and biting at him, Pwent went into a wild and furious gyration, a violent convulsion, a seizure of sorts, it seemed.

The dwarf's ridged armor tore apart the beast's flesh, fast reducing the monster to a misshapen lump of pulped meat.

"Bwahaha!" Athrogate cheered, grinning, saluting and belly-laughing as he leaped past Pwent and went into an arm-rolling assault of morningstar over morningstar at the next beast coming in.

The blunt weapons weren't quite as lethal against the thick and malleable flesh, which gave way under the weight of their punishment. A typical fighter with a normal morningstar would have found himself in sorry shape against the shadowy crawlers, but Athrogate was no typical fighter. His strength was that of a giant, his skills honed over centuries of battle, and his morningstars, too, were far from the usual.

He worked the weapons expertly, maneuvering himself right in front of the battered creature before coming in with a mighty overhead chop that splattered the crawler across the stone before him.

He had no time to salute himself, and just enough time to tell Pwent to get up, before another three beasts came in hard at him, with many more following.

Black clawing hands reached at him repeatedly, but Athrogate kept his morningstars spinning, driving them back. Out of the corner of his eye, though, the dwarf saw another monster, on the branch of a tree not far away, and when that beast leaped at him, Athrogate had no manner of defense.

He did manage to close his eyes.

* * * * *

Bruenor reminded himself that Catti-brie lay helpless behind him in the wagon. With that thought in the dwarf's mind, the first crawler dragging itself at him got cut in half, head to crotch, by a mighty two-handed overhead chop. Ignoring a fountain of blood and gore, Bruenor kicked his way through the mess and took out a second with a sidelong cut, blocking the third's slashing claws with his heavy buckler.

He felt a fourth coming from the other way and instinctively cut across hard with his axe, not realizing until it was too late that it was a drow, not a fleshy beast.

But the nimble Jarlaxle leaped up and tucked in his legs. "Careful, friend," he said as he landed, though he slurred his words for the wand he carried in his teeth. He stepped in front of the surprised dwarf, stabbing forward with two swords, popping deep holes in the chest of the next approaching monster.

"Could've warned me," Bruenor grumbled, and went back to chopping and slashing. A screech behind him and to his right warned him that the beasts had reached the mules.

* * * * *

Drizzt didn't even have a moment to take in the sight of Bruenor and Jarlaxle fighting side by side, something he never expected to see. He rushed in front of the duo, slashing with every stride, and into a fast spin, blades cutting hard and barely even slowing when they sliced through the meaty body of a crawler. A second spin followed, the mighty ranger moving along as he turned, and he came out of it with three running strides, stabbing repeatedly. He pulled up short and turned, then leaped and flipped sidelong over another of the creatures, managing to stab down twice as he went over. Drizzt landed lightly on the other side of it, immediately falling into another spin, his scimitars humming through the air and through gray-black flesh all around him.

The drow turned back toward the wagon then, and took heart in seeing Jarlaxle's nightmare punishing any crawlers that came too near, the hellish steed stomping its hooves and blasting out miniature fireballs.

Drizzt cut in behind it, his eyes going wide as he saw a beast coming over the opposite side rail. The drow hit the jockey box in full stride and leaped over the rail without slowing. He darted in front of Catti-brie at full speed, his scimitars cutting apart the beast as he passed.

How he wanted to stay with her! But he couldn't, not with the mules tugging and thrashing in terror.

He sprang down right between them, agilely avoiding their kicks and stomps, and deftly clearing away enemies with precision thrusts and stabs.

Just behind the mules, he stopped and veered again, thinking to re-run the route.

No need, he realized as soon as he took note of Jarlaxle and Bruenor, fighting together as if they had shared a mentor and a hundred battles. Jarlaxle's fighting style, favoring forward-rolling his blades and stabbing, compared to Drizzt's wide-armed slashes, complemented Bruenor's straight-ahead ferocity. In tandem, they worked in short, angled bursts for one to engage a creature, then hand it off to his partner for the killing blow.

With a surprised grin, Drizzt slipped behind them instead of in front of them, running a circuit of the wagon and taking care to give the furiously thrashing nightmare a wide berth.

* * * * *

Athrogate yelled out, thinking himself doomed, but a second form flew through the air, head down, helmet spike leveled. Thibbledorf Pwent hit the leaping crawler squarely, skewering it with his spiked helm and pushing it aside with him as he crashed to the rocky ground. He bounced up and began hopping about, the fleshy beast bouncing atop his head, fully stuck and dying fast.

"Oh, but that's great!" Athrogate cried. "That's just great!"

Too enraged to hear him, the fierce battlerager charged into a group of the beasts, thrashing and punching and kneeing and kicking, even biting when one clawed hand came too near his face.

Athrogate rushed up beside him, morningstars spinning furiously, splattering black flesh with every powerful swing. Side by side, the dwarves advanced, enemies flying all about, one still bobbing in its death throes atop the helmet spike of Thibbledorf Pwent.

Bruenor and Jarlaxle fought a more defensive battle, holding their ground with measured chops and stabs. As the ranks of monsters thinned and the wagon became secure, Drizzt hopped up on the bench, retrieved his bow, and began firing toward the tree line with flashing arrows, further thinning the horde coming at Bruenor and Jarlaxle.

Pwent and Athrogate, their rocky campsite cleared, joined the others, and Drizzt again dropped the bow and drew out his scimitars. With a communal nod and knowing grins, the five went out in a line of devastation, sweeping clear the grassy patch near the road and sweeping clear the road as well before turning and running as one back to the wagon.

With nothing left to hit, four of the group, the dwarves and Jarlaxle, each took up positions north, south, east, and west around the wagon. Drizzt scrambled into the wagon bed beside Catti-brie, Taulmaril the Heartseeker in hand, ready to support his comrades.

His attention was soon turned to his beloved cargo, though, and he looked down to see Catti-brie jerking spasmodically, standing upright though she was not trying to walk. She floated off the ground, her eyes rolling back in her head.

"Oh, no," Drizzt muttered, and he had to fall back. Most agonizing of all, he had to step away from his tortured wife.

CHAPTER

Danica and Cadderly rushed through the hallways of Spirit Soaring to see what the commotion was all about. They had to push through a bevy of whispering wizards and priests to squeeze their way out the door, and the grand front porch of the structure was no less crowded.

"Stay up here!" a mage called to Danica as she squirmed through and jumped down the steps to the cobblestones. "Cadderly, don't let her . . ."

The man eased up on his protests as Cadderly lifted a hand to silence him. The priest trusted in Danica, and reminded the others to do the same. Still, Cadderly was more than a little perplexed by the sight before him. Deer, rabbits, squirrels, and all manner of animals charged across the lawn of Spirit Soaring, in full flight.

"There was a bear," an older priest explained.

"A bear is scaring them like this?" Cadderly asked with obvious skepticism.

"Bear was running just as fast, just as frightened," the priest clarified, and as Cadderly frowned in disbelief, several others nodded, confirming the wild tale.

"A bear?"

"Big bear. Has to be a fire."

But Cadderly looked to the south, from whence the animals came, and he saw no smoke darkening the late afternoon sky. He sniffed repeatedly, but found no scent of smoke in the air. He looked at Danica, who was making her way to the southern tree line. Somewhere beyond her came the roar of another bear, then one of a great cat.

Cadderly pushed his way to the front steps and cautiously descended. A deer bounded out of the trees, leaping frantically across the lawn. Cadderly clapped his hands, figuring to frighten the creature enough to make it veer to the side, but it never seemed to hear or even see him. It went leaping by, knocking him back as it passed.

"I told you!" the first mage cried at him. "There's no sensibility in them."

In the woods, the bear roared again, more powerfully, more insistently.

"Danica!" Cadderly called.

The bear was roaring out in protest and in pain, its threatening growls interspersed with higher-pitched squeals.

"Danica!" Cadderly cried again, more insistently, and he started toward the trees. He stopped abruptly as Danica burst out of the brush.

"Inside! Inside!" she yelled to them all.

Cadderly looked at her questioningly, then his eyes widened in surprise and horror as a horde of crawling beasts, long arms propelling them along at tremendous speed, charged out of the trees behind her.

The priest had studied the catalogs of Faerûn's many and varied animals and monsters, but he had never seen anything quite like these. In that instant of identification, Cadderly got the image of a legless man crawling on long, powerful arms, but that reflexive thought did not hold under closer scrutiny. Wide, hunched shoulders surmounted squat torsos, and the dark-skinned creatures used their arms to walk. They had something resembling feet at the end of their stubby legs, like a sea mammal's flippers. Their locomotion was half hop, half drag. Had they stood straight up, they would nearly match an average man, despite their vestigial feet and their compressed heads, a sort of half-sphere set on their shoulders.

Their faces were far from human in appearance, with no forehead to speak of, a flat nose, nostrils open forward, and shining yellow eyes—malignant eyes. But their mouths, all toothy and vicious, most alarmed Cadderly and everyone else staring at the beasts. They stretched almost the width of their elongated faces, with a hinged bottom jaw that protruded forward and seemed to project right from the top of the chest, snapping upward hungrily in an eager underbite.

Danica was ahead of the monstrosities, and a fast runner, but one of them closed fast on her, cutting an intercepting angle.

Cadderly started to call out to her with horror, but bit it off as she dropped her weight to her heels and skidded to a stop, threw herself around in a circle, and leaped into the air, tucking her legs up high as the creature came in under her. It too stopped fast, long arms reaching up, but Danica's legs were faster and they drove down hard against the monster's upturned face. She used the press as a springboard and leaped away. The monster bounced under the weight of the blow.

Danica put her head down and ran with all speed, sparing a heartbeat to wave Cadderly back into the cathedral, to remind him with her desperate expression that he, too, was in grave danger.

As the priest turned, he saw just how grave that danger was. Coming out of the woods were more of the crawling beasts, many more. That unseen but oft-heard bear lumbered out, too, thrashing and stumbling, covered with the shadowy creatures.

His heart pounding, Cadderly leaped to the stairs, but on the porch, the many wizards and priests were in a panic, crushing against the door with few actually getting inside. To both sides of the double doors, windows flew open, those inside beckoning their companions to dive in from the porch.

They weren't going to make it, Cadderly realized as he glanced back at Danica. How he wished he had his hand crossbow, or even his walking stick! But he had come down thinking that nothing was seriously out of sorts. Physically, he was unarmed.

But he still had Deneir.

Cadderly turned on the top step and closed his eyes, falling into prayer, praying for some solution. He began spellcasting before he even realized what he was attempting.

He opened his eyes and threw his arms wide. Danica hit the bottom step and sprang up past him, a host of creatures right behind her.

A blast of energy rolled out from Cadderly across the ground and through it in a great, rolling wave, lifting the cobblestones and grass, and many of the creatures.

More waves came forth, washing the beasts back in a series of rolling semicircles, like a ripple of waves from the shore of a still pond. The hungry beasts tried to fight past it, but inevitably lost ground, washing farther and farther backward.

"What is that?" a wizard asked in obvious awe, and despite his concentration, Cadderly heard the woman.

He had no answer.

None, that is, except that his spell had bought them the time they needed, and into Spirit Soaring they all went, Danica and Cadderly coming last, with Danica practically pulling her stunned husband in behind her.

* * * * *

Danica was relieved to hear other people calling out commands to guard the windows and doors, because Cadderly could do little at that moment, and he needed her. She looked around only briefly, suddenly realizing that someone was missing. Spirit Soaring was a huge place of many, many rooms, so she hadn't noticed the absence before. But in that moment of urgency and danger, she knew that the Spirit Soaring family was incomplete.

Where was Ivan Bouldershoulder?

Danica glanced around again, trying to recall when last she had seen the boisterous dwarf. But Cadderly's gasp brought her back to the situation at hand.

"What did you do out there?" Danica asked him. "I have never seen—"

"I know not at all," he admitted. "I went to Deneir, seeking spells, seeking a solution."

"And he answered!"

Cadderly looked at her with a blank expression for a moment before shaking his head with concern. "The *Metatext*, the Weave . . ." he whispered. "He is part of it now."

Danica stared at him, puzzled.

"As if the two—perhaps the three of them, Deneir, *Metatext*, and Weave—are no longer separate," Cadderly tried to explain.

"But save for Mystra, the gods were never a part of—"

"No, more than that," Cadderly said, shaking his head more forcefully. "He was writing to the Weave, patterning it with numbers, and now . . ."

The sound of breaking glass, followed by shouts, followed by screams, broke short the conversation.

"They come," said Danica, and she started off, pulling Cadderly behind her.

They found their first battle in the room only two doors down from the

146

foyer, where a group of priests met the incursion of a pair of the beasts head on. Smashing away with their maces, and mostly armored, the priests had the situation well in hand.

Cadderly took the lead, running fast to the central stairwell and sprinting up three steps at a time to get up to the fourth floor and his private quarters. Just inside the doorway, he grabbed his belt, a wide leather girdle with a holster on either side for his hand crossbows. He looped a bandolier of specially crafted bolts around his neck and sprinted back to join Danica, loading the crossbows as he went.

They started for the stairs, but then discovered an unwelcome talent of the strange, crawling beasts: they were expert climbers. Down the hall a window shattered, and they heard thumps as one of the creatures pull itself through.

Danica moved in front of Cadderly as he dashed that way, but as they reached the room and kicked the door wide, he pushed her aside and lifted his arm, leveling the crossbow.

A beast was in the room, a second in the window frame, and both opened wide their mouths in vicious snarls.

Cadderly fired, the bolt flashing across the room to strike the chest of the beast in the window. The dart's side supports folded inward, collapsing on themselves and crushing the small vial they held. That concussion ignited magical oil in an explosive burst that blew a huge hole in the monster's black flesh. The force blew the crawler back out the window.

Cadderly aimed his second crossbow at the remaining creature, but turned his arm aside as Danica charged it. She stutter-stepped at the last moment, brought her left leg across to her right, and swept it back powerfully, deflecting both clawing arms aside. She expertly turned her hips as she went, gaining momentum, for as her left foot touched down, she snap-kicked with her right, driving the tip of her foot into the beast's left eye.

It howled and thrashed, arms swinging back furiously, predictably, and Danica easily stepped out of reach, then followed through with a forward step and front kick to the creature's chest that drove it back against the wall.

Again it reacted with fury, and again she easily leaped out of reach.

This was the way to fight the creatures, she decided then. Strike hard and back out, repeatedly, never staying close enough to engage those awful claws.

Cadderly was more than glad that she had the situation under control when they heard the window in the adjoining room shatter. He spun around the jamb, turning to kick open the next door, and swept into the room with his left arm upraised.

The beast huddled right before him, waiting to spring at him.

With a startled cry, Cadderly fired the hand crossbow, the bolt hitting the charging crawler barely two feet away, close enough that he felt the rush of concussive force as the dart exploded. Then the beast was gone, blown back across the room where it settled against the wall, its long arms out wide and trembling, a hole in its torso so large that Cadderly realized he could slide his fist into it with ease.

His breathing came in surprised gasps, but he heard a commotion just outside. He dropped the hand crossbow from his left hand—it bounced off his mid thigh, for it was securely tethered—and worked fast to reload the other weapon.

He nearly dropped the explosive dart when Danica rushed into the hall behind him, slamming the door of the first room.

"Too many!" she cried. "And they're coming in all around us. We've got to call up help from below."

"Go! Go!" Cadderly yelled back, fumbling with the dart as a shadowy form filled the window across the room.

Danica, hardly noticing the nearby enemy, ran for the stairwell. The fleshy beast hurled itself at Cadderly.

The crossbow string slipped from his grasp, and he was lucky to stop the dart from falling out of its grooved table. His eyes flashed from bow to beast and back again, and back, to see a filthy clawed hand slashing at his face.

* * * * *

The center stairs at Spirit Soaring ran down a flight, turned around a landing, then ran down another flight in the opposite direction, two flights for every story of the building. Danica didn't actually run down the steps. She went halfway down the first flight and hopped the railing, landing lightly halfway down the second flight. She didn't bounce right to the third set of stairs, but leaped down to the landing to reconnoiter the third floor.

As she had feared, she was met by the sound of breaking glass. She yelled down the stairs again and sprang halfway down the next stairway, then leaped to the fourth set of steps. She heard the commotion of many people running up the stairs.

"Break into patrols to secure each floor!" Danica yelled to them, her point accentuated when the lead group reached the landing to the second story and immediately encountered a pair of the beasts rushing down the hallway at them.

Waggling fingers sent bolts of magical force reaching out. Armored clerics crowded into the doorway to shield the unarmored wizards.

Few at Spirit Soaring were untested or unseasoned in battle, and so several broke off from the first group with precision and discipline, most continuing up the stairs.

Danica was already gone from the spot, sprinting back up three steps at a time. She had been away from Cadderly for longer than she had anticipated, and though she trusted in him—how could she not, when she had seen him face down a terrible dragon and a vampire, and when she had watched him, through sheer willpower and divine magic, create the magnificent library cathedral?—she knew that he was alone up there on the fourth floor.

Alone and with more than two dozen windows to defend in that wing alone.

* * * * *

He cried out in alarm and turned away from the blow, but not enough to avoid the long, vicious claws. He felt the skin under his left eye tear away, and the weight of the blow nearly knocked him senseless.

Cadderly wasn't even aware that he had pulled the trigger of his hand crossbow. The bolt wasn't set perfectly on the table, but it snapped out anyway, and good fortune alone had the weapon turned in the correct direction. The bolt stabbed into the monster's flesh, collapsed, and exploded, throwing the beast backward. It flew against the wall, shrieking in a ghastly squeal. Clawed hands grabbed at the blasted-open wound.

Cadderly heard the scream, but couldn't tell whether it was pain, defeat, or victory. Bent low, he stumbled out of the room, blood streaming down his face and dripping on the floor. The blow hadn't touched his eye, but it was already swollen so badly he could see only splashes of indistinguishable light.

Staggering and disoriented, he heard more creatures dragging themselves through other rooms. Load! Load! his thoughts silently screamed, and he fumbled to do just that, but quickly realized that he hadn't the time.

He closed his eyes and called out to Deneir.

All he found were numbers, patterns written on the Weave.

His confusion lasted until a creature burst into the hall before him. The numbers formed a pattern in his mind, and a spell issued from his lips.

A gleaming shield of divine energy enwrapped the priest as the creature rushed in, and though Cadderly instinctively recoiled from its bashing, clawing attacks, they did not, could not, seriously harm him.

They couldn't penetrate the magical barrier he had somehow enacted.

Another spell flowed into his thoughts, and he wasted no time in uttering the words, dropping his hand crossbows to hang by their tethers and throwing his hands high into the air. He felt the energy running through him, divine and wonderful and powerful, as if he pulled it out of the air. It tingled down his arms and through his torso, down his legs and into the floor, and there it rolled out in every direction, an orange-red glow spider-webbing through the floor planks.

The creature whacking at him immediately began to howl in pain, and Cadderly ambled down the hall, taking the consecrated ground with him. Too stupid to realize its error, the fleshy beast followed and continued to scream out, its lower torso sizzling under the burn of radiant energy.

More creatures came at him and tried to attack, but began howling as they entered the circle of power. The magic still moved with Cadderly as he turned toward the stairs.

There, the mighty priest saw Danica gawking at him.

The first creature died. Another one fell, then a third, consumed by the power of Deneir, the power of the unknown dweomer Cadderly had cast. He waved for Danica to run away, but she didn't, and went to join him instead.

As soon as she drew near, she too began to glisten under the light of his divine shield.

"What have you done?" she asked him.

"I have no idea," Cadderly replied. He wasn't about to stand there and question his good fortune.

"Let's clear the floor," Danica said, and together they moved down the hallway.

Danica led with a flurry of kicks and punches that finished off two of the beasts as they writhed in pain when the consecrated ground came under them.

One creature tried to scramble into a side room, and Danica turned toward it. But Cadderly cast forth a pointing finger and cried out another prayer. A shaft of light, a lance of divine energy, shot out and skewered the beast, which howled and crashed into the doorjamb as Danica neared.

The crawler survived the spearlike energy, but it sparkled and glowed, making it easy for the expert Danica to line up her blows and quickly dispatch it.

By the time five bloodied and battered priests arrived on the landing of the stairs to support the couple, one wing of the fourth floor had been swept clear of monsters. Cadderly still emanated the circle of power flowing around him, and discovered too that his wounds were magically mending.

The other priests looked at him with puzzlement and intrigue, but he had no answers for them. He had called to Deneir, and Deneir, or some other being of power, had answered his prayers with unknown dweomers.

There was no time to sit and contemplate, Cadderly knew, for Spirit Soaring was a gigantic structure full of windows, full of side rooms and alcoves, plus narrow back passages and a multilevel substructure.

They fought throughout the night and into the early dawn, until no more monsters came through the windows. Still they fought throughout the morning, weary and battered, and with several of their companions dead, painstakingly clearing the large spaces of Spirit Soaring.

Cadderly and Danica both knew that many rooms remained to be explored and cleared, but they were all exhausted. The task began to reinforce the windows with heavy boards, to tend the wounded, and to organize battle groups for the coming night and the next possible attack.

"Where is Ivan?" Danica asked Cadderly when they finally had a few moments alone.

"He went to Carradoon, I thought."

"No, just Pikel, with Rorey and . . ." the names caught in Danica's throat. All three of her children had gone to Carradoon, had traveled through the mountain forests from which those hideous creatures had come.

"Cadderly?" she whispered, her voice breaking. He, too, had to take a deep breath to stop himself from falling over in fear.

"We have to go to them," he said.

But Danica was shaking her head. "You have to stay here," she replied. "You cannot—"

"I can move more quickly on my own."

"We have no idea what precipitated this," Cadderly complained. "We don't even know what power we're up against!"

"And who better than I to find out?" his wife asked, and she managed a little grin of confidence.

A very little grin of confidence.

CHAPTER

She wore a little knowing smile, a smile at odds with her eyes, which had rolled again to white. She was floating off the ground.

"Ye mean to kill him?" she asked, as if she were talking to someone standing before her. As she spoke, her eyes came back into focus.

"The accent," Jarlaxle remarked as Catti-brie's shoulders shifted back—as if she thought she was leaning back in a chair, perhaps.

"If ye be killing Entreri to free Regis and to stop him from hurting anyone else, then me heart says it's a good thing," the woman said, and leaned forward intently. "But if ye're meaning to kill him to prove yerself or to deny what he is, then me heart cries."

"Calimport," Drizzt whispered, vividly recalling the scene.

"Wha—?" Bruenor started to ask, but Catti-brie continued, cutting him short.

"Suren the world's not fair, me friend. Suren by the measure of hearts, ye been wronged. But are ye after the assassin for yer own anger? Will killing Entreri cure the wrong?

"Look in the mirror, Drizzt Do'Urden, without the mask. Killin' Entreri won't change the color of his skin—or the color of yer own."

"Elf?" Bruenor asked, but at that shocking moment, Drizzt couldn't even hear him.

The weight of that long-ago encounter with Catti-brie came cascading back to him. He was there again, in the moment, in that small room, receiving one of the most profound slaps of cold wisdom anyone had ever cared enough about him to deliver. It was the moment he realized that he loved Catti-brie, though it would be years before he dared act on those feelings.

He glanced at Bruenor and Jarlaxle, a bit embarrassed, too much overwhelmed, and turned again to his beloved, who continued that old conversation—word for word.

". . . if only ye'd learn to look," she said, her lips turned in that disarming, charming smile that she had so often flashed Drizzt's way, each time melting any resistance he might have to what she was saying.

"And if only ye'd ever learned to love. Suren ye've let things slip past, Drizzt Do'Urden."

She turned her head, as if some commotion had occurred nearby, and Drizzt remembered that Wulfgar had entered the room at that moment. Wulfgar was Catti-brie's lover at that time, though she'd just hinted that her heart was for Drizzt.

And it was, he knew, even then.

Drizzt began to shake as he remembered what was to come. Jarlaxle moved up behind him then, and reached around Drizzt's head. For an instant, Drizzt tensed, thinking the mercenary had a garrote. It was no garrote, however, but an eye patch, which Jarlaxle tied on securely before shoving Drizzt forward.

"Go to her!" he demanded.

Only a step away, Drizzt heard again the words that had, in retrospect, changed his life, the words that had freed him.

"Just for thoughts, me friend," Catti-brie said quietly, and Drizzt had to pause before continuing to her, had to let her finish. "Are ye more trapped by the way the world sees ye, or by the way ye see the world seein' ye?"

Tears streaming from his lavender eyes, Drizzt fell over her in a great hug, pulling down her outstretched arms. He didn't cross into that shadowed plane, protected as he was by Jarlaxle's eye patch. Drizzt pulled Catti-brie down to him and hugged her close, and kept on hugging her until she finally relaxed and slipped back to a sitting position.

At last, Drizzt looked at the others, at Jarlaxle in particular.

"I am not your enemy, Drizzt Do'Urden," he said.

"What'd'ye do?" Bruenor demanded.

"The eye patch protects the mind from intrusion, magical or psionic,"

Jarlaxle explained. "Not fully, but enough so that a wary Drizzt would not be drawn again into that place where . . ."

"Where Regis's mind now dwells," said Drizzt.

"Be sure that I'm not knowin' a bit o' what ye're talking about," said Bruenor, planting his hands firmly on his hips. "What in the Nine Hells is going on, elf?"

Drizzt wore a confused expression and began to shake his head.

"It is as if two planes of existence, or two worlds from different planes, are crashing together," Jarlaxle said, and all of them looked at him as if he had grown an ettin's second head.

Jarlaxle took a deep breath and gave a little laugh. "It is no accident that I found you on the road," he said.

"Ye think we ever thinked it one, ye dolt?" asked Bruenor, drawing a helpless chuckle from the drow mercenary.

"And no accident that I sent Athrogate there—Stuttgard, if you will— into Mithral Hall to coax you on the road to Spirit Soaring."

"Yeah, the Crystal Shard," Bruenor muttered in a tone that showed obvious skepticism.

"All that I told you is true," Jarlaxle replied. "But yes, good dwarf, my tale was not complete."

"Me heart's skippin' to hear it."

"There is a dragon."

"There always is," said Bruenor.

"I and my friend here were being pursued," Jarlaxle explained.

"Nasty buggers," said Athrogate.

"Pursued by creatures who could raise the dead with ease," said Jarlaxle. "The architects of the Crystal Shard, I believe, who have somehow transcended the limitations of this plane."

"Yup, ye're losing me in the trees again," said Bruenor.

"Creatures of two worlds, like Catti-brie," Drizzt said.

"Maybe. I cannot know for certain. That they are of, or possess the ability to be of two dimensions, I am certain. From this hat, I can produce dimensional holes, and so I did, and threw one such item at the creature pursuing me."

"The one what kept melting before me morningstars could flatten it out," Athrogate explained.

"Plane shifting," Jarlaxle said. "And it did so as my dimensional hole fell over it, and the combination of two extra-dimensional magics tore a rift to the Astral Plane."

"Then the creature's gone," said Bruenor.

"Forever, I expect," Jarlaxle agreed.

"And ye're needin' us and needin' Cadderly why, then?"

"Because it was an emissary, not the source. And the source . . ."

"The dragon," said Drizzt.

"Always is," Bruenor said again.

Jarlaxle shrugged, unwilling to commit to that. "Whatever it is, it remains alive, and with the terrible power to send its thoughts across the world, and send its emissaries out as well. It's been calling forth minions from the realm of the dead with abandon, and perhaps"—he paused and looked back to the scene of the slaughtered beasts around them—"the power to call forth minions from this other place, this dark place."

"What're ye about, ye durned elf?" Bruenor demanded. "What did ye pull us along to?"

"Along the road that will find an answer for your dear daughter's plight, I hope," Jarlaxle replied without hesitation. "And yes, I put you beside Athrogate and I in our own quest, as well."

"Ye dropped us in the middle of it, ye mean!" Bruenor growled.

"I'm wantin' to punch yer skinny face!" Pwent shouted.

"We were already in the middle of it," Drizzt said, and when all turned to regard him as he knelt there hugging Catti-brie, it was hard for any to disagree. Drizzt looked at Jarlaxle and said, "The whole world is in the middle of it."

CHAPTER

SCOUTS' DISMAY

14

"We cannot just wait here for them to assail us again at twilight!" a young wizard cried, and many others took up that refrain.

"We do not even know if that will happen," reminded Ginance, an older woman, a priest of Cadderly's order who had been cataloging scrolls at Spirit Soaring since its earliest days. "We have never encountered such creatures as these . . . these lumps of ugly flesh! We know not if they have an aversion to sunlight, or if they broke off the attack at dawn for strategic reasons."

"They left when the dawn's light showed in the east," the first protested. "That tells me we've a good place to start in our counterattack, and counter we must—aggressively."

"Aye!" several others shouted.

The discussion in the nave of Spirit Soaring had been going on for some time, and thus far Cadderly had remained quiet, gauging the demeanor of the room. Several wizards and priests, all of them visitors to the library, had been killed in the brutal assault of the previous night. Cadderly was glad to see that the remaining group, some seventy-five men and women, most highly trained and skilled in the arcane or divine arts, had not given in to despair after that unexpected battle. Their fighting spirit was more than evident, and that, Cadderly knew, would be an important factor if they were to sort through their predicament.

He focused again on Ginance, his friend and one of the wisest and most knowledgeable members of his clergy.

"We don't even know if Spirit Soaring is cleared of the beasts," she said, quieting the exuberance.

"None are out biting at us, the vicious creatures!" the first mage argued. Ginance seemed at a loss to overcome the tidal wave of shouts that followed, all calling for action beyond the confines of the cathedral.

"You presume that they're mindless, or at least stupid," Cadderly finally put in, and though he hadn't shouted the words, as soon as he started talking, the room went silent and all eyes focused his way.

The priest took a deep breath at that reminder, yet again, of his importance and reputation. He had built Spirit Soaring, and that was no small thing. Still, he remained unnerved by the reverence shown him, particularly given that many of his guests were far more seasoned in the art of warfare than he. One group of priests from Sundabar had spent years traversing the lower planes, battling demons and devils. Yet even they stared at him, hanging on his every word.

"You assume they ran away because they didn't like the sunlight, rather than for tactical reasons," Cadderly explained, carefully choosing his words. He shook his foolish nervousness away by reminding himself of his missing children, and the missing Bouldershoulder brothers. "And now you assume that if there were any more of the beasts still inside Spirit Soaring, they would rush right out ravenously instead of hiding away to strike at more opportune moments."

"And what do you believe, good Cadderly?" asked the same young wizard who had been so fiery and obstinate with Ginance. "Do we sit and fortify, to prepare for the next onslaught, or do we go out and find our enemies?"

"Both," Cadderly replied, and many heads, particularly the older veterans, nodded in agreement. "Many of you did not come here alone, but with trusted friends and associates, so I will leave it up to you to decide on the sizes and dispositions of battle groups. I would suggest both brawn and magic, and magic both divine and arcane. We don't know when this . . . plague will end, or whether or not it will get worse, so we must do our best to cover all contingencies."

"I would suggest groups of no less than seven," said one of the older wizards.

They began talking amongst themselves again, which Cadderly thought best. Those men and women didn't need his guidance on the details. Ginance came over to him then, still troubled about the notion that Spirit Soaring might be hosting some uninvited guests.

"Are all of our brethren available after last night?" Cadderly asked her.

"Most. We have two score or so brothers ready to scour Spirit Soaring— unless you would have some go out with the others."

"Just a few," Cadderly decided. "Offer our more worldly brothers—those who have spent the most time gathering herbs that might be used medicinally, who best know the terrain surrounding the library—to the various scouting teams sorted out by our many guests. But let us keep most of our own inside Spirit Soaring, as they know best the many catacombs, tunnels, and antechambers. That is your task, of course."

Ginance took that great compliment with a bow. "Lady Danica would be most helpful, as would Ivan . . ." She paused at the sour look Cadderly flashed her way.

"Danica will be out of Spirit Soaring within a short time," Cadderly explained. "Mostly in search of Ivan, who seems to be missing, and . . ."

"They're safely in Carradoon," Ginance assured him. "All three, and Pikel, too."

"Let us hope," was all Cadderly could reply.

* * * * *

A short while later, Cadderly sat on the balcony of his private room, looking southeast, toward Carradoon. So many thoughts fought for his attention as he worried about his children, about Danica who had gone out to look for them and for the missing Ivan Bouldershoulder. He feared for his home, Spirit Soaring, and the implications its downfall might have on his order and more personally, upon him. The horde of unknown monsters that had come against them so violently and determinedly had done little true damage to the cathedral's structure, but Cadderly had felt the shatter of every window upon his own body, as if someone had flicked a finger hard against his skin. He was intimately bound to the place, and in ways that even he didn't truly yet understand.

So many worries, and not least among them, Cadderly Bonaduce worried about his god and the state of the world. He had gone there, to the Weave, and had found Deneir, he was sure. He had been granted spells the likes of which he had never before known.

It was Deneir, but it was not Deneir, as if the god was changing before his very eyes, as if Deneir, his god, the rock of philosophical thought that Cadderly had used as the foundation of his very existence, was becoming part of something else, something different, perhaps bigger . . . and perhaps darker.

It seemed to Cadderly as if Deneir, in his attempt to unravel the mystery of the unraveling, was writing himself into the fabric of the Weave, or trying to write the Weave into the *Metatext* and taking himself with it in the process!

A flash of fire from a wooded valley to the east brought Cadderly back to the present. He stood up and walked to the railing, peering more intently into the distance. A few trees were on fire—one of the scouting wizards had enacted a fireball, or a priest had called down a column of flame, no doubt.

Which meant that they had encountered monsters.

Cadderly swept his gaze to the south, in line with distant Carradoon, off beyond the lower peaks. He could see the western bank of Impresk Lake on that clear day, and he tried to take some solace in the water's calm appearance.

He prayed that their near catastrophe was local to Spirit Soaring, that his children and Pikel had gone to Carradoon oblivious to the deadly horde that had come into the mountains behind them.

"Find them, Danica," he whispered to the late morning breezes.

* * * * *

She had gone out from Spirit Soaring first that day. Going alone allowed Danica to move more swiftly. Trained in stealth and speed, the woman quickly put the library far behind her, moving southeast down the packed-dirt road to Carradoon. She stayed just to the side of the open trail, moving through the brush with ease and speed.

Her hopes began to climb as the sun rose behind her, with no sign of monsters or destruction.

But then the smell of burned flesh filled her nostrils.

Cautious, but still moving with great speed, Danica ran to the top of an embankment beside the road, overlooking the scene of a recent battle: a ruined wagon and charred ground.

The Baldurian wizards.

She descended the steep decline, noting the piles of melted flesh and having no difficulty recognizing them as the remains of the same type of monsters that had assaulted Spirit Soaring the night before.

After a quick inspection revealed no human remains, Danica glanced back to the northwest, toward Spirit Soaring. Ivan had been out gathering wood the night those four had left, she recalled, and typically, the dwarf did so to the sides of the eastern road—the very road upon which she stood.

Danica's hopes for her friend began to sink. Had he encountered a similar shadowy horde? Had he seen the Baldurian wizards' fight and come down to aid them?

Neither scenario boded well. Ivan was as tough a fighter as Danica had ever known, capable and smart, but was out alone, and the sheer numbers that had come against Spirit Soaring, and had obviously hit the four mighty wizards on the road, could surely overwhelm anyone.

The woman took a deep, steadying breath, forcing herself not to jump to pessimistic conclusions regarding the wizards, Ivan, or the implications for her own children.

They were all capable, she reminded herself again, supremely so.

And there were no human or dwarf bodies that she could identify.

She began to look around more carefully for clues. Where had the monsters come from, and where had they gone?

She found a trail, a swath of dead trees and brown grass leading northward.

With a glance to the east, toward Carradoon, and a quick prayer for her children, Danica went hunting.

* * * * *

The blood on Ginance's face told Cadderly that his concern that some beasts hid within Spirit Soaring had been prudent.

"The catacombs crawl with the creatures," the woman explained. "We're clearing them room by room, crypt by crypt."

"Methodically," Cadderly observed.

Ginance nodded. "We leave no openings behind us. We will not be flanked."

Cadderly was glad to hear the confirmation, the reminder that the priests who had come to the call of Spirit Soaring over the last years were intelligent and studious. They were disciples of Deneir and of Gond, after all, two gods who demanded intelligence and reason as the cornerstones of faith.

Ginance held up her light tube, a combination of magic and mechanics using an unending spell of light and a tube of coated material to create a perpetual bulls-eye lantern. Every priest at Spirit Soaring had one, and with implements such as those, they could chase the darkness out of the deepest recesses.

"Leave nothing behind you," Cadderly said, and with a nod, Ginance took her leave.

Cadderly paced his small room, angry at his own inactivity, at the responsibilities that held him there. He should be with Danica, he told himself. But he shook that notion aside, knowing well that his wife could travel more swiftly, more stealthily, and more safely by herself. Then he thought he should be clearing the library with Ginance.

"No," he decided.

His place wasn't in the catacombs, but neither was it in his private quarters. He needed time to recuperate and mentally reset both his determination and his sense of calm before going back into the realm of the spiritual in his search to find Deneir.

No, not to find him, he realized, for he knew where his god had gone. Into the *Metatext*.

Perhaps for all time.

It fell on Cadderly to sort it out, and in doing so, to try to unravel the strange alterations of the divine spells that had come to him unbidden.

But not just then.

Cadderly strapped on his weapon belt and refilled his dart bandolier before looping it over his shoulder and across his chest. He considered his spindle-disks, a pair of hard, fist-sized semicircular plates bound by a small rod, around which were wrapped the finest of elven cords. Cadderly could send the disks spinning to the end of their three-foot length and back again at great speed, and could alter the angle easily to strike like a snake at any foe. He wasn't certain how much effect the weapon might have on the malleable flesh of the strange invaders, but he put the weapons in his belt pouch anyway.

He started toward the door, passing the wall mirror as he went, and there he paused and considered himself and his purpose, and the most important duty before him, that of leadership.

He looked fine in his white shirt and brown breeches, but he decided those weren't enough, especially since he looked very much like a young man, as young as his own children. With a smile, the not-so-young priest went to his wardrobe and took out his layered light blue traveling cloak and looped it over his shoulders. Then came his hat, also light blue, wide-brimmed and with a red band bearing the candle-over-eye emblem of Deneir set in gold on the front. A smooth walking stick, its top carved into the likeness of a ram's head, completed the look, and Cadderly took a moment to pause before the mirror again, and to reflect.

He looked so much like the young man who had first discovered the truth of his faith.

What a journey it had been! What adventure! In constructing Spirit Soaring, Cadderly had been forced into a moment of ultimate sacrifice. The creation magic had aged him, swiftly, continually, and greatly, to the point where all around him, even his beloved Danica, had thought he would surely perish for the effort. At the completion of the magnificent structure, Cadderly was prepared to die, and seemed about to. But that had been no more than a trial by Deneir, and the same magic that had wearied him then reinvigorated him after, reversing his aging to the strange point where he appeared and felt like a man of twenty once again, full of the strength and energy of youth, but with the wisdom of a weathered veteran more than twice his apparent age.

And he was being called again to the struggle, but Cadderly feared the implications were greater to the wider world even than the advent of the chaos curse.

He looked at himself in the mirror carefully, at the Chosen of Deneir, ready for battle and ready to reason his way through chaos.

In Spirit Soaring, Cadderly gained confidence. His god would not desert him, and he was surrounded by loyal friends and mighty allies.

Danica would find their children.

Spirit Soaring would prevail and they would lead the way to whatever might come when the time of magical turbulence sorted out.

He had to believe that.

And he had to make sure that everyone around him knew that he believed it.

Cadderly went down to the main audience hall of the first floor and left the large double doors open wide, awaiting the return of the scouts.

He didn't have to wait for long. As Cadderly entered the hall under the arch from the stairwell, the first group of returning scouts stumbled into Spirit Soaring's front doors—half the group, at least. Four members had been left dead on the field.

Cadderly had barely taken his seat when a pair of his Deneirrath priests entered, flanking a young and burly visiting priest—surrounding and supporting him, with one trying to bandage the man's ripped and burned shield arm.

"They were everywhere," the scout explained to Cadderly. "We were attacked less than half a league from here. A wizard tried a fireball, but it blew up short and smoked my arm. A priest tried to heal me on the field, but his spell caused an injury instead—to himself. His whole chest burst open, and . . . bah, we can't depend on any magic now!"

Cadderly nodded grimly through the recounting. "I saw the fight from my balcony, I believe. To the east . . . ?"

"North," the priest scout corrected. "North and west."

Those words stung Cadderly, for the fireball he had witnessed was opposite that direction. The priest's claim that "they were everywhere" reverberated in Cadderly's thoughts, and he tried hard to tell himself that his children were safe in Carradoon.

"Without reliable magic, our struggle will be more difficult," Cadderly said.

"Worse than you think," said one of the Spirit Soaring escorts, and he looked to the scout to elaborate.

"Four of our nine were slain," the man said. "But they didn't stay dead."

"Resurrection?" Cadderly asked.

"Undead," the man explained. "They got back up and started fighting again—this time against the rest of us."

"There was a priest or a wizard among the monsters' ranks?"

The man shrugged. "They fell, they died, they got back up."

Cadderly started to respond but bit it short, his eyes going wide. In the fight at Spirit Soaring the night before, at least fifteen men and women had been killed, and had been laid in a side room on the first level of the catacombs.

Cadderly leaped from his chair, alarm evident on his face.

"What is it?" the priest scout asked.

"Come along, all three," he said, scrambling toward the back of the room. He veered to a side door to corridors that would allow him to navigate the maze of the great library more quickly.

* * * * *

Danica picked her way carefully but quickly along the trail, staying just to the side of the swath of devastation. It ran anywhere from five to ten long strides across, with broken trees and torn turf along its center, as if some great creature had ambled through. She saw only patches of deadness along the edges—not complete decay as she found in the middle of the trail, but spotty areas where sections of trees seemingly had simply died—along both sides.

The monk was loath to walk across that swath, or even enter the area of deepest decay, but when she saw a print on an open patch of ground, she knew that she had to learn more. She held her breath as she approached, for she recognized it as a footprint indeed, a giant footprint, four-toed and with great claws, the impression of a dragon's foot.

Danica knelt low and inspected the area, taking particular interest in the grass. Not all of it was dead on the trail, but the nearer to the footprints, the more profound the devastation. She stood up and looked around at the standing trees along the sides, and envisioned a dragon walking through, crushing down any trees or shrubs in its path, occasionally flexing its wings, perhaps, which would have put them in contact with the bordering trees.

She focused on the dead patches of those trees, so stark in contrast with the vibrancy of the forest itself. Had the mere touch of the beast's wings killed them?

She looked again at the footprint, and at the profound absence of life in the vegetation immediately surrounding it.

A dragon, but a dragon that killed so profoundly with a mere touch?

Danica swallowed hard, realizing that the hunched, fleshy crawlers might be the least of their problems.

CHAPTER

15

They're less likely to take comfort in his dwarf heritage if they think him an idiot," Hanaleisa explained to Temberle, who was more than a little upset at the whispers he was hearing among the ranks of the Carradden refugees.

Temberle had insisted that Pikel, the only dwarf in the group and the only one who seemed able to conjure magical light in the otherwise lightless tunnels, would lead them through the dark. Though a few had expressed incredulity at the notion of following the inarticulate, green-bearded dwarf, none had openly disagreed. How could they, after all, when Pikel had undeniably been the hero of the last fight, freezing the water and allowing a retreat from certain disaster?

But that was yesterday, and the march of the last few hours had been a series of starts and stops, of backtracking and the growing certainty that they were lost. They had encountered no walking dead, at least, but that seemed cold comfort in those dank and dirty caves, crawling through tunnels and openings that had even the children on all fours, and with crawly bugs scurrying all around them.

"They're scared," Temberle whispered back. "They'd be complaining no matter who took the lead."

"Because we're lost." As she spoke, Hanaleisa nodded her chin at Pikel, who stood up front, lighted shillelagh tucked under his stumped arm while he scratched at his thick green beard with his good hand. The strange-looking dwarf stared at a trio of tunnels branching out before him, obviously without a clue.

"How could we *not* be lost?" Temberle asked. "Has anyone been through here, ever?"

Hanaleisa conceded that point with a shrug, but pulled her brother along as she moved to join the dwarf and Rorick, who stood by Pikel's side, leaning on a staff someone had given him to aid his movement with his torn ankle.

"Do you know where we are, Uncle Pikel?" Hanaleisa asked as she approached.

The dwarf looked at her and shrugged.

"Do you know where Carradoon is? Which direction?"

Without even thinking about it, obviously sure of his answer, Pikel pointed back the way they had come, and to the right, what Hanaleisa took to be southeast.

"He's trying to get us higher into the mountains before finding a way out of the tunnels," Rorick explained.

"No," Temberle was quick to reply, and both Rorick and Pikel looked at him curiously.

"Eh?" said the dwarf.

"We have to get out of the tunnels," Temberle explained. "Now."

"Uh-uh," Pikel disagreed, and he grabbed up his cudgel and held both of his arms out before him, mimicking a zombie to accentuate his point.

"Certainly we're far enough from Carradoon to escape that madness," said Temberle.

"Uh-uh."

"We're not that far," Rorick explained. "The tunnels are winding back and forth. If we came out on a high bluff, Carradoon would still be in sight."

"I do not disagree," said Temberle.

"But we have to get out of the tunnels as soon as possible," Hanaleisa added. "Dragging a gravely wounded man through these narrow and dirty spaces is sure to be the end of him."

"And going above ground is likely to be the end of all of us," Rorick shot back.

Hanaleisa and Temberle exchanged knowing looks. Watching the dead rise and come against them had profoundly unnerved Rorick, and certainly, the older twins shared that disgust and terror.

Hanaleisa walked over and draped her arm across Pikel's shoulders. "Get us in sight of the open air, at least," she whispered to him. "These close quarters and the unending darkness is playing on the nerves of all."

Pikel reiterated his zombie posture.

"I know, I know," Hanaleisa said. "I don't want to go out and face those things again, either. But we're not dwarves, Uncle Pikel. We can't stay down here forever."

Pikel leaned on his cudgel and gave a great, heaving sigh. He tucked the club under his stump and stuck a finger in his mouth, slurping about for a moment before pulling it forth with a hollow popping sound. He closed his eyes and began to chant as he held the wet finger up before him, magically sensitizing himself to the current of air.

He pointed to the right-hand corridor.

"That will get us out?" Hanaleisa asked.

Pikel shrugged, apparently unwilling to make any promises. He took up his glowing cudgel and led the way.

* * * * *

"We require the other four," decided Yharaskrik, still in the body of Ivan and speaking through the dwarf's mouth. "The lich First Grandfather Wu is lost to us, for now at least, but four others are missing and awaiting recall."

"They are busy," Hephaestus insisted.

"No matter is more important than the one before us."

The dracolich emitted a low, threatening growl. "I will have them," he said.

"The drow and the human?"

"You know who I mean."

"We already have lost First Grandfather Wu to the drow," Yharaskrik reminded. "It is possible that Jarlaxle was killed in that same conflict."

"We do not know what happened to First Grandfather Wu."

"We know that he is lost to us, that he is . . . gone. There is nothing more we need know. He found Jarlaxle and was defeated, and whether the drow was also killed—"

"Is something we would know if you cared to search!" Hephaestus said, and there it was, the true source of his simmering rage.

"Do not overreach," the illithid in the dwarf's body retorted. "We are great and mighty, and our power will only multiply as more minions are brought through the rift, and more undead are called to our service—perhaps we will soon learn how to raise the bodies of the crawlers, then our army will be unending. But mighty, too, are our enemies, and none more so than the one we have here, within our reach, at the place they call Spirit Soaring."

"Magic is failing."

"But it has not failed. It is unpredictable, of course, but potent still."

"Fetchigrol and Solmé have bottled this mighty enemy up in his hole," Hephaestus argued with dismissive sarcasm, his voice dripping as he referred to Cadderly as "mighty."

"They are out on the trails even now."

"Where many have been killed!"

"A few, no more," Yharaskrik said. "And many of our minions were consumed in the battle. They do not issue from an inexhaustible source, great Hephaestus."

"But the walking dead do—millions and millions will answer our call. And as they kill, their ranks increase," the dracolich proclaimed.

"The summoning is easy for those of this world who have fallen," Yharaskrik agreed. "But it is not without cost to the power of Crenshinibon—and who more likely than the powerful Cadderly to discover a countering magic?"

"I will have them!" Hephaestus roared. "The drow and his human companion—that Calishite. I will have them and I will devour them!"

The body of Ivan Bouldershoulder settled back on its heels. The illithid within was shaking the yellow-haired head with dismay and resignation. "A creature of centuries should know more of patience," Yharaskrik scolded quietly. "One enemy at a time. Let us destroy Cadderly and Spirit Soaring, then we can go hunting. We recall the four apparitions—"

"No!"

"We will need all of our power to—"

"No! Two in the north and two in the south. Two for the drow and two for the human. If First Grandfather Wu returns, then bring him back to our side, but the other four will hunt until they have found the drow and the human. I will have those treacherous fools. And fear not for Cadderly and his forces. We will peck at them until they are weak, then the catastrophe of Hephaestus will fall over them. I went out to Solmé this very day and the ground beneath me died at my passing, and the touch of my wings rotted the trees. I fear no mortal, not this Cadderly nor anyone else. I am Hephaestus, I am catastrophe. Look upon me and know doom!"

With a large part of his enormous consciousness still residing within the coil of the dragon, sharing that body with Hephaestus and Crenshinibon, Yharaskrik understood that it could not convince the dragon otherwise. The illithid also realized, to its dismay, that Hephaestus was gaining the upper hand in the competition for the alliance of Crenshinibon.

Perhaps the illithid had erred in abandoning that coil with so much of its consciousness. Perhaps it was time to return to the others within the life-force of Hephaestus, to better battle the stubborn dragon.

A smile creased the face of Ivan Bouldershoulder—an ironic one indeed, Yharaskrik thought, because he was at that moment concluding that sacrificing the dwarf to the rage of Hephaestus might placate the dragon for a while, long enough for Yharaskrik to regain some measure of dominance.

* * * * *

A chorus of weary cheers erupted when at last the beleaguered refugees of Carradoon saw a stream of daylight. Never had any imagined how deep and dark mountain tunnels could be—except for Pikel, of course, who had been raised in dwarven mines.

Even Rorick, who had warned against going outside, couldn't hide his relief at learning that there was indeed an ending to those lightless corridors. With great hopes, they turned a long and curving corner leading to daylight.

And arrived with a communal, profound, and disappointed sigh.

"Uh-oh," said Pikel, for they had not come to the end of the tunnel, but merely to a natural chimney, and a very long and narrow one at that.

"We're deeper than I believed," Temberle admitted, staring up the shaft, which extended upward for more than a hundred feet. Most of it could not be climbed, and was too narrow in many places for any attempt, even for nimble Hanaleisa or Rorick, who were the slimmest of the group.

"Did you know we were this far down?" Hanaleisa asked Pikel, and in reply the dwarf began drawing mountains in the air, then merely shrugged.

His reasoning was correct, Hanaleisa and the other onlookers knew, for their current depth was likely more dependent upon the contours of the mountainous land above than the relatively mild grade of the tunnels they had been traversing.

The high shaft confirmed, though, that they were indeed moving deeper into the Snowflakes.

"You have to get us out," Temberle said to Pikel.

"To battle hordes of undead?" Rorick reminded him, and Temberle shot his brother an irritated look.

"Or at least, you have to show us . . . show *them*"—he glanced back at the many Carradden moving into sight around the corner—"that there is a way out. Even if we don't go outside," he added, looking pointedly at his little brother, "it remains important that we know we *can* go outside again. We're not dwarves."

A cry sounded down the line. "They're fighting in the back!" a woman yelled. "Undead! Undead sailors again!"

"We know there's a way out," Hanaleisa said somberly, "because now we know there's a way in."

"Even if it's the way we already came," Temberle added, and he and Hanaleisa made their way along the line to take up arms once again, to battle bloodthirsty monsters in an unending nightmare.

By the time Hanaleisa and Temberle arrived at the scuffle, the small skirmish had ended, leaving a trio of waterlogged and rotted zombies crumpled in the corridor. But one of the Carradden, too, had fallen, caught by surprise. Her neck had been broken in the opening salvo.

"What are we to do with her?" a man asked, speaking above the wails of the woman's husband, a fellow sailor.

"Burn her, and be quick!" another shouted, which elicited many cries of protest and many more shouts of assent. Both sides in the debate became more insistent with each passing shout, and it seemed as if the whole argument would explode into more fighting then and there.

"We cannot burn her!" Hanaleisa yelled above it all, and whether by deference to one of Cadderly's children or simply because of the strength and surety in her voice, Hanaleisa's yell interrupted the cacophony of the brewing storm, at least for the moment.

"Ye'd have her stand up, then, to walk like one o' them?" an old seadog argued. "Better to burn her now and be sure."

172

"We haven't any fire, nor any tools for making fire," Hanaleisa shot back. "And even if we did, would you have us trudging through tunnels filled with such a smell and reminder as that?"

The dead woman's husband finally tore away from those trying to hold him back, and shoved his way through the crowd to kneel beside his wife. He took up her head, cradling it in his arms, his strong shoulders bobbing with sobs.

Hanaleisa and Temberle looked at each other, not knowing what to do.

"Cut off her head, then!" someone yelled from the back, and the dead woman's husband lifted a hateful and threatening gaze in the direction of the gruesome suggestion.

"No!" Hanaleisa yelled, again quieting the crowd. "No. Find some rocks. We'll bury her under a cairn, respectfully, as she deserves."

That seemed to mollify the distraught husband somewhat, but some in the crowd began to protest all the more loudly.

"And if she comes to a state of undeath like all the others, and charges at us?" a nearby dissenter remarked to Hanaleisa and Temberle. "Are you two going to have the will to cut her down, and in front of this poor man here? Are you sure you're not being cruel in thinking to be kind?"

Hanaleisa found it a hard point to argue, and the weight of responsibility for the calamity pressed down heavily on her young shoulders. She looked back at the husband, who obviously recognized her dilemma. He stared at her pleadingly.

"A few heavier rocks, then," Hanaleisa said. "If whatever abomination that is animating the dead reaches her, which I think unlikely," she added for the sake of the distraught man, "then she will not be able to rise against us, or anyone else."

"No, she'll be trapped flailing under our heavy stones, and what an eternity that's to be!" the old seadog said. More yelling ensued, and again the husband's expression fell as he hugged his dear dead wife more closely.

"Aye, so if we cut off her head and that happens, then she can tuck it under one arm, what, and walk about forever like that?" another man chided the first.

"I hate this," Temberle whispered to his sister.

"We've no choice," Hanaleisa reminded him. "If we don't lead, who will?"

In the end, they settled on Hanaleisa's suggestion, building a cairn of heavy rocks to securely inter the dead woman. At Hanaleisa's private suggestion, Pikel then performed a ceremony to consecrate the ground around the cairn, with Hanaleisa assuring all, particularly the husband, that such a ritual would make it very unlikely that any necromantic magic could disturb her rest.

That seemed to calm the bereaved husband somewhat, and mollify the protestors, though in fact, Pikel had no such real ceremony to offer and the impromptu dance and song he offered was no more than a show.

At that dark time, in that dark place, Hanaleisa thought a show was just as good.

She realized it was better than the alternatives, of which she could not think of even one.

CHAPTER
D A R K H O L E S

Danica saw the cave entrance far in the distance, long before she realized that the trail of death led to that spot. She knew instinctively that such a creature as had caused that withering and decay would not long bask in sunlight.

The trail meandered a bit, but soon bent toward the dark face of the distant mountain, where it ended abruptly. Likely, the dragon had taken flight.

When Danica at last arrived at the base of the mountain, she looked up at the black mouth of the cavern. It was indeed large enough to admit a great wyrm, a subtle crease high in the mountain wall, inaccessible to any unable to fly.

Or unable to climb with the skill of a master monk.

Danica closed her eyes and fell inside herself, connecting mind and body in complete harmony. She envisioned herself as lighter, as unbounded by the press of gravity. Slowly, the woman opened her eyes again, lifting her chin to scan a path among the stones. Few others would have seen much possibility there, but to Danica, a ridge no wider than a finger seemed as inviting as a ledge upon which five men could stand abreast.

She mentally lifted her body, then reached up to a narrow ledge and locked her fingers in place, counting out the cadence of the next few movements. She scrambled like a spider, seeming effortless, walking the wall on all fours, hands and feet reaching and stretching. Danica moved horizontally as well as vertically, shifting toward better ridges, more broken stones and better handholds.

The sun crossed its midpoint, and still Danica climbed. The wind howled around her, but she ignored its cold bite, and would not let it dislodge her. Of more concern to her was her timing. Her estimate in beginning her ascent was that the creature she sought was a beast of the darkness, and the last place she wanted to be when it emerged from its hole was splayed out on a cliff face, hundreds of feet above the ground.

With that unsettling thought in mind, Danica pushed on, her fingers and toes finding holds, however tentatively. She constantly shifted her weight to minimize the pull against any one limb or even one digit. As she neared the cave opening, the ascent became more broken and not so steep, with several stretches where she could pause and catch her breath. One long expanse was more a walk than a climb. Danica took her time along that trail and paid extra care to use any cover she could find among the many tumbled stones along the path that led to the stygian darkness of the waiting cave.

* * * * *

Numbers.

He was counting and adding, subtracting and counting some more. A compulsion dominated his every thought, to count and to add, to seek patterns in the many numbers that flitted though his thoughts.

Ivan Bouldershoulder had always been fond of numbers. Designing a new tool or implement, working through the proper ratios and calculating the necessary strength of each piece had been among the dwarf craftsman's greatest joys. As when Cadderly had come to him with a tapestry depicting dark elves and their legendary hand crossbows. Working from that image and his knowledge and intuition alone, Ivan had replicated those delicate weapons to near perfection.

Numbers. It was all about numbers. Everything was about numbers—at least, that's what Cadderly had always argued. Everything could be reduced to numbers and deconstructed at will from that point forward, if only the intelligence doing the reducing was great enough to understand the patterns involved.

That was the difference between the mortals and the gods, Cadderly had often remarked. The gods could reduce life itself to numbers.

Such thoughts had never found a home in the far less theorizing and far more pragmatic Ivan Bouldershoulder, but apparently, he realized, Cadderly's sermons had created a far bigger imprint on his brain than he had assumed.

He thought of the implication of numbers, and that memory of a long-ago conversation was the only thing that made the befuddled dwarf realize that the numbers constantly flashing before him just then were nothing more than a purposeful and malicious distraction.

Ivan felt as if he were waking up beside a babbling brook, that moment of recognition of the sound giving him a real space outside of his dreams, a piece of solidity and reality from which to bring his thoughts fully to the waking world.

The numbers continued to flash more insistently. The patterns flickered and disappeared.

Distraction.

Something was keeping him off balance and out of sorts, away from consciousness itself. He couldn't close his eyes against the intrusion, because his eyes were already closed.

No, not closed, he suddenly understood—whether they were closed or not was of no practical consequence, because he wasn't the one using them, or seeing through them. He was lost, wandering aimlessly within the swirl of his own thoughts.

And something had put him there.

And something had kept him there—some force, some creature, some intellect that was inside him.

The dwarf had broken the enchantment of distraction and lashed out from the cocoon of numbers, though he flailed blindly.

A memory flashed quickly through his thoughts, of fighting on a rocky slope north of Mithral Hall, of a piece of shale spinning through the air and taking the arm from his brother.

As abruptly as Pikel's arm, the memory was gone, but Ivan kept running through the darkness of his own mind, seeking flashes and moments of his own identity.

He found another recollection, a time when he had flown on a dragon. It wasn't anything substantial, just a sensation of freedom, the wind blowing through his hair, dragging his beard out behind him.

A brief flicker of mountains' majesty unfolding before him.

It seemed a fitting metaphor to the dwarf. He felt the same way, but within himself. It was as if his mind had been lifted above the landscape of all that was Ivan Bouldershoulder, as if he were overlooking himself from afar, a spectator in his own thoughts.

But at least he knew. He had escaped the distraction and knew again who he was.

Ivan began to fight. He grabbed at every memory and held it fast, steeling his thoughts to ensure that what he remembered was true. He saw Pikel, he saw Cadderly, he saw Danica and the kids.

The kids.

He had watched them grow from drooling, helpless critters to adulthood, tall and straight and full of potential. He took pride in them as if they were his own children, and he would not let that notion go.

No creature in all the multiverse was more stubborn than a dwarf, after all. And few dwarves were as far-thinking as Ivan Bouldershoulder. He began immediately to use his recognition of the creature telepathically dominating him to begin a flow of information back the other way.

He knew his surroundings through the memory of that other being. He understood the threats around him, to some extent, and he felt keenly the power of the dracolich.

If he wanted to survive, if there was any way to survive, he knew, in that moment when he would at last find a way to reassert control of his mortal coil, that he couldn't allow himself to be confused and couldn't allow himself to be surprised.

* * * * *

The face of Ivan Bouldershoulder, controlled solely by Yharaskrik the illithid, smiled.

The dwarf was waking up.

Because of the illithid's own uncertainty, Yharaskrik knew, for as it had begun to consider the wisdom of returning fully to consciousness within the draconic host of Crenshinibon, so it had also, unavoidably, lessened its grasp on the dwarf.

Yharaskrik understood well that once a possessed creature of strong intellect and determination—a dwarf perhaps more than any other race—had broken out of the initial mental invasion of psionic power, it was like a trickle of water through an earthen dam.

It couldn't be stopped, even if Yharaskrik had decided that it was critical to stop it. It could be temporarily plugged, perhaps, but never fully stopped, for all of the mental cobwebs Yharaskrik had enacted to keep the dwarf locked in a dark hole were beginning to erode.

The illithid amused itself with a notion of freeing the dwarf right before the waiting maw of fearsome Hephaestus. He thought of departing the dwarf's mind almost fully, but leaving just a bit of consciousness within Ivan so that it could feel the desperate terror and the last moments of the dwarf's life.

What, after all, could be more invasive and intrusive than being so intimate a part of another being's final moments?

And indeed, Yharaskrik had done that very thing many times before, as it pondered the truth of death. To the illithid's frustration, however, never had it been able to send its own consciousness over into the realm of death with that of its host.

It didn't matter, the illithid decided as it pushed away those past failures with a mental sigh. It still enjoyed those voyeur moments, of sharing those ultimate sensations and fears uninvited, of intruding upon the deepest privacy any sentient creature could ever know.

Through the eyes of Ivan Bouldershoulder, Yharaskrik looked upon Hephaestus. The dracolich lay curled at the back of the largest chamber in the mountain cavern, not asleep, for sleep was for the living, but in a state of deep meditation and plotting, and fantasizing of the victories to come.

No, the illithid decided as it sensed the dragon's continuing feelings of superiority. Yharaskrik would not give Hephaestus the satisfaction of that particular kill.

Methodically, the illithid in the dwarf's body walked over to retrieve Ivan's antlered helmet and his heavy axe, formulating the plan as it went. It wanted to feel the dwarf's extended terror, his fury and his fear. Yharaskrik moved out of the cave, signaling the four undead wizards to follow, and stepped out onto the rocky descent a short way, then paused, calling Fetchigrol to its side.

On Yharaskrik's command, the specter crossed the unseen threshold once more, past the realm of death and into the other world, the Shadowfell, that had been opened to them through the power of the falling Weave.

Yharaskrik paused only a moment longer, to taunt the thoughts of Ivan Bouldershoulder.

Then it let the dwarf have the control and sensibilities of his mortal coil back once more, surrounded by enemies and with nowhere to run, and no way to win.

* * * * *

Ivan knew where he was and what was coming against him—he had garnered that from the consciousness of his possessor. He felt no shock from the illithid departing, and so Ivan Bouldershoulder woke up swinging. His axe hummed through the air in great sweeping cuts. He smashed the burned wizard, sending up a cloud of flecks of blackened skin. His backhand opened wide the chest of a second zombie and sent the horrid creature tumbling away. When another came in at him behind the arc of that cut, Ivan lowered his head and butted hard, the deer antlers on his helmet poking deep holes in the charging beast.

With a groan, the undead wizard fell backward off the helmet spikes, just in time to catch the dwarf's axe swing right in the side of its head. The axe blew through and dived into the fourth as it shuffled up to grasp at the dwarf.

By that time, Ivan's initial fury played out, more enemies swarmed toward him: huddled, fleshy beasts.

Ivan sprinted down the trail, away from the cave, though he knew from memory that the route was surely a dead end, a long drop. But the invading consciousness still hovered over him, he sensed, anticipating just such a run.

So Ivan turned and bulled his way through the close pursuit of a pair of crawling beasts, knocking them aside with sheer ferocity and strength. He ran all the faster, right for the cave mouth, and straight into it.

And there lay the moldering skeleton of a titanic dragon, itself imbued with the animate power of the undead. It was already moving when Ivan came upon it, leaping up onto its four legs with amazing dexterity.

The sight nearly knocked the breath out of Ivan. He knew that something big and terrible was in that cave before he'd fully awakened, but he couldn't have anticipated a catastrophe of such proportions.

A lesser dwarf, a lesser warrior, would have hesitated right there at the entrance, and the huddled beasts would have fallen over him from behind, and even had he somehow prevailed in that crush, the great monster before him would have had him.

But Ivan did not hesitate. He lifted his axe high and charged the dra-colich, bellowing a war cry to his god, Moradin. He had no doubt he was going to die, but he would do so in a manner of his choosing, in the manner of a true warrior.

* * * * *

The first sounds of battle alerted Danica. She scrambled around a stone and her heart fell, for there she saw Ivan, fighting valiantly against overwhelming odds of crawling beasts and a few horribly maimed walking dead. Behind them, directing them, Danica sensed, was some spectral being, huddled and shadowy and shimmering like simultaneously thinning and thickening gray smoke. Danica's first instinct was to go to Ivan, or rush behind the pursuing throng and attack the leading creature, but even as she digested the awful scene, the dwarf turned and sprinted away, up the trail toward the great cave.

The monsters pursued. The specter rushed behind them.

Danica followed.

Into the cave went Ivan. Into the cave went the monsters and the zombies and the specter. To the edge of the entrance went Danica, and there she skid-ded to an abrupt stop, and there she saw Ivan's doom, saw her own doom, saw the doom of all the world.

Danica couldn't even catch her breath in the sight of the great dracolich, and enough of the dragon remained intact for her to recognize the red scales of the wyrm. Her gaze locked on the beast's face, half-rotted, white bone showing, eye sockets burned out horribly, and a peculiar, green-glowing horn protruding from the very middle of its forehead.

She felt the power emanating from that horn.

Awful power.

Ivan's battle cry broke her trance, and she looked down at the dwarf's charge, his axe up high over his head as if he meant to tear his way right through the beast. He charged at the dracolich's front leg, and the wyrm lifted its foot at the last moment.

Ivan dived, and so did a trio of huddled fleshy beasts and one of the undead—one of the wizards from Baldur's Gate, Danica recognized with a heavy heart.

The beast stamped with power that shook the whole of the mountain spur, sending cracks spiderwebbing across the stone floor.

The air around its foot was sprayed with blood and gore, a crimson mist of ultimate destruction, a stamp of pure finality.

Danica couldn't contain her gasp.

A few of the creatures that had not followed the dwarf to doom, falling back and stumbling every which way from the sheer concussion of the stomp, noted that faint noise.

Then Danica was running away from the cave, hungry beasts in close pursuit. She sprinted down the trail, trying to figure out how or where she might go, for the navigable angle of decline would not hold, not in any direction.

She glanced over her shoulder, turned back, and cut fast behind a stone outcropping, and cut the other way around another, trying to gain some distance so that she could get over a ledge and begin her descent down the cliff face.

But there were too many, and every turn did no more than put different monsters close on her tail.

She ran out of room and skidded to the edge of the cliff, perched at the point of the longest drop, for not only did it rise above the hundreds of feet of cliffs that had led Danica to that awful place, it went far deeper on one side, into a gorge low in the foothills of the Snowflakes.

Danica turned around, then fell flat as a beast leaped at her. It sailed over her, its hungry cry turning to a scream of terror, fast receding as it plummeted to oblivion.

Up hopped Danica, kicking out to knock back the next monster in line. The third, as if oblivious to the fate of the first, leaped into the air and tumbled at her. Again she ducked, though not as fully, and the creature brushed her as it went over. Danica fought hard and regained her balance just in time.

But the creature's flailing claw caught her shoulder and tugged her back.

All the fury and tumult of the moment seemed to stop suddenly and Danica's ears filled with the emptiness of a mournful wind.

And she was falling.

She twisted around, looking down a thousand feet and more to the tops of very tall trees.

She thought of Cadderly, of her children, of a life not yet complete.

PART
3

THE SUM OF THEIR PARTS

THE SUM OF THEIR PARTS

We live in a dangerous world, and one that seems more dangerous now that the way of magic is in transition, or perhaps even collapse. If Jarlaxle's guess is correct, we have witnessed the collision of worlds, or of planes, to the point where rifts will bring newer and perhaps greater challenges to us all.

It is, I suspect, a time for heroes.

I have come to terms with my own personal need for action. I am happiest when there are challenges to be met and overcome. I feel in those times of great crisis that I am part of something larger than myself—a communal responsibility, a generational duty—and to me, that is great comfort.

We will all be needed now, every blade and every brain, every scholar and every warrior, every wizard and every priest. The events in the Silver Marches, the worry I saw on Lady Alustriel's face, are not localized, but, I fear, resonate across the breadth of Toril. I can only imagine the chaos in Menzoberranzan with the decline of the wizards and priests; the entire matriarchal society might well be in jeopardy, and those greatest of Houses might find themselves besieged by legions of angry kobolds.

Our situation on the World Above is likely to be no less dire, and so it is the time for heroes. What does that mean, to be a hero? What is it that elevates some above the hordes of fighters and battle-mages? Certainly circumstance plays a role—extraordinary valor, or action, is more likely in moments of highest crisis.

And yet, in those moments of greatest crisis, the result is, more often than not, disaster. No hero emerges. No savior leads the charge across the battlefield, or slays the dragon, and the town is immersed in flames.

In our world, for good or for ill, the circumstances favorable to creating a hero have become all too common.

It is not, therefore, just circumstance, or just good fortune. Luck may play a part, and indeed some people—I count myself among them—are more lucky than others, but since I do not believe that there are blessed souls and cursed souls, or that this or that god is leaning over our shoulders and involving himself in our daily affairs, then I do know that there is one other necessary quality for those who find a way to step above the average.

If you set up a target thirty strides away and assemble the hundred best archers in any given area to shoot at it, they'd all hit the mark. Add in a bet of gold and a few would fall away, to the hoots of derision from their fellows.

But now replace the target with an assassin, and have that assassin holding at dagger-point the person each successive archer most loves in the world. The archer now has one shot. Just one. If he hits the mark—the assassin—his loved one will be saved. If he misses the assassin, it is certain doom for his beloved.

A hero will hit that mark. Few mere archers would.

That is the extra quality involved, the ability to hold poise and calm and rational thought no matter how devastating the consequences of failure, the ability to go to that place of pure concentration in times most emotionally and physically tumultuous. Not just once and not by luck. The hero makes that shot.

The hero lives for that shot. The hero trains for that shot, every day, for endless hours, with purest concentration.

Many fine warriors live in the world, wielding blade or lightning bolt, who serve well in their respective armies, who weather the elements and the enemies with quiet and laudable stoicism. Many are strong in their craft, and serve with distinction.

But when all teeters precariously on the precipice of disaster, when victory or defeat rests upon matters beyond simple strength and courage and valor, when all balances on that sword-edged line between victory or defeat, the hero finds a way—a way that seems impossible to those who do not truly understand the give and take of battle, the ebb and flow of sword play, the logical follow-up to counter an enemy's advantage.

For a warrior is one trained in the techniques of various weaponry, one who knows how to lift a shield or parry a thrust and properly counter, but a true warrior, a hero, extends beyond those skills. Every movement is instinctual, is engrained into every muscle to flow with perfect and easy coordination. Every block is based on clear thinking—so clear that it is as much anticipatory as reflexive. And every weakness in an opponent becomes apparent at first glance.

The true warrior fights from a place of calm, of controlled rage and quelled fear. Every situation comes to sharpened focus, every avenue of solution shines its path clearly. And the hero goes one step beyond that, finding a way, any way, to pave a path of victory when there is no apparent route.

The hero finds a way, and when that way is shown, however difficult the path, the hero makes the thrust or the block or the last frantic riposte, stealing his opponent's victory. As when Regis used his ruby pendant to paralyze a battle-mage in Luskan. As when Wulfgar threw himself at the yochlol to save Catti-brie. As when Catti-brie made that desperate shot in the sewers of Calimport to drive off Entreri, who had gained the advantage over me. As when Bruenor used his cunning, his strength, and his unshakable will to defeat Shimmergloom in the darkness of Mithral Hall.

Certain doom is a term not known in the vocabulary of the hero, for it is precisely at those times when doom seems most certain—when Bruenor rode the flaming shadow dragon down to the depths of Garumn's Gorge—that the warrior who would be hero elevates himself above the others. It is, instinctually, not about him or his life.

The hero makes the shot.

We are all to be tested now, I fear. In this time of confusion and danger, many will be pulled to the precipice of disaster, and most will fall over that dark ledge. But a few will step beyond that line, will find a way and will make that shot.

In those moments, however, it is important to recognize that reputation means nothing, and while past deeds might inspire confidence, they are no guarantee of present or future victory.

I hope that Taulmaril is steady in my hands when I stand upon that precipice, for I know that I walk into the shadows of doom, where black pits await, and I need only to think of broken Regis or look at my beloved Catti-brie to understand the stakes of this contest.

I hope that I am given that shot at this assassin, whomever or whatever it may be, who holds us all at dagger-point, for if so, I intend to hit the mark.

For that is the last point to make about the hero. In the aforementioned archery contest, the hero wants to be the one chosen to take that most critical shot. When the stakes are highest, the hero wants the outcome to be in his hands. It's not about hubris, but about necessity, and the confidence that the would-be hero has trained and prepared for exactly that one shot.

—Drizzt Do'Urden

CHAPTER

NOTHING BUT THE WIND

17

I t all stopped. Everything. The battle, the fear, and the chase. It was over, replaced by only the sound of the wind and the grand view from on high. A sensation of emptiness and solitude washed over the monk. Of freedom. Of impending death.

A twist, a shift, and pure control had Danica upright immediately, and she turned around to face the cliff from which she had just tumbled. She reached out and lunged forward, her eyes scanning before her and below her, all in an instant, yielding a sudden recognition and complete sorting of the larger jags and angles. She slapped her palm against the stone, then the other one, then back and forth repeatedly. With each contact her muscles twitched against the momentum of the fall.

A jut of stone far below and to the left had her thrusting her left foot out that way, and as she slapped the stone with both hands together, she gave the slightest push, again and again, ten times in rapid succession as she descended, subtly shifting to the left.

Her toe touched a jag and she threw her weight to that foot, bending her leg to absorb the impact. She couldn't begin to stop the momentum of her descent with just that, but she managed to push back with some success, stealing some of her speed.

It was the way of the monk. Danica could run down the wall of a tall building and land without injury. She had done it on more than one occasion. But of course, a tall building was nowhere near the height of that cliff, and the grade was more difficult, sometimes sheer and straight, sometimes less than sheer, sometimes more than sheer. But she worked with all her concentration, her muscles answering her demands.

Another jag gave her the opportunity to break a bit more of her momentum, and a narrow ledge allowed her to plant both feet and work her leg muscles against the relentless pull of gravity.

After that, halfway to the ground, the woman looked more like a spider running frantically along a wall, her arms and legs pumping furiously.

A dark form fell past her, startling her and nearly stealing her concentration. One of the fleshy beasts, she recognized, but she didn't begin to speculate on how it might have fallen.

She had no time for that, no time for anything but absolute concentration on the task before her.

Nothing but the wind filled her senses, that and the contours of the cliff.

She was almost to the ground, still falling too quickly to survive. Danica couldn't hope to land and roll to absorb the tremendous impact. So she hooked her feet together against the stone and threw herself over backward, rolling over just in time to see the tall pines she had viewed from above.

Then she was crashing through the branches, needles flying, wood splintering. A broken branch hooked her and tore a fair slice of skin out of her side and ripped away half her shirt. A heavier branch not much farther below didn't break, but bent, and Danica rolled off it head over heels, tumbling and crashing, rebounding off the heaviest lower branches and breaking through amidst a spray of green needles, and still with thirty feet to fall.

Half blinded by pain, barely conscious, the monk still managed to sort herself out and spin to get her feet beneath her.

She bent and rolled sidelong as she landed. Over and over she went, three times, five times, seven times. She stopped with a gasp, explosions of pain rolling up from her legs, from her torn side, from a shoulder she knew to be dislocated.

Danica managed to turn over a bit, to see a lump of splattered black flesh.

At least she didn't look like that, she thought. But though she had avoided the mutilation suffered by the crawlers, she feared that the result would be the same and that she would not survive the fall.

Cold darkness closed in.

But Danica fought it, telling herself that the dracolich would come looking for her, reminding herself that she was not safe, that even if she somehow managed to not die from the battering she had taken in the fall, the beast would have her.

She rolled to her belly and pushed up on her elbows, or tried to, but her shoulder would not allow it and the waves of agony that rippled out overwhelmed her. She propped herself up on one arm, and there vomited, gasping. Tears filled her almond-shaped eyes as her retching, and the spasms in her ribs, elicited a whole new level of agony.

She had to move, she told herself.

But she had no more to give.

The cold darkness closed in again, and even mighty Danica could not resist.

* * * * *

Looking out the door of the side room in the darkened gorge, Catti-brie could barely make out the forms of her companions in the other chamber's flickering torchlight. They were all trapped at the apparent dead end, shadow hounds coming in swift pursuit, a dragon blocking the way before them. Drizzt was lost to them, and Wulfgar, beside Catti-brie, had taken the brunt of the dragon's breath, a horrid cloud of blackness and despair that had left him numb and nearly helpless.

She peered out the door, desperate for an answer, praying that her father would find a way to save them all. She didn't know what to make of it when Bruenor took off the gem-studded helmet and replaced it with his broken-horned old helm.

When he handed the crown to Regis and said, "Keep the helm safe. It's the crown of the King of Mithral Hall," his intent became all too clear.

The halfling protested, "Then it is yours," and the same gripping fear that coursed through Catti-brie was evident in Regis's voice.

"Nay, not by me right or me choice. Mithral Hall is no more, Rumble—Regis. Bruenor of Icewind Dale, I am, and have been for two hundred years, though me head's too thick to know it!"

Catti-brie barely heard the next words as she gasped and understood all too clearly what Bruenor was about to do. Regis asked him something she couldn't hear, but understood that it was the very same question whose awful answer screamed at her in her own thoughts.

Bruenor came into clear sight then, running out of the room and charging straight for the gorge. "Here's one from yer tricks, boy!" he yelled, looking at the small side chamber concealing Catti-brie and Wulfgar. "But when me mind's to jumping on the back of a worm, I ain't about to miss!"

There it was, spoken openly, a declaration of the ultimate sacrifice for the sake of the rest of them, trapped deep in the bowels of the caverns once known as Mithral Hall by a great dragon of shadow.

"Bruenor!" Catti-brie heard herself cry, though she was hardly conscious of speaking, so numbed was she by the realization that she was about to lose the dwarf, her beloved adoptive father, the great Bruenor who had served as the foundation of her entire life, the strength of Catti-brie Battlehammer.

The world moved in slow motion for the young woman at that terrible moment, as Bruenor sprinted across the floor to the gorge, reaching over his shoulder to set his cloak afire—and under it was a keg of oil!

The dwarf didn't waver and didn't slow as he reached the lip and went over, axe high, back aflame.

Compulsion and terror combined to drag Catti-brie over to that ledge, arriving at the same time as Regis, both gawking down at the burning dwarf, locked upon the back of the great shadow dragon.

Bruenor had not wavered, but his actions had taken all the strength from Catti-brie, to be sure! She could hardly hold herself upright as she watched her father die, giving his life so that she, Wulfgar, and Regis could cross the gorge and escape the darkness of Mithral Hall.

But she'd never find the strength to make it, she feared, and Bruenor would die in vain.

Wulfgar was beside her then, grimacing against the magical despair, fighting through it with the determination of a barbarian of Icewind Dale. Catti-brie could hardly comprehend his intent as he lifted his wondrous warhammer high and flung it down at the dragon.

"Are ye mad?" she cried, grabbing at him.

"Take up your bow," he told her, and he was Wulfgar again, freed of the dragon's insidious spell. "If a true friend of Bruenor's you be, then let him not fall in vain!"

A true friend? The words hit Catti-brie hard, reminding her poignantly that she was so much more than a friend to that dwarf, her father, the anchor of her life.

She knew that Wulfgar was right, and took up her bow in shaking hands, and sighted her target through tear-filled eyes.

She couldn't help Bruenor. She couldn't save him from the choice he had made—the choice that had possibly saved the three of them.

It was the toughest shot she had ever had to make, but she had to make it, for Bruenor's sake.

The silver-flashing arrow streaked away from Taulmaril, its lightning flash filling Catti-brie's wet eyes.

* * * * *

Someone grabbed her and pulled her arms down to her side. She heard the hiss of a distant whisper, but could make out no words, nor could she see the one whose touch she felt.

It was Drizzt, she knew from the tenderness and strength in those delicate hands.

But Drizzt was lost to her, to them all. It made no sense.

And Bruenor. . . .

But the gorge was gone, the dragon was gone, her father was gone, all the world was gone, replaced by that land of brown mists and crawling, shadowy beasts, coming at her, clawing at her.

They could not reach her, they could not hurt her, but Catti-brie found little comfort in the emptiness. She felt nothing, was aware of nothing but the crawling, misshapen, ugly forms in a land she did not recognize.

In a place where she was completely alone.

And worse than that, worst of all, a line of division between two realities so narrow and blurry that the sheer incongruence of it all stole from Catti-brie something much more personal than her friends and familiar surroundings.

She tried to resist, tried to focus on the feeling of those strong arms around her—it had to be Drizzt!—but she realized that she couldn't even feel the grasp any longer, if it was there.

The huddled images began to blur. The two worlds competed with flashing scenes in her mind and a discordant cacophony of disconnected sounds, a clash of two realities from which there was no escape.

She fell within herself, trying to hold on to her memories, her reality, her individuality.

But there was nothing to hold onto, no grounding pole to remind her of anything, of Catti-brie, even.

She had no cogent thought and no clear memories, and no self-awareness.

She was so utterly lost that she didn't even know that she was utterly lost.

* * * * *

A speck of bright orange found its way past Danica's closed eyelid, knifing through the blackness that had taken her senses. Wearily, she managed to crack open that eye, to be greeted by the sunrise, the brilliant orb just showing its upper edge in the east, in the V-shaped crook between two mountains. It almost seemed to Danica as if those distant mountains were guiding the light directly to her, to her eyes, to awaken her.

The events of the previous day played out in her thoughts, and she couldn't begin to sort out where dreams had ended and awful reality had begun.

Or had it all been a dream?

But then why was she lying in a canyon beside a great cliff?

Slowly the woman started to unwind it all, and the darkness receded.

She pulled herself up to her elbows, or tried to until waves of agony in her shoulder laid her low once more. Wincing against the pain, her eyes tightly closed, Danica recalled the fall, the tumble through the trees, then she back-tracked from there to the scene atop the cliff in the lair of the undead dragon.

Ivan was dead.

The weight of that hit Danica hard. She heard again the stomp of the dracolich and saw once more the splattering flesh flying about the cavern. She thought of all the times she had seen Ivan with her kids, the doting uncle offering the wisdom wrought of tough lessons, unlike the doting Pikel, who was so much softer-edged than his brother.

"Pikel," she whispered into the grass, overwhelmed by the thought of telling him about Ivan.

The mention of Pikel brought Danica's thoughts careening back to her own children, who were out, somewhere, with the dwarf.

She opened her eyes—the lower rim of the sun was visible, the morning moving along.

Her children were in trouble. That notion seemed inescapable. They were either in trouble or the danger had already found them and taken them, and that, Danica would not allow herself to accept.

With a growl of defiance, the monk pulled up to one arm and tucked her legs under her, then threw herself up and back into a kneeling position, her left arm hanging limp, not quite at her side but a bit behind her. She couldn't turn her head against the pain to look at her shoulder, but she knew it was dislocated.

That wouldn't do.

Danica scanned the area behind her, the stone of the cliff wall. With a determined nod, she leaped to her feet, and before the pain could slow her, she rushed toward the wall, jumped into the air, and turned as she descended, slamming the back of her injured shoulder against the stone.

She heard a loud popping sound and knew it was a prelude to agony. Indeed, the waves that came at her had her doubled over and vomiting.

But she could see her shoulder, aligned once more, and the pain fast subsided. She could even move her arm again, though the slightest motion hurt badly.

She stood leaning against the stone wall for a long while, falling within herself to find a place of calm against the furious storm that roiled in her battered form.

When she at last opened her eyes, she first focused upon one of the fallen crawlers, flattened and splattered against the ground. She managed to look up behind her, up the cliff, thinking of the dracolich and what she had to do to warn those who might help her defeat the beast.

She looked south, guided by her mothering instincts, toward the road to Carradoon and her children, and there she desperately wanted to go. But she focused on an area not so far to the south, trying to get a sense of the valley in proportion to the direct north-south trail to Spirit Soaring.

Danica nodded, recognizing that she wouldn't have to cross the mountainous barrier to find that road. Fairly certain of her location—she was in a deep valley several miles from the cathedral—she started away on unsteady legs, her ankle threatening to roll under her with each step.

Soon after, she was leaning on a walking stick, fighting the pain and dreading the trail up to her home. The road was much steeper than the trail from Carradoon, and she toyed with the idea of continuing all the way around to the port city, then using the more passable pathways instead.

She couldn't help but laugh at herself for that feeble justification. She'd lose a day and more of travel time taking that route, a day and more Cadderly and the others didn't have to spare.

She came upon the north-south road some time after highsun, her strength sapped, her clothes sticking to her with sweat. Again she looked southeast toward unseen Carradoon, and thought of her children. She closed her eyes and turned south, then looked upon the road home, the road she needed to take for all their sakes.

She recalled that the road continued fairly flat for about a quarter of a mile, then began an onerous climb up into the Snowflakes. She had to make that climb. It was not a choice, but a duty. Cadderly had to know.

And Danica meant to walk all through the night to tell him. She started off at a slow pace, practically dragging one foot and leaning heavily on the walking stick in her right hand, her left arm hanging loose at her side. Every step jolted that shoulder, and so Danica paused and tore off a piece of her already torn shirt, fashioning it into a makeshift sling.

With a sigh of determination, the woman started away again, a little more quickly, but with her strength fast waning.

She lost track of time, but knew the shadows were lengthening around her, then she heard something—a rider or a wagon—approaching from behind. Danica shuffled off the trail and threw herself down behind a bush and a rock, crawling into a place to watch the road behind her. She chewed hard on her bottom lip to keep from gasping out in pain, but even that notion and sensation were soon lost to her as her curious quarry came into view.

She saw the horse first, a skeletal black beast with fire around its hooves. It snorted smoke from its flared nostrils. A hell horse, a nightmare, and as Danica noted the wagon driver—or more particularly, the driver's great, wide-brimmed and plumed hat, and the ebon color of his skin—she remembered him.

"Jarlaxle?" she whispered, and more curious still, he sat with another dark elf Danica surely recognized.

The thought of that rogue Jarlaxle riding along with Drizzt Do'Urden knocked Danica even more emotionally off-balance. How could it be?

And what did it mean, for her and for Cadderly?

As the wagon neared, she made out a couple of heads above the rail of the backboard. Dwarves, obviously. A squeal from the side turned her attention to a third dwarf riding a pig that looked like it grazed on the lower planes right beside the nightmare pulling the wagon.

Danica told herself that it couldn't be Drizzt Do'Urden, and warned herself that it was not out of the realm of possibility that the fiendish Jarlaxle might be behind all of the trouble that had come to Erlkazar. She couldn't risk going to them, she told herself repeatedly as the wagon bounced along the trail, nearing her hiding place.

Despite those very real and grounded reservations, as the wagon rolled up barely ten feet from her, the nightmare snorting flames and pounding the road with its fiery hooves, the desperate woman, realizing instinctively that she was out of options, pulled herself up to her knees and called out for help.

"Lady Danica!" Jarlaxle cried, and Drizzt spoke her name at the same time.

Together the two drow leaped down from the wagon and ran to her, moving to opposite sides of her and falling on bended knee. Together they gently cradled and supported her, and glanced at each other with equal disbelief that anything could have so battered the magnificent warrior-monk.

"What'd'ye know, elf?" one of the dwarves called, climbing from the back of the wagon. "That Cadderly's girl?"

"Lady Danica," Drizzt explained.

"You must . . ." the woman gasped. "You must get me to Cadderly. I must warn him . . ."

Her voice trailed off and she faltered, her consciousness slipping away.

"We will," Drizzt promised. "Rest easy."

* * * * *

Drizzt looked at Jarlaxle, grave concern evident on his face. He wasn't sure Danica could survive the journey.

"I have potions," Jarlaxle assured him, but with less confidence than Drizzt would have hoped for. Besides, who could be sure what effects his potions might produce in such a time of wild magic?

They made Danica as comfortable as they could in the back of the wagon, laying her beside Catti-brie, who sat against the backboard and still seemed totally unaware of her surroundings. Jarlaxle stayed beside the monk, spooning magical healing potions into her mouth, while Bruenor drove the wagon as fast as the nightmare could manage. Drizzt and Pwent ran near flank, fearing that whatever had hit Danica might not be far afield. On Jarlaxle's bidding, Athrogate and the hell boar stayed near, riding just in front of the nightmare.

"It's getting steeper," Bruenor warned a short time later. "Yer horse ain't for liking it."

"The mules are rested now," Jarlaxle replied. "Go as far as we can, then we'll put them back up front."

"Night'll be falling by then."

"Perhaps we should ride through."

Bruenor didn't want to agree, but he found himself nodding despite his reservations.

"Elf?" the dwarf asked, seeing Drizzt approach from some brush to the side of the trail.

"Nothing," Drizzt answered. "I have seen no sign of any monsters, and no trail to be found save Danica's own."

"Well, that's a good thing," Bruenor said. He reached over and grabbed at Drizzt's belt to help the drow hop up the side of the rolling wagon.

"Her breathing is steady," Drizzt noted of Danica, and Jarlaxle nodded.

"The potions have helped," said Jarlaxle. "There is a measure of predictable magic remaining."

"Bah, but she ain't said a word," said Bruenor.

"I've kept her in a stupor," Jarlaxle explained. "For her own sake. A simple enchantment," he added reassuringly when both Drizzt and Bruenor looked at him with suspicion. He pulled from his vest a pendant with a dangling ruby, remarkably like the one worn by Regis.

"Hey, now!" Bruenor protested and pulled hard on the reins, bringing the wagon up short.

"It's not Regis's," Jarlaxle assured him.

"You had his, in Luskan," Drizzt remembered.

"For a time, yes," said Jarlaxle. "Long enough to have my artisans replicate it." As Bruenor and Drizzt continued to stare at him hard, Jarlaxle just shrugged and explained, "It's what I do."

Drizzt and Bruenor looked at each other and sighed.

"I did not steal anything from him, and I could have, easily enough," Jarlaxle argued. "I did not kill him, or you, and I could have—"

"Easily enough," Drizzt had to agree.

"When can you free her of the trance?" Drizzt asked.

Jarlaxle glanced down at Danica, the monk seeming much more at ease, and he started to say, "Soon." Before the word got out of his mouth, Danica's hand shot up and grasped the dangling chain that held the ruby pendant. With a twist and turn that appeared so subtle and simple as she sat up from the wagon bed, she spun the startled Jarlaxle around and jerked the chain behind him, twisting it even more to hold the drow fast in a devastating chokehold.

"You were told never to return, Jarlaxle Baenre," Danica said, her mouth right beside the dark elf's ear.

"Your gratitude overwhelms me, Lady," the drow managed to gasp in reply.

He stiffened as Danica pulled and twisted. "Move your fingers a bit more into position to grasp a weapon, drow," she coaxed. "I can snap your neck as easily as a dry twig."

"A little help?" Jarlaxle whispered to Drizzt.

"Danica, let him go," Drizzt said. "He is not our enemy. Not now."

Danica loosened her grip, just a bit, and stared skeptically at the ranger, then looked to Bruenor.

Drizzt nudged the silent dwarf.

"Good to meet ye at last, Lady Danica," Bruenor said. "King Bruenor Battlehammer, at yer ser—"

Drizzt elbowed him again.

"Aye, let the rat go," Bruenor bade her. " 'Twas Jarlaxle that gived ye the potions that saved yer hide, and he's been a help with me daughter there."

Danica glanced from one to the other, then looked over at Catti-brie. "What's wrong with her?" she asked as she released Jarlaxle, who shifted forward to get away from her.

"I never thought I would see Jarlaxle caught so easily," Drizzt remarked.

"I share your surprise," the mercenary admitted.

Drizzt smiled, briefly enjoying the moment. He came over the rail of the wagon then, stepping past Jarlaxle to go to Danica, who leaned against the tailgate.

"I'll not underestimate that one again," Jarlaxle promised quietly.

"You must get me to Spirit Soaring," Danica said, and Drizzt nodded.

"That is where we were going," he explained. "Catti-brie was touched by the falling Weave—some kind of blue fire. She is trapped within her own mind, it seems, and in a dark place of huddled, crawling creatures."

Danica perked up at that description.

"You have seen them?" Jarlaxle remarked.

"Long-armed, short-legged—almost no-legged—gray-skinned beasts attacked Spirit Soaring in force last night," she explained. "I was out scouting . . ." Her voice trailed off as she gave a great sigh.

"Ivan Bouldershoulder is dead," she said. Bruenor cried out and Drizzt winced. From the side of the wagon, Thibbledorf Pwent wailed. "The dragon—a dracolich, an undead dragon . . . and something more . . ."

"A dracolich?" Jarlaxle said.

"Dead dragon walking—dead dragon talking, dead dragon furious, I'm thinking that curious!" Athrogate rhymed, and Thibbledorf Pwent nodded in appreciation, drawing a scowl from Bruenor.

A dumbfounded Danica stared at the bizarre Athrogate.

"You have to admit that one does not see a dracolich every day," Jarlaxle deadpanned.

Danica seemed even more at a loss.

"Something stranger still, you mentioned?" Jarlaxle prompted.

"Its touch is death," the monk explained. "I found it by following a trail of utter devastation, a complete withering of everything the beast had touched. Trees, grass, everything."

"Never heared o' such a thing," said Bruenor.

"When I saw the beast, gigantic and terrible, I knew my guess to be correct. Its mere touch is death. It is death incarnate, and something more—a horn in its head, glowing with power," Danica went on, her eyes closed as if she had to force herself to remember things she did not want to recall. "I think it was . . ."

"Crenshinibon, the Crystal Shard," said Jarlaxle, nodding with every word.

"Yes."

"That durned thing again," Bruenor grumbled. "So there ye go, elf. Ye didn't break it."

"I did," Jarlaxle corrected. "And that is part of the problem, I fear."

Bruenor just shook his hairy head.

Danica pointed to a tall peak not far behind them and to the north. "He controls them." She looked directly at Jarlaxle. "I believe the dragon is Hephaestus, the great red wyrm whose breath destroyed the artifact, or so we thought."

"It is indeed Hephaestus," Jarlaxle assured her.

"Ye think ye might be tellin' us what ye're about anytime soon?" Bruenor grumbled.

"I already told you my fears," Jarlaxle said. "The dragon and the liches, somehow freed of the prison artifact of their own creation—"

"The Crystal Shard," said Danica, and she tapped her forehead. "Here, on the dracolich."

"Joined by the magic of the collapsing Weave," said Jarlaxle, "merged by the collision of worlds."

Danica looked at him, incredulous.

"I know not either, Lady Danica," Jarlaxle explained. "It's all a guess. But this is all related, of that I am certain." He looked at Catti-brie, her eyes wide open but unseeing. "Her affliction, these beasts, the dragon risen from the dead . . . all of it . . . all part of the same catastrophe, the breadth of which we still do not know."

"And so we have come to find out," said Drizzt. "To bring Catti-brie to Cadderly in the hope that he might help her."

"And I'm thinking that ye'll be needin' our help, too," Bruenor said to Danica.

Danica could only sigh and nod in helpless agreement. She glanced at the distant cliff, the lair of the dracolich and the Crystal Shard, the grave of Ivan Bouldershoulder. She tried not to look past that point, but she couldn't help herself. She feared for her children.

CHAPTER

It was more than independent thought, Yharaskrik knew. It was independent desire.

Such a thing could not be tolerated. The seven liches that had created the Crystal Shard were represented by the singular power of Crenshinibon only. They had no say in the matter, and no opinions or wants that were pertinent.

But to the perceptive illithid, there was no missing the desire behind Fetchigrol's request. The creature wasn't acting purely on expediency or any compulsion to please its three masters joined as the Ghost King. Fetchigrol wanted something.

And Crenshinibon's addition to the internal debate brewing within the Ghost King was nothing but supportive of the lich-turned-specter.

Yharaskrik telepathically appealed to Hephaestus to deny the lich, and tried to imbue a sense of the depth of his trepidation, but he had to walk a fine line, not wanting the Crystal Shard to recognize that concern.

The illithid couldn't tell whether the dragon caught its subtle inflection of thought, or whether Hephaestus, still less than enamored with Yharaskrik, simply didn't care. The dragon's response came back in the form of eagerness, exactly as Fetchigrol had requested.

"How greatly might we tap the minions of the reformed Shadowfell before we cease to be their masters in this, our world?" Yharaskrik said aloud.

Hephaestus wrestled full control of the dracolich's mouth to respond. "You fear these huddled lumps of flesh?"

"There is more to the Shadowfell than the crawlers," Yharaskrik replied after a brief struggle to regain the use of the voice. "Better that we use the undead of our plane for our armies—their numbers are practically unlimited."

"And they are ineffective!" the dracolich roared, shaking the stone of the chamber. "Mindless . . ."

"But controllable," the illithid interrupted, the words twisting as both creatures fought for physical control.

"We are the Ghost King!" Hephaestus bellowed. "We are supreme."

Yharaskrik started to fight back, but paused as he considered Fetchigrol standing before him and nodding. He could feel the satisfaction coming from the shadowy creature, and he knew that Crenshinibon had sided with Hephaestus, that permission had been given to Fetchigrol to fly back to Carradoon and raise a great army of crawlers to catch and slaughter those people who had fled into the tunnels.

The satisfaction of that creature! Why could not Hephaestus understand the danger in any independent emotions emanating from one of the seven? They were to have no satisfaction, other than in serving, but Fetchigrol was acting on his own personal ego, not a compulsion to serve the greater host. He had been shown up by Solmé, who went to the Shadowfell to raise an army while Fetchigrol merely reanimated dead flesh to do his bidding. The escape of so many from Carradoon had added to that sense of failure in the specter, and so the creature was trying to rectify the situation.

But the specter should not have cared. Why could Hephaestus not understand that?

We are greater with competent generals, came a thought, and Yharaskrik knew it to be Crenshinibon, who would not speak aloud with the dragon's voice.

"They would not dare cross us," Hephaestus agreed.

Let us use their anger.

To what possible gain? Yharaskrik thought, but was careful to shield from the others. What gain would they garner by pursuing the fleeing Carradden? Why should any of them waste their moments concerned about the fate of refugees?

"Your caution grows wearying," the dracolich said as Fetchigrol exited the cavern, bound for Carradoon. Yharaskrik's initial recognition that it was Hephaestus speaking was given pause by the word choice and the timbre of the voice, reflecting more a reasoned remark than the bellow typical of Hephaestus. "Can we not simply destroy for the enjoyment of the act?"

The illithid had no physical body of its own, so it possessed no heels, but Yharaskrik surely fell back on its heels at that revealing moment. It had not adequately shielded its concerns from the other two. The mind flayer had no place to hide from . . .

From which?

The Ghost King, the mind of the dragon answered, reading every thought as if it were his own.

Yharaskrik understood at that moment that the bond between Hephaestus and Crenshinibon was tightening, that they were truly becoming one being, one mind.

The illithid couldn't even begin to hide its fear that the same fate awaited it. As a mind flayer, Yharaskrik was well-versed in the notion of a hive mind—in its Underdark homeland, hundreds of its kind would join together in a common receptacle of intelligence and philosophy and theory-craft. But those were other illithids, equal beings of equal intelligence.

"And the Ghost King is greater than your kin," the dracolich's voice answered. "Is that your fear?"

Its every thought was open to them!

"There is a place for you, Yharaskrik," the Ghost King promised. "Hephaestus is the instinct, the anger, and the physical power. Crenshinibon is the collection of near-eternal wisdom and the dispassion—hence judgment—of a true god. Yharaskrik is the freedom of far-reaching projection and the understanding of the surrealism of worlds joined."

One word, buried in the middle of that declaration of power, revealed to Yharaskrik the truth: judgment. Of the parts of the proposed whole, judgment sat atop the hierarchy, and so it was Crenshinibon that meant to hold its identity. The dragon would be the reactive, the illithid would serve as the informative, and Crenshinibon would control it all.

And so it was Crenshinibon, Yharaskrik realized in that awful moment, who was granting the liches a greater measure of autonomy, and only because the Crystal Shard knew with full confidence that they would ever remain slaves to it, their ultimate creation.

Yharaskrik's only chance would be to get through to Hephaestus, to convince the dragon that he would lose his own identity in that ultimately subservient role.

In response to that unhidden notion, the dracolich laughed, a horrid, scraping noise.

* * * * *

Solmé had bested Fetchigrol. Centuries before, they and five others had joined in common purpose, a complete unification into a singular artifact of great power and infinite duration. Fetchigrol wasn't supposed to care that Solmé had outdone him. Crenshinibon's explanation had been instructive, not a chastisement.

The apparition, an extension of something greater than Fetchigrol, a tool for the furthering of Crenshinibon and nothing more, wasn't supposed to care.

But he did. When Fetchigrol stood at the docks of ruined Carradoon later that same night and reached through the planes to the Shadowfell, he felt elation. His own, not Crenshinibon's.

And when his consciousness returned to Toril, rift in hand, and tore open the divide, he took great satisfaction—his own, not Crenshinibon's—in knowing that the next instructive lecture would be aimed at Solmé and not at himself.

Huddled crawlers poured through the rift. Fetchigrol didn't control them, but he guided them, showing them the little inlet just north of the docks, where the waters of Impresk Lake calmed and the tunnel complex began. The crawlers didn't fear the tunnels. They liked the dark recesses, and no creature in all the multiverse more enjoyed the hunt than the ravenous, fleshy beasts of the dark Shadowfell.

More came through as the rift swirled in on itself and started to mend, to return to the stasis of natural order.

Fetchigrol, Crenshinibon's blessing clear in his eager thoughts, tore it open wide again.

And he ripped it open again when it began to diminish sometime later, knowing all the while that each reopening weakened the fabric of separation between the two worlds. That fabric, that reality of what had always been, was the only real means of control. Gradually, the third tear began to mend.

Fetchigrol tore it wide yet again!

Fewer crawlers came through with each rift, for the shadowy gray region the apparitions had been inhabiting was nearly emptied of the things.

Fetchigrol, who would not lose to Solmé, reached deeper into the Shadow-fell. He recklessly widened his call to the far edges of the gray plain, to regions he could not see.

He never saw or heard it coming, for the beast was a creature of shadow, and silent as such. A black cloud descended over the apparition, fully engulfing him.

In that terrible instant, he knew he had failed. It didn't matter the issue, for there was no anchor to the specific disaster.

Just failure. Utter, complete, and irrevocable. Fetchigrol felt it profoundly. It devoured any thoughts he might have for the situation at hand.

The shadow dragon couldn't get through the rift, but it managed to snake its head out far enough to snap its great jaws over the despairing apparition.

And Fetchigrol had no escape. To plane shift would merely place him more fully before the devouring dragon on the other side of the tear. Nor did he have any desire to escape, for the despair wrought by the shadow dragon's black cloud of breath made Fetchigrol understand that obliteration was preferable.

And so he was obliterated.

* * * * *

In the Shadowfell, the dragon receded, but marked the spot of the tear, expecting that soon it might widen enough for it to pass through. When it left, other beasts found their way to the opening.

Nightwings, giant black bats, opened wide their leathery wings and took flight above the ruins of Carradoon, eager to feast on the lighter flesh of the material world.

Fearsome dread wraiths, humanoid, emaciated, and cloaked in tattered dark rags, who could leach the life-force of a victim with a touch, crawled through in hunting packs.

And a nightwalker, a giant, hairless humanoid twenty feet tall, all sinewy and with the strength of a mountain giant, squeezed its way through the rift and onto the shores of Impresk Lake.

* * * * *

In the cave on the cliff, the Ghost King knew.

Fetchigrol was gone, his energy winked out, lost to them.

Yharaskrik was an illithid. Illithids were creature of callous logic and did not gloat, but dragons were creatures of emotion, and so when the illithid pointed out that it had been right in its condemnation of Fetchigrol's plan, a wall of rage came back at it.

From both Hephaestus and Crenshinibon.

For a moment, Yharaskrik didn't understand the Crystal Shard's agreement with the volatile beast. Crenshinibon, too, was an artifact of pragmatic and logical thinking. Unemotional, like the illithid.

But unlike Yharaskrik, Crenshinibon was also ambitious.

And so Yharaskrik knew at that moment that the bond would not hold, that the triumvirate in the dracolich's consciousness would not and could not remain tenable. It thought to find a host outside the dragon's body, but dismissed the notion immediately, realizing that nothing was as mighty as the dracolich, after all, and Hephaestus would not suffer the illithid to survive.

It had to fight.

Hephaestus was all anger and venom, that wall of rage, and the illithid went at him methodically, poking holes with logic and reasoning, reminding its opponent of the inarguable truths, for those truths alone—the recklessness of opening wide a gate to an unknown plane, and the needed caution in continuing against a foe as powerful as the combined might of Spirit Soaring—could serve as a premise on which to build its case.

By every measure of the principles of debate, Yharaskrik was far beyond its opponent. The simple truth and logic were on its side. The illithid poked its holes and appealed to reason over rage, repeatedly, thinking to turn the favor of Crenshinibon, who, he feared, would ultimately decide the outcome of their struggle.

The battle within became a wild assault without, as Hephaestus's dracolich form thrashed and clawed at the stone, breathed fire that melted stone and minion alike, and bull-rushed walls, shaking the entire mountain in great tremors.

Gradually, Hephaestus began to play out his rage, and the internal battle diminished as it became a session of dialogue and discourse. With Yharaskrik leading the way, the Ghost King began to sort how it might correct for the loss of Fetchigrol. The Ghost King began to accept the past and look to the next move in the wider, and more important struggle.

Yharaskrik took some small comfort in the victory, fully recognizing that it might be temporary in nature and fully expecting that it would battle Hephaestus many more times before things were finally settled.

The illithid turned its thoughts and arguments to the very real possibility that Fetchigrol's demise indicated that the apparition had reached too far into what had once been the Plane of Shadow. But for reasons still unknown to the Ghost King, the Plane of Shadow had become something more, something bigger and more dangerous. It also seemed to be somehow moving closer to the Prime Material Plane, and in that event, what consequences might result?

Crenshinibon seemed not to care, reasoning that out of chaos, the Ghost King could only grow stronger.

And if a dangerous and too-powerful organized force had come through the rift, the Ghost King could simply fly away. The Crystal Shard, Yharaskrik understood implicitly, was far more concerned about the loss of two of the seven.

For Hephaestus, there remained only unrelenting and simmering anger, and most of all, the dragon's consciousness growled at the thought of not being able to exact revenge on those who had so ruined the beast in life.

While Yharaskrik thought of times to come and how to shape the wider path, and Crenshinibon considered the remaining five and whether any repairs were called for, the dragon only pressed, incessantly, for an immediate assault on Spirit Soaring.

They were not one, but three, and to Yharaskrik, the walls separating the triumvirate that was the Ghost King seemed as impenetrably thick and daunting as ever. And from that came the illithid's inescapable conclusion that it must find a way to dominate, to force oneness under its own commanding will and intellect.

And it hoped it could hide that dangerous ambition from its too-intimate fellows.

CHAPTER

19

W e are nothing! There is nothing!" the priest screamed, storming about the audience hall in Spirit Soaring, accentuating every word with an angry stomp of his foot. His point was furthered by the blood matting his hair and caked about the side of his face and shoulder, a wound that looked worse than it was. Of the five who had been with him out and about the Snowflakes, he had been the most fortunate by far, for the only other survivor had lost a leg and the other seemed doomed to amputation—and only if the poor woman even survived.

"Sit down, Menlidus, you old fool!" one of his peers yelled. "Do you think this tirade helpful?"

Cadderly hoped Menlidus, a fellow priest of Deneir, would take that advice, but he doubted it, and since the man was more than a decade his senior—and looked at least three decades older than Cadderly—he hoped he wouldn't have to intervene to forcibly silence the angry man. Besides, Cadderly understood the frustration behind the priest's rant, and didn't wholly dismiss his despairing conclusions. Cadderly, too, had gone to Deneir and feared that his god had been lost to him forever, as if Deneir had somehow simply written himself into the numerical maze that was the *Metatext*.

"I am the fool?" Menlidus said, stopping his shouting and pacing, and tapping a finger to his chest as he painted a wry smile on his face. "I have called pillars of flame down upon those who are foes of our god. Or have you forgotten, Donrey?"

"Most surely, I have not," Donrey replied. "Nor have I forgotten the Time of Troubles, or any of the many desperate situations we have faced before, and have endured."

Cadderly appreciated those words, as apparently, he saw in looking around at the large gathering, did everyone else in the room.

Menlidus, though, began to laugh. "Not like this," he said.

"We cannot make that judgment until we know what this silence is truly all about."

"It is about the folly of our lives, friend," the defeated Menlidus said quietly. "All of us, and do look at us! Artists! Painters! Poets! Man and woman, dwarf and elf, who seek deeper meaning in art and in faith. Artists, I say, who evoke emotion and profundity with our paintings and our scribblings, who cleverly place words for the effect dramatic." His snicker cut deep. "Or are we illusionists, I wonder?"

"You do not believe that," said Donrey.

"Who believe our own illusions," Menlidus qualified. "Because we have to. Because the alternative, the idea that there is nothing more, that it is all a creation of imagination to maintain sanity, is too awful to contemplate, is it not? Because the truth that these gods we worship are not immortal beings, but tricksters promising us eternity to extract from us fealty, is ultimately jarring and inspiring despair, is it not?"

"I think we have heard enough, brother," said a woman, a renowned mage who also was possessed of significant clerical prowess.

"Have we?"

"Yes," she said, and there was no mistaking the edge to her voice, not quite threatening but certainly leading in that direction.

"We are priests, one and all," Menlidus said.

"Not so," several wizards pointed out, and again the bloody priest gave a little laugh.

"Yes, so," Menlidus argued. "What we call divine, you call arcane—our altars are not so different!"

Cadderly couldn't help but wince at that, for the notion that all magic emanated from one source brought him back to his younger days in the Edificant Library. Then he had been an agnostic priest, and he too had wondered if the arcane and the divine were no more than different labels for the same energy.

"Save that ours accepts the possibility of change, as it is not rooted in dogma!" one wizard cried, and the volume began to rise about the chamber, wizards and priests lining up against each other in verbal sparring.

"Then perhaps I speak not to you," Menlidus said after Cadderly locked him with a scowl. "But for us priests, are we not those, above all others, who claim to speak the truth? The divine truth?"

"Enough, brother, I beg," Cadderly said then, knowing where Menlidus was going despite the man's temporary calm, and not liking it at all.

He moved toward Menlidus slowly, wearing a carefully maintained expression of serenity. Having heard nothing from Danica or his missing children, Cadderly was anything but serene. His gut churned and his thoughts whirled.

"Do we not?" Menlidus shouted at him. "Cadderly of Deneir, above all others, who created Spirit Soaring on the good word and power of Deneir, should not doubt my claim!"

"It is more complex than that," said Cadderly.

"Does not your experience show that our precepts are not foolish dogma, but rather divine truth?" Menlidus argued. "If you were but a conduit for Deneir in the construction of this awe-inspiring cathedral, this library for all the world, do you not laugh in the face of such doubts as expressed by our secular friends?"

"We all have our moments of doubt," Cadderly said.

"We cannot!" Menlidus exclaimed, stamping his foot. That movement seemed to break him, though, a sudden weariness pulling his broad shoulders down in a profound slump. "And yet, we must, for we are shown the truth." He looked across the room at poor Dahlania, one leg gone, as she lay near death. "I begged for a blessing of healing," he mumbled. "Even a simple one—any spell at all to alleviate her pain. Deneir did not answer that plea."

"There is more to this sad tale," Cadderly said quietly. "You cannot blame—"

"All my life has been in service to him. And this one moment when I call upon him for my most desperate need, he ignores me."

Cadderly heaved a sigh and placed a comforting hand on Menlidus's shoulder, but the man grew agitated and shrugged that touch away.

"Because we are priests of *nothing!*" Menlidus shouted to the room. "We feign wisdom and insight, and deceive ourselves into seeing ultimate truth in the lines of a painting or the curves of a sculpture. We place meaning where there is none, I say, and if there truly are any gods left, they must surely derive great amusement from our pitiful delusions."

Cadderly didn't have to look around the room at the weary and beleaguered faces to understand the cancer that was spreading among them, a trial of will and faith that threatened to break them all. He thought to order Menlidus out of the room, to chastise the man loudly and forcefully, but he dismissed that idea. Menlidus wasn't creating the illness, but was merely shouting it to the rafters.

Cadderly couldn't find Deneir—his prayers, too, went unanswered. He feared that Deneir had left him forever, that the too-inquisitive god had written himself into the Weave or had become lost in its eternal tangle. Cadderly had found power, though, in the fight against the fleshy beasts of shadow, casting spells as mighty as any he might have asked from Deneir.

But those spells, he believed—he feared—hadn't come from the one he had known as Deneir. He didn't know what being, if any being, had bestowed within him the power to consecrate the ground beneath his feet with such blessed magic.

And that was most troubling of all.

For Menlidus's point was well taken: If the gods were not immortal, then was their place for their followers any more lasting?

For if the gods were not powerful and wise enough to defeat the calamity that had come to Faerûn, then what hope for men?

And worse, *what was the point of it all?* Cadderly dismissed that devastating thought almost as soon as it came to him, but it indeed fluttered through his mind, and through the minds of all those gathered there.

Menlidus spat his devastating litany one emphatic last time. "Priests of nothing."

* * * * *

"We are leaving," Menlidus said to Cadderly early the next morning, after an eerily quiet night. That respite had not set well with poor Cadderly, however, for Danica had not yet returned.

No word from his wife, no word of his missing children, and perhaps worst of all, Cadderly still found no answers to his desperate calls to Deneir.

"We?" he replied.

Menlidus motioned through the door, across the hall and into a side chamber, where a group of about a dozen men and women stood dressed for the road.

"You're all leaving?" Cadderly asked, incredulous. "Spirit Soaring is under a cloud of assault and you would desert—"

"Deneir deserted me. I did not desert him," Menlidus replied sharply, but with a calm surety. "As their gods deserted them, and as the Weave abandoned three of them, wizards all, who find their life's pursuit a sad joke, as is mine."

"It didn't take much of a test to shake your faith, Menlidus," Cadderly scolded him, though he wanted to take the words back as soon as he heard them escape his mouth. The poor priest had suffered a failing of magic at the very worst moment, after all, and had watched a friend die because of that failure. Cadderly knew that he was wrong to judge such despair, even if he didn't agree with the man's conclusion.

"Perhaps not, Cadderly, Chosen of Nothing," Menlidus replied. "I only know what I feel and believe—or no longer believe."

"Where are you going?"

"Carradoon first, then to Cormyr, I expect."

Cadderly perked up at that.

"Your children, of course," said Menlidus. "Fear not, my old friend, for though I no longer share your enthusiasm for our faith, I will not forget my friendship to Cadderly Bonaduce and his family. We will seek out your children, do not doubt, and make sure that they are safe."

Cadderly nodded, and wanted nothing more than that. Still, he felt compelled to point out the obvious problem. "Your road is a dangerous one. Perhaps you should remain here—and I'll not lie to you, we need you here. We barely repelled that last attack, and have no idea of what may come against us next. Our dark enemies are out there, in force, as many of our patrols painfully learned."

"We're strong enough to punch our way through them," Menlidus replied. "I would counsel you to convince everyone to come with us. Abandon Spirit Soaring—this is a library and a cathedral, not a fortress."

"This is the work of Deneir. I can no more abandon it than I can abandon that who I am."

"A priest of nothing?"

Cadderly sighed, and Menlidus patted him on the shoulder, a symbolic reversal of fortunes. "They should all leave with us, Cadderly, my old friend.

For all our sakes, we should go down to Carradoon as one mighty group. Escape this place, I counsel, and raise an army to come back and—"

"No."

Menlidus looked at him hard, but there was no arguing against that tone of finality in Cadderly's voice.

"My place is Spirit Soaring," Cadderly said.

"To the bitter end?"

Cadderly didn't blink.

"You would condemn the others here to the same fate?" Menlidus asked.

"Their choices are their own to make. I do think we're safer here than out there on the open trails. How many patrol parties met with disaster, your own included? Here, we have a chance to defend. Out there, we're fighting on a battlefield of our enemy's choosing."

Menlidus considered Cadderly for just a moment longer, then snorted and waved his hand, motioning to the people across the hall. They hoisted bags, shields, and weapons and followed the man down the corridor.

"We're left with less than fifty to defend Spirit Soaring," Ginance remarked, coming to Cadderly as the angry fallen priest departed. "If the crawling beasts come at us with the ferocity of the first fight, we will be hard-pressed."

"We are more ready for an attack now," Cadderly replied. "Implements are more reliable than spells, it would seem."

"That is the consensus, yes," said Ginance. "Potions and wands did not fail in the field, even as spellcasting misfired or fell empty."

"We have many potions. We have wands and rods and staves, enchanted weapons and shields," said Cadderly. "Make certain that they are properly distributed as you sort our defenses. Power to every wall."

Ginance nodded and started away, but Cadderly stopped her by adding, "Catch up to Menlidus and offer him all that we can spare to take with him on his journey. I fear that his party will need all that we can give, and a fair measure of good luck, to get down the mountainside."

Ginance paused at the door, then smiled and nodded. "Simply because he abandons Deneir does not mean that Deneir should abandon him," she said.

Cadderly managed a weak smile at that, all the while fearing that Deneir, though perhaps inadvertently and through circumstances beyond his control, had already done exactly that, to all of them.

But Cadderly had no time to think about any of that, he reminded himself, no time to consider his absent wife and missing children. He had found some measure of powerful magic in his moment of need. For all their sakes, he had to learn the source of that magic.

He had barely begun his contemplation when shouts interrupted him.

Their enemies had not waited for sunset.

Cadderly rushed down the stairs, strapping on his weapons as he went, nearly running over Ginance at the bottom.

"Menlidus," she cried, pointing to the main doors, which stood open.

Cadderly ran there and fell back with a gasp. Menlidus and all the others of his band were returning, walking stiff-legged, arms hanging at their sides, vacant stares through dead eyes—for those who still had their eyes.

All around the zombies came the crawling beasts, dragging and hopping at full speed.

"Fight well!" Cadderly called out to his defenders. All about the first and second floors of Spirit Soaring, manning every wall, window, and doorway, priests and wizards lifted shields and weapons, wands and scrolls.

* * * * *

A couple of hundred yards ahead, a burst of flames erupted far above them—above the branches of distant trees on a high ridge on the mountain road. Drizzt, Jarlaxle, and Bruenor sat up straight on the wagon's jockey box, startled, and behind them, Danica stirred.

"That's Spirit Soaring," Drizzt remarked.

"What is?" Danica asked, scooting forward to the back of the seat and peering up between Drizzt and Bruenor.

A column of black smoke began to climb into the sky above the tree line.

"It is," Danica said breathlessly. "Drive them faster!"

Drizzt glanced at Danica and had to blink in amazement at how quickly the woman had healed. Her training and discipline, combined with Jarlaxle's potions and monk abilities, had restored the woman greatly.

Drizzt made a mental note to speak with Danica about her training, but he ended the line of thought abruptly and nudged Bruenor. Understanding his intent, the dwarf nodded and jumped off the side of the wagon, with Drizzt fast following. Bruenor called for Pwent as they ran around the back, setting themselves against the tailgate.

"Push them hard!" Drizzt called to Jarlaxle when the three were set, and the drow snapped the reins and clicked at the mules, while the three in back put their shoulders to the wagon and shoved with all their strength, legs pumping furiously, helping the wagon up the steep incline.

Danica was out beside them in a heartbeat, and though she winced when she braced her injured shoulder against the wagon, she kept pushing.

As they crested a ridge, Jarlaxle shouted, "Jump!" and the four grabbed on tightly and lifted their legs as the wagon gained speed. It was a short-lived burst, though, for another steep incline lay before them. The mules strained, the foursome strained, too, and the wagon moved along slowly.

The huddled forms of crawlers crept out on the trail before them, but before Jarlaxle could yell out a warning, another form, a dwarf on a fiery hell boar, burst through the brush on the opposite side of the road, wisps of smoke rising from the branches behind him. Athrogate plowed into the crawlers, the demon boar hopping and stomping its hooves, sending out rings of fiery bursts. One crawler was gored and sent flying, another trampled under smoking hooves, but a third, near the other side of the road, had time to react and use its powerful arms to twist and leap up high above the snorting boar, right in the path of Athrogate.

"Bwahaha!" the dwarf howled, his morningstars already spinning in opposing circles.

The weapons swung around at the monster simultaneously, right low, left high, both connecting to send the crawling thing into an aerial sidelong spin. Athrogate expertly curled his right arm under his left in the follow-through, then reversed his momentum and snapped that weapon back in a fierce backhand that smacked the creature in its ugly face—and to add a finishing touch, the dwarf enacted the morningstar's magic after the first strike, its nubby spikes secreting explosive oil onto the weapon head.

A pop and a flash revealed the magic to the onlookers. Even without the explosion, they quickly knew that added power was behind the strike as the creature executed several complete rotations before it hit the ground.

Hardly slowing, Athrogate charged his mount right through the brush on the far side, morningstars spinning, boar snorting fire.

He emerged after the wagon had passed, chasing and battering a crawler with every step, and as the creature fell dead, Athrogate squeezed his legs and twisted the boar into line, running fast after his companions.

He caught up to them just as the wagon came over the last ridge, the road twisting through a narrow tree line onto the open grounds of the magnificent Spirit Soaring.

The lawn was crawling with fleshy beasts, as were Spirit Soaring's walls. The upper corner of the building was burning, belching black smoke from several windows.

Athrogate skidded his boar to a stop beside Bruenor and Pwent. "Come on, ye dwarfs, and kick yer heels! We'll give 'em a beatin' that'll make 'em squeal!"

Bruenor gave only a cursory glance at the nodding Drizzt before scrambling around the side of the wagon bed, leaping up, and retrieving his many-notched axe. Pwent already carried his weapons, and was first to Athrogate's side.

"Ye protect me king!" Pwent demanded of him, and Athrogate gave a hearty "Bwahaha!" in reply. That was good enough for Thibbledorf Pwent, whose idea of "defend" was to charge ahead so quickly and madly that the many enemies flanking him could never catch up.

"Ye keepin' the pig?" Bruenor asked as he rambled up.

"Aye, she's a good way to introduce meself!"

Athrogate spearheaded the three-dwarf wedge, trotting his boar at a pace that the two runners could easily match.

Behind them, Jarlaxle kept firm control of the mules and the wagon, and looked to Danica and Drizzt.

"To the side door on the right side!" Danica called to the dwarves.

Drizzt, scimitars drawn, ran up beside Jarlaxle.

"Go, go, go," Danica bade them as she scrambled over the wagon rail and into the bed. "I'll keep the wagon clear and Catti-brie safe."

Drizzt gave her a pleading look, not wanting to drive the helpless Catti-brie into the middle of such a tumultuous fight.

"We've nowhere to run," Jarlaxle said, answering that concern. "We go forward or we go back, but if Cadderly loses here, our fate will surely be the same."

Drizzt nodded and turned to his companion.

"Clear a short path and move up the wagon," Jarlaxle explained. "Clear a bit more and move a bit more."

"When we get into the open, they'll swarm," Drizzt said with another nervous glance at the wagon bed, which held his defenseless beloved.

"More to kill, and more quickly, then," Jarlaxle said with a tip of his hat—a tip that left the giant feather in his hand. He snapped the dagger from his enchanted bracer into the same hand, then flicked his wrist several times to elongate the magical weapon into a long sword.

Drizzt grabbed the bridle of the nearest mule and tugged the creature along with him, breaking through the tree line and out into the open, in full view of the monstrous hordes.

Directly ahead, he watched Bruenor and the other dwarves wade in with abandon.

* * * * *

Athrogate howled, kicked his boar into a charge, and threw his arms up, rolling over backward, executing a perfect dismount that left him on his feet behind the snorting hell beast.

Monsters swarmed at them head on and from both sides. As the boar met the frontal assault with bursts of flame from its stomping hooves, and wild and vicious head swings, Athrogate diverted to the right, morningstars spinning. He clashed with the attackers and flesh splattered far and wide, crawlers verily exploding under the weight of his swings.

Not to be outdone, Thibbledorf Pwent hit a line of charging crawlers with a sidelong tackle, as if daring them to find a weakness in his devastating armor. The Gutbuster thrashed, kicked, punched, kneed, elbowed, and head-butted with gleeful ferocity, using all of his many weapons to tear at the enemy. Thibbledorf Pwent was known as the most ferocious warrior of Mithral Hall—no small claim!—and Athrogate had been similarly regarded many years before among an even larger clan of dwarves. One after another, the crawlers were mowed down before them.

But any watching who might have thought that the pair were warriors protecting their king were soon disavowed of any notion that this particular king needed any protection.

The demon-boar faltered under a tangle of clawing arms and biting fangs. A final burst of stinging fire singed black flesh as the boar faded back to its home plane. Before those crawlers could recover from its sudden evaporation, a new enemy was among them.

Bruenor hit the group with a heavy shield rush, his solid shield cracking into one fleshy beast with enough force to imprint its foaming mug heraldry into the creature's chest. The crawler was thrown back under the weight of the blow. Bruenor opened up, throwing his shield arm out to the left to slam a second creature, and coming across with a mighty chop of his axe that cracked the collarbone of a third enemy, driving it down with tremendous force. Barely had he finished that stroke when Bruenor tore free his axe and cut left to right with a devastating backhand. He hopped as he went out to the end of that swing, and strengthened his momentum with a sudden pirouette.

Another crawler fell away, mortally wounded.

Bruenor landed awkwardly, though, and a crawler got its arm over his shield to scratch at his face.

The dwarf just growled and threw his shield arm up, taking the crawler's arm high with it, and as the beast tried to slash at Bruenor with its free hand, so too did Bruenor bring his axe across. The heavy axe and the powerful dwarf easily parried that strike, and worse for the crawler, Bruenor's swing was hardly slowed by the collision, his fine weapon opening wide the crawler's midsection.

Bruenor gave a second hoist and shoved with his shield to throw that beast away, then chopped back the other way with his axe, cracking it into the skull of another attacker. A sudden twist and reangled tug broke apart the skull and freed the axe. Bruenor waded along, flanked by his devastating team.

* * * * *

Twenty strides behind the ferocious dwarves, Drizzt and Jarlaxle didn't have the luxury of watching the devastating display of martial prowess, for they, too, were quickly hard-pressed.

Drizzt broke center and right, Jarlaxle center and left, each facing their respective foes with typical drow speed and sword play. With his straight blades, Jarlaxle quick-stepped front and back, rolling his hands only so much as to align his blade tips for more deadly stabs. Every step of Jarlaxle's dance was punctuated by forward-prodding sword blades. Those crawlers who ventured too near to Jarlaxle fell back full of small, precise holes.

For Drizzt, with his curving blades, the dance was more one of swinging swaths, each blade slicing across with such force, precision, and momentum that all before it, reaching limbs and pressing monsters, fell back or fell to the ground. While Jarlaxle rarely turned in his battle, Drizzt rarely faced the same direction for more than a heartbeat or two. Quickly realizing that his best attribute against the monsters was his agility, the drow ranger twirled and leaped, spun and dropped low as he came around.

Then up into the air he went again, once even quick-stepping atop the heads of two crawlers that futilely tried to keep pace with his movements.

Drizzt landed right behind them, with more monsters coming at him, but it was all a ruse, for he was up in the air once more, leaping backward and high, tucking his legs in a back flip over the pair of crawlers he had just trod upon. Because they turned in their efforts to keep up with him, he found himself once again behind them.

Down came his scimitars and down went the two crawlers, skulls creased.

More were there to take their places, the fearless and ravenous beasts coming on with abandon. Though both drow fought brilliantly, the pair made little headway toward Spirit Soaring.

And despite their best efforts, crawlers slipped in behind them, rushing for the wagon.

* * * * *

Bruenor saw them first. "Me girl!" he screamed, glancing back at a beast pulling itself up the side of the wagon.

"We're too far!" he scolded his companions, dwarf and drow. "Turn back!"

Pwent and Athrogate, covered in the gore of splattered creatures, immediately spun around. Bruenor pivoted the formation, the three beginning a second and even more ferocious charge back the way they'd come.

"Drizzt! Elf!" Bruenor yelled with every step, desperate for his friend to reach Catti-brie's side.

* * * * *

Drizzt, too, understood that the beasts had been cunning enough to get in behind them. He attempted the same kind of turn that Bruenor and his companions had taken.

But he was hard-pressed, as was Jarlaxle, each alone with crawlers intent on keeping them from retreating to the wagon. Drizzt could only fight on and hope to find a gap, and yell back warnings to Danica.

A crawler pulled itself over the rail of the wagon's side and Drizzt sucked in his breath.

"Jarlaxle!" he begged.

Five strides away from him, Jarlaxle nodded and threw down the feather. Immediately a gigantic flightless bird stood beside the mercenary.

"Go!" Jarlaxle yelled, maneuvering to Drizzt's side as the bird commanded the field.

Side by side they went, trying to find some rhythm, some compliment to their varied styles. But Drizzt knew that they could not reach the wagon in time.

And Bruenor, screaming from behind him, knew it too.

But all five, drow and dwarves alike, breathed easier when a form stood tall before the crawler on the wagon, for up popped Danica, her sling hanging empty, her fists balled before her chest. Up went one leg, straight above her head, and her amazing dexterity was matched by her strength as she drove her foot down atop the crawler's head.

With a sickening *crack,* that head flattened even more and the beast dropped from the side of the wagon as surely and swiftly as if a mountain had fallen atop it.

All five of the companions fighting to approach the wagon shouted out to Danica as a crawler leaped over the other side of the wagon at her back. But she needed no such warning, coming out of her devastating stomp with a perfect pivot to back-kick the second beast in its ugly face. It, too, bounced away.

A third creature clambered over the rail and a circle kick suddenly filled its grinning maw. Danica remained up on her right leg and went up to the ball of her foot to execute a complete spin and slam a fourth crawler.

Yet another beast climbing up the side was met with a flurry of fists, a rapid explosion of ten short punches that turned its face to mush. Before it could fall away, Danica hooked it under the armpit and turned powerfully, launching it across the wagon to bowl over and dislodge another of its companions.

The woman turned fast and fell into a defensive crouch, seeing a pair of monsters up front on the jockey box. One jerked weirdly and the other followed, then fine drow swords exploded out of their chests. Both crawlers were jerked off opposite sides of the wagon and the swords slipped free. Jarlaxle stood on the seat alone.

With a smile, the drow snapped his right wrist up, and his magical blade transformed from sword to dirk. With a wink, Jarlaxle launched the dagger toward Danica—right past her, to impale a crawler and knock it off the wagon's backside.

He tipped his hat, flicked another dagger from his wrist, and turned to rejoin Drizzt, who had defeated a quartet of crawlers as they had tried to attack the mules.

"You three, with the wagon," Drizzt told the dwarves as they arrived.

As Jarlaxle leaped down beside him and gave a nod to his fellow drow, Drizzt led the way forward toward the screeching, pecking, stomping diatryma.

"You lead, I secure," Jarlaxle said, the command ringing clearly to Drizzt Do'Urden.

In that short charge and retreat, in that moment of desperation to rescue the wagon, the two had found a level of confidence and complement that Drizzt had never thought possible. His beloved wife was in that wagon, helpless, and yet he had stopped to engage the first line of crawlers near the mules, fully confident that Jarlaxle would secure the jockey box and reinforce Danica's desperate defense of Catti-brie.

So on they went, fighting as one. Drizzt led the way with his leaps and slashing cuts while a series of daggers reached out behind him, flew out around him. Every time he lifted a scimitar, a dagger whistled under his arm. Every time he dived and rolled right, a dagger shot past his left—or a stream of daggers, for Jarlaxle's bracers gave him an inexhaustible and ready supply.

To their side, the crawling beasts finally pulled down the diatryma, but it didn't matter, for behind the drow, Bruenor tugged the mules and wagon along while Pwent and Athrogate flanked him, throwing themselves at any monsters venturing too near. Danica held the wagon bed, striking with devastating effect at any who dared try to climb aboard.

Finally they were rolling along, their enemies thinning before them. Drizzt darted left and right, taking great chances, diving into rolls and leaping into spins, confident every time that a dagger would fly his way in support if any monster found a hole in his defenses.

* * * * *

Inside Spirit Soaring, word of the allies' charge began to spread among the priests and wizards, and they began to call out their support and to cheer with great relief the unexpected reinforcements. And from more than one came a cry of relief at the return of Lady Danica!

All around the library, the calls went out and the defenders took heart, none more so than Cadderly. With his hand crossbows and devastating darts, he had methodically cleared most of the second story balconies of invaders, and had left a dozen dead before the front door for good measure, shooting down from on high.

But with his wife in sight, flanked by heroes of great renown, the priest was so overcome that he forgot how to breathe. He stared at the wagon, creeping across the courtyard toward Spirit Soaring, where Drizzt Do'Urden and Jarlaxle—Jarlaxle!—sprinted back and forth, working as if they were a single, four-armed warrior, Drizzt leaping and spinning, mowing down crawlers whose arms went up to grab at him always a heartbeat too late.

And Jarlaxle came behind like god-thrown lightning, stabbing the beasts with short, deadly strokes and nimbly dancing through them as they fell to the ground, mortally wounded.

There were dwarves, too, and Cadderly recognized King Bruenor from that legendary one-horned helm and the foaming mug shield, working his axe with deadly efficiency and tugging the mules along, while two other dwarf warriors flanked the team. Any beasts that ventured too near were crushed by a blur of spinning morningstars on one side, or torn apart by the multitude of spikes and ridges adorning the wild dwarf on the other.

There was Danica, and oh, but she had never looked more beautiful to Cadderly than at that very moment. She had been battered, he could see, and that stung his heart, but her warrior spirit ignored her wounds, and she worked her dance magnificently about the wagon bed. Not a creature could get close to clearing the rails.

Below the balcony where he stood, Cadderly heard his fellow priests shouting to "Form up!" and he knew they meant to go out and meet the incoming band. When he took a moment to stop gawking at the magnificence of the six warriors in action, he realized that help would be sorely needed.

Many monsters became aware of fresh meat on the approaching wagon. The attack on the building had all but ceased. Every ravenous eye turned toward easy prey.

Cadderly realized the awful truth. For all the power of those six, they would never make it. A horde of monsters stood poised to wash over them like breaking waves on a low beach.

His beloved wife would never come home.

From the balcony, he turned into the cathedral, thinking to rush to the stairwell. He skidded to an abrupt stop, hearing a distant call—as he had in that previous moment of desperation when he had been caught alone on the upper floors with the attacking crawlers.

He turned, his eyes guided to a cloud in the sky above. He reached for that cloud and called to it, and a portion of it broke away. A chariot of cloud, pulled by a winged horse, raced down from on high. Cadderly climbed atop the balcony's rail and the speeding chariot swooped down before him. Hardly even thinking about his actions, for he was leaping onto a cloud, the priest jumped aboard. The winged horse followed his every mental command, sweeping down from the balcony right before the astonished eyes of the priests and wizards who were gathering to charge out the front door. As one, they gasped and fell back into the cathedral. Cadderly's chariot soared out above the frightened crawlers.

Some of the undead, Menlidus among them, turned to intercept the new foe, but Cadderly looked upon them and channeled the divinity flowing within him, releasing a mighty burst of radiance that knocked the undead monsters back and blasted them to ash.

He grimaced at the destruction of his dear friend, but Cadderly pushed away the sadness and continued on, fast nearing the wagon and the six warriors and the host of crawlers battling them. Again he cast a spell, though he knew not what it was, simply trusting the power he felt within. He looked at the largest mob of monsters and shouted a single word—not just any word, but a thunderous word, an explosion of vocal power aimed at enemies alone, for it did not affect the spiked-armored dwarf, who thrashed wildly in the middle of the throng.

But the wild dwarf was struck dumbfounded and confused when all the monsters clawing and biting at him were yanked away. Through the air they went, flailing helplessly against the weight of the priest's thunder. They landed hard some thirty steps distant, bouncing and tumbling, scrambling away, wanting no part of the godlike priest and his words of doom.

Cadderly paid them no more heed, bringing his chariot up beside the wagon and bidding his friends to climb aboard. He spoke another word of power and a great light ignited around him and the wagon. All of the crawlers caught within it began to thrash and burn, but the others, the drow, the dwarves, and the two women, felt no pain. Instead, they were washed with healing warmth, their many recent wounds mending in the brilliant yellow beams of magical light.

Bruenor yelled at Drizzt, who had told him to climb aboard the chariot. When the dwarf king hesitated, Athrogate and Pwent, running along beside him, hooked him under the arms and dragged him up.

Drizzt sprang aboard the wagon and into the bed, catching Danica's eye. "Watch those beasts for me," he said, trusting her fully. He sheathed his blades, went to his beloved, and scooped her into his arms. With Danica leading, they made the chariot easily.

Jarlaxle did not follow, but waved Cadderly away. He threw daggers into the nearest thrashing crawler for good measure, then brought forth his nightmare, summoning it before the terrified team. The drow ran around the mules, conjuring another sword from his enchanted bracer as he went, while his nightmare pounded the ground with fiery hooves. A few clever slashes set the mules free, and Jarlaxle, reigns in hand, ran between and past them, and jumped upon his nightmare.

He kicked the steed into a charge, galloping along the path cleared by Cadderly's cloud chariot. He tugged the mules along and guided them up on the porch and through the open front doors before any of the crawlers could intercept him.

Priests slammed the doors closed behind the drow and his four-legged escorts. Jarlaxle immediately dismissed his nightmare and handed the mules off to astonished onlookers.

"It would not do to waste a perfectly good team," he explained. "And these two have taken us a long way." He finished with a laugh—which lasted only as long as it took him to turn and come face to face with Cadderly.

"I told you never to return to this place," the priest said, ignoring the many curious onlookers crowding around him, demanding to know what sort of magic he had found to conjure a chariot of cloud, to speak thunder, to glow with the radiance of a healing god, to reduce the undead to ashes with a single word. They, who could not reliably cast the simplest of dweomers any longer, had witnessed a display of power that the greatest priests and wizards of Faerûn could hardly imagine.

Jarlaxle bowed low in response, tipping his unfeathered hat. He didn't answer, though, other than to motion to Drizzt, who came fast to his side, as Danica was fast to Cadderly's.

"He is not our enemy," Danica assured her husband. "Not any more."

"I keep trying to tell you that," Jarlaxle agreed.

Cadderly looked to Drizzt, who nodded his agreement.

"Enough of that, and who truly cares?" a wizard yelled, bulling his way up to Cadderly. "Where did you find such power? What prayers were those? To throw a multitude of enemies aside with a mere word! A chariot of cloudstuff? Pray tell, good Cadderly. Is this Deneir, come to your call?"

Cadderly looked at the man hard, looked at them all, his face a mask of studious concentration. "I know not," he admitted. "I do not hear the voice of Deneir, yet I believe that he is involved somehow." He looked directly at Drizzt as he finished. "It is as if Deneir is giving this answer to me, one last gift . . ."

"Last?" Ginance called out with alarm, and many others mumbled and grumbled.

Cadderly looked at them and could only shrug, for he truly didn't know the answer to the riddle that was his newfound power. He shifted his gaze to Jarlaxle. "I trust my wife, and I trust Drizzt, and so you are welcome here in this time of mutual need."

"With information you will find valuable," Jarlaxle assured him, but the drow was cut short by a sharp cry from the back of the gathering. All eyes turned toward Catti-brie. Drizzt had set her down on a divan at the side of the foyer, but she was floating in the air, her arms out as if she were under water, her eyes rolled to white and her hair floating around her, again as if she were weightless.

She turned her head and spat, then snapped back the other way as if someone had slapped her across the face. Her eyes once more shone blue, though they were surely seeing something other than that which was before her.

"She is demon-possessed!" a priest cried.

Drizzt donned the eye patch Jarlaxle had given to him and rushed to his wife, grabbing her in a hug and gently pulling her down.

"Take care, for she is in a dark place that welcomes new victims," Jarlaxle said to Cadderly as he moved to join Drizzt. Cadderly looked at him curiously but went in anyway, taking Catti-brie's hand.

Cadderly's form jolted as if shocked by lightning. His eyes twitched and his entire form changed, a ghostly superimposition of an angelic body, complete with feathery wings, over his normal human form.

Catti-brie cried out then and so did Cadderly. Jarlaxle grabbed the priest and tugged him back. The ghostly lines of Cadderly's form disappeared, leaving him gawking at the woman.

"She is caught between worlds," Jarlaxle said.

Cadderly looked at him, licked his suddenly dry lips, and did not disagree.

CHAPTER

A DWARF'S STUBBORNNESS

He felt the sensation seeping into his consciousness, the willpower of another being trying to possess him. But Ivan Bouldershoulder was ready for it. He was no simpleton, and no novice to any kind of warfare. He had felt the dominating willpower of a vampire—right before he had utterly destroyed the thing—and he had studied the methods of wizards and illusionist, and even illithids, like any well-prepared dwarf warrior.

The creature had caught him by surprise with the first intrusion, true. Spirit Soaring and the Snowflakes had been a peaceful place for years, the one notable exception being the arrival of Artemis Entreri, Jarlaxle Baenre, and the Crystal Shard, but since Cadderly had completed the new library, Ivan and everyone else had come to think of the place as home, as peaceful, as safe.

Even with the turbulence of the wider world and the current problems with magic—the types of problems that had never really concerned the likes of Ivan Bouldershoulder, who trusted his muscle more than any waggling fingers—Ivan hadn't been ready for the onslaught of the Ghost King. And he'd certainly not been ready for the intrusion that had overwhelmed him and stolen from him his very body. But for nearly the entire time he had been possessed, Ivan had studied his possessor. Rather than flail against an opaque wall he could not penetrate, the dwarf had bided his time, gathering what information he could, trying to take from his possessor even as it continued to rob him.

Thus, when Yharaskrik had released him on that high mountain plateau, Ivan was ready for the fight—or more accurately, for the flight. And the illithid had inadvertently shown him the way: a crack in the floor beneath the dracolich that was more than a crack, that was indeed a shaft leading down into the mountains and, Ivan had hoped, into the catacomb of tunnels that wound through the lower stones.

With nowhere else to go, and doom certain if he stayed above, Ivan had scrambled straight for that route, counting on surprise to get him past the crushing claws of the great beast.

To his good fortune, when the dragon's foot had stomped, a host of the fleshy beasts had been right behind him, and the splatter and spray of flesh and gore and blood had provided wonderful cover for his desperate dive.

To his ultimate good fortune, the shaft had not run straight down for very far, gradually winding to the side and easing the impact as he connected with the dirt and stone. And it had widened, allowing him to twist in his descent and get his heavy boots out in front of him, digging them in against the slide. The last drop had hurt—twenty feet straight down with nothing but dark air around him as he broke through the roof of an underground chamber, but even there, the dwarf had found that extra bit of heroism, the one heroes only rarely discussed openly: good luck.

He had landed in water. It wasn't very deep and wasn't very clean, but it was enough to cushion his fall. He had lost his antlered helm up above but had retrieved his axe, and he was alive, and in a place where the monstrous dracolich couldn't follow.

Luck had given him a chance.

Soon after, though, Ivan Bouldershoulder figured that his luck had run out.

For the rest of the day, he had wandered in the darkness, splashing, for he could find no dry land in the chamber, and no exit. He had felt some movement around his legs in the thigh-deep murk, and figured there might be some fish or some other crawly things in the underground pool, so maybe he could catch them and figure out a way to survive for some time.

Either way, he believed that he would surely die alone and miserable in the dark.

So be it.

Then the illithid had come calling, whispering into his subconscious, trying to pry its way back into control.

Ivan put up a wall of anger and sheer dwarven stubbornness that held the creature at bay, and he knew with confidence that he could hold it indefinitely, that he would not be possessed again.

"Go away, ye silly beast," he said. He focused and concentrated on every word as he spoke. "What'd'ye want with me in here, where there's no way out?"

It seemed a logical enough refutation. Indeed, what did the illithid have to gain?

But still the creature seeped into his thoughts, demanding control.

"What, can ye make me fly, then, ye fool?" Ivan shouted into the darkness. "Fly me back up to yer dead dragon and the little beasties ye so love?"

He felt the anger then, and the revulsion, and understood that he had caught the mind flayer a bit off its guard, though just for a fleeting moment.

Ivan let his own guard slip, just a bit.

He felt the other being inside his mind clearly then, striving for dominance. A wave of utter disgust nearly buckled the dwarf's knees. But he held fast, and purposely lowered his guard just a bit more.

He was soon walking toward the northern end of the wide chamber. He could barely make out the boulders piled along that wall. Guided by Yharaskrik's will, counting on the illithid having a wider view of his surroundings than he, the dwarf climbed up onto the lower stones. He pulled one aside and felt the slightest breeze, and as his eyes adjusted to the more intense gloom beyond, he saw that a long, wide tunnel lay before him.

Done with ye! his thoughts screamed and Ivan Bouldershoulder began the fight of his life. He pushed back against the overwhelming intellect and willpower of the mind flayer with every measure of stubbornness and anger a dwarf could muster. He thought of his brother, of his clan, of King Bruenor, of Cadderly and Danica and the kids, of everything that made him who he was, that gave joy to his life and strength to his limbs.

He denied Yharaskrik. He screamed at Yharaskrik, aloud and in his every thought. He thrashed physically, hurling himself against the stones, tearing at the tunnel opening to widen it, ignoring the falling rocks that banged off his arms and shoulders. And he thrashed mentally as well, screaming at the wretched beast to be gone from his mind.

From *his* mind!

Such rage enveloped him that Ivan tore the rocks free with bloody fingers and felt no pain. Such strength accompanied that rage that he flung the stones, some half his weight, far behind him to splash into the murky pool. And still he ignored the bruises and cuts, and the strain on his corded muscles. He let the rage take him fully and hold him, a wall of denial, a demand that the illithid get out.

The hole was wide enough to crawl through—wide enough for two Ivans to crawl through side by side—and still the dwarf dug at the stones with his battered hands, using that physical sensation to give focus to his rage.

He had no idea how long he went on like that, a few heartbeats or a few thousand, but finally, an exhausted Ivan Bouldershoulder fell through the opening and rolled into the tunnel. He landed flat on his face and lay there, gasping, for a long while.

Despite the pain, a wry grin widened on his hairy face, for Ivan knew that he was truly alone.

The tentacle-faced beast had been denied.

He slept, then, right there in the mud, amidst the stones, keeping himself mentally ready to fend off another intrusion and hoping that no wandering creature of the Underdark would find him and devour him as he lay exhausted and battered in the darkness.

* * * * *

Rorick dived to the floor, just under the clawing feet of a huge black bat. "Uncle Pikel!" he screamed, beseeching the druid to do something.

Pikel balled up his fist, pumped his arms, and stamped his feet in frustration, for he had nothing, nothing at all, to offer. Magic was gone—even his natural affinity with animals had flown. He thought back to only a few days earlier, when he had coaxed the roots out of the walls to secure the barricades—a temporary thing, apparently, since pursuit came from that direction. The dwarf knew he couldn't reach that level of magic, perhaps not ever again, and his frustration played out, in that dark chamber deep beneath the Snowflakes.

"Ooooh!" he whined, and he stamped his sandaled feet harder. His whine became a growl as he saw the same bat that had sent Rorick diving for cover angle its wings and come around directly at him.

Pikel blamed the bat. It made no sense, of course, but none of it made a lot of sense to Pikel just then. So he blamed the bat. That bat. Only that bat. That one bat had caused the failure of magic, and had chased away his god.

He squatted and picked up his cudgel. It wasn't enchanted anymore, no longer a magical shillelagh, but it was still a solid club, as the bat found out.

The black leathery thing swooped at Pikel, and the dwarf leaped and spun, launching the most powerful strike he had ever managed with his strong arm, even from the days when he had the use of both. The hard wood crunched against bat skull, shattering the bone.

The nightwing fell as surely as if a huge boulder had fallen upon it from on high, crashing down atop Pikel, the two of them rolling away in a tumble of dwarf and black bat.

Pikel head-butted and kicked with abandon. He bit and poked with his stubby arm. He swung his cudgel with short but heavy strokes, battering the creature relentlessly.

Nearby, a man screamed as a nightwing swooped in and caught him by the shoulders in its huge clawed feet, but Pikel didn't hear it. Several others cried out, and a woman shrieked in horror when the bat flew straight for a wall and let loose its prey, hurling the poor man against the rocks, where his bones shattered with a sickening crackle.

Pikel didn't hear it. He was still swinging his club and kicking with fury, though the bat that enwrapped him with those great wings was already dead.

"Get up, Uncle Pikel!" Hanaleisa yelled at him as she leaped past.

"Huh?" the dwarf replied, and he pulled one wing down from in front of his face and followed the sound to see Hanaleisa sprinting toward Rorick, who was still flat on the ground. Standing above him, Temberle cut his greatsword back and forth in long sweeping arcs above his head, trying to cut at a stubborn nightwing that fluttered up and down above him as if to taunt him. He couldn't hit the agile bat.

But Hanaleisa did, leaping high into the air as she rushed past Temberle, somersaulting as she went to enhance the power of her kick. She kicked the bat solidly in the side, sending it several feet away as she tumbled over and landed, still in a run.

The nightwing turned its attention her way as it righted itself in the air, and swooped to give chase.

With that distraction, Temberle's sword at last caught up to it, slashing a leathery wing back to front. The nightwing flopped weirdly in the air and fluttered down, and Hanaleisa and Temberle were upon it before it managed to get the wounded wing out from under itself.

Hanaleisa was the first to break away, calling out orders, trying to establish some measure of order and supporting lines of defense. But the whole of the wide chamber was in a frenzy, with nightwings fluttering all around them, with wounded men and woman, backs torn wide, one scalped by a raking claw, screaming and running and diving for cover.

A group of more than a dozen grabbed up all of the precious torches stored at the far end of the hall, at the mouth of a tunnel the group had planned to traverse after their rest stop, and went running away.

Others followed in the chaos.

Temberle knocked down another bat, and Hanaleisa matched him.

Other nightwings swept out of the chamber in pursuit down the tunnels.

When it finally ended, just over a score of refugees remained, with three of those badly wounded.

"It won't hold," Hanaleisa said to her brothers and uncle as they gathered together their scant supplies and few remaining torches. "We need to find a way out of here."

"Uh-uh!" Pikel emphatically disagreed.

"Then light your staff!" Hanaleisa yelled at him.

"Ooooh," said the dwarf.

"Hana!" Rorick scolded.

The monk held forth her hands and took a deep breath, composing herself. "I'm sorry. But we need to move along, and quickly."

"We cannot stay here," Temberle agreed. "We need to get as close to Spirit Soaring as we can manage, and we need to get out of these tunnels."

He looked at Pikel, but the dwarf just shrugged, hardly confident.

"We have no other option," Temberle assured him.

A commotion behind them turned them around, and Rorick said, "The scout returns!"

They rushed to the fisherman, Alagist, and even in the torchlight, they could see that he was thoroughly shaken. "We feared you dead," Hanaleisa said. "When the bats came in—"

"Forget the damned bats," the man replied, and the punctuation of his sentence came as a thump from the distant corridor, like a rumble of thunder.

"What—?" Temberle and Rorick said together.

"A footstep," Alagist said.

"Uh-oh," said Pikel.

"What magic?" Hanaleisa asked the dwarf.

"Uh-oh," he repeated.

"Gather up the wounded!" Temberle called to all still in the chamber. "Take everything we can carry! We must be gone from this place!"

"He can't be moved," a woman called from beside an unconscious man.

"We have no choice," Temberle said to her, rushing over to help.

The chamber shuddered under the reverberations of another heavy footstep.

The woman didn't argue as Temberle hoisted the wounded man over one shoulder.

Pikel, torch in hand, led the way out of the chamber.

* * * * *

"Come on, then!" Ivan yelled into the darkness. "Not with yer head, ye damned squid, but all o' ye! Come and play!" He didn't have his axe, but he hoisted a pair of rocks and banged them together with enthusiasm bordering on murderous glee.

That physical manifestation of anger echoed the dwarf's sheer rage, and once more, the intrusions of Yharaskrik faded to nothingness. If the illithid had come to him that time with any hope of possessing him again, Ivan believed with confidence, that delusion had come to an end.

But the dwarf was still alone, battered and bloody and lost in the dark, with no real expectation that there was a way out of those forever-twisting tunnels. He glanced over his shoulder to the watery cavern, and considered for a moment going back and trying to figure out a way in which he could survive on the fish, or whatever those swimming things might be. Could he somehow strain or heat the murky water enough to make it potable?

"Bah!" he snorted into the darkness, and decided that it was better to die trying than to simply exist in a dark and empty hole!

So off Ivan trudged, rocks in hands, a scowl on his face, and a wall of rage within him just looking for an outlet.

He walked for hours, often stumbling and tripping, for though his eyes adjusted quickly to the darkness, he still had to feel his way along. He found many side passages, some that led to dead ends, and others he took simply because they "felt" more promising. Even with his dwarf's senses, so at home underground, Ivan had little idea of where he actually was in relation to the

World Above, and even in relation to where he had first dropped down into the murky underground pond. With every turn, Ivan held his breath, hoping he wasn't just going in circles.

At every turn, too, the dwarf tucked one of his stone weapons under his armpit, wetted his finger, and held it aloft in search of air currents.

Finally, he felt the slightest breeze on that upraised finger. Ivan held his breath and stared into the blackness. He knew it could be but a crack, a teasing, impassable chimney, a torturous wormhole he could never squeeze through.

He slammed his rocks together and stomped along, clinging to optimism and armoring himself with anger. An hour later, he was still in darkness, but the air felt lighter to him, and he felt a distinct sensation on that wetted finger whenever he lifted it.

Then he saw a light. A tiny spark, far away, rebounding off many turns and twists. But a light nonetheless. Along the walls, rocks took more definitive shape to the dwarf's fine underground vision. The darkness was surely less absolute.

Ivan rumbled along, thinking about how he could organize a counterstrike against the dracolich and the illithid and their huddled, shadowy minions. His fears went from his own dilemma to his friends up above, to Cadderly and Danica, the kids and his brother. His pace increased, for Ivan was always one who would fight like a badger for his own sake, but who would fight like a horde of hell-spawned badgers when his friends were involved.

Soon, though, he slowed again, for the light was not daylight, he came to realize, nor was it any of the glowing fungi so common in the Underdark. It was firelight—torchlight, likely.

Down there, that probably meant the light of an enemy.

Ready for a fight, Ivan crept ahead. Knuckles whitening on stones, Ivan gritted his teeth and imagined the sensation of crushing a few skulls.

A single voice stole that bellicose attitude and had him blinking in astonishment.

"Oo oi!"

CHAPTER

Cadderly emerged from the room after spending more than half the morning with Catti-brie, his face ashen, his eyes showing profound weariness.

Drizzt, waiting in the anteroom, looked to him with hope, and Jarlaxle, who stood beside Drizzt, looked instead at his dark elf companion. The mercenary recognized the truth splayed on Cadderly's face even if Drizzt did not—or could not.

"You have found her?" Drizzt asked.

Cadderly sighed, just slightly, and handed the eye patch to him. "It is as we believed," he said, speaking to Jarlaxle more than Drizzt.

The drow mercenary nodded and Cadderly turned to face Drizzt. "Catti-brie is caught in a dark place between two worlds, our own and a place of shadow," the priest explained. "The touch of the falling Weave has had many ill effects upon wizards and priests across Faerûn, and no two maladies appear to be the same, from what little I have seen. For Argust of Memnon, the touch proved instantly fatal, turning him to ice—just empty ice, no substance, no flesh beneath it. The desert sun reduced him to a puddle in short order. Another priest carries with him a most awful disease, with open sores across his body, and is surely failing. Many stories . . ."

"I care not of them," Drizzt interrupted, and Jarlaxle, hearing the edge creeping into the ranger's voice, put a comforting hand on Drizzt's shoulder. "You have found Catti-brie, caught between the worlds, you say, though in truth I fear it is all a grand illusion masking a sinister design—perhaps the Red Wizards, or—"

"It is no illusion. The Weave itself has come undone, some of the gods have fled, died . . . we're not yet certain. And whether it is the cause of the falling Weave, or a result of it, a second world is falling all around ours, and that junction seems also to have increased the expanse of the Plane of Shadow, or perhaps even opened doorways into some other realm of shadows and darkness," said Cadderly.

"And you have found her—Catti-brie, I mean—trapped between this place and our own world. How do we retrieve her fully, and bring her back . . ." His voice trailed off as he stared into Cadderly's too-sympathetic face.

"There is a way!" Drizzt shouted, and he grabbed the priest by the front of his tunic. "Do not tell me that it is hopeless!"

"I would not," Cadderly replied. "All sorts of unexplained and unexpected events are occurring all around us, on a daily basis! I have found spells I did not know I possessed, and did not know Deneir could grant, and with all humility and honesty, I say that I am not certain it is even Deneir granting them to me! You ask me for answers, my friend, and I do not have them."

Drizzt let him go, the drow's shoulders sagging, along with his aching heart. He offered a slight nod of appreciation to Cadderly. "I will go and tell Bruenor."

"Let me," said Jarlaxle, and that brought a surprised look from Drizzt. "You go to your wife."

"My wife cannot feel my touch."

"You do not know that," Jarlaxle scolded. "Go and hold her, for both your sakes."

Drizzt looked from Jarlaxle to Cadderly, who nodded his agreement. The distraught drow put on the magical eye patch as he entered the adjacent chamber.

"She is lost to us," Jarlaxle said softly to Cadderly when they were alone.

"We do not know that."

Jarlaxle continued to stare at him, and Cadderly, grim-faced, could not disagree. "I see no way for us to retrieve her," the priest admitted. "And even if we could, I fear that the damage to her mind is already beyond repair. By any means I can fathom, Catti-brie is forever lost to us."

Jarlaxle swallowed hard, though he was not surprised by the prognosis. He wouldn't tell King Bruenor quite everything, he decided.

* * * * *

Another defeat, Yharaskrik pointed out.

We weakened them!

We barely scratched their walls, the illithid imparted. *And now they have new and powerful allies.*

More of my enemies in one place for me to throttle!

Cadderly and Jarlaxle and Drizzt Do'Urden. I know this Drizzt Do'Urden, and he is not to be taken lightly.

I know him as well. Crenshinibon unexpectedly joined the internal dialogue, and the illithid detected a simmering hatred behind the simple telepathic statement.

We should fly from this place, Yharaskrik dared to suggest. *The rift has brought uncontrollable beasts from the shadowy plane, and Cadderly has found unexpected allies . . .*

No cogent response came from the dragon, just a continuous, angry growl reverberating through the thoughts of the triumvirate that was the Ghost King, a wall of anger and resentment, and perhaps the most resounding "no" Yharaskrik had ever heard.

Through the far-reaching mental eyes of the illithid, its consciousness flying wide to scout the region, they had seen the rift in Carradoon. They had seen the giant nightwalkers and the nightwings and understood that a new force had come to the Prime Material Plane. And through the eyes of the illithid, they had witnessed the latest battle at Spirit Soaring, the coming of the dwarves and the drow, the power revealed by Cadderly— that unknown priestly magic had unnerved Yharaskrik most of all, for he had felt the magical thunder in Cadderly's ward and had retreated from the brilliance of the priest's beam of light. Yharaskrik, ancient and once part of a great communal mind flayer hive, thought it knew of every magical dweomer on Toril, but it had never seen anything like the power of the unpredictable priest that day.

The melted flesh of crawlers and the ash piles of the raised dead served as grim reminders to the mind flayer that Cadderly was not to be underestimated.

Thus, the dracolich's continuing growl of denial was not a welcome echo in Yharaskrik's expansive mind. The illithid waited for the sound to abate, but it did not. It listened for a third voice in the conversation, one of moderation, but heard nothing.

Then it knew. In a sudden insight, a revelation of a minuscule but all-important shift, the mind flayer realized that the Ghost King was no longer a triumvirate. The resonance of the growl deepened, more a chorus of two than the grumble of one. Two that had become one.

No words filtered out of that rumbling wall of anger, but Yharaskrik knew its warnings would go unheeded. They would not flee. They—the mind flayer and that dual being with whom it shared the host dragon corpse, for no longer could Yharaskrik count Hephaestus and Crenshinibon as separate entities!—would show no restraint. Not the rift, not Cadderly's unexplained new powers, not the arrival of powerful reinforcements for Spirit Soaring, would slow the determined vengeance of the Ghost King.

The growl continued, a maddening and incessant wall, a pervasive answer to the illithid's concerns that brooked no intelligent debate, or, the creature understood, no room for a change of plans, whatever new circumstances or new enemies might be revealed.

The Ghost King meant to attack Spirit Soaring.

Yharaskrik tried to send its thoughts around the growl, to find Crenshinibon, or what remained of the Crystal Shard as an independent sentience. It tried to construct logic to stop the dracolich's angry vibrations.

It found nothing, and every path led to one road only: eviction.

It was no longer a disagreement, no longer a debate about their course of action. It was a revolt, full and without resolution. Hephaestus-Crenshinibon was trying to evict Yharaskrik, as surely as had the dwarf in the tunnels below.

Unlike that occasion, however, the mind flayer had nowhere else to go.

The growl rolled on.

Yharaskrik threw wave after wave of mental energy at the dragon-shard mind. It gathered its psionic powers and released them in ways subtle and clever.

The growl rolled on.

The illithid assailed the Ghost King with a wall of discordant notions and emotions, a cacophony of twisted notes that would have driven a wise man mad.

The growl rolled on.

It attacked every fear buried within Hephaestus. It conjured images of the exploding Crystal Shard from those years before, when the light had burned the eyes from Hephaestus's head.

The growl rolled on. The mind flayer found no wedge between the dragon and the artifact. They were one, so completely united that even Yharaskrik couldn't fathom where one ended and the other began, or which was in control, or which even, to the illithid's great surprise and distress, was initiating the growl.

And it went on, unabated, unflinching, incessant and forevermore if necessary, the illithid understood.

Clever beast!

There was nothing left there for the mind flayer. It would have no control of the great dracolich limbs. It would find no conversation or debate. It would find nothing there but the growl, heartbeats and days and years and centuries. Just the growl, just the opaque wall of a singular note that would forevermore dull its own sensibilities, that would steal its curiosity, that would force it to stay within, confined to an endless battle.

Against Hephaestus alone, Yharaskrik knew it could prevail. Against Crenshinibon alone, Yharaskrik held confidence that it would find a way to win.

Against both of them, there was only the growl. It all came clear to the illithid, then. The Crystal Shard, as arrogant as Yharaskrik itself, and as stubborn as the dragon, as patient as time, had chosen. To the illithid, that choice at first seemed illogical, for why would Crenshinibon side with the lesser intellect of the dragon?

Because the Crystal Shard was more possessed of ego than the illithid had recognized. More than logic drove Crenshinibon. By joining with Hephaestus, the Crystal Shard would dominate.

The growl rolled on.

Time itself lost meaning in the rumble. There was no yesterday and no tomorrow, no hope nor fear, no pleasure nor pain.

Just a wall, not thickening, not thinning, impenetrable and impassable.

Yharaskrik couldn't win. It couldn't hold. The Ghost King became a creature of two, not three, and those two became one, as Yharaskrik departed.

The disembodied intellect of the great mind flayer began to dissipate almost immediately, oblivion looming.

* * * * *

All the wizened and experienced minds remaining at Spirit Soaring gathered in lectures and seminars, sharing their observations and intuition about the crash of worlds and the advent of the dark place, a reformed Plane of Shadow they came to call the Shadowfell. All reservations were cast aside, priest and mage, human, dwarf, and drow.

They were all together, plotting and planning, seeking an answer. They were quick to agree that the fleshy beasts crawling over Spirit Soaring were likely of another plane, and no one argued the basic premise of some other world colliding, or at least interacting in dangerous ways, with their own world. But so many other questions remained.

"And the walking dead?" Danica asked.

"Crenshinibon's addition to the tumult," Jarlaxle explained with surprising confidence. "The Crystal Shard is an artifact of necromancy more than anything else."

"You claimed it destroyed—Cadderly's divination showed us the way to destroy it, and we met those conditions. How then . . . ?"

"The collision of worlds?" Jarlaxle asked more than stated. "The fall of the Weave? The simple chaos of the times? I do not believe that it has returned to us as it was—that former incarnation of Crenshinibon was indeed destroyed. But in its destruction, it is possible that the liches who created it have come free of it. I believe that I battled one, and that you encountered one as well."

"You make many presumptions," Danica remarked.

"A line of reasoning to begin our investigation. Nothing more."

"And you think these things, these liches, are the leaders?" asked Cadderly.

Before Jarlaxle could answer, Danica cut him short. "The leader is the dracolich."

"Joined with the remnants of Crenshinibon, and thus with the liches," said Jarlaxle.

"Well, whatever it is, something bad's going on, something badder than anything I e'er seen in me long years o' living," said Bruenor, and he looked toward the doorway to Catti-brie's room as he spoke. An uncomfortable silence ensued, and Bruenor harrumphed a great and profound frustration and took his leave to be with his wounded daughter.

To the surprise of all, especially Cadderly, the priest found himself beside Jarlaxle as the conversation resumed. The drow had surprising insights on the dual-world hypothesis. He had experience with the shadowy form they both understood to be one of the liches that had created

Crenshinibon in that long-lost age. These ideas seemed to Cadderly the most informative of all.

Not Drizzt, nor Bruenor, not even Danica fathomed as clearly as Jarlaxle the trap into which Catti-brie had fallen, or the dire, likely irreparable implications of a new world imprinting on the old, or of a shattering of the wall between light and shadow. Not the other mages nor the priests quite grasped the permanence of the change that had found them all, of the loss of magic and of some, if not all the gods. But Jarlaxle understood.

Deneir was gone, Cadderly had come to accept, and the god was not coming back, at least not in the form Cadderly had come to know. The Weave, the source of Toril's magic, could not be rewound. It appeared as though Mystra herself—all of her domain—was simply there one moment, gone the next.

"Some magic will continue," Jarlaxle said as the discussion neared its end. It had become little more than a rehash of belabored points. "Your exploits prove that."

"Or they are the last gasps of magic dying," Cadderly replied. Jarlaxle shrugged and reluctantly nodded at the possibility of that theory.

"Is this world that is joining with ours a place of magic and gods?" Danica asked. "The beasts we have seen—"

"Have nothing to do with the new world, I think, which may be imbued, as is our own, with both magic and brute force," Jarlaxle interrupted without reservation. "The crawlers come from the Shadowfell." Cadderly nodded agreement with the drow.

"Then, is their magic dying?" Drizzt asked. "Has this collision you speak of destroyed their Weave, as well?"

"Or will the two intertwine in new ways, perhaps with this Plane of Shadow, this Shadowfell, between them?" Jarlaxle said.

"We cannot know," said Cadderly. "Not yet."

"What next?" asked Drizzt, and his voice took on an unusual timbre, one of distinct desperation—desperation wrought by his fears for Catti-brie, the others knew.

"We know what tools we have," Cadderly said, and he stood up and crossed his arms over his chest. "We will match strength with strength, and hope that some magic, at least, will find its way to our many spellcasters."

"You have shown as much already," said Jarlaxle.

"In a manner I cannot predict, much less control or summon."

"I have faith in you," Jarlaxle replied, and that statement gave all four of them pause, for it seemed so impossible that Jarlaxle would be saying that of Cadderly—or anyone!

"Should Cadderly extend similar confidence?" Danica said to the drow.

Jarlaxle burst into laughter, helpless and absurd laughter, and Cadderly joined him, and Danica joined them, too.

But Drizzt could not, his gaze sliding to the side of the room, to the door behind which Catti-brie sat in unending darkness.

Lost to him.

* * * * *

Desperation gripped the normally serene Yharaskrik as the reality of its situation closed in around it. Memories flew away and equations became muddled. It had known physical oblivion before, when Hephaestus had released his great fiery breath upon Crenshinibon, blasting the artifact. Only through an amazing bit of good fortune—the falling Weave touching the residual power of the artifact with the remnants of Yharaskrik nearby—had the illithid come to consciousness again.

But oblivion loomed once again, and with no hope of reprieve. The disembodied intellect flailed without focus for just a few precious moments before the desperate mind flayer reached out toward the nearest vessel.

But Ivan Bouldershoulder was ready, and the dwarf put up such a wall of denial and rage that Yharaskrik couldn't begin to make headway into his consciousness. So shut out was the illithid that Yharaskrik had no understanding of where it was, or that it was surrounded by lesser beings that might indeed prove susceptible to possession.

Yharaskrik didn't even fight back against that refusal, for it knew that possession would not solve its problem. It could not inhabit an unwilling host forever, and should it insert all of its consciousness into the physical form of a lesser being, should it fully possess a dwarf, a human, or even an elf, it would become limited by that being's physiology.

There was no real escape. But even as it rebounded away from Ivan Bouldershoulder, the mind flayer had another thought, and cast a wide net, its consciousness reaching out across the leagues of Faerûn. It needed another awakened intellect, another psionicist, a fellow thinker.

It knew of one. It reached for one as its homeless intellect began to flounder.

THE GHOST KING

In a lavish chamber beneath the port city of Luskan, many miles to the northwest, Kimmuriel Oblodra, lieutenant of Bregan D'aerthe, second-in-command behind only Jarlaxle Baenre, felt a sensation, a calling.

A desperate plea.

CHAPTER

A   W H I S P E R   I N   T H E   D A R K

The night was quiet, the forest beyond the wide courtyard of Spirit Soaring dark and still.

Too quiet, Jarlaxle thought as he stared out from a second-story balcony, where he kept his assigned watch. He heard others in the hallways behind him expressing hope at the calm, but to Jarlaxle, the deceptive peace was just the opposite. The pause revealed to him that their enemies were not foolhardy. The last attack had become a massacre of fleshy crawling beasts—their burned and blasted lumps littered the lawn still.

But they weren't finished, to be sure. Given Danica's report, given Jarlaxle's understanding of the hatred toward him and toward Cadderly and Danica, he saw no possibility that Spirit Soaring would suddenly be left in peace.

This night was peaceful, though—undeniably so, paradoxically so, eerily so. And in that quiet, with not even the breath of wind accompanying it, Jarlaxle, and Jarlaxle alone, heard a call.

His eyes widened despite his near-perfect control over his emotions, and he reflexively glanced around. He knew how tentative his—and Athrogate's—welcome was at Spirit Soaring, and he could hardly believe his misfortune as another ally, one who would not likely be accepted by any at Spirit Soaring, demanded an audience.

He tried to push that quiet but insistent call away, but its urgency only heightened.

Jarlaxle looked to the forest and focused his thoughts on one large tree, just behind the foliage border. Then, with another glance around, the drow slipped over the balcony railing and nimbly climbed to the ground. He disappeared into the darkness, making his careful way across the wide courtyard.

* * * * *

"Bah, just as I told ye, elf," a sneering Bruenor Battlehammer said to Drizzt as they watched Jarlaxle slip down from his perch. "Ain't no friend to any other'n Jarlaxle, that one."

A profound sigh reflected Drizzt's deep disappointment.

"I'll go get Pwent and bottle up that damned annoying dwarf ol' big-hat there brung with him." Bruenor started to turn away, but Drizzt caught him by the shoulder.

"We don't know what this is about," he reminded them. "More scouting? Did Jarlaxle see something?"

"Bah!" Bruenor snorted, pulling away. "Go and see if ye got to see, but I'm already knowing."

"Await my return," Drizzt said.

Bruenor glared at him.

"Please, trust me in this," Drizzt begged. "There is too much at stake for all of us, for Catti-brie. If anyone can help us solve the riddle of her troubles, it is Jarlaxle."

"Thought it was Cadderly. Ain't that why we're here?"

"Him, too," said Drizzt, and as Bruenor visibly relaxed, he slipped out the window and moved after Jarlaxle. Not a wary creature stirred at his silent passing.

* * * * *

Ever do I find you in curious places, Kimmuriel Oblodra's fingers waggled to Jarlaxle, using the intricate hand language of the drow. *With Cadderly Bonaduce and his pathetic priests? Truly?*

In this time, we all share concerns, and profit from . . . accommodations of mutual benefit, Jarlaxle's fingers answered. *The situation here is desperate, even grave.*

I know more about it than you do, Kimmuriel assured him, and Jarlaxle wore a puzzled expression.

"About the failing of the Weave, perhaps . . . ?" he said quietly.

Kimmuriel shook his head and responded aloud. "About your predicament. About Hephaestus and Crenshinibon."

"And the illithid," Jarlaxle added.

"Because of the illithid," Kimmuriel corrected. "Yharaskrik, without form and dissipating, found me in Luskan. He is no more a part of this creature they call the Ghost King. He was cast out, to fade to nothingness."

"And he seeks revenge?"

"Revenge is not the way of illithids," Kimmuriel explained. "Though no doubt Yharaskrik enjoyed the bargain I offered."

Do tell, said Jarlaxle, with his fingers and his amused expression.

"Its only hope was to journey to the Astral Plane, a place of consciousness without corporeal restraint," Kimmuriel explained. "With the failure of conventional magic and divine magic, its best opportunity for such a journey was a fellow practitioner of psionics—me. Without its own body as anchor, the mind flayer could not facilitate the flight alone."

"You let it go?" Jarlaxle asked, raising his voice just a bit. He wasn't as angry as intrigued, however, revealed by the way he reached up to tug at the diatryma feather that was nearly fully regrown in his enchanted hat.

"To survive as the years pass, Yharaskrik must find a mind hive of illithids. We of psionic power are not unaffected by that which is occurring across the multiverse, and having such allies. . . ."

"They are wretched creatures."

Kimmuriel shrugged. "They are among the most brilliant of all the mortal beings. I know not what will happen to my powers, nor to magic, divine or arcane. I know only that the world is changing—has changed. Even shifting here through the dimensions proved a great risk, but one that I needed to take."

"To warn me."

"To warn and to instruct, for in return for passage, Yharaskrik revealed to me all it knows about the Ghost King, and about the remnants of the artifact, Crenshinibon."

"I am touched at your concern for me."

"You are necessary," said Kimmuriel, drawing a laugh from Jarlaxle.

"Do tell me, then," Jarlaxle said. "How might I, might we, defeat this Ghost King?"

Kimmuriel nodded and recounted it all in detail then, echoing Yharaskrik's lecture about the being that was both Hephaestus and Crenshinibon, about its powers and its limitations. He explained the minions and the gates that brought them to Faerûn. He talked of one such rift he had sensed, though had not yet inspected, still opened wide in the lakeside town to the southeast. He spoke of human and dwarf refugees hiding in tunnels.

"You trust this mind flayer?" Jarlaxle asked in the end.

"Illithids are trustworthy," Kimmuriel replied. "Loathsome, at times, fascinating always, but as long as their goals are understood, their logic is easily followed. In this case, Yharaskrik's goal was survival. Its plight was real and immediate, and caused by the Ghost King. Knowing that truth, as I did, I trust in its recounting."

Jarlaxle believed that he held some insight into the mindset of illithids as well, for he had been a companion of Kimmuriel Oblodra for a long, long time, and if someone had ever deigned to put a squishy octopoid head on that particular drow, it surely would have fit Kimmuriel well.

* * * * *

In the brush not far away, Drizzt Do'Urden listened to it all with interest, though much of it was no more than a confirmation of that which they had already surmised about their mighty enemy. Then he listened to Jarlaxle's reply and instructions, with wide-eyed disbelief, and truly he felt vindicated in trusting Jarlaxle.

"You cannot demand of me that I take such a risk with Bregan D'aerthe," he heard Kimmuriel argue.

"It is worth the potential gain," Jarlaxle replied. "And think of the opportunity here for you to discern so much more of the mystery that is occurring all around us!"

That last line apparently had the desired effect on Kimmuriel, for the drow bowed to Jarlaxle, turned to the side, and literally cut the air with an outstretched finger, leaving a sizzling vertical blue line in its wake. With a wave, Kimmuriel turned that two-dimensional blue line into a doorway and stepped through, disappearing from sight.

Jarlaxle stood for a bit, hands on hips, digesting it all. Then, with a shake of his head, one of disbelief, even bemusement, the mercenary headed back for Spirit Soaring.

By the time Drizzt arrived, only moments after Jarlaxle, the summons was already out for him and Bruenor to an audience with Cadderly.

And Jarlaxle, of course.

CHAPTER

GAUNTLET THROWN

The Ghost King emerged from its cave with a deafening roar and a stomp of clawed feet that sent fleshy crawlers flying. The magnificent creature stepped out without heed to the scrambling beasts. Its great tail, part skeletal and part rotting dragon flesh, swept aside any too near. Its torn leathery wings buffeted those to either side with a great wind.

No plotting guided the attack, no care for minions or any role they might play. Rage drove the Ghost King. Freed of the caution of Yharaskrik, the great beast followed its emotions. The Ghost King could not be defeated by mere mortals, whose magic was failing. The Ghost King need not plot and connive and tread with fearful caution.

Wings wide, the Ghost King leaped from the pinnacle and rode the updrafts to climb above the Snowflakes. With eyes magical, the Ghost King saw across the miles to the symbol of its enemies, the place on which it focused its rage.

Higher it climbed, above the few wispy clouds that dulled part of the starry night sky. And there it circled, gathering speed, gathering its hatred. And like a bolt from on high, the Ghost King folded its wings, tipped down its huge head, and plummeted for Spirit Soaring.

Though Hephaestus's lips were mostly withered away, any watching would have noted a wicked smile upon the dracolich's face.

* * * * *

Twenty-one priests and wizards, almost half the contingent of residents and visitors remaining at Spirit Soaring, licked dry lips and clutched stones coated in explosive oil. The other half tried to sleep in the too-quiet night. They checked and rechecked their other implements, weapons and armor, magical rings and wands, scrolls and potion bottles, nervously awaiting the attack they knew would come.

It would be a greater beast, too, Cadderly had informed them after his meeting with the newcomers, the drow and the dwarves. A dragon, an undead dracolich, the master of the many minions they had slaughtered, would lead the next attack, so Cadderly had assured them with confidence.

More than a few of them had seen a dragon before, a handful had even witnessed the awful splendor of a dracolich. They were seasoned veterans, after all, travelers mostly, who had come to Spirit Soaring to try to make sense of a dangerous world gone mad.

Their mouths were dry, to a man and woman, for what sort of previous experiences could have offered them—could have offered anyone—solace at that desperate time?

They stood alert, spread over every vantage point of Spirit Soaring, their counterparts sleeping in small groups nearby, weapons at their sides. The attack would come soon, Cadderly had said. Perhaps that very night.

In the central chamber of the second floor, with easy access to corridors that would deliver them to any wall in short order, Cadderly, Danica, the two drow, and the three dwarves waited as well, none of them finding sleep. All of them expected, with each arrival of Ginance and her roving patrol group, to hear that the beast was upon them.

Spirit Soaring was alert, was ready.

But nothing could have truly prepared the fifty-four souls in the cathedral for the advent of the Ghost King. Some few sentries near the northeastern corner of the great building noted the movement from high above and pointed at the giant missile hurtling down at Spirit Soaring. A few managed to scream out a warning, and one lifted a shield in ridiculous defense.

With strength unimaginable, the Ghost King pulled up from its plummet just before it slammed the building, extending its great hind legs out before it and crashing in.

Not a person, not even King Bruenor, so strong on his feet, not even Athrogate, possessed of the low center of balance of a dwarf and the strength of a mountain giant, remained on his feet under the weight of that collision. Spirit Soaring shook to its foundation, glass shattering all over the structure under the sheer force of the impact and the twist of the magical building's indomitable frame. Doors popped open and corridors twisted. Bricks fell from every chimney.

The thunderous sound of a dragon's roar muted every scream, crash, and shatter.

The defenders pulled themselves up and did not shy from the fray. By the time Cadderly and his elite group arrived on the scene, where the wall had been torn away and the Ghost King stood, a dozen rocks had already been thrown, their magical oil exploding at they hit the flesh and bone of the beast.

The Ghost King swiveled its great head on a serpentine neck, fiery eyes selecting a group of annoying rock-throwers, but before the beast could bring its rage to bear on those men and woman, a wizard's fireball, thrown from a necklace of enchanted rubies, engulfed its face in biting flames.

Lightning blasts followed. A pillar of divine fire swept down from above to scorch the back of the dracolich's neck.

And the beast roared, and the beast thrashed, and the building shook, and again men and women, elf and drow and dwarf, tumbled. A swipe of the dracolich's mighty tail slapped the length of the building, shattering more glass, breaking stone facing and cracking thick timber supports.

The room lay broken open, the beast clearly visible to Cadderly's approaching group. The three dwarves spearheading did not hesitate in the face of that catastrophe, and could not slow. They had to be the focus of the battle, by the plans Cadderly had drawn.

As soon as he had felt the thunder of the initial impact, the wound to the place built of his magic, Cadderly had felt the assault on his own body. As the dracolich came into sight, Cadderly felt the magic building within him. Wrought of his desperation, his anger, his denial of the horror of it, the power of spells unknown began to stir.

Whether sensing that power or just recognizing Cadderly, the Ghost King locked its eyes on the approaching group and opened wide its jaws.

"Dive!" Bruenor yelled, and Thibbledorf Pwent dived into Bruenor and knocked him aside, the two of them falling atop the rolling Athrogate.

Flanking the dwarves, Drizzt, Jarlaxle, and Danica easily sidestepped from the direct line to the beast.

But Cadderly didn't move left or right. He thrust his hands forward, hand crossbow in one, walking stick in the other, and chanted in words he did not know.

Dragonfire poured forth from the beast, filling the room in front of them. While Spirit Soaring's magical structure diminished the effect on the walls and floor, the furniture, books, and bric-a-brac went up in bursts of flame, and the gout of immolation rushed across the floor at its living targets, jetting for the open doorway. And there it was stopped by Cadderly's ward.

As the conflagration lessened, the priest fired his hand crossbow, more an act of defiance and challenge than to inflict true damage to the mighty beast, though Cadderly did smile as the bolt exploded against the dracolich's face.

Into the burning room ran the seven, meeting the beast head on. Rocks flew in from left and right, smacking the dracolich and exploding with sudden bursts of magical flame. More magic roared in as well, a hornet's nest of stings, a hurricane of lightning, a god's wrath of fire.

Wings beat against Spirit Soaring in reply. The great tail slapped left and right, crushing stone and wood and throwing wizards and priests aside. But the beast did not turn its focus from that one room, from those seven puny heroes.

"And so we meet," the Ghost King said, its voice shaking the smoldering timbers.

Cadderly fired another dart into its ugly face.

Bruenor, Athrogate, and Pwent didn't pause, bursting through the doorway and charging across the room.

Dragonfire drove them back.

"In together!" Cadderly demanded, and the seven tightened ranks around the priest, with his fire ward and his protection from the dracolich's withering touch.

Spell after spell came forth from the priest, in words none of them understood, and each of the defenders felt hardened against the deadly touch of the beast. On they went, marching right into the blinding roil of the Ghost King's breath. Those fires parted around them and reformed behind them as the dracolich continued its long exhale, so that the group of seven was fully surrounded by opaque walls of streaming flames.

But they moved forward, and as soon as the Ghost King finished, Cadderly cried for a charge.

And charge they did, Bruenor lifting high his axe, Athrogate beside him and spinning his morningstars, and Thibbledorf Pwent darting right between them, leaping at the beast with abandon. The battlerager latched on to one of the dracolich's great hind legs, dug his leg spikes in for support, and began whacking away with both hands, shaving skin and bone with his ridged armor as he thrashed.

Drizzt and Danica moved right behind the dwarves— Drizzt started to, but Cadderly grabbed him by the arm, then cupped his hand over Drizzt's right fist as Drizzt held his scimitar.

"You are the agent of all that is good!" Cadderly charged the surprised drow. The priest spoke another few words that neither he nor Drizzt understood, and Icingdeath glowed more brightly with a divine white light, one that overwhelmed its normal bluish hue. "Vanquish the beast!" Cadderly demanded, except it wasn't truly Cadderly, or *only* Cadderly talking, Drizzt realized to his hope and his horror. It was as if someone else, some*thing* else, some god or angel, had possessed the priest and placed that power and responsibility upon the drow.

Drizzt blinked but didn't dare hesitate other than to call forth Guenhwyvar. He spun back with such fury that it left him stumbling at the dracolich. He moved beside Danica, who leaped and spun and kicked out wide, hitting the beast with rapid and heavy blows. The Ghost King bit down at her, but she was too quick to be caught like that, and she threw herself aside at the last moment.

The snapping jaws cracked in the empty air, and Drizzt rushed in, glowing weapon in hand. He stabbed with Twinkle, the fine blade knifing through some rotting skin to crack against bone, then he slashed with Icingdeath, with his scimitar Cadderly had somehow infused with the power of divine might.

The strike sounded like the drop of a gigantic boulder, a sudden and sharp retort that dwarfed the boom of a fireball and made Athrogate's oil-soaked strikes seem like the tapping of a bird. The Ghost King's head flew back, a great chunk of its cheekbone and upper jaw flying from its face to the courtyard below.

Flying, too, went Guenhwyvar, a great leap that brought the panther clawing at the beast's ugly face.

Everyone else, even wild Pwent, paused a moment to stare in disbelief.

"Impressive," Jarlaxle congratulated, standing beside the gawking Caddderly. The drow threw down his plume, bringing forth the giant diatryma bird. Then he lifted his arms, a wand in each hand. From one came thundering lightning, from the other a line of viscous globs of green goo that the drow aimed to splatter across the wyrm's face, hoping to blind it or hinder its snapping jaws.

What a force they were!

But what an enemy they had found.

The Ghost King did not lift away and flee, did not shy even from Drizzt and that awful weapon. It stomped its leg, crushing through the support beams and driving straight down through the ceiling of the structure's first floor. Poor Pwent was ground by the walls and fell away, all twisted, to the main level.

The Ghost King shook its head wildly and Guenhwyvar went flying away. Then the beast swung its head back with battering ram force at Drizzt, a blow that would have killed him had it hit him squarely. But no one ever hit Drizzt Do'Urden squarely. As the head swung in, Drizzt dived over sideways, just ahead of it. Still, the sheer weight of the glancing blow forced him to roll repeatedly in an attempt to absorb the force. He tumbled out of room, slamming hard into the wrecked chamber's side wall, a burst of embers flying up behind him.

Stung and a bit dazed but hardly down, Drizzt rushed back at the beast. He watched Athrogate sail up in the air before him, caught by a foreleg. The dwarf's oil-soaked morningstar crashed and exploded against the bone, splintering it, but still the Ghost King managed to throw the dwarf far.

"Me head to shake, me bones to break!" the indomitable Athrogate yelled out even as he flew across the room and crashed to the floor. "He flinged me, a flat stone across a still lake!" he finished as he skipped up from the floor and slammed the corner of the wall near the outer break—only the word "lake" came out "la-*aa-aa-aa*-ke" as he fell to the ground outside.

With the two dwarves and Guenhwyvar out of the fray, Danica and Bruenor were sorely pressed. Bruenor pushed back hits from under his shield, his legs bowing but not buckling, his axe ever ready to respond with a heavy chop. Danica leaped and spun, rolled and somersaulted through the air, always half a step ahead of claw or bite.

"We can't hold it!" Jarlaxle said through gritted teeth. Even when Drizzt got back into the fight, his divinely weighted scimitar driving hard against the beast, the mercenary's grim visage didn't soften.

Jarlaxle spoke the painful truth. For all their power and gallant efforts, they were inflicting only minor wounds on the beast, and attrition was already working against them. Then cries went out that crawlers were swarming from the forest, and many on the periphery of the fight had to turn their attention outward.

In that awful moment of honesty, it seemed that all would end for Spirit Soaring and her defenders.

Cadderly reached up with his arms, and up further with his magic, and to all witnessing the event, it seemed as if the mighty priest had plucked a star or the sun itself from the sky and pulled it down over his own body.

Cadderly shone with such radiance that beams of his emanating light streamed through every crack in Spirit Soaring's planking. Beyond the broken wall, the courtyard and the forest shone as though lit by a clear midday.

The night was completely gone, and so too were the wounds of all those near the priest. Pain and fatigue were replaced by warmth and invigoration, the likes of which they had never known.

The opposite effect jarred the Ghost King, and the beast recoiled in shock and torturous pain.

Beyond the wall, the approaching crawlers fell back on their flat feet, long arms flailing to try, futilely, to block the heavenly light. Wisps of smoke rose from their black skins. Those that could roll backward scrambled for the shadows of the trees.

The Ghost King's roar shook the building to its foundation yet again. The beast did not fly away, but flailed all the more wildly, thumping Bruenor, who took every blow with a snarl and a swipe of retribution. The creature's foreleg cut nothing but air as it swiped at Danica, whose acrobatics defied gravity as she lifted and twisted and turned. The dracolich's great jaws snapped down on the diatryma and lifted the flailing bird into the air, where the massive head thrashed right and left and bit down, cutting the bird in half.

The creature tried to bite at the dodging woman, but there was Drizzt, rushing in, his blades rolling left and right and straight overhead, every swipe of the enchanted Icingdeath stabbing out a bit farther, slicing through dragon scale, melting dragon flesh, and exploding dragon bone.

The Ghost King slipped back from the ledge, its hind legs reaching to find footing on the ground. Barely had it stepped down before Thibbledorf Pwent hit it with a flying head butt, his helmet spike digging into the beast's calf and securing his hold. From the other side came Athrogate, one morningstar in hand, the other lost in the fall. He spun the heavy ball above his head in both hands, brought forth its oily might, and struck the Ghost King's other leg with such force that a red scale disintegrated beneath the blow and the beast's desiccated flesh splintered and dissolved all the way to the bone, which cracked loudly.

And above all the pain from those furious warriors, above the continuing sting of Jarlaxle's lightning bolts and the hindrance of the drow's viscous globs, there was the ever-intrusive agony of Cadderly's light. That awful light, divine spurs that permeated every inch of the Ghost King's being.

The beast breathed its fire into the room again, but Cadderly's ward remained to repel the effect, and his light healed his friends as soon as they were stung by the flames.

The effort cost the Ghost King dearly, for all the while it locked its great head in position to fill the room with its fires, Drizzt, who scrambled onto its leg and up to its neck, found the unhindered opportunity to pummel the dragon's skull. Again and again, Icingdeath came down with fury, bone and flesh and scales exploding under each thunderous strike.

The dragon's fiery breath ended abruptly with Drizzt's last strike. The Ghost King shuddered with such force that all, Drizzt and Athrogate included, were thrown aside. The creature leaped back, far out into the courtyard.

"Finish it!" Jarlaxle cried to all, and indeed, it seemed at that moment that the dracolich was in its last throes, that a concerted assault could actually bring the beast down.

And so they tried, but their weapons and spells and missiles passed through the Ghost King without consequence. For there was suddenly nothing tangible to the beast, just its shape outlined in blue light. Thibbledorf Pwent went charging out from the base of Spirit Soaring, roaring as only a battlerager could bellow, and leaped with abandon—right through the intangible beast to bounce down on the turf.

Even more significant to Drizzt, as he moved to follow Pwent, was the apparition of Guenhwyvar across the courtyard. The panther did not charge at the Ghost King. Ears flattened with uncharacteristic trepidation, Guenhwyvar, never afraid of anything, turned and fled.

Drizzt gawked in surprise. He looked to the beast on the field, to Pwent as he ran all around the glowing form, inside it even, thrashing to no effect.

Then suddenly, nothing at all remained to be seen of the Ghost King as the beast faded, just faded to nothingness. It was gone.

The defenders looked on with shock. Cadderly stared with amazement after the blue-white image and gasped at his memories of the Prophecies of Alaundo and of this year, 1385, the Year of Blue Fire. Coincidence, or fitting representation of their greater catastrophe? Before he could delve any deeper into his contemplations, from a room much farther inside Spirit Soaring, Catti-brie screamed in abject terror.

PART
4

SACRIFICE

S A C R I F I C E

The recognition of utter helplessness is more than humbling; it is devastating. On those occasions when it is made clear to someone, internally, that willpower or muscle or technique will not be enough to overcome the obstacles placed before him, that he is helpless before those obstacles, there follows a brutal mental anguish.

When Wulfgar was taken by Errtu in the Abyss, he was beaten and physically tortured, but on those few occasions I was able to coax my friend to speak of that time, those notes he sang most loudly in despair were those of his helplessness. The demon, for example, would make him believe that he was free and was living with the woman he loved, then would slaughter her and their illusionary children before Wulfgar's impotent gaze.

That torture created Wulfgar's most profound and lasting scars.

When I was a child in Menzoberranzan, I was taught a lesson universal to male drow. My sister Briza took me out to the edge of our cavern homeland where a gigantic earth elemental waited. The beast was harnessed and Briza handed me the end of the rein.

"Hold it back," she instructed.

I didn't quite understand, and when the elemental took a step away, the rope was pulled from my hand.

Briza struck me with her whip, of course, and no doubt, she enjoyed it.

"Hold it back," she said again.

I took the rope and braced myself. The elemental took a step and I went flying after it. It didn't even know that I existed, or that I was tugging with all my insignificant strength to try to hinder its movement.

Briza scowled as she informed me that I would try again.

This test must be a matter of cleverness, I decided, and instead of just bracing myself, I looped the rope around a nearby stalagmite, to Briza's approving nods, and dug in my heels.

The elemental, on command, took a step and whipped me around the stone as if I were no more than a bit of parchment in a furious gale. The monster didn't slow, didn't even notice.

In that moment, I was shown my limitations, without equivocation. I was shown my impotence.

Briza then held the elemental in place with an enchantment and dismissed it with a second one. The point she was trying to make was that the divine magic of Lolth overwhelmed both muscle and technique. This was no more than another subjugation tactic by the ruling matron mothers, to make the males of Menzoberranzan understand their lowly place, their inferiority, particularly to those more in Lolth's favor.

For me, and I suspect for many of my kin, the lesson was more personal and less societal, for that was my first real experience encountering a force supremely beyond my willpower, utterly beyond my control. It wasn't as if had I tried harder or been more clever I might have changed the outcome. The elemental would have stepped away unhindered and unbothered no matter my determination.

To say I was humbled would be an understatement. There, in that dark cavern, I learned the first truth of both mortality and mortal flesh.

And now I feel that terrible measure of impotence again.

When I look at Catti-brie, I know that she is beyond my ability to help. We all dream about being the hero, about finding the solution, about winning the moment and saving the day. And we all harbor, to some degree, the notion that our will can overcome, that determination and strength of mind can push us to great ends—and indeed they can.

To a point.

Death is the ultimate barrier, and when faced with impending death, personally or for someone you love, a mortal being will encounter, most of all, ultimate humility.

We all believe that we can defeat that plague or that disease, should it befall us, through sheer willpower. It is a common mental defense against the inevitability we all know we share. I wonder, then, if the worst reality of a lingering death is the sense that your own body is beyond your ability to control.

In my case, the pain I feel in looking at Catti-brie is manifold, and not least among the variations is my own sense of helplessness. I deny the looks that Cadderly and Jarlaxle exchanged, expressions that revealed their hearts and minds. They cannot be right in their obvious belief that Catti-brie is beyond our help and surely doomed!

I demand that they are not right.

And yet I know that they are. Perhaps I only "know" because I fear beyond anything I have ever known that they are correct, and if they are, then I will know no closure. I cannot say goodbye to Catti-brie because I fear that I already have.

And thus, in moments of weakness, I lose faith and know that they are right. My love, my dearest friend, is lost to me forever—and there again lurches my stubbornness, for my first instinct was to write "likely forever." I cannot admit the truth even as I admit the truth!

So many times have I seen my friends return from the brink of death: Bruenor on the back of a dragon, Wulfgar from the Abyss, Catti-brie from the dark plane of Tarterus.

So many times have the odds been beaten. In the end, we always prevail!

But that is not true. And perhaps the cruelest joke of all is the confidence, the surety, that our good fortune and grand exploits have instilled in my friends, the Companions of the Hall.

How much worse becomes the cruel reality when at last we are touched by inescapable tragedy.

I look at Catti-brie and I am reminded of my limitations. My fantasies of saving the moment and the day are dashed against jagged and immovable rocks. I want to save her and I cannot. I look at Catti-brie, wandering lost, and in those moments when I can accept that this state is forever, my hopes become less about victory and more about . . .

I can hardly think it. Have I truly been reduced to hoping that this woman I love will pass on quickly and peacefully?

And still the fight goes on around us, I am sure, in this world gone mad. And still will my scimitars be put to use in a struggle that has, I fear, only just begun. And still will I be needed to mediate between Bruenor and Jarlaxle, Cadderly and Jarlaxle. I cannot skulk away and be alone with my mounting grief and pain. I cannot abrogate my responsibilities to those around me.

But it all, so suddenly, seems less important to me. Without Catti-brie, what is the point of our fight? Why defeat the dracolich when the outcome will not change, since we are all doomed in the end? Is it not true that that which we deem important is, in the grand scheme of the millennia and the multiverse, utterly and completely irrelevant?

This is the demon of despair wrought of impotence. More profound than the helplessness created by Shimmergloom the shadow dragon's dark cloud of breath. More profound than the lesson of the drow matron mothers. For that question, "What is the point?" is the most insidious and destructive of all.

I must deny it. I cannot give in to it, for the sake of those around me and for the sake of myself, and yes, for the sake of Catti-brie, who would not allow me to surrender to such a concept.

Truly this inner turmoil tests me more than any demon, any dragon, any horde of ravaging orcs ever could.

For as this dark moment shows me the futility, so too it demands of me the faith—the faith that there is something beyond this mortal coil, that there is a place of greater understanding and universal community than this temporary existence.

Else it is all a sad joke.

—Drizzt Do'Urden

CHAPTER

WANDERING IN THE DARKNESS

24

"How can I be tellin' ye what I ain't for knowing?" Ivan grumbled, putting Temberle back on his heels.

"I thought . . . you might know . . ." the young man stammered.

"You are a dwarf," Hanaleisa added dryly.

"So's he!" Ivan fumed, poking a finger Pikel's way. His obstinate expression melted when he looked back to the Bonaduce siblings, both wearing skeptical expressions. "Yeah, I know," Ivan agreed with an exasperated sigh.

"Doo-dad," said Pikel, and with an imperious "harrumph" of his own, he walked away.

"He's durned good in the higher tunnels, though," Ivan said in his brother's defense. "When there's roots pokin' through. He talks to 'em, and the damned things talk back!"

"Our current plight?" Rorick reminded, walking over to join the discussion. "The folk are sick of tunnels and growing ever more agitated."

"They'd rather be out in Carradoon, would they?" Ivan retorted. It was sarcasm, of course, but to everyone's surprise, Rorick didn't blink.

"They're saying that very thing," he informed the others.

"They forget what chased us here in the first place," said Temberle, but Rorick shook his head with every word.

"They forget nothing—and we've been fighting those same monsters in the tunnels, anyway."

"From defensible positions, on ground of our choosing," said Hanaleisa, to which Rorick merely shrugged.

"Do ye think ye might be finding yer way back to the tunnels near to Carradoon?" Ivan asked Temberle and Hanaleisa.

"You cannot . . ." Temberle started, but Hanaleisa cut him short.

"We can," she said. "I've been marking the tunnels at various junctures. We can get back close to where we started, I'm sure."

"Might be our best option," said Ivan.

"No," said Temberle.

"We're not knowin' what's still there, boy," Ivan reminded. "And we know what's waiting for us in the mountains, and I know ye didn't see nothing the size o' that damned wyrm in Carradoon, else ye'd all be dead. I'd like to give ye a better choice—I'd like a better choice for meself!—but I'm not for knowing another way out o' these tunnels, and the one I came down can't be climbed, and I wouldn't be climbing back that way anyhow!"

Temberle and Hanaleisa exchanged concerned looks, and both glanced across the torchlit chamber to the haggard refugees. The weight of responsibility pressed down upon them, for their decisions would affect everyone in that chamber, perhaps fatally.

"Choice ain't for ye, anyway," Ivan blustered a few heartbeats later, as if reading their thoughts, certainly reading their expressions. "Ye done good in gettin' these folk from Carradoon, and I'll be sure to tell yer Ma and Da that when we get back to Spirit Soaring. But I'm here now, and last time I bothered to look, I've got a bit o' rank and experience on the both o' ye put together.

"We can't stay down here. Yer brother's right on that. If we were all kin dwarves, we'd just widen a few holes, put up a few walls, call the place home, and be done with it. But we ain't, and we got to get out, and I can't be getting us out unless we're going back the way ye came in."

"We'll be fighting there," Hanaleisa warned.

"More the reason to go, then!" Ivan declared with a toothy grin.

And they went, back the way they had come, and when they weren't sure of either left or right, because Hanaleisa's markings were neither complete nor always legible, they guessed and pressed on. And when they guessed wrong, they turned around and marched back, double-time, by the barking commands of Ivan Bouldershoulder.

Bark he did, but he added a much-needed enthusiasm, full of optimistic promise. His energy proved contagious and the group made great headway that first day. The second went along splendidly as well, except for one unusually long detour that nearly dropped Ivan, who insisted on leading the way, into a deep pit.

By the third day, their steps came smaller and the barks became mere words. Still they went along, for what choice did they have? When they heard the growls of monsters echoing along distant tunnels, though they all cringed at the notion of more fighting, they took hope that such sounds meant they were nearing the end of their Underdark torment. Hungry, as they had fed on nothing more than a few mushrooms and a few cave fish, thirsty, as most of the water they found was too fetid to drink, they took a deep breath and pushed forward.

Around a bend in the corridor, where the tunnel soon widened into a large chamber, they saw their enemies—not undead monsters, but the crawling fleshy beasts that Ivan knew so well—at the same time their enemies saw them. Driven by the knowledge that he had led those poor, beleaguered folks, including Cadderly's precious children, into danger, Ivan Boulder-shoulder was fast to the charge. Fury drove his steps, and determination that he would not be the cause of disaster brought great strength to his limbs. The dwarf hit the advancing enemy line like a huge rock denying the tide. Crawlers flowed around him, but those nearest exploded under the weight of Ivan's mighty axe.

Flanking him left came Temberle and Hanaleisa, a great slash of the blade and a flurry of fists, and to the right came Pikel and Rorick. Rorick attempted only one spell, and when it utterly failed, he took up the dagger he carried on his belt and was glad that he, like his siblings, had been taught how to fight.

For Pikel, there was no magical glow to his club, no shillelagh enchantment to add weight to his blows. But like his brother, Pikel had gone to a deeper place of anger, a place where he was fighting not just for himself, but for others who could hardly defend against such enemies.

"Oo oi!" he yelled repeatedly, emphasizing each shout by cracking his cudgel across the head of a crawling beast. He could only swing with one arm, it was true, and swung a weapon absent its usual enchantment, but crawler after crawler was bowled back or fell straight to the ground, shuddering in its death throes, its skull battered to shards.

With that living prow of five skilled fighters, the embattled refugees pushed on and drove their enemies back. Any thought that they should slow and close ranks, or flee back the way they had come, was denied by Ivan—not with words, but because he would neither slow nor turn. He seemed as if he cared not if those flanking and supporting him kept up.

For Ivan, this wasn't about tactics, but about anger—anger at all of it: at the dragon and at the danger that threatened Cadderly's children; at the frustration of his brother, who felt abandoned by his god; at the loss of security in the place he called home. Left and right went his axe, with no thought of defense—not a blocking arm or a creature leaping at him deterred his cuts. He sliced a grasping arm off where his axe hit it, and more than one fleshy beast did leap upon him, only to get a head-butt or a jab in the face from the pommel of the axe. Then, as the foolish creature inevitably fell away, Ivan kicked and spat and ultimately split the thing's head wide with that double-bladed, monstrous weapon he carried.

He waded along, the floor slick with blood and gore, with brains and slabs of flesh.

He got too far ahead of the others, and creatures came at him from every side, even from behind.

And creatures died all around the frenzied dwarf.

They grabbed at him and clawed at him. Blood showed on every patch of Ivan that was not armored, and creatures died with strands of his yellow hair in their long fingers. But he didn't slow, and his blows rained down with even more strength and fury.

Soon enough, even the stupid crawlers understood to stay away from that one, and Ivan could have walked across the rest of the chamber unhindered. Only then did he turn back to support the line.

The fight went on and on, until every swing of a weapon came with aching arms, until the whole of the refugee band gasped for every breath as they struggled to continue the battle. But continue they did, and the crawlers died and died. When it was at last over, the remnants of the strange enemy finally fleeing down side corridors, the wide chamber full of blood and bodies, the ranks of the refugees had not significantly thinned.

But if there was an end to their battle, none of them could see it.

"To Carradoon," the indomitable Hanaleisa bade Ivan and Pikel, raising her voice so that all could hear, and hoping against hope that her feigned optimism would prove contagious.

The meager food, the constant fighting, the lack of daylight, the smell of death, and the grieving of so many for so many had depleted the band, she knew, as did everyone else. The reprieve that was Ivan, adding his bold, confident, and fearless voice, had proven a temporary uplift.

"We'll be fighting, every step!" complained one of the fishermen, sitting on a rock, his face streaked with blood—his own and that of a crawler—and with tears. "My stomach's growling for food and my arms are aching."

"And there's nothing back the way we came but dark death!" another shouted at him, and so yet another argument ensued.

"Get us out of here," Hanaleisa whispered to Ivan. "Now."

They didn't bury their dead under piles of heavy stones, and they made no formal plans for their wounded, just offered each a shoulder and dragged themselves along. They were moving again soon after the fight, but it seemed an inch at a time.

"If it comes to fightin' again, the two of ye will make us win or make us lose," Ivan informed Temberle and Hanaleisa. "We can't move along as fast, 'tis true, but we can't fight any slower or we die. They'll be lookin' to you two. Ye find that deeper place and pull out the strength ye need."

The twins exchanged fearful glances, but those fast became expressions of determination.

* * * * *

In a quiet chamber not far from where the Bouldershoulders, the Bonaduce children, and the other refugees earned their hard-fought victory, the absolute darkness was interrupted by a blue-glowing dot, hovering more than six feet above the stone floor. As if some unseen hand was drawing with it, the dot moved along, cutting the blackness with a blue line.

It hung there, sizzling with magical power for a few moments, then seemed to expand, moving from two dimensions to three, forming a glowing doorway.

A young drow male stepped through that doorway, materializing from thin air, it seemed. Hand crossbow in one hand, sword in the other, the warrior slipped in silently, peering intently down the corridor, one way, then another. After a quick search of the area, he moved in front of the portal, stood up straight, and sheathed his sword.

On that signal, another dark elf stepped into the corridor. Fingers waggling in the silent language of the race, he ordered the first scout to move back behind the magical entry and take up a sentry position.

More drow stepped out, moving methodically and with precision and discipline, securing the area.

The portal sizzled, its glow increasing. More dark elves stepped through, including Kimmuriel Oblodra, who had created the psionic dimensional rift. A drow beside him began to signal with his fingers, but Kimmuriel, showing great confidence, grabbed his hand and bade him to whisper instead.

"You are certain of this?" the drow, Mariv by name, asked.

"He is following Jarlaxle's recommendation and request," answered the second drow who had come through the portal, Valas Hune, a scout of great renown. "So, no, Mariv, our friend is not certain because he knows that Jarlaxle is not certain. That one is always acting as if he is sure of his course, but all of his life's been a gamble, hasn't it?"

"That is his charm, I fear," said Kimmuriel.

"And why we follow him," Mariv said with a shrug.

"You follow him because you agreed to follow him, and promised to follow him," Kimmuriel reminded, clearly uncomfortable with, or condescending toward, such a line of reasoning. Kimmuriel Oblodra, after all, was perhaps the only drow close enough to Jarlaxle to understand the truth of that one: the appearance of a great gamble might be Jarlaxle's charm, but Kimmuriel knew that the source of the charm was truly a farce. Jarlaxle seemed to gamble all the time, but his course was rarely one of uncertainty. That was why the logical and pragmatic, never-gambling Kimmuriel trusted Jarlaxle. It had nothing to do with charm, and everything to do with the realization of that which Jarlaxle promised.

"You may, of course, change your mind," he finished to Mariv, "but it would not be a course I would advise."

"Unless he'd prefer you dead," Valas Hune remarked to Mariv with a sly grin, and he moved away to make sure the perimeter was secure.

"I know you're uncomfortable with this mission," Kimmuriel said to Mariv, and such empathy was indeed rare, almost nonexistent, from the callous and logical drow psionicist. Mariv had been Kimmuriel's appointee, and had climbed the ranks of Bregan D'aerthe during Jarlaxle's absence, when the band had been fully under Kimmuriel's direction. The young wizard was in Kimmuriel's highest favor, one of three in the third tier of the mercenary band where Kimmuriel was undisputed second and Jarlaxle was undisputed leader. Even with the drawdown and current unpredictability of magic, the resourceful Mariv retained Kimmuriel's good graces, for he was possessed of many magical items of considerable power and was no novice with the blade as well. Well-versed with the sword, having graduated from Melee-Magthere, the drow martial school, before his tenure at Sorcere, the academy for wizards, Mariv remained a potent force even in a time of the collapsing Weave.

Kimmuriel stood quiet then, and waved away all other conversation, waiting for the rest of his strike force to come through the gate, and for all the preparations around him to be completed. As soon as those things were done, all eyes turned his way.

"You know why we have come," Kimmuriel said quietly to those around him. "Your orders are without exception. Strike true and strike as instructed—and *only* as instructed."

The psionicist knew that more than a few of the Bregan D'aerthe warriors remained confused about their mission, and some were even repulsed by it. He didn't care. He trusted his underlings to perform as instructed, for to do otherwise was to face the wrath of not only the ultimately deadly Jarlaxle, but of Kimmuriel, and no one could exact exquisite torture more profoundly than a psionicist.

Two score of Bregan D'aerthe's force had entered the tunnels beneath the Snowflakes not far from the destroyed town of Carradoon. They moved out, silent, methodical, deadly.

CHAPTER

It started hesitantly, one cheer of victory among a sea of doubting and skeptical expressions. For those outside of Spirit Soaring, the dwarves on the ground and the wizards and priests fighting from the balconies and rooftops, they saw only that single image of the great dracolich dematerializing before their astonished eyes, fading to seeming nothingness under the brilliant light of Cadderly's conjured sun.

It was gone, of that they were all certain, and the assault of its minions had also ended with the disappearance of the great wyrm. The wizards didn't even bother sending magical bolts out at the retreating hordes, so intent were they on the empty spot where the dracolich had been.

Then that one cheer became a chorus of absolute relief. Clapping, whistling, and shouting with joy, they moved toward the spot where the beast had departed the field as if pulled by gravity.

The cheers grew louder, shouts of joy and hope. Wizards proclaimed that the Weave itself would mend. Priests cried out in joy that they would once more be able to speak with their gods. Cheers for Cadderly rolled across the walls, some proclaiming him a god, a deity who could bring the sun itself to bear on his enemies.

"All fear Cadderly!"

But that was outside Spirit Soaring. That euphoria was for those who could not hear Catti-brie screaming.

With magical anklets speeding his strides, Drizzt outpaced Cadderly, Danica, and even Bruenor, desperate as the dwarf king was to reach his daughter. The drow scrambled through the corridors, leaped a banister to the fifth step of a rising staircase, and sprinted up to the third floor three steps at a time. He banged against walls so he didn't have to slow in his turns down the side corridors, and when he came to her door, Jarlaxle's eye patch in hand, along with his divinely weighted scimitar, he shouldered right through it.

Jarlaxle was waiting for him, though how the mercenary had beaten him to the room, Drizzt could not fathom and didn't have time to consider.

Catti-brie huddled against the back wall, screaming no more, but trembling with abject terror. She shielded her face with upraised arms, and between those intervening limbs, Drizzt could see that her white eyes were wide indeed.

He leaped toward her, but Jarlaxle caught him and tugged him back.

"The patch!" Jarlaxle warned.

Drizzt had enough of his senses remaining to pause for a moment and don the enchanted eye patch, dropping Icingdeath to the floor in the process. He went to his beloved and enveloped her, wrapping her in a great hug and trying to calm her.

Catti-brie seemed no less frightened when the other three arrived a few heartbeats later.

"What's it about?" Bruenor demanded of both Cadderly and Jarlaxle.

Jarlaxle had his suspicions and started to answer, but he bit his response off short and shook his head. In truth, he had no real evidence, nor did Cadderly, and they all looked to Drizzt, whose eye—the one not covered by the patch—like his wife's, had gone wide with horror.

* * * * *

They had not destroyed the Ghost King—that much was obvious to Drizzt as he hugged Catti-brie close and slipped into the pit of despair that had become her prison.

Her eyes looked into that alien world. He, briefly, resided in a gray shadow of the world around him, mountainous terrain to mimic the Snowflakes, in the Shadowfell.

The Ghost King was there.

On the plain before Catti-brie, the dracolich thrashed and roared in defiance and pain. Its bones shone whiter, its skin, where the scales had fallen away, showed an angry red mottled by great blisters. Seared by holy light, the beast seemed out of its mind with pain and rage, and though he had just faced it in battle, Drizzt could not imagine standing before it at that horrible time.

Cadderly had stung the beast profoundly, but Drizzt could easily recognize that the wounds would not prove mortal. Already the beast seemed on the mend, and that act of reconstitution was the most terrifying of all.

The beast reared up in all of its fiendish glory, and it began to turn, faster and faster, and from its spinning form emanated shadows, like demonic arms of darkness. They reached across the plain, grasping scrambling crawlers, who shrieked, but only once, then fell dead.

Drizzt had never witnessed anything like it, and he concentrated on only a small portion of the spectacle. For the sake of his own sanity, he had to keep his emotional and mental distance from the conduit that was Catti-brie.

The Ghost King was leaching the life energy out of anything it could reach, was stealing the life-force from the crawlers and using that energy to mend its considerable wounds.

Drizzt knew that the monster would recover fully, and soon. Then the Ghost King would return to Spirit Soaring.

With great effort and greater remorse, the drow pulled himself away from his beloved wife. He couldn't comfort her. She felt not at all his embrace, and heard not at all his gentle calls.

He had to return to his companions. He had to warn them. Finally, he managed to let go, then broke the mental link to Catti-brie. The effort left him so drained that he collapsed on the floor of the room.

He felt strong hands grab him and hoist him upright, then guide him to sit on the edge of the small bed.

Drizzt opened his eyes, pulling back the eye patch.

"Bah, but another of her fits?" said Athrogate, who had just come to the door, Thibbledorf Pwent beside him.

"No," answered Cadderly, who stared at Drizzt. All eyes went to the priest, and many of them, Danica most of all, gasped in surprise at the sight of the man.

He wasn't young any more.

For years, it had taken first-time visitors to Spirit Soaring considerable effort to reconcile the appearance of Cadderly Bonaduce, the accomplished and venerable priest whose remarkable exploits stretched back two decades, for he appeared as young as his own children. But before the disbelieving stares of the three dwarves, two drow, and his wife, that youth had dissipated.

Cadderly looked at least middle-aged, and more. His skin sagged, his shoulders slumped a bit, and his muscles thinned even as the others stood gawking. He looked older than Danica, older than he was, nearer to sixty than to fifty.

"Cadderly," Danica gasped. He managed a smile back at her and held his hand up to keep her and the others at bay.

He seemed to stabilize, and he appeared as a man in his fifties, not much older than his actual age.

"Humans," Athrogate snorted.

"The magic of the cathedral," Jarlaxle said. "The wounded cathedral."

"What do you know?" Danica snapped at the drow mercenary.

"The truth," said Cadderly, and Danica turned to him, approached him, and he allowed her a hug. "My youth, my health—are wound within the walls of Spirit Soaring," he explained to them. "The beast wounded it—wounded us!" He gave a helpless little laugh. "And surely wounded me."

"We will fix it," Danica breathlessly promised.

But Cadderly shook his head. "It isn't a matter of wood and nails and stone," he said.

"Then Deneir will fix it with you," Jarlaxle said, drawing curious stares with his unexpected compassion.

Cadderly started to shake his head, then looked at the drow and nodded, for it was no time for any expression of pessimism.

"But first we must ready ourselves for the return of the Ghost King," Jarlaxle remarked, and he led everyone's gaze to Drizzt Do'Urden, who sat on the bed staring helplessly at Catti-brie.

"What's she seeing, elf?" Athrogate demanded. "What memory this time?"

"No memory," Drizzt whispered. He could hardly even find his voice. "She cowers before the raging Ghost King."

"In the Shadowfell," Cadderly reasoned, and Drizzt nodded.

"It is there, in all its fury, and there it heals its wounds," the drow said, looking so pitifully, so helplessly, at his lost and terrified wife. He couldn't reach her. He couldn't help her. He could only look on and pray that somehow Catti-brie would find her way out of darkness.

For a fleeting moment, it occurred to Drizzt Do'Urden that his wife might truly be better off dead, for it seemed that her torment might have no end. He thought back to that quiet morning on the road from Silverymoon when, despite the troubles with the ways of magic, all had seemed so right in his world, beside the woman he loved. It had been only a matter of tendays since that falling magical strand had descended upon Catti-brie and had taken her from Drizzt, but to him, sitting on that bed, so near and yet so distant from his wife, it truly seemed a lifetime ago.

All of that pain and confusion showed on his face, he realized, when he looked at his companions. Bruenor stood in the doorway, trembling with rage, tears streaking his hairy cheeks, his strong fists balled at his sides so tightly that his grip could have crushed stone. He studied Danica, so troubled by her own spouse's dilemma, still taking the time to alternate her gaze between Cadderly, whom she stood beside, and Drizzt, and with equal sympathy and fear showing for both.

Jarlaxle put a hand on Drizzt's shoulder. "If there's a way to get her back, we will find it," he promised, and Drizzt knew he meant every word. When Drizzt looked past him to Bruenor, he recognized that the dwarf understood Jarlaxle's sincerity.

But both also knew that it wouldn't do any good.

"It heals, and it will return," Cadderly said. "We must prepare, and quickly."

"To what end?" asked a voice from the hallway, and they all turned to see Ginance and the others standing there. The speaker, a wizard, held one arm in close, for his robe's sleeve had fallen to tatters and the arm underneath it had withered to dried skin and bone. One of the dracolich's tail swipes had touched him there.

"If we defeat it again, will it not simply retreat once more to this other world of which you speak?" Ginance asked. Cadderly winced at the devastating question from his normally optimistic assistant.

Everyone understood Cadderly's grimace, particularly Drizzt, for the simple truth of Ginance's remark could not be denied. How could they defeat a beast who could so readily retreat, and so easily heal, as Drizzt had witnessed when he had hugged Catti-brie?

"We will find a way," Cadderly promised. "Before Spirit Soaring, in the old structure that was the Edificant Library, we fought a vampire. That creature, too, could run from the field if the battle turned badly. But we found a way."

"Aye, yer dwarfs sucked the gassy thing into a bellows!" howled Thibble-dorf Pwent, who had made Ivan Bouldershoulder tell him that story over and over again during the time Ivan and Pikel had spent at Mithral Hall. "And spat him out into a running stream under the sunshine!"

"What're ye saying?" Athrogate demanded, his eyes wide with intrigue and awe. "Are ye speaking true?"

"He is," Caderly confirmed, and he tossed a wink at the rest of the crew, all of them glad for the light-hearted respite.

"Bwahaha!" roared Athrogate. "I'm thinking that we're needin' a song for that one!"

The faces around them, particularly those in the hallway, didn't change much, however, as the weight of the situation quickly pressed the brief respite away.

"We need to prepare," Caderly said again, when all had muted to an uncomfortable silence.

"Or we should leave this place, and quickly," said the wizard with the withered arm. "Run fast for Baldur's Gate, or some other great city where the beast daren't approach."

"Where an army of archers will greet it with doom too sudden for its clever retreat!" another voice chimed in from beyond the room's door.

Drizzt watched Caderly through it all, as the chorus for retreat grew louder and more insistent, and Drizzt understood the priest's personal turmoil. Caderly could not disagree with the logic of swift departure, of running far from that seemingly doomed place.

But Caderly could not go. Damage to Spirit Soaring manifested in his personal being. And Caderly and Danica could not go far, since their children were still missing and might be out there, or in Carradoon.

Drizzt looked to Bruenor for guidance.

"I ain't leaving," the dwarf king said without hesitation, commanding the gathering. "Let the beast come back, and we'll pound it into dust."

"That is foolish . . ." the wizard with the withered arm started to argue, but Bruenor's expression stopped the debate before it could begin, and made the man blanch almost as surely as had the sight of the dracolich.

"I ain't leaving," Bruenor said again. "Unless it's to go find Caderly's kids, or to go and find me missing friend, Pikel, who stood beside me and me kin in our time o' trial. He's lost his brother, so Lady Danica tells me, but he's not to lose his friends from Mithral Hall."

"Then you'll be dead," someone in the hall dared to say.

"We're all to die," Bruenor retorted. "Some of us're already dead, though we're not knowin' it. For when ye're to run and leave yer friends behind, then ye're surely dead."

Someone started to reply with an argument, but Cadderly shouted, "Not now!" So rare was it that the priest raised his voice in such a way that all conversation in the room and without stopped. "Go and assess the damage," Cadderly instructed them all. "Count our wounds . . ."

"And our dead," the withered wizard added with a hiss.

"And our dead," Cadderly conceded. "Go and learn, go and think, and do so quickly." He looked at Drizzt and asked, "How long do we have?"

But the drow could only shrug.

"Quickly," Cadderly said again. "And for those who would leave, organize your wagons as fast as you can. It would not do you well to be caught on the road when the Ghost King returns."

* * * * *

His giant hat in hand, Jarlaxle entered the private quarters of Cadderly and Danica, who sat around the priest's desk, staring at his every step.

"You surprise me," Cadderly greeted him.

"You surprise everyone around you with this new magic you've found," Jarlaxle replied, and he took the chair Danica indicated, beside her and opposite Cadderly.

"No," Cadderly replied. "I have not found any new magic. It has found me. I can't even begin to explain it, and so how can I claim ownership of it? I know not from where it comes, or if it will be there when I need it in the next crisis."

"Let us hope," said Jarlaxle.

Outside the room's south window came a commotion, horses whinnying and men calling out orders.

"They're all leaving," Jarlaxle said. "Even your friend Ginance."

"I told her to go," said Cadderly. "This is not her fight."

"You would flee, too, if you could," Jarlaxle gathered from his tone.

With a heavy sigh, Cadderly stood up and walked to the window to glance at the activity in the courtyard. "This battle has confirmed an old fear," he explained. "When I built Spirit Soaring, weaving the magic Deneir allowed to flow through this mere mortal coil, it aged me. As the cathedral neared completion, I became an old man."

"We had already said our farewells," Danica added.

"I thought I had reached the end of my life, and that was acceptable to me, for I had fulfilled my duty to my god." He paused and looked at Jarlaxle curiously. "Are you religious?" he asked.

"The only deity I grew up knowing was one I would have preferred not to know," the drow answered.

"You are more worldly than that," said Cadderly.

"No," Jarlaxle answered. "I follow no particular god. I thought to interview them first, to see what paradise they might offer when at last I have left this life."

Danica crinkled her face at that, but Cadderly managed a laugh. "Always a quip from Jarlaxle."

"Because I do not consider the question a serious one."

"No?" Cadderly asked with exaggerated surprise. "What could be more serious than discovering that which is in your heart?"

"I know what is in my heart. Perhaps I simply do not feel the need to find a name for it."

Cadderly laughed again. "I would be a liar if I told you I didn't understand."

"I would be a liar if I bothered to answer your ignorance. Or a fool."

"Jarlaxle is no fool," Danica cut in, "but of the former charge, I reserve judgment."

"You wound me to my heart, Lady Danica," said the drow, but his grin was wide, and Danica couldn't resist a smile.

"Why haven't you left?" Cadderly asked bluntly. It was that question, Jarlaxle knew, that was the reason he'd been asked to join the couple. "The road is clear and our situation seems near to hopeless, and yet you remain."

"Young man . . ."

"Not so young," Cadderly corrected.

"By my standards, you will be young when you have passed your one-hundredth birthday, and young still when you have spent another century rotting in the ground," said Jarlaxle. "But to the point, I have nowhere to run that this Ghost King cannot find me. It found me in the north, outside of Mirabar. And as it found me, I knew it would find you."

"And Artemis Entreri?" Danica asked, to which Jarlaxle shrugged.

"Years have passed since I last spoke with him."

"So you came here hoping that I would have an answer to your dilemma," said Cadderly.

Again the drow shrugged. "Or that we might work together to find a solution to our common problem," he answered. "And I did not come without powerful allies to our cause."

"And you feel no guilt in involving Drizzt, Bruenor, Catti-brie, and that Pwent creature in such a desperate struggle?" Danica asked. "You would march them to near-certain doom?"

"Apparently I have more faith in us than you do, Lady," Jarlaxle quipped, and turned to Cadderly. "I was not disingenuous when I proposed to Bruenor and Drizzt that they would do well in bringing Catti-brie to this place. I knew that many of the great minds of our time had no doubt come to Spirit Soaring in search of answers—and what could provide a greater clue to the reality that has descended upon us than the affliction of Catti-brie? Even regarding the Ghost King, I believe it is all connected—more so now that Drizzt has told us that she is watching the beast in that other world in which her mind is trapped."

"They are connected," Cadderly agreed, speaking before Danica could respond. "Both are manifestations of the same catastrophe."

"In one, we may find clues to the other," said Jarlaxle. "We already have! Thank your god that Catti-brie was here, that we could discern the truth of the Ghost King's defeat, and know that the beast would return."

"If I could find my god, I would thank him," Cadderly replied dryly. "But you are correct, of course. So now we know, Jarlaxle. The beast will return, whole, angry, and wiser than in our first battle. Do you intend to remain to battle it again?"

"Such a course offers me the best chance to prevail, I expect, and so yes, good sir Cadderly, with your permission, I and my dwarf companion would like to stand beside you for that next battle."

"Granted," Danica said, cutting Cadderly short, and when she looked at him, he flashed her a smile of appreciation. "But do you have any ideas? They say you are a clever one."

"You have not witnessed enough of me to come to that conclusion on your own?" Jarlaxle said to her, and he patted his heart as if she had wounded him profoundly.

"Not really, no," she replied.

Jarlaxle burst out in laughter, but only briefly. "We must kill it quickly—that much is obvious," he said. "I see no way to hinder its ability to walk between the worlds, and so we must defeat it abruptly and completely."

"We struck at it with every magic I could manage," said Cadderly. "I merely hope to be able to replicate some of those spells—I hold no illusions that there are greater powers to access."

"There are other ways," Jarlaxle said, and he nodded his chin toward Cadderly's hand crossbow and bandolier.

"I shot it repeatedly," Cadderly reminded him.

"And a hundred bees might sting a man to little effect," the drow replied. "But I have been to a desert where the bees were the size of a man. Trust me when I tell you that you would not wish to feel the sting of but one of those."

"What do you mean?" asked Danica.

"My companion, Athrogate, is a clever one, and King Bruenor more so than he," Jarlaxle replied.

"Would that Ivan Bouldershoulder were still with us!" said Cadderly, his tone more full of hope than of lament.

"Siege weapons? A ballista?" Danica asked, and Jarlaxle shrugged again.

"Drizzt, Bruenor, and his battlerager will remain as well," Jarlaxle informed Cadderly, and the drow stood up from his chair. "Ginance and some others offered to take Catti-brie away, but Drizzt refused." He looked Cadderly directly in the eye as he added, "They don't intend to lose."

"Catti-brie should have been allowed to go," said Danica.

"No," Cadderly replied, and when both looked at him, they saw him staring out the window. Danica could see that he was suddenly deep in thought. "We need her," he said in a tone that revealed him to be certain of his claim, though not yet sure why.

* * * * *

"Copper for yer thoughts, elf," Bruenor said. He moved behind Drizzt, who stood on a balcony overlooking the courtyard of Spirit Soaring, staring out at the ruined forest where the dracolich had passed.

Drizzt glanced back at him and acknowledged him with a nod, but didn't otherwise reply—just gazed into the distance.

"Ah, me girl," Bruenor whispered, moving up beside him, for how could Drizzt be thinking of anything else? "Ye think she's lost to us."

Still Drizzt didn't reply.

"I should smack ye one for losing faith in her, elf," Bruenor said.

Drizzt looked at him again, and he withered under that honest gaze, the level of the dwarf's own confidence overwhelming his bluster.

"Then why're we stayin'?" Bruenor managed to ask, a last gasp of defiance to the drow's irresistible reasoning.

Drizzt wore a puzzled look.

"If not for bringing me girl back, then why're we staying here?" Bruenor clarified.

"You would leave a friend in need?"

"Why're we keepin' her here, then?" Bruenor went on. "Why not put her on one o' them wagons rolling away, bound for a safer place?"

"I don't believe half of them will make it out of the forest alive."

"Bah, that's not what ye're thinking!" Bruenor scolded. "Ye're thinking that we'll find a way. That as we kill this dragon thing, we'll also find a way to get me girl back. It's what ye're thinking, elf, and don't ye lie to me."

"It is what I'm hoping," Drizzt admitted, "not thinking. The two are not the same. Hoping against reason."

"Not so much, else ye wouldn't keep her here, where we're all likely to die."

"Is there a safe place in all the world?" Drizzt asked. "And something else. When the dracolich began to shift to the other plane, Guenhwyvar fled."

"Smart cat would've run off long before that," said Bruenor.

"Guenhwyvar fears no battle, but she understands the dilemma of dimensions joined. Remember when the crystal tower in Icewind Dale collapsed?"

"Aye," said Bruenor, his face brightening just a bit. "And Rumblebelly rode the damned cat to her home."

"Remember Pasha Pook's palace in Calimport?"

"Aye, a sea o' cats following yer Guenhwyvar from her home. What're ye thinking, elf? That yer cat might get you to me girl on the other plane, and might bring ye both back?"

"I don't know," Drizzt admitted.

"But ye're thinking there might be a way?" Bruenor asked in a tone as desperately hopeful as any the drow had ever heard from his dwarf friend.

He fixed Bruenor with a stare and a grin. "Isn't there always a way?"

Bruenor managed a nod at that, and as Drizzt turned his gaze outward from the balcony, he looked to the trees.

"What are they doing?" Drizzt asked a moment later, when Thibbledorf

Pwent and Athrogate bobbed out of the forest, carrying a heavy log shoulder to shoulder.

"If we're meaning to stay and fight, then we're meaning to win," said Bruenor.

"But what are they doing, exactly?" Drizzt asked.

"I'm afraid to ask them two," Bruenor admitted, and he and Drizzt shared a much-needed chuckle.

"Ye going to bring in the damned cat again this fight?" Bruenor asked.

"I fear to. The seam between these worlds, between life and death as well, is too unpredictable. I would not lose Guen as I have lost . . ."

His voice trailed off, but he didn't need to finish the thought for Bruenor to understand.

"World's gone crazy," the dwarf said.

"Or maybe it always was."

"Nah, but don't ye start talking like that," Bruenor scolded. "We've put a lot o' good years and good work under our girdles, and ye know it."

"And we even made peace with orcs," said Drizzt, and Bruenor's face tightened and he let out a little growl.

"Ye're a warm fire on a cold winter night, elf," he muttered.

Drizzt smiled all the wider, stood up straight, and stretched his arms and back. "We're staying and we're fighting, my friend. And one more thing we're doing . . ."

"Winning," said Bruenor. "We might get me girl back and we might not, elf, but I'm meaning to stay mad for a bit."

He punched Drizzt in the shoulder.

"Ye ready to kill us a dragon, elf?"

Drizzt didn't answer, but the look he gave to Bruenor, his lavender eyes full of a fire the dwarf king had seen so many times before, made Bruenor almost pity the dracolich.

Down on the courtyard below, Pwent, who was leading the pair, stumbled and the two dwarves crashed down in a heap with their heavy cargo.

"If them two don't kill us all with their plannin', that wyrm ain't getting back to its hiding place," Bruenor declared. "Or if it does, then I'm meaning to find a way to chase it there and be done with it!"

Drizzt nodded, more than ready for the fight, but mixed with his expression of determination was a bit of intrigue at that last statement. His hand went to his belt pouch, to Guenhwyvar, and he wondered.

He had traveled the planes with the cat before, after all.

"What're ye thinking, elf?" Bruenor asked.

Drizzt flashed him those eyes again, so full of determination and simmering anger.

Bruenor nodded and smiled, no less determined and no less angry.

* * * * *

"Is there no way to learn?" Danica asked Cadderly.

Cadderly shook his head. "I've tried. I've asked, of Deneir or of any sentience I might find anywhere."

"I can't do this any more," Danica admitted. She slumped in her chair and put her hands over her face. Cadderly was at her side in a heartbeat, hugging her, but he had little to offer. He was no less tormented than she.

Their children were out there somewhere, maybe alive and maybe, very possibly, dead.

"I have to go back out," Danica said, straightening and taking a deep, steadying breath. "I have to go to Carradoon."

"You tried already, and it nearly killed you," Cadderly reminded. "The forest is no less—"

"I know!" Danica snapped at him. "I know and I don't care. I can't stay here and just wait and hope."

"I cannot go!" Cadderly shouted back at her.

"I know," Danica said softly, tenderly, and she reached up and ran her fingers across Cadderly's cheek. "You are bound here, tied to this place, I know. You cannot desert it, because if it falls, you fall, and our enemies win. But I have recovered from my wounds, and we have driven off the beast for now." Cadderly started to interrupt, but Danica silenced him by putting a finger over his lips. "I know, my love," she said. "The Ghost King will return and attack Spirit Soaring once more. I know. And it is a fight I welcome, for I will see that creature destroyed. But . . ."

"But our children are out there," Cadderly finished for her. "They're alive—I know they are! If any of them had fallen, Spirit Soaring would feel the loss."

Danica looked at him, curious.

"They are of me, as this place is of me," Cadderly tried to explain. "They are alive, I am sure."

Danica fell back a bit and stared at her husband. She understood his confidence, but knew, too, that it was based more on a need to believe that the children were alive and well than on anything substantive.

"You cannot stay here," Cadderly said, surprising her, and she sat up straight, her eyes wide.

"You are about to fight the most desperate battle of your life, and you would send me away?"

"If the Ghost King returns and is to be defeated . . ." Cadderly paused there, seeming almost embarrassed.

"It will be by the power of Cadderly, and not the fists of Danica," she reasoned.

Cadderly shrugged. "We are a powerful team, we seven, each armed in our own ways to do battle with such a beast as the Ghost King."

"But I least of all," the woman said. She held up her empty hands. "My weapons are less effective than Bruenor's axe, and I haven't the tricks of Jarlaxle."

"There is no one I would rather have fighting beside me than you," Cadderly said. "But truly, there is no one in all the world who might better elude the monsters in the forest and find our children. And if we don't have them, then . . ."

"Then what is the point?" Danica finished for him. She leaned in and kissed him passionately.

"They are alive," Cadderly said.

"And I will find them," Danica whispered back.

She was out of Spirit Soaring within the hour, moving among the trees alongside the road to Carradoon, invisible and silent in the dark night.

CHAPTER

D A W N

26

"W hy aren't we fighting?" Temberle whispered to Ivan. Even his hushed tone seemed to echo in the too-quiet tunnels.

"Not for knowin'," Ivan replied to Temberle and to all the remaining refugees in the group, which numbered less than twenty. "Hoping it's your da's work."

"Boom," Pikel said hopefully, and loudly, drawing gasps from all the others. "Oops," the green-bearded dwarf apologized, slapping his hand over his mouth.

"Or they're setting a trap for us," Hanaleisa interjected. Ivan was nodding as she spoke, about to make the same observation. "Perhaps they've learned from the slaughter."

"So what are we to do?" asked Rorick, and when she looked at her younger brother, Hanaleisa saw real fear there, and put a comforting hand on his shoulder.

"We go on, for what choice do we got?" said Ivan, and he purposely lifted his voice. "If they be lying in wait for us, then we'll just kill 'em and walk on over their rottin' bodies."

Ivan slapped his bloodstained axe across his open hand and nodded with determination, then stomped away.

"Oo oi!" Pikel agreed, and adjusted his cooking pot helmet and scrambled to follow.

Not far from that site, the beleaguered band entered a room that presented yet another puzzle, but a welcome one at first glance. The chamber floor was littered with dead crawlers and dead giant bats, and even a dead giant.

The group scanned for clues, mostly looking for the bodies of those who had fought the beasts. Was it another fleeing refugee group?

"Did they kill each other?" Temberle asked, voicing a question they were all asking themselves.

"Not unless they use tiny bows," one of the refugees answered. Temberle and the others moved to the man's position, bringing the meager torchlight to bear. They found him holding a small dart, like those Cadderly used with his hand crossbows.

"Father!" Rorick said hopefully.

"If it was, he was busy," said Hanaleisa as she moved around, finding the same darts littering the floor and the bodies. She shook her head with doubt. Only two such hand crossbows were kept at Spirit Soaring, but dozens, perhaps hundreds, of darts had been fired in that fight. She pulled one from the corpse of a crawler and held it up, shaking her head even more. None of the darts showed her father's added feature: the collapsible center where the tiny vials of explosive oil were stored.

"These ain't Cadderly's," Ivan confirmed a moment later. Since he had designed and built Cadderly's hand crossbows and its quarrels, his words carried undeniable truth.

"Then who?" asked Rorick.

"We weren't that far away," Temberle added. "And this battle's not so old. This happened fast, and it happened quietly." He looked with great alarm at his sister and his Uncle Ivan.

"Poison-tipped," said Hanaleisa.

More than a few eyes widened at that, for most folk knew the dire implications of poison-tipped hand crossbow darts.

"Has the whole world gone upside down, then?" asked Ivan, his tone more sober—even somber—than ever. "I'm thinking the sooner we get to the surface, the better we'll be."

"Uh-huh," Pikel agreed.

On they marched, swiftly, and with all feeling that the enemy of their enemy would most certainly not prove to be their friend.

* * * * *

The hairless, black-skinned giant lurched forward another step.

Click. Click. Click.

The monster groaned as three more darts punctured its skin, adding to the drow sleep poison coursing its veins. Its next step came heavier, foot dragging.

Click. Click. Click.

The giant went down on one knee, barely conscious of the movement. Small, dodging forms came at it, left, right, and center, slender blades gleaming with magic. The nightwalker waved its arms, trying to deflect the approaching enemies, to block and to swat aside the dark elves as though they were gnats. But every swing, waved under the weight of a most profound weariness, was waved too slowly to catch the agile warriors. Every block failed to drive off the stabs and thrusts and slashes, and the giant nightwalker swatted nothing but the cavern's stagnant air.

They didn't maul the giant. Every strike landed precisely and efficiently in an area that would allow the smoothest and swiftest flow of blood. The behemoth didn't get hit a hundred times, not more than a score even, but as it settled to a prone position on the floor, overcome by poison and loss of blood, the nightwalker's wounds were surely mortal.

The last group, Valas Hune signaled to Kimmuriel. *The way is clear.*

Kimmuriel nodded and followed his lead team through the chamber. Another giant bat crashed down against the far wall, coaxed to sleep in mid flight. Many crawlers still thrashed on the floor, their movements uncoordinated and unfocused but defiant until one of the drow warriors found the time to finish the job with a sure stroke to the neck.

Out of that chamber, the Bregan D'aerthe force moved down a corridor to an area of tunnels and chambers puddled by lake water. After only a few more twists and turns, every dark elf squinted against the brightness of the surface. Night had fallen long ago, but the moon was up, and sensitive drow eyes stung under the brilliance of Selûne's glow.

Can we not simply leave this place? more than one set of fingers dared flash Kimmuriel's way, but they were met one and all with a stern look that offered no compromise.

He had determined that they needed to go to the ruined town on the lakeshore before leaving the uncivilized reaches between Old Shanatar and Great Bhaerynden, and so to the place known as Carradoon they would go.

They exited the tunnels in the cove north of the city and easily scaled the cliffs to the bluff overlooking the ruined town. More than half the structures had burned to the ground, and less than a handful of those remaining had avoided the conflagration. The air hung thick with smoke and the stench of death, and skeletons of ship masts dotted the harbor, like markers for mass graves. The dark elves moved down in tight formation, even more cautious outside than in the more familiar environ of the tunnels. A giant nightwing occasionally flew overhead, but unless it ventured too near, the disciplined drow held their shots.

Led by Valas Hune, scouts broke left and right, flanking, leading, and ensuring that no pursuit was forthcoming.

What do you seek in this ruin? Valas's fingers asked of Kimmuriel soon after they had entered the city proper.

Kimmuriel indicated that he wasn't quite certain, but assured the scout that something there was worth investigating. He sensed it, felt it keenly.

A commotion to the side broke the discussion short as both drow contemplated the beginnings of a battle along a road parallel to their path. Another giant nightwalker had found the band and foolishly came on. The tumult increased briefly as the closest drow engaged and lured the behemoth to a narrow stretch between two buildings, a place where drow hand crossbows could not miss the huge target.

Kimmuriel and the bulk of his force continued along before the thing was even dead, confident in the discipline and tactics of the skilled and battle-proven company.

A scout returning from the quay delivered the report Kimmuriel had awaited, and he led swiftly to the spot.

"That bodes ill," Valas Hune remarked—the first words spoken since they had come out of the tunnels—when they came in sight of the rift. Every dark elf viewing the spectacle knew it immediately for what it was: a tear in the fabric of two separate worlds, a magical gate.

They stopped a respectful distance away, defenders sliding out like tentacles to secure the area as only Bregan D'aerthe could.

"Purposeful? Or an accident of misfiring magic?" Valas Hune asked.

"It matters not," answered Kimmuriel. "Though I expect that we will encounter many such rifts."

"A good thing, then, that drow never tire of killing."

Valas Hune fell silent when he realized that Kimmuriel, eyes closed, was no longer listening. He watched as the psionicist settled back, then lifted his hands toward the dimensional rift and popped wide his eyes, throwing forth his mental energy.

Nothing happened.

"Purposeful," Kimmuriel answered. "And foolish."

"You cannot close it?"

"An illithid hive could not close it. Sorcere on their strongest day could not close it," he said, referring to the great academy of the magical Art in Menzoberranzan.

"Then what?"

Kimmuriel looked to Mariv, who produced a thick wood-and-metallic rod the length of his forearm. Delicate runes of red and brown adorned the cylindrical item. Mariv handed it to Kimmuriel.

"The rod that cancels magical effects?" Valas Hune asked.

Kimmuriel looked to a young warrior, the same who had led the way through the gate in the tunnels, bidding him forth. He signaled the rod's command words with the fingers of his free hand as he passed the powerful item to the younger drow.

Licking dry lips, the drow moved toward the rift. His long white hair started to dance as he neared, as if tingling with energy, or struck, perhaps, by winds blowing on the other side of the dimensional gate.

He glanced at Kimmuriel, who nodded for him to proceed.

The young drow lifted the rod up to the rift, licked his lips again, and spoke the words of command. The magical implement flared with a brief burst of power that flowed its length and leaped out at the rift.

Back came a profound darkness, a gray mist that rolled through the conduit and surged into the hand of the drow warrior, who wasn't wise enough or quick enough to drop the rod in time.

He did drop it when his arm fell limp. He looked at Kimmuriel and the others, his face stretching into the most profound expression of terror any of them had ever witnessed as his life-force withered to shadowstuff and his empty husk fell dead to the ground.

No one went to aid him, or even to investigate.

"We cannot close it," Kimmuriel announced. "We are done here."

He led them away at a swift pace, Valas recalling his scouts as they went.

As soon as he thought them far enough so that the rift's continuing fields wouldn't interfere, Kimmuriel enacted another of his dimensional doorways.

"Back to Luskan?" Mariv asked as the next least of the band was brought forward to ensure the integrity of the gate.

"For now, yes," answered Kimmuriel, who was thinking that perhaps their road would lead them much farther than Luskan, all the way back into the Underdark and Menzoberranzan, where they would become part of a drow defense comprised of twenty thousand warriors, priestesses, and wizards.

The young drow stepped through and signaled from the other side, from the subterranean home Kimmuriel's band had constructed under the distant port city on the Sword Coast.

The Bregan D'aerthe force departed the Barony of Impresk as swiftly and silently as they had come.

* * * * *

The human refugees' eyes, too, stung as they came in sight of the surface world after several long and miserable days of wandering and fighting in the dark tunnels. Squinting against the sunrise reflecting across Impresk Lake, Ivan led the group to the edge of the cave at the back of the small cove.

The rest of the group crowded up beside him, eager to feel the sun on their faces, desperate to be out from under tons of rock and earth. Collectively, they took great comfort in the quiet of the morning, with no sounds other than the songs of birds and the lap of waves against the rocks.

Ivan brought them quickly into the open air. They had found more slaughtered nightwings, nightwalkers, and crawlers. Convinced that the tunnels were infested with dark elves, Ivan and the others were happy indeed to be out of them!

Getting out of the cove took longer than expected. They didn't dare venture out near the deeper water, having seen too much of the undead fish. Getting up the cliff face, for they had come down with magical help from Pikel, was no easy task for the weary humans or the short-legged dwarves. They tried several routes unsuccessfully and eventually crossed the cove and climbed the lower northern rise. The sun was high in the eastern sky when they at last managed to circle around and come in sight of Carradoon.

For a long, long while, they stood on the high bluff looking down at the ruins, saying not a word, making not a sound other than the occasional sob.

"We got no reason to go in there," Ivan asserted at length.

"We have friends—" a man started to protest.

"Ain't nothing alive in there," Ivan interrupted. "Nothing alive ye're wantin' to see, at least."

"Our homes!" a woman wailed.

"Are gone," Ivan replied.

"Then what are we to do?" the first man shouted at him.

"Ye get on the road and get out o' here," said Ivan. "Meself and me brother're for Spirit Soaring . . ."

"Me brudder!" Pikel cheered, and pumped his stump into the air.

"And Cadderly's kids with us," Ivan added.

"Shalane is no farther, and down a safer road," the man argued.

"Then take it," Ivan said to him. "And good luck to ye." It seemed as simple as that to the dwarf, and he started away to the west, a route to circumvent the destroyed Carradoon and pick up the trail that led into the mountains and back to Spirit Soaring.

"What is happening to the world, Uncle Ivan?" Hanaleisa whispered.

"Durned if I know, girl. Durned if I know."

CHAPTER

ELSEWHERE LUCIDITY

Cadderly tapped a finger against his lips as he studied the woman playing out the scene before him. She was talking to Guenhwyvar, he believed, and he couldn't help but feel like a voyeur as he studied her reenactment of a private moment.

"Oh, but she's so pretty and fancy, isn't she?" Catti-brie said, her hand brushing the air as if she were petting the great panther as it curled near her feet. "With her lace and finery, so tall and so straight, and not a silly word to pass those painted lips, no, no."

She was there, but she wasn't, Cadderly sensed. Her movements were too complete and too complex to be merely a normal memory. No, she was reliving the moment precisely as it had occurred. Catti-brie's mind was back in time while her physical form was trapped in the current time and space.

With his unique experience regarding physical aging and regression, Cadderly was struck by the woman's apparent madness. Was she really mad, he wondered, or was she, perhaps, trapped in a bona fide but unknown series of disjointed bubbles in the vast ocean of time? Cadderly had often pondered the past, had often wondered if each passing moment was a brief observance of an eternal play, or whether the past was truly lost as soon as the next moment was found.

Watching Catti-brie, it seemed to him that the former wasn't as unrealistic as logic implied.

Was there a way to travel in time? Was there a way to bring foresight to those unanticipated preludes to disaster?

"Do ye think her pretty, Guen?" Catti-brie asked, drawing him from his contemplation.

The door behind Cadderly opened, and he glanced to see Drizzt enter the room, the drow wincing as soon as he recognized that Catti-brie had entered another of her fits. Cadderly begged him to silence with a wave and a finger over pursed lips, and Drizzt, Catti-brie's dinner tray in hand, stood very still, staring at his beloved wife.

"Drizzt thinks her pretty," Catti-brie continued, oblivious to them. "He goes to Silverymoon whenever he can, and part o' that's because he's thinking Alustriel pretty." The woman paused and looked up, though surely not at Cadderly and Drizzt, and wore a smile that was both sweet and pained. "I hope he finds love, I do," she told the panther they could not see. "But not with her, or one o' her court, for then he's sure to leave us. I'm wantin' him happy, but that I could'no' take."

Cadderly looked at Drizzt questioningly.

"When first we retook Mithral Hall," he said.

"You and Lady Alustriel?" Cadderly asked.

"Friends," Drizzt replied, never taking his eyes off his wife. "She allowed me passage in Silverymoon, and there I knew I could make great strides toward finding some measure of acceptance in the World Above." He motioned to Catti-brie. "How long?"

"She has been in this different place for quite a while."

"And there she is my Catti," Drizzt lamented. "In this elsewhere of her mind, she finds herself."

The woman began to shake then, her hands twitching, her head going back, her eyes rolling up to white. The purple glow of faerie fire erupted around her once more and she rose a bit higher from the floor, arms going out wide, her auburn hair blowing in some unfelt wind.

Drizzt put the tray down and adjusted the eye patch. He hesitated only a few moments, at Cadderly's insistence, as the priest moved closer to Catti-brie, even dared touch her during the dangerous time of transition. Cadderly closed his eyes and opened his mind to the possibilities swirling in the discordant spasms of the tortured woman.

He fell back, quickly replaced by Drizzt, who wrapped Catti-brie in a tight hug and eased her to the floor. The drow looked at Cadderly, his expression begging for an explanation, but he saw the priest even more perplexed, wide-eyed and staring at his hand.

Drizzt, too, took note of the hand that Cadderly had placed upon Catti-brie. What appeared as a blue translucence solidified and became flesh tone once more.

"What was that?" the drow asked as soon as Catti-brie settled.

"I do not know," Cadderly admitted.

"Words I hear too often in these times."

"Agreed."

"But you seem certain that my wife cannot be saved," said Drizzt, a sharper tone edging into his voice.

"I do not wish to give such an impression."

"I've seen the way you and Jarlaxle shake your heads when the conversation comes to her. You don't believe we can bring her back to us—not whole, at least. You have lost hope for her, but would you, I wonder, if it was Lady Danica here, in that state, and not Catti-brie?"

"My friend, surely you don't—"

"Am I to surrender my hope as well? Is that what you expect of me?"

"You're not the only one here clinging to desperate hope, my friend," Cadderly scolded.

Drizzt eased back a bit at that reminder. "Danica will find them," he offered, but how hollow his words sounded. He continued in a soft voice, "I feel as if there is no firmament beneath my feet."

Cadderly nodded in sympathy.

"Should I battle the dracolich with the hope that in its defeat, I will find again my wife?" Drizzt blurted, his voice rising again. "Or should I battle the beast with rage because I will never again find her?"

"You ask of me . . . these are questions . . ." Cadderly blew a heavy sigh and lifted his hands, helpless. "I do not know, Drizzt Do'Urden. Nothing can be certain regarding Catti-brie."

"We know she's mad."

Cadderly started to reply, "Do we?" but he held it back, not wishing to involve Drizzt in his earlier ponderings.

Was Catti-brie truly insane, or was she reacting rationally to the reality that was presented to her? Was she re-living her life out of sequence or was she truly returning to those bubbles of time-space and experiencing those moments as reality?

The priest shook his head, for he had no time to travel the possibilities of such a line of reasoning, particularly since the scholars and sages, and the great wizards and great priests who had visited Spirit Soaring had thoroughly dismissed any such possibility of traveling freely through time.

"But madness can be a temporary thing," Drizzt remarked. "And yet, you and Jarlaxle think her lost forever. Why?"

"When the madness is tortured enough, the mind can be permanently wounded," Cadderly replied, his dour tone making it clear that such was an almost certain outcome and not a remote possibility. "And your wife's madness seems tortured, indeed. I fear—Jarlaxle and I fear—that even if the spell that is upon her is somehow ended, a terrible scar will remain."

"You fear, but you do not know."

Cadderly nodded, conceding the point. "And I have witnessed miracles before, my friend. In this very place. Do not surrender your hope."

That was all he could give, and all that Drizzt had hoped to hear, in the end. "Do you think the gods have any miracles left in them?" the dark elf quietly asked.

Cadderly gave a helpless laugh and shrugged. "I grabbed the sun itself and pulled it to me," he reminded the drow. "I know not how, and I didn't try to do it. I grabbed a cloud and made of it a chariot. I know not how, and didn't try to do it. My voice became thunder . . . truly, my friend, I wonder why anyone would bother asking me questions at this time. And I wonder more why anyone would believe any of my answers."

Drizzt had to smile at that, and so he did, with a nod of acceptance. He turned his gaze to Catti-brie and reached out to gently stroke her thick hair. "I cannot lose her."

"Let us destroy our enemy, then," Cadderly offered. "Then we will turn all of our attention, all of our thoughts, and all of our magic to Catti-brie, to find her in her . . . elsewhere lucidity . . . and bring her sense back to our time and space."

"Guenhwyvar," Drizzt said, and Cadderly blinked in surprise.

"She was petting the cat, yes."

"No, I mean in the next fight," Drizzt explained. "When the Ghost King began to leave the field, Guenhwyvar fled faster. She does not run from a fight. Not from a raging elemental or a monstrous demon, and not from a dragon or dracolich. But she fled, ears down, full speed away into the trees."

"Perhaps she was hunting one of the crawlers."

"She was running. Recall Jarlaxle's tale of his encounter with the specter he believes was once a lich of the Crystal Shard."

"Guenhwyvar is not of this plane, and she feared creating a rift as the Ghost King opened a dimensional portal," Cadderly reasoned.

"One that perhaps Guenhwyvar could navigate," Drizzt replied. "One that perhaps I could navigate with her, to that other place."

Cadderly couldn't help but smile at the reasoning, and Drizzt offered a curious expression. "There is an old saying that great minds follow similar paths to the same destination," he said.

"Guen?" Drizzt asked hopefully, patting his belt pouch. But Cadderly was shaking his head.

"The panther is of the Astral Plane," the priest explained. "She cannot, of her own will, go to where the Ghost King resides, unless someone there possessed a figurine akin to your own and summoned her."

"She fled the field."

"Because she feared a rift, a great tear that would consume all near to her, and the Ghost King, if their dangerous abilities came crashing together. Perhaps that rift would send our enemy to the Astral Plane, or to some other plane, but likely the creature is anchored enough both here and in the Shadowfell that it could return." He was still shaking his head. "But I have little faith in that course and fear a potential for greater disaster."

"Greater?" Drizzt asked, and he began a hollow laugh. "Greater?"

"Are we at the point where we reach blindly for the most desperate measures we can find?" Cadderly asked.

"Are we not?"

The priest shrugged again. "I don't know," he admitted, his gaze fixing on Catti-brie again. "Perhaps we will find another way."

"Perhaps Deneir will deliver a miracle?"

"We can hope."

"You mean pray."

"That, too."

* * * * *

He lifted the spoon to her lips and she did not resist, taking the food methodically. Drizzt dabbed a napkin into a small bowl of warm water and wiped a bit of the porridge from her lips.

She seemed not to notice, as she seemed not to notice the taste of the food he offered. Every time he put a spoonful into Catti-brie's mouth, every time she showed no expression at all, it pained Drizzt and reminded him of the futility of it all. He had flavored the porridge exactly as his wife liked, but he understood with each spoonful that he could have skipped the cinnamon and honey and used bitter spices instead. It wouldn't have mattered one bit to Catti-brie.

"I still remember that moment on Kelvin's Cairn," he said to her. "When you relived it before my eyes, it all came back into such clear focus, and I recalled your words before you spoke them. I remember the way you had your hair, with those bangs and the uneven length from side to side. Never trust a dwarf with scissors, right?"

He managed a little laugh that Catti-brie seemed not to hear.

"I did not love you then, of course. Not like this. But that moment remained so special to me, and so important. The look on your face, my love—the way you looked inside of me instead of at my skin. I knew I was home when I found you on Kelvin's Cairn. At long last, I was home.

"And even though I had no idea for many years that there could ever be more between us—not until that time in Calimport—you were ever special to me. And you still are, and I need you to come back to me, Catti. Nothing else matters. The world is a darker place. With the Ghost King and the falling Weave, and the implications of this catastrophe, I know that so many trials will fall before me, before all goodly folk. But I believe that I can meet those challenges, that we together will find a way. We always find a way!

"But only if you come back to me. To defeat a mighty foe, a warrior must *want* to defeat a mighty foe. What is the point, my love, if I am alone once more?"

He exhaled and sat there, staring at her, but she didn't blink, didn't react at all. She hadn't heard him. He might pretend differently for the sake of his own sanity, but Drizzt knew in his heart that Catti-brie wasn't lurking there, just beneath the damaged surface, taking it all in.

Drizzt wiped a tear from his lavender eyes, and as the moisture went away, it was replaced by that same look that had at once shaken and encouraged Bruenor, the promise of the Hunter, the determination, the simmering rage.

Drizzt leaned forward and kissed Catti-brie on the forehead and told himself that it had all been wrought by the Ghost King, that the dracolich was the source of all that had gone so very wrong in the world, not a result of some larger disaster.

No more tears for Drizzt Do'Urden. He meant to destroy the beast.

CHAPTER

They knew their enemy would return, and they knew where they wanted to fight it, but when it happened, as expected as it was, sturdy Athrogate and Thibbledorf Pwent gasped more profoundly than they cried out.

The Ghost King came back to the material world of Toril in exactly the same place that it had departed, appearing first and briefly in its translucent blue-white glow. Quickly it was whole again, on the courtyard outside the cathedral, and even as Pwent and Athrogate shouted out, their bellows echoing through the deserted hallways, the great beast leaped into the air and took wing, flying high into the night sky.

"It's up there! It's up there, me king!" Pwent cried, hopping up and down and pointing skyward. Bruenor, Drizzt, and the others arrived in the room adjacent to the balcony from which the two dwarves had been keeping watch.

"The dracolich appeared in the same place?" Cadderly asked, clearly interpreting some importance in that fact.

"Just like ye guessed," Athrogate answered. "Glowin' and all, then it jumped away."

"It's up there, me king!" Pwent shouted again.

Drizzt, Cadderly, Bruenor, and Jarlaxle exchanged determined nods. "It doesn't get away from us this time," said Bruenor.

All eyes went to Cadderly at that proclamation, and the priest's nod was one of confidence.

"Inside," Cadderly ordered them all. "The beast will return with fury and fire. Spirit Soaring will protect us."

*****

Danica took a deep breath and grabbed at a nearby tree trunk to steady herself when she heard the awful, otherworldly shriek of the dracolich taking flight. She couldn't help but glance back toward Spirit Soaring, already miles behind her, and she had to remind herself that Cadderly was surrounded by powerful allies, and that Deneir, or some other divine entity, miraculously heard his pleas.

"They will prevail," Danica said softly—very softly, for she knew that the forest about her was full of monsters. She had watched groups of crawlers scratch by on the road and had felt the thunderous steps of some gigantic black behemoth, the likes of which she had never before known.

She was halfway to Carradoon and had hoped to be there already, but the going had been slow and cautious. As much as she wanted a fight, Danica could ill afford one. Her focus was Carradoon and Carradoon alone, to find her children, while Cadderly and the others dealt with the Ghost King at Spirit Soaring.

That was the plan—they knew the undead dragon would return—and Danica had to steel herself against any second-guessing. She had to trust Cadderly. She couldn't turn back.

"My children," she whispered. "Temberle and Rorick, and Hana, my Hana . . . I will find you."

Behind her, high in the sky, the Ghost King's shriek split the night as profoundly as a bolt of lightning and the roar of thunder.

Danica ignored it and focused on the trees before her, picking her careful and swift way through the haunted woods.

"Kill him, Cadderly," she said under her breath, over and over again.

*****

Without the cautionary interference of Yharaskrik, the Ghost King reveled in its flight, knowing that its vulnerable target lay below, knowing that soon enough it would destroy Spirit Soaring and the fools who had remained within.

The sweet taste of impending revenge filled Hephaestus's dead throat, and the dragon wanted nothing more than to dive at the building at full speed and tear it to kindling. But surprisingly to both entities that made up the Ghost King, recklessness was tempered by the pain of their recent defeat. The Ghost King still felt the blinding sting of Cadderly's fires, and the weight of Drizzt's scimitar. Though confident that its second assault would be different, the Ghost King meant to take no unnecessary chances.

And so from on high, up among the clouds, the beast called upon its minions once more, summoning them from the forests around Spirit Soaring, compelling them to soften the ground.

"They will not kill Cadderly," the beast said into the high winds. "But they will reveal him!"

The Ghost King folded its wings and dived, then opened them wide and rode the momentum and the currents in a spiraling pattern above the building, its magically enhanced eyesight scouring the land below.

Already the forest was alive with movement as crawlers and nightwings, huddled wraiths, and even a giant nightwalker swarmed toward Spirit Soaring.

The Ghost King's laugh rumbled like distant thunder.

* * * * *

They heard the break of glass, one of the few panes left intact from the previous assault, but the building did not shudder.

"By the gods," Cadderly cursed.

"Damned crawlers!" Bruenor agreed.

They were in the widest audience hall on the first story of the building, a windowless affair with only a few connecting corridors. Pwent and Athrogate stood at the rail on the northern balcony with their tied-off logs, some twenty-five feet above the others. Bruenor, Cadderly, and the rest stood on the raised dais where Cadderly usually held audience, across from the double doors and the main corridor that led to the cathedral's foyer. Drizzt stood at the open doorway of a small, secure anteroom, where lay Catti-brie.

Drizzt bent low to tuck a blanket more tightly around his wife, and whispered, "He won't get you. On my life, my love, I will kill that beast. I will find a way back to you, or a way to lead you back to us."

Catti-brie didn't react, but lay staring into the distance.

Drizzt leaned in and kissed her on the cheek. "I promise," he whispered. "I love you."

Not far from them, Drizzt heard wood splintering. He stood up straight and moved out of the small anteroom, securing the door behind him.

Cadderly shivered as he felt the unclean beasts crawling into the broken windows of Spirit Soaring.

"Clear the place?" Athrogate yelled down.

"No, hold your positions!" Cadderly ordered, and even as he spoke, the door on the balcony nearest the two dwarves began to rattle and bang. Cadderly fell within himself, trying to join with the magic that strengthened Spirit Soaring, begging the cathedral, begging Deneir, to hold strong.

"Come on, then," Cadderly whispered to the Ghost King. "Lead the way."

"He learned from his loss," Jarlaxle remarked as Drizzt rejoined them. "He's sending in the fodder. He's not to be trapped alone as before."

Cadderly flashed an alarmed look at Drizzt and Bruenor.

"I'll bring him in," Drizzt promised, and he charged across the room to the double doors, the other three close behind.

Cadderly grabbed him before he could leave the room. As Drizzt turned, the priest gripped his right hand, in which he held Icingdeath, then reached for the hilt of Twinkle with his other hand. Cadderly closed his eyes and chanted, and Drizzt felt again an infusion of power into both his weapons.

"Bruenor, the door," Jarlaxle said, drawing out a pair of black metal wands. "And do duck aside."

Jarlaxle nodded to Drizzt, then to Bruenor, who flung wide the double doors. Beyond them, the corridor to the foyer teemed with crawlers, and nightwings fluttered above them.

A lightning bolt blasted from Jarlaxle's wand to sear the darkness. The second wand responded in kind, then the first took its turn, and the second fired again. Flesh smoldered, bats tumbled, a stench filled the holy place.

A fifth bolt followed, a sixth fast behind. Monsters scrambled to get out of the corridor, or melted where they stood. The seventh blast shook the walls of Spirit Soaring.

"Go!" Jarlaxle ordered Drizzt, and loosed yet another explosive line of sizzling energy.

And right behind it went Drizzt Do'Urden, running and leaping, spinning and slashing with seeming abandon. But every stroke was planned and timed perfectly, clearing the way and propelling Drizzt along. A nightwing dived at him, or fell at him—the beast was badly scored from the many lightning bolts. Drizzt hit it with a solid backhand and his divinely-weighted scimitar threw the giant bat aside, the blade tearing its flesh with brutal ease.

The drow leaped atop the heads of a pair of trembling, dying crawlers and sprang away onto a third, bowling it over, spinning as he went and cutting another beast in half as he twirled around. He reached the foyer doors, both hanging loose from the battering of the eight lightning bolts.

"Jarlaxle!" Drizzt cried, and he skidded down and kicked the doors open, revealing a foyer stuffed with enemies.

Lightning bolts streaked over the hunched drow, one, two, blasting, burning, blinding, and scattering the beasts. Then Drizzt was up behind them, his mighty scimitars battering the creatures aside.

Out the door Drizzt went, into the courtyard.

"Fight me, dragon!" he yelled. A foolish nightwing dived at Drizzt from on high and was met by a flashing scimitar that cleaved through flesh and bone and infused a web of searing divine light into the creature of darkness. The batlike beast went spinning backward, up into the air, dead long before it tumbled and flopped to the ground.

From all around, from the walls and broken windows of Spirit Soaring, everything seemed to pause for just a moment. Drizzt had drawn attention to himself, indeed, and the monsters swarmed his way, leaping from the trees across the courtyard and from the walls of Spirit Soaring.

A wicked grin creased the dark elf's face. "Come on, then," he whispered, and he gave a private nod to Catti-brie.

* * * * *

"We got to go to him!" cried Bruenor. Along with Cadderly and Jarlaxle, he had eased out of the audience chamber and crept nearer the foyer, gaining a view of the open courtyard beyond.

"Hold, dwarf," Jarlaxle replied. He was looking to Cadderly as he spoke and taking note of the priest's equal confidence in Drizzt.

Bruenor started to reply, but bit it short with a gasp as he saw the first wave of monsters swarm at Drizzt.

The drow ranger exploded into motion, leaping and spinning, stepping atop monstrous heads and backs, slashing with devastating speed and precision. One after another, crawlers crumbled to heaps of quivering flesh or went sailing back, launched by a swinging, divinely-weighted blade. Drizzt leaped from a beast's back and hit the ground in a fast run up atop another, where he double stabbed, spun to the side, and caught yet another crawler with a deadly backhand. The drow continued his spin and darted out of it past the first dying beast to stab a fourth, slash a fifth, and leap above a sixth, thrusting down to mortally wound that one as he passed overhead with Twinkle, slashing up high to take the legs from a swooping nightwing in the same movement.

"You've known him a long time . . ." Jarlaxle said to Bruenor.

"Ain't never seen that," the dumbfounded dwarf admitted.

Drizzt, whirling like a maelstrom, moved beyond their line of sight then, past the angle of the open double doors. But the erupting sounds and shrieks told the friends that his furious charge had not slowed. He veered back into view, sprinting the opposite way, cutting a swath of devastation with every stride, every thrust, and every swing. Crawlers flew and crumbled, nightwings tumbled dead from on high, but the divine glow on Drizzt's scimitars did not diminish, even seemed to flare with more purpose and anger.

A crash in the room behind them turned the three around to see a crawler thrashing in its death throes in the middle of the floor. A second dropped down from above, accompanied by the glee-filled cackle of Thibbledorf Pwent.

"Trust in Drizzt!" Cadderly commanded the other two, and the priest led the charge back into the audience hall, the battlefield of their choosing.

* * * * *

The sheer exuberance of Thibbledorf Pwent held the breach at the broken doorway. Thrashing and punching, the dwarf laughed all the harder with every bit of gore that splattered his ridged armor and with every sickening puncture of a knee-spike or a gauntlet.

"Get out o' the way!" Athrogate yelled at him repeatedly, the equally-wild dwarf wanting a chance to hit something.

"Bwahaha!" Thibbledorf Pwent responded, perfectly mimicking Athrogate's signature cry.

"Huh," Athrogate said, for that gave him pause. Only a brief pause, however, before he let out a hearty "Bwahaha!" of his own.

Thibbledorf Pwent dived out of the way and a pair of crawlers rushed onto the balcony to confront Athrogate, who promptly buried them under a barrage of his powerful morningstars, setting free another heartfelt howl of laughter.

Pwent, meanwhile, went right to the corridor exit, battering the next beasts in line. He hooked one with a glove spike and did a deft, swift turn and throw, launching the flailing thing over the balcony. Then the dwarf fell back, inviting more crawlers into the room, where he and Athrogate, side by side, destroyed them.

* * * * *

He did not slow and did not tire. The image of his wounded wife stayed crystal clear in his thoughts and drove him on, and because he felt no fatigue, he began to wonder if the power Cadderly had infused into his weapons was somehow providing strength and stamina to him, as well.

It was a fleeting thought, for the present predicament crowded out all but his most intense warrior instincts. Drizzt gave himself no time to reflect, for every turn brought him face-on with enemies, and every leap became a series of contortions and tucks to avoid a host of reaching arms or raking claws.

But it mattered not how many of those claws and arms came at Drizzt Do'Urden. He stayed ahead of them, every one, and his blades, so full of fury and might, cleared the way, whichever way he chose to go. Carnage piled around him and a mist of monster blood filled the air. Every other step fell atop the fleshy corpse of a dead enemy.

"Fight me, dragon!" he yelled, and his voice rang with an almost mocking glee. "Come down from on high, coward!"

In the space of those two sentences, another four crawlers fell dead, and even the stupidly vicious beasts were beginning to shy from the mad drow warrior. The trend continued—instead of rushing to avoid enemies, Drizzt found himself chasing them. And all the while, he continued calling out his challenges to the Ghost King.

That challenge was answered, not by the dragon, but by another creature, a gigantic nightwalker, that stepped from the forest and thundered at the dancing drow.

Drizzt had fought one of those behemoths before, and knew well how formidable they were, their deceptively thin limbs tightly wound with layers of muscle that could crush the life from him with hardly a thought.

Drizzt smiled and charged.

* * * * *

As they shied from Drizzt, many of the monsters charged in through the open double doors of Spirit Soaring and down the corridor leading to the audience hall. The leading crawler almost got through the door, but Bruenor was beside that entryway, his back to the wall, and he perfectly timed the mighty two-handed sweep of his axe, burying it in the crawler's chest and stopping the thing dead in its tracks.

A yank from the dwarf sent the thing rolling away, and as he did, he released his left hand, jerked his arm back to reposition his shield, and threw himself into the next beast scrambling through the door. Dwarf and crawler rolled aside, leaving the path open to Jarlaxle and his lightning bolts, one, two, flashing down the crowded hallway.

Behind those stepped Cadderly, right up to the doorway, and he threw his arms up high and pulled down magical power, releasing it through his feet and spreading it in a glowing circle right there in the archway. The priest fell back and the stubborn crawlers came on, and as they stepped upon Cadderly's consecrated ground, they were consumed by devastating radiance. They shrieked and they smoldered and they crumbled down, writhing in mortal agony.

Jarlaxle threw another pair of lightning bolts down the corridor.

Another crawler came flying over the balcony from above, but up there, as in the audience room, the situation was fast quieting.

"Come on, ye little beasties!" Athrogate yelled down the empty corridor above.

"Come on, dragon," Cadderly said in reply.

"Come on, Drizzt," Bruenor had to add.

* * * * *

With brutal speed and ferocity, the black-skinned behemoth snapped a punch out at the charging drow, and a lesser warrior than Drizzt would have been crushed by that blow. The ranger, though, with his speed multiplied by his anklets, and his razor-edged reflexes, stepped left as the giant began its swing. Anticipating that the behemoth would react to that movement, Drizzt fast-stepped back the other way so he ran unhindered as the creature's fist plowed through the air.

Drizzt didn't slow as he charged past the giant, but he did leap and spin to gain momentum as he slashed out with Icingdeath. He meant to strike the giant's kneecap, and to use that impact to reverse his momentum and his spin so he could scramble to the side, but to Drizzt's surprise, he felt no sense of impact.

Drizzt landed almost as if he had hit nothing solid at all, and despite his previous experiences with his divinely-infused weapons, he found himself almost stupefied by the reality that he had cut right through the behemoth's leg.

Improvising, Drizzt flipped diagonally to his left, lifting himself over and twisting around as he did to place himself directly behind the giant. A further twist stabbed Icingdeath up into the back of the giant's other thigh, and the howling creature had to rise up on its tiptoes even as it lurched to grab at its other severed leg.

Drizzt retracted Icingdeath, but only to make way for Twinkle as that blade slashed across, taking with it the giant's remaining leg.

Down crashed the massive beast, its screams reaching out to the Ghost King more than Drizzt's spoken challenges ever could.

Drizzt didn't bother finishing the giant—it would bleed out and die on its own—and instead positioned himself for a run to the cathedral. Everything fled before him, nightwings fluttering into the darkness and crawlers climbing all over each other to get away. He caught a few and killed each with a single, devastating stroke, and ran a more circuitous route to his planned position to further scatter the horde.

A cry from above rent the night, a scream painful in its intensity and sheer volume. Drizzt dived into a somersault and rolled to his feet, planting them firmly and facing that scream. He saw the dracolich's fire-filled eyes first, like shooting stars diving toward him, then saw the green glow of Crenshinibon, the beast's newest horn.

"Come on!" Drizzt shouted, and he slapped his scimitars together, sparks flying from the impact.

In a single movement, he sheathed them and pulled Taulmaril from his shoulder. Grinning wickedly, Drizzt let fly a silver-streaking arrow, then a second, then a line of them, reaching out and stinging the beast as it plummeted from on high.

CHAPTER

CHASING IT TO THE ENDS OF REALITY

There!" Rorick cried, pointing at the sky high above the mountains.

They had heard the shriek of doom, and following Rorick's gaze, they saw the Ghost King as it glided across the starry canopy.

"Over our home," Hanaleisa said, and all five began to run. With every tenth step, though, Ivan called for a halt. Finally, the others slowed, gasping for breath.

"We stay together or we're suren dead," the yellow-bearded dwarf scolded. "I can'no' run with ye, girl!"

"And I cannot watch from afar as my home is attacked," Hanaleisa countered.

"And ye can'no' get there," said Ivan. "Half a day and more o' walking—hours of running. Ye mean to run for hours, do ye?"

"If I—" Hanaleisa started to retort, but she went quiet at Pikel's "Shh!" All eyes focused on the green-bearded dwarf as he hopped about, pointing into the dark forest.

A moment later, they heard the shuffling of many creatures moving swiftly through the underbrush. As one, the group braced for an attack, but they quickly realized that those creatures, minions of the Ghost King, they believed, were not coming for them but were running flat out to the west, up the hillsides toward Spirit Soaring. Their enemies swarmed to the distant battle.

"Quick, then, but not running," Ivan ordered. "And stay close, all o' ye!"

Hanaleisa spearheaded the charge, and at a swift pace. With her intensive training in stealth and stamina, and the graceful manner of her movements, she was sure that she could indeed run all the way home, as far as it was, even though the path was mostly uphill. But she couldn't abandon the others, surrounded by enemies, and particularly Rorick with his torn ankle, struggling with every step.

"Mother and Father are surrounded by a hundred capable mages and priests," Temberle tried to reassure her—and reassure himself, she sensed from the tone of his voice. "They will defeat this threat."

Soon after, with nearly a mile behind them, the group had to slow, both from exhaustion and because the forest around them teemed with shadowy creatures. On more than one occasion, Hanaleisa held up her hand to stop those behind her and fell low behind a tree trunk or a bush, expecting a fight. Every time, though, the noisy beasts scrambling ahead or to the sides seemed possessed of a singular purpose, and that purpose had nothing to do with the little band of Carradden refugees.

Gradually, Hanaleisa began to press on even when enemies sounded very near—a part of her hoped that some would come against them, she had to privately admit. Anything they killed out in the wilds would be one less attacker at the gates of Spirit Soaring.

But then Hanaleisa sensed something different, some movement that seemed intent upon them. She slid behind a broad tree and motioned for the others to stop, then held her breath as something approached very near, opposite her on the other side of the tree.

She jumped out as her opponent did the same, and launched a series of blows that would have leveled a skilled warrior.

But every strike was intercepted by an open hand that slapped her attacks aside. It took Hanaleisa only a moment to understand her defeat, only a heartbeat to recognize her opponent as the woman who had trained her all her life.

"Mother!" she cried, and Danica fell over her in the tightest hug she had ever known.

Rorick and Temberle echoed Hanaleisa's call and they, along with Ivan and Pikel, rushed up to embrace Danica.

Tears of profound relief and sheer joy filled Danica's eyes as she crushed each of her children close to her, and as she fell over Pikel. And those tears streaked a face full of confusion when she looked upon Ivan.

"I saw you die," she said. "I was on the cliff, outside the cave, when the dracolich crushed you."

"Crushed them what was chasing me, ye mean," Ivan corrected. "Dumb thing didn't even know it was standing above a hole—small for a dragon, but a tunnel for meself!"

"But . . ." Danica started. She just shook her head and kissed Ivan on his hairy cheek.

"You found a way," she said. "We'll find a way."

"Where's Father?" Hanaleisa asked.

"He remains at Spirit Soaring," Danica replied, and she glanced nervously up the mountains, "facing the Ghost King."

"He's surrounded by an army of wizards and warrior priests," Rorick insisted, but Danica shook her head.

"He's with a small group of powerful allies," Danica corrected, and she looked at Ivan and Pikel. "King Bruenor and one of his battleragers, and Drizzt Do'Urden."

"Bruenor," Ivan gasped. "Me king, come to us in our time o' need."

"Drizzit Dudden," Pikel added with a signature giggle.

"Lead on, Milady," Ivan bade Danica. "Might that we'll get there when there's still something to hit!"

* * * * *

The Ghost King didn't open wide its wings to break out of the stoop. Down it came, a missile from on high, wings folded, eyes burning, jaws wide. At the very last moment, right before it crashed, the Ghost King snapped its head up and flipped its wings out, altering nothing but its angle of descent. It hit the ground and plowed through the turf, digging a trench as it skidded at its prey. And if that alone were not enough to put a fast end to the fool who would challenge a god, the Ghost King breathed forth its flaming breath.

On and on it went, consuming all in its path, reaching to the very doorway of Spirit Soaring. The flesh of dead crawlers bubbled and burst and disintegrated beneath the conflagration, grass charred and obliterated.

"Drizzt!" Bruenor, Cadderly, and Jarlaxle yelled together from inside the cathedral, knowing their friend was surely consumed.

The gout of flames might have continued much longer, for it seemed an endless catastrophe, but a scimitar swung by a drow who should have been buried in that assault smashed hard against the side of the Ghost King's face.

Jolted, stunned that Drizzt had been quick enough to get out of the way, the Ghost King tried to turn its fury upon him.

But a second blow, so heavy with magical power, snapped the dracolich's head to the side yet again.

The Ghost King hopped up to its hind legs, towering over the drow even though it stood in a trench deeper than two tall men, a hollow torn by the weight of its cometlike impact.

Barely had it stood when the beast bit down at the drow, spearlike teeth snapping loudly, and in Spirit Soaring's doorway, Bruenor gasped, thinking his friend taken whole.

But again Drizzt moved ahead of his enemy, again the drow, so intent on the image of his wounded bride, so perfect in his focus and so adroit his reflexes, dived at precisely the right angle, forward and inside the reach of the Ghost King. As he came up, three lightning-fast steps brought him to the beast's right hind leg, where his scimitars bit deep.

Yet the power of Cadderly's magic and the fury of Drizzt Do'Urden could not do to that godlike being what he had done in dismembering the nightwalker, and for all of his rage and fury and focus, Drizzt never lost one simple truth: He could not beat the Ghost King alone.

And so he was moving again, and with all speed, even as he struck hard. Again the dragon snapped its killing fangs at him, and again he dodged and ran, at a full sprint away from the dracolich and toward Spirit Soaring.

Instinctively, Drizzt swerved out wide and dived again, and felt the heat at his back as the Ghost King breathed forth its murderous fires once more. Drizzt crossed that blackened line back the other way the moment it ended, again just ahead of the pursuing, biting monster.

He bolted through the double doors just ahead of the Ghost King and called out for Cadderly, for there was nowhere to turn.

And as he knew would happen, the Ghost King's fires followed him inside, rushing fast for his back and engulfing him fully, filling the passageway behind and in front with dragonfire.

* * * * *

Cadderly groaned in pain as roiling flames gnawed at Spirit Soaring, at the magic that sustained the priest and his creation. He held his radiant hands out before him, reaching for the corridor, reaching for Drizzt, praying he had reacted quickly enough.

Only when Drizzt scrambled into the room, out of the blast of dragonfire, did Cadderly allow himself to breathe. But his relief, the relief of them all, lasted only a moment before the whole of the great structure shuddered violently.

Cadderly fell back and grimaced, then again as another explosion rocked Spirit Soaring. Its walls, even for their magic, could not withstand the fury of the Ghost King, who crashed in, tearing with tooth and claw, battering aside walls, wood and stone alike, with its skull. Ripping, shredding, and battering its way along, the Ghost King moved into the structure, widening the passageway and crashing through the lower ceiling outside the audience chamber.

Inside that hall, the four companions fell back, step by step, trying to hold their calm and their confidence. A look at Cadderly did nothing to bolster their resolve. With every crash and tear against Spirit Soaring, the priest shuddered—and aged. Before their astonished eyes, Cadderly's hair went from gray to white, his face became creased and lined, his posture stooped.

The front wall of the audience chamber cracked, then blew apart as the monster slammed through. The Ghost King lifted its head and issued a deafening wail of pure hatred.

The building shook as the wyrm stomped into the room, then shook again with its next heavy step, which brought it within striking distance of its intended prey.

"For me king!" yelled Thibbledorf Pwent, who sat atop a tied-off log up on the high balcony. Right before him, standing on the rail, Athrogate cut free the lead log and gave it a heave to send it swinging down from on high.

The giant spear stabbed into the side of the Ghost King, hitting it squarely just under its shoulder, just under its wing, and indeed, the creature lurched, if only a bit, under the weight of that blow.

An inconsequential weight, though, against the godlike dracolich.

Except that Thibbledorf Pwent then cut loose the second log, the one on which he sat. "Wahoo!" he yelled as he swung past Athrogate, who gave a shove for good measure, and followed the same trajectory as the first beam.

More than the dwarf's added weight enhanced the blow as log hit log, end to end, for the front end of that second log had been hollowed out and filled with explosive oil. Like a gigantic version of Cadderly's hand crossbow bolts, the dwarven version collapsed in on itself and exploded with the force of a thunderbolt.

The front log blew forward, lifting the Ghost King and throwing it far and fast against the opposite wall. The back log blew to splinters, and the dwarf who had been sitting upon it flew forward, arms and legs flailing, and chased the dracolich through the air to the wall, catching it like a living grapnel even as the ceiling crumbled down atop the stunned Ghost King. Like a biting fly on the side of a horse, Thibbledorf Pwent scrambled and stabbed.

The Ghost King ignored him, though, for on came Drizzt, leading the charge, Bruenor behind. Still beside the shaken Cadderly, Jarlaxle lifted his wands and began a barrage.

Taulmaril's stinging arrows led Drizzt's assault, flashing at the Ghost King's face to keep the creature occupied. As he neared, Drizzt threw the bow aside and reached for his blades.

He unsheathed only Icingdeath, however, his eyes sparking with sudden inspiration.

* * * * *

He felt his bones cracking like the beams of Spirit Soaring itself. His back twisted in a painful hunch, and his arms trembled from the effort of trying to hold them up before him.

But Cadderly knew that the moment of truth was at hand, the moment of Cadderly and Spirit Soaring and Deneir—somehow he sensed that it was the Scribe of Oghma's last moment, his god's final act.

He needed power then, and he found it, and as he had done in the previous battle with the Ghost King, the priest seemed to reach up and bring the sun itself down upon him. Allies drew strength and healing energy—so much so that Athrogate hardly groaned as he leaped down from the balcony, his twisted ankles untwisting before the pain even registered.

The Ghost King felt the brutal sting of Cadderly's light, and the priest advanced. The dracolich filled the room with dragonfire, but Cadderly's ward held strong and the sting did not stop the assault.

The Ghost King focused on Drizzt instead, determined to be rid of that wretched warrior, but again it could not bite quickly enough to catch the dancing elf, and as it tried to position its strikes to corner Drizzt against the rubble of the broken wall, it found itself cornered instead.

Drizzt leaped up against the dracolich and caught hold with his free hand on the monster's rib, exposed by the wide hole blown into it by the dwarven bolt, and before the Ghost King or anyone else could begin to analyze the drow's surprising move, Drizzt pulled himself right inside the beast, right into the lung, torn wide.

The Ghost King shuddered and thrashed with abandon, out of its mind with agony as the drow, both weapons drawn, began tearing it apart from the inside. So violent was its movements, so shattering its cries, so furious its breath that the other combatants staggered to a stop and pressed hands over their ears, and even Pwent fell off the creature.

But inside, Drizzt played out his fury, and Cadderly held forth his radiant light to bolster his allies and consume his enemy.

The Ghost King pushed away from the wall, stumbling and kicking, smashing a foot right through the floor to crash down into the catacombs below. It shrieked and breathed its fire, and the weakened magic of Spirit Soaring could not resist the bite of those flames. The smoke grew thick, dulling the blinding brilliance of Cadderly's light, but not weakening its effect.

"Kill it, and quickly!" Jarlaxle yelled as the beast shuddered and shook with agony. Bruenor raised his axe and charged, Athrogate set his morning-stars to spinning, and Thibbledorf Pwent leaped onto a leg and thrashed as only a battlerager could.

A blue glow overwhelmed the yellow hue of Cadderly's radiance, and the three dwarves felt their weapons hitting only emptiness.

Drizzt fell through the insubstantial torso, landing lightly on the floor, but sliding and slipping on the blood and gore that covered him. Pwent tumbled face down with an "Oomph!"

"It flees!" Jarlaxle shouted, and behind him, in the small room, Catti-brie cried out. In the main hall, the Ghost King vanished.

Cadderly was first to the anteroom, though every step seemed to pain the old man. He pulled the latch and threw open the door, and from under his white shirt produced the ruby pendant Jarlaxle had loaned to him.

Before him, Catti-brie trembled and cried out. Behind him, Drizzt pulled out the onyx figurine. Cadderly looked at Drizzt and shook his head.

"Guenhwyvar will not get you there," said the priest.

"We cannot allow it to escape us again," Drizzt said. He moved inexorably toward Catti-brie, drawn to her in her pain.

"It will not," Cadderly promised. He gave a profound sigh. "Tell Danica that I love her, and promise me that you will find and protect my children."

"We will," Jarlaxle answered, and Drizzt, Bruenor, and Cadderly all looked at him in astonishment. Had not the weight of the situation been pressing so enormously upon all of them at that moment, all three would have burst out in laughter.

It was a fleeting moment of relief, though. Cadderly nodded his appreciation to Jarlaxle and turned back to Catti-brie, bringing the ruby pendant up before her. With his free hand he gently touched her face and he moved very near to her, falling into her thoughts and seeing through her eyes.

A collective gasp sounded from the two drow and the three dwarves, and Cadderly began to glow with the same bluish-white hue of the departing Ghost King. That gasp became a cry as the priest faded to nothingness.

Catti-brie cried out again, but more in surprise, it seemed, than in fear.

With a determined grunt, Drizzt again reached for Guenhwyvar, but Jarlaxle grabbed his wrist. "Don't," the mercenary bade him.

A crash behind them stole the moment, and all turned to see a giant support beam lying diagonally from the balcony to the floor, thick with flames.

"Out," Jarlaxle said, and Drizzt moved to Catti-brie and scooped her up in his arms.

* * * * *

It was a shadow image of the world he had left, absent the fabricated structures, a land of dull resolution and often utter darkness, of huddled ugly beasts and terrifying monsters. But in those clouds of shadowstuff shone a singular brilliance, the light of Cadderly, and before him loomed the most profound darkness of all, the Ghost King.

And there the two did battle, light against darkness, the radiance of Deneir's last gift to his Chosen against the combined powers of perversion. For a long, long while, light seared through shadows, and the flowing shadows rolled back to cover the radiance. For a long, long while, neither seemed to gain an advantage, and the other creatures of the dark plane looked on in awe.

Then those creatures fell back, for the shadow could not grow against that radiance, that unrelenting warmth of Cadderly Bonaduce. Possessed of great draconic intelligence and the wisdom of centuries, the Ghost King knew the truth as well.

For the king had been usurped and the new Ghost King stood amidst the darkness, and in that final struggle, Cadderly could not be defeated.

With a cry of protest, the dracolich lifted away and fled, and Cadderly, too, did not remain. For it was not his place, and there, he cared not if the evil beast lived or died.

But he could not allow the creature to return to his homeland.

He knew the sacrifice before him. He knew that he could not cross back through the membrane between worlds, that he was trapped by duty to Deneir, to what was right, and to his family and friends.

With a smile of contentment, certain of a life well-lived, Cadderly left that world of darkness for a place almost, but not quite, his home.

CHAPTER

THE LAST MEMORIES OF CHANGING GODS

30

She did not lie limp in Drizzt's arms, but rather seemed to be watching an awe-inspiring spectacle, and from her twitches and gasps, Drizzt could only imagine the battle his friend Cadderly was waging with the Ghost King.

"Kill it," he found himself whispering as he stumbled out of the ruined cathedral, through the double doors and onto the wide porch. What he really meant was a private prayer to Cadderly to find a way to bring Catti-brie back to him. "Kill it," meant all of it, from the tangible and symbolic dracolich to the insanity that had gripped the world and had entrapped Catti-brie. It was his last chance, he believed. If Cadderly could not find a way to break the spell over his beloved wife, she would remain forever lost to him.

To the relief of them all, no monsters remained to confront them as they escaped the building. The courtyard was littered with dead, killed by Drizzt or by the ferocious assault of the Ghost King. The lawn, once so serene and beautiful, showed the blackened scar of dragonfire, great brown swaths of dead grass from the dracolich's touch, and the massive trench dug by the diving wyrm.

Jarlaxle and Bruenor led the way out of the structure, and when they looked back at the grand cathedral, at the life's work of Cadderly Bonaduce, they understood better why the assault had taken such a toll on the priest. Fires leaped from several places, most dramatically from the wing they had just departed. Where the initial assault of dragonfire had been muted by the power of the cathedral's magic, the protective spells had worn thin. The fire wouldn't consume the place entirely, but the damage was extensive.

"Put her down, friend," Jarlaxle said, taking Drizzt's arm.

Drizzt shook his head and pulled away, and at that moment, Catti-brie's eyes flickered, and for a moment, just a moment, Drizzt thought he saw clarity there, thought he saw, within her—she recognized him!

"Me girl!" Bruenor cried, obviously seeing the same.

But a fleeting thing it was, if anything at all, and Catti-brie settled almost immediately back into the same lethargic state that had dominated her days since the falling Weave had wounded her.

Drizzt called to her repeatedly and shook her gently. "Catti! Catti-brie! Wake up!"

But he received no response.

As the weight of her condition sank in, Athrogate gave a cry, and all eyes went to him, then followed his gaze to the cathedral's open doorway.

Out walked Cadderly. Not flesh and blood, but a translucent, ghostly form of the old priest, hunched but walking with a purpose. He approached them and walked right through them, and everyone shuddered with a profound sense of coldness as he neared and passed.

They called to him, but he could not hear, as if they didn't exist. And so, they knew, in Cadderly's new reality, they did not.

The old priest ambled to the tree line, the other six following, and against the backdrop of leaping orange flames, Cadderly began to walk and whisper, bending low, his hand just off the ground. Behind him, a line of blue-white light glowed softly along the grass, and they realized that Cadderly was laying that line as he went.

"A ward," Jarlaxle realized. He tentatively stepped over it, and showed relief indeed when it did not harm him.

"Like the barrier in Luskan," Drizzt agreed. "The magic that was put down to seal off the old city, where the undead walk."

Cadderly continued his circuit, indeed walking the perimeter of Spirit Soaring.

"If the Ghost King returns, it must be to this spot," Jarlaxle said, though he seemed less than confident of his assessment and his reasoning sounded more like a plea. "The undead will not be able to cross out of this place."

"But how long's he got to weave it?" Bruenor asked.

"He knew," Drizzt gasped. "His words for Danica . . ."

"Forever," Jarlaxle whispered.

It took a long while for the priest to complete his first circuit, and he began his second anew, for the magic ward where he had started was already fading. Barely after Cadderly commenced the second pass, a voice called out from the darkness of the forest. "Father!" cried Rorick Bonaduce. "He is old! Mother, why does he look so old?"

Out of the trees rushed Danica and her children, with Ivan and Pikel. Joyful greetings and reunions had to wait, though, dampened by the pain that lay evident on the faces of three young adults, and on the woman who had so loved Cadderly.

Drizzt felt Danica's pain profoundly as he stood holding Catti-brie.

"What happened?" Danica asked, hurrying to join them.

"We drove it off, and hurt it badly," said Jarlaxle.

"Cadderly chased it when it left," said Bruenor.

Danica looked past them to the burning Spirit Soaring. She knew why her ghostly husband seemed so old, of course. Spirit Soaring was ruined, its magic diminished to near nothingness, and that magic supported Cadderly as surely as it held strong the timbers, stone, and glass of Deneir's cathedral. The magic had made Cadderly young, and had kept him young.

The spell had been destroyed.

Her husband had been destroyed, too, or . . . what? She looked at him and did not know.

"His last thoughts were of you," Drizzt said to her. "He loved you. He loves you still, as he serves Deneir, as he serves us all."

"He will come back from this," Hanaleisa said with determination. "He will finish his task and return to us!"

No one contradicted her, for what was to be gained? But a look from Danica told Drizzt that she, too, sensed the truth. Cadderly had become the Ghost King. Cadderly, his service to Spirit Soaring and to the wider world, was eternal.

The ghostly priest was halfway through his third circuit when dawn broke over the eastern horizon, and the others, exhausted, continued to follow him.

His glow diminished with the rising sun until he was gone from sight entirely, to the gasps—hopeful and horrified—of his children.

"He's gone!" Temberle cried.

"He's coming back to us," Rorick declared.

"Not gone," Jarlaxle said a moment later, and he motioned the others over to him. The glowing line continued on its way, and near to its brightest point, its newest point, the air was much colder. Cadderly was still there, unseen in the daylight.

The fires had diminished greatly in Spirit Soaring, but the group did not go back inside the cathedral, instead setting a camp just outside the front door. Weariness alone brought them some sleep, in cautious shifts, and as dusk descended, the Ghost King, the apparition of Cadderly, returned to view, walking, forever walking, his lonely circuit.

Soon after, some crawlers returned, a small group seeming intent on again attacking Spirit Soaring. They broke out of the forest and shrieked as one as they neared Cadderly's glowing line. Off they ran, into the darkness.

"Cadderly's ward," Bruenor said. "A good one."

The group rested a little easier after that.

"We have to leave this place," Jarlaxle remarked to them all later that night, and that drew many looks, few appreciative. "We do," the drow insisted. "We have to tell the world what has happened here."

"You go and tell them, then," Hanaleisa growled at him, but Danica put her hand on her daughter's forearm to quiet her.

"The monsters have retreated, but they remain out there," Jarlaxle warned.

"Then we stay in here where they can't get at us," Rorick argued.

"The dracolich can return inside that ward," Jarlaxle warned. "We must lea—"

Drizzt stopped him with an upraised hand and turned to Danica. "In the morning, first light," he bade her.

"This is our home. Where will we go?"

"Mithral Hall, and Silverymoon from there," Drizzt answered. "If there is an answer to be found, look to Lady Alustriel."

Danica turned to her children, who frowned as one, but had no words to counter the obvious reality. The food they could salvage from inside the structure couldn't sustain them forever.

As a compromise, they waited another two nights, but by then, even Hanaleisa and Rorick had to admit that their father was not coming back to them.

And so it was a solemn caravan that made its way out of Spirit Soaring one bright morning. The wagon hadn't been badly damaged out in the courtyard, and with five skilled dwarves supplying the know-how, they managed to repair it completely. Even better news followed when they found the poor mules, frightened and hungry but very much alive, roaming a distant corridor of the cathedral's first floor, their magical shoes intact.

They set a slow pace down to empty, ruined Carradoon, then north to the road to Mithral Hall. They knew they would find enemies in the Snowflakes, and so they did, but with the combined strength of the five dwarves, the Bonaduce family, and the two drow, no sufficient number of crawlers, giant bats, or even nightwalkers could pose any real threat.

They set an easier pace than the fury that had brought them south, and two tendays later, they crossed the Surbrin and entered Mithral Hall.

* * * * *

Hunched and uncomplaining, the Ghost King Cadderly circled the ruins of Spirit Soaring that night.

And every night, forevermore.

* * * * *

It was all a blur, all a swirl, an overriding grayness that defied lucidity. Flashes of images, most of them terrifying, stabbed at her sensibilities and jolted her from memory to memory, to senses of the life she had known.

It was all an ungraspable blur.

But then Catti-brie saw a dot within that sea of movement, a focal point, like the end of a rope reaching out to her through the fog. In her mind and with her hand she reached out for that point of clarity and to her surprise, she touched it. It was firm and smooth, the purest ivory.

The clouds swirled out, retreating from that point, and Catti-brie saw with her eyes clearly then, and in the present, for the first time in tendays. She looked to her lifeline, a single horn. She followed it.

A unicorn.

"Mielikki," she breathed.

Her heart pounded. She tried to fight through the confusion, to sort out all that had transpired.

The strand of the Weave! She remembered the strand of the Weave touching her and wounding her.

It was still there, inside of her. The gray clouds roiled at the edges of her focus.

"Mielikki," she said again, knowing beyond doubt that it was she, the goddess, who stood before her.

The unicorn bowed and went down on its front knees, inviting her.

Catti-brie's heart beat furiously; she thought it would jump out of her chest. Tears filled her eyes as she tried to deny what was coming next, and she silently begged to delay.

The unicorn looked at her, great sympathy in its large dark eyes. Then it stood once more and backed away a step.

"Give me this one night," Catti-brie whispered.

She rushed out of the room and padded on bare feet to the next door in Mithral Hall, the one she knew so well, the one she shared with Drizzt.

He lay on the bed in fitful sleep when she entered the room, and she released the bindings of her magical garment and let it drop to the floor as she slid in beside him.

He started, and turned, and Catti-brie met him with a passionate kiss. They fell together, overwhelmed, and made love until they collapsed into each other's arms.

Drizzt's sleep was more profound then, and when she heard the soft tap of the unicorn's horn on the closed door, Catti-brie understood that Mielikki was compelling him to slumber.

And calling her to her destiny.

She slid out from under Drizzt's arm, raised up on one elbow, and kissed him on the ear. "I will always love you, Drizzt Do'Urden," she said. "My life was full and without regret because I knew you and was completed by you. Sleep well, my love."

She slipped out of the bed and reached for her magical blouse. But she stopped and shook her head, moving instead to her dresser. There she found clothes Alustriel of Silverymoon had given to her: a white, layered gown full of pleats and folds, but sleeveless and low-cut, and with no even hemline. It was a wrap designed to flow with her every movement, and to enhance, not hide, her beauty of form.

She took a hooded black cloak and threw it over her shoulders, and gave a twirl to see it trailing.

She went out on bare feet. She didn't need shoes any more.

The unicorn was waiting, but offered no protest as Catti-brie quietly led it down the dim corridor, to a door not far away. Within lay Regis, tormented, emaciated, hanging on to life by a thread and by the near-continual efforts of the loyal priests of Mithral Hall, one of whom sat in a chair near the halfling's bed, deep in slumber.

Catti-brie didn't have to undo the bindings holding Regis's arms and legs, for there was much she would leave behind. Regis broke free of his fleshy coil then, and the woman, his guide and companion, gently lifted him into her arms. He started to groan, but she whispered to him softly, and with the magic of Mielikki filling her breath, the halfling calmed.

Out in the hall, the unicorn went down to its knees and Catti-brie sat sidesaddle upon its back. They started down the corridor.

* * * * *

A cry from a familiar voice awakened Drizzt, its panic so at odds with the wonderful, lingering warmth of the previous night.

But if Bruenor's frantic call didn't fully break the sleepy spell, the image that came into focus, at the same time Drizzt became aware of the sensations of his touch, surely did.

Catti-brie was there with him, in his bed, her eyes closed and a look of serenity on her face, as if she was asleep.

But she wasn't asleep.

Drizzt sat bolt upright, gagging and choking, eyes wide, hands trembling.

"Catti," he cried. "Catti, no!" He fell over her, so cool and still, and lifted her unresponsive form to him. "No, no, come back to me."

"Elf!" Bruenor shrieked again—shrieked and not yelled. Never before had Drizzt heard such a keen from the stoic and level-headed dwarf. "Oh, by the gods, elf!"

Drizzt lowered Catti-brie to the bed. He didn't know whether to touch her, to kiss her, to try to breathe life into her. He didn't know what to do, but Bruenor's third cry had him rolling out of bed and stumbling through his door.

He burst out into the hall, naked and sweating, and nearly ran over Bruenor, who was shaking and stumbling down the corridor, and carrying in his arms the lifeless form of Regis.

"Oh, elf."

"Bruenor, Catti-brie. . . . " Drizzt stammered, but Bruenor interrupted him.

"She's on the damned horse with Rumblebelly!"

Drizzt looked at him dumbfounded, and Bruenor nodded his chin down the corridor and stumbled toward the nearest connecting hallway. Drizzt supported him and pulled him along, and together they turned the corner. There ahead of them, they saw the vision that had accounted for no small part of Bruenor's frantic cry.

A unicorn carried Catti-brie, riding sidesaddle and cradling Regis in her arms. Not the equine creature or the woman looked back, despite the commotion of pursuit and drow and dwarf calling out to them.

The corridor turned sharply again, but the unicorn did not.

It walked right into the stone and was gone.

Drizzt and Bruenor stumbled to a halt, gasping and stuttering over words that would not come.

Behind them came a commotion as other dwarves reacted to the cries of their king, and Jarlaxle, too, ran up to the horrified pair. Many cries went up for Regis, lying dead in Bruenor's arms, for the halfling who had served well as steward of Mithral Hall and as a close advisor to their greatest king.

Jarlaxle offered his cloak to Drizzt, but had to put it on the ranger, who was out of his mind with terror and pain. Finally, Drizzt focused on Jarlaxle, grabbing the mercenary by the folds of his shirt and running him up against a wall.

"Find her!" Drizzt begged, against all logic, for he knew where the woman lay, still and cold. "You must find her! I'll do anything you demand . . . all the riches in the world!"

"Mithral Hall and everything in it!" Bruenor yelled.

Jarlaxle tried to calm the ranger and Bruenor. He nodded and he patted Drizzt's shoulder, though of course he had no idea where to begin, or what precisely he would be looking for—Catti-brie's soul?

Their promises of fealty and riches rang strangely discordant to Jarlaxle at that moment. He would find her, or would try, at least. Of that, he had no doubt.

But to Jarlaxle's surprise, he had no intention of taking a copper for his efforts, and wanted no promise of fealty from Drizzt Do'Urden.

Maybe something else compelled him then.

EPILOGUE

She felt it like a heartbeat beneath her bare feet, the land alive, the rhythm of life itself, and it compelled her to dance. And though she had never been a dancer, her movements were fluid and graceful, a perfect expression of the springtime forest into which she had been placed. And though her hip had been wounded badly—forever wounded, they had all believed—she felt no pain when she lifted her leg high, or leaped and spun in an inspired pirouette.

She came upon Regis sitting in a small field of wildflowers, looking out at the ripples on a small pond. She offered a smile and a laugh, and danced around him.

"Are we dead?" he asked.

Catti-brie had no answer. There was the world out there, somewhere beyond the trees of the springtime forest, and there was . . . here. This existence. This pocket of paradise, an expression of what had been from the goddess Mielikki, a gift given to her and to Regis, and to all Toril.

"Why are we here?" the halfling, who was no longer tormented by shadowy, huddled monsters, asked.

Because they had lived a good life, Catti-brie knew. Because this was Mielikki's gift—to Drizzt as much as to them—an expression of wondrous memory from the goddess who knew that the world had changed forever.

Catti-brie danced away, singing, and though she had never been a singer, her voice sounded with perfect pitch and tone, another effect of the enchanted wood.

They remained on Toril, though they didn't know it, in a small pocket of an eternal springtime forest amidst a world growing dark and cold. They were of that place, as surely as, and even more so, than Cadderly had been of Spirit Soaring. To leave would be to invite the nightmares and the stupor of abject confusion.

For any others to enter would invite unto them variations of the same.

For the glen was the expression of Mielikki, a place of possibilities, of what could be and not of what was. There were no monsters there, though animals abounded. And the gift was a private one and not to be shared, a secret place, the goddess Mielikki's indelible mark, Mielikki's fitting monument, on a world that had moved in a new direction.

* * * * *

Two piles of rocks.

Two cairns, one holding Regis and one holding Catti-brie. Just over a month earlier, Drizzt and Catti-brie had been on the road to Silverymoon, and despite the trouble with the Weave, it had been a joyous journey. For more than eight years, Drizzt had felt complete, had felt as if all the joys had been doubled and all the pain halved as he danced through his life arm-in-arm with that wonderful woman who had never shown him anything less than honesty and compassion and love.

Then it was gone, stolen from him, and in a way he simply could not comprehend. He tried to take solace in telling himself that her pain had ended, that she was at peace—with Mielikki, obviously, given the vision of the unicorn. She had been suffering those last tendays, after all.

But it didn't work, and he could only shake his head and fight to hold back his tears, and hold back his desire to throw himself across that cold and hard cairn assembled in a decorated lower chamber of Mithral Hall.

He looked to the smaller stone pile and remembered his journey with Regis to Luskan, then thought back much farther, to their first days together in Icewind Dale.

The drow dropped his hand on Guenhwyvar, whom he had called for the ceremony. It was fitting that the panther was there, and if he had known any way to accomplish it, it would have been fitting to have Wulfgar there. Drizzt resolved then to go to Icewind Dale to inform his barbarian friend face-to-face.

Then it all broke. The notion of telling Wulfgar finally cracked the stoic posture of Drizzt Do'Urden. He began to sob, his shoulders bobbing, and he felt himself sinking toward the floor, as if the stones were rising up to bury him—and how he wished they would!

Bruenor grabbed him, and cried with him.

Drizzt shook himself out of it in short order, and stood tall with a cold grimace, and such a look it was that it chilled everyone in the room.

"It's goin' to be all right, elf," Bruenor whispered.

Drizzt only stared straight ahead with cold, hard, unfocused anger.

He knew he would never be the same; he knew that the inner growling would not diminish with the passing of days, of tendays, of months, or years, or decades perhaps. There was no shining and hopeful light at the end of that dark passage.

Not this time.

* * * * *

When Regis wanted to find something he could use as a fishing line, he found it. When he searched for a hook and pole, those, too, were readily discovered. And when he pulled his first knucklehead trout from the small pond, the halfling gasped in surprise and wondered if perhaps he was in Icewind Dale!

But no, he knew, for even if that strange forest was located in that land it was not of that land.

Scrimshaw tools were not far away, and Regis was not surprised to find them. He wanted them and they were there, and so he began to wonder if the place itself was a dream, a grand illusion.

Heaven or hell?

Would he wake up?

Did he want to?

He spent his days fishing and at his scrimshaw, and he was warm and happy. He ate meals more delicious than anything he had ever known, and went to sleep with his belly full and dreamed beautiful dreams. And the song of Catti-brie filled the forest air, though he saw her only in fleeting moments, far away, leaping onto sunbeams and moonbeams as if they were ladders to the heavens.

Dancing, always dancing. The forest was alive through her movements and her song, and the songs of birds accompanied her gaily in the sunshine, and with haunting beauty in the soft darkness of the night.

He was not unhappy and not frustrated, but many times, Regis, for the sake of his own curiosity, tried to walk in a straight line, to veer neither left nor right a single step in an attempt to find the end of the forest.

But every time, somehow, inexplicably, he found himself back where he had started, on the banks of a small pond.

He could only put his hands on his hips and laugh—and retrieve his fishing pole.

* * * * *

And so it went, and time became meaningless, the days and the seasons mattering not at all.

It snowed in the forest, but it was not cold, and the flowers did not stop blooming, and Catti-brie, the magical soul of Mielikki's expression, did not slow her dance nor quiet her song.

It was her place, her forest, and there, she knew happiness and serenity and peace of mind, and if challenges came against the forest, she would meet them. Regis knew all of that, too, and knew that he was a guest there, welcome forevermore, but not as intricately tied to the land as was his companion.

And so the halfling took it upon himself to become a caretaker of sorts. He cut a garden and tended it to perfection. He built himself a home within a hillside, with a round door and a cozy hearth, with shelves of wondrous scrimshaw he had sculpted and plates and cups of wood, and a table always set . . .

. . . for guests who never came.